THE THERAPIST

Helene Flood

THE THERAPIST

Translated from the Norwegian by
Alison McCullough

MACLEHOSE PRESS
QUERCUS · LONDON

First published in the Norwegian language as *Terapeuten*
by H. Aschehoug & Co, Oslo, in 2019
First published in Great Britain in 2021 by

MacLehose Press
An imprint of Quercus Editions Ltd
Carmelite House
50 Victoria Embankment
London EC4Y 0DZ

An Hachette UK company

A CIP catalogue record for this book is available from the British Library.

ISBN (HB) 978 1 52940 602 3
ISBN (TPB) 978 1 52940 601 6
ISBN (Ebook) 978 1 52940 600 9

This book is a work of fiction. Names, characters, businesses, organisations, places
and events are either the product of the author's imagination or are used fictitiously.
Any resemblance to actual persons, living or dead, events or locales is entirely coincidental.

10 9 8 7 6 5 4 3 2 1

Designed and typeset in Cycles by Libanus Press, Marlborough
Printed and bound in Great Britain by Clays Ltd, Elcograf S.p.A

For Frédéric

Friday, March 6: The message

It was dark outside when he left. I woke as he leaned over me and kissed me on the forehead.

"I'm going now," he whispered.

Still half-asleep, I turned. He was wearing his coat, had his bag slung over his shoulder.

"O.K.," I mumbled.

"Just go back to sleep," he said.

I heard his footsteps on the stairs, but must have been asleep before the door clicked shut behind him.

———

When I wake I'm alone in the bed. There's a gap between the blind and windowsill that admits a weak shaft of sunlight, which hits me in the eyes and stirs me. It's 7.30 a.m. – not a bad time to get up.

I pad barefoot to the bathroom in defiance of the wall-to-wall carpet of chipboard tiles in the hall, the wet wooden pallets that cover the clay floor in the bathroom. We don't have a ceiling light in here, but Sigurd set up a work lamp when he was pulling up the tiles and it's still standing there, disconcertingly permanent. Luckily, it's light enough that I don't need to use the lamp. It's starkly functional, in the way that work lamps are, and gives off a hard white light that makes me feel as if I'm showering in the revealing brightness of a secondary school changing room. I turn on the water, let it warm up as I take off my nightgown.

The boiler needs changing, but Sigurd showers quickly and I don't plan on washing my hair today, so it'll do.

The shower cabinet is plastic – this, too, was meant to be temporary. Sigurd has designed a shower for us, a brick cubicle with glass doors and tiny blue-flecked and white tiles. In all the half-finished rooms in the house, the standstill is most obvious in the bathroom. The old tiles are gone, the new ones not yet laid. We have no lights, no proper curtains to speak of, pallets to walk on so we don't damage the floor, a hole in the wall where the water runs out, and this provisional shower cabinet, an ancient relic from Sigurd's grandfather. I once saw the house as it would be when it was finished as I walked through this abandoned building site: the blue-flecked tiles, the shining glass bricks, the recessed lights – would feel the heated tiles beneath the soles of my feet, the hot water perfectly meted out from a modern showerhead with several settings. Now all I can see is just how much time it's all going to take. As I stick my hand into the stream of water, feeling it begin to warm up, it occurs to me that I've somehow stopped believing the house will ever be finished.

Under the hot water I wake up – it's cold in here; the temperature is O.K. in the bedroom, but the bathroom is freezing. The winter has been a long one, and every morning I've stood here naked and waited for the heat with a hand in the stream of water. Now the season is slowly moving into spring. The shower does me good as it hammers against my cold, goose-pimpled skin. I collect water in my palms and dip my face in it; feel it jerk me fully from the night, feel the day taking hold.

Friday. Three patients – the usual Friday gang. First Vera, then Christoffer, and finally Trygve. It's a bad idea to see Trygve last thing on a Friday, but it's so tempting to just schedule the same time next week at the end of our sessions together. I gather another handful of water, dip my face into it, rub my hands along my cheeks. Sigurd will be at his friend's cabin in Norefjell until Sunday. I'll be alone all weekend.

Unable to stand the cold bathroom for a second longer than necessary I go back into the bedroom to get dressed. The sheets lie in a crumpled heap on the bed. The air is dense with the smell of sleep – mine, at least – and perhaps his, too. I didn't see what time it was when he left, it could be several hours ago already. We don't have any wardrobes, but between the chimney and the wall Sigurd has installed a metal rail where we keep our clothes. Sigurd's hang there messily, any old way, while my dresses, shirts and jackets are arranged by colour in a neat row. Looking at Sigurd's clothes it seems there may be some missing, but then he is supposed to be going straight to the mountains. The bag that was on the floor is gone, and now I remember he had it over his shoulder when he left. I put on a soft, pigeon-blue shirt and trousers, a smart, neutral outfit for the day, thinking that it's only a matter of hours before I can come up here again and grab some workout clothes should I decide to go to the gym, or put on my pyjama bottoms and an oversized T-shirt if not. Only three patients first.

Actually, three patients is too few. I need to have four every day, and at least a day or two every week with five. Those were the figures I had calculated when I started freelancing. "There's less paperwork in private practice," I said to Sigurd as we made our plans, sitting in the kitchen of our old apartment by Torshovparken and drawing up a budget on an Excel spread-sheet. "I can manage four patients a day, possibly five. Five, most days. Or one day a week, anyway – although a little extra money wouldn't hurt." We laughed.

"Don't work yourself to death now," Sigurd said.

"Says you," I said.

Sigurd started working for himself at the same time, had plotted his own calculations on the same Excel spreadsheet. A minimum of eight clients simultaneously, preferably ten. He'd help the other partners when they needed it; every hour would count.

"There'll be some overtime," we said to each other, "but we'll make good money, put a little extra in the piggy bank." So far I only have three patients on most days, and very rarely five. Why did it turn out this way? It's more difficult to find patients than I expected, and the younger ones often cancel, but that's only part of the reason. I do up the last of my shirt buttons, all neatly, decently closed. I'd forgotten to include one important thing when I sat there in the kitchen in Torshov, Sigurd's old desk lamp providing the light above my computer and the sheets of paper on which we'd scribbled our notes. The human factor. I enjoy my own company, but even I need others. I had erased my colleagues with the stroke of a pen, never guessing that I would feel so lonely. That it would make me passive. A year ago, if anyone had told me how difficult it would feel to advertise for and pull in more patients – how I would shrink from it – I wouldn't have believed them.

Breakfast is the best meal of the day, in my opinion. I sit at our kitchen island with the newspaper, a slice of bread and a cup of coffee. I prefer to eat alone. Sigurd always leaves early after downing his coffee while standing beside the kitchen counter, but I like to take my time. Read the *Aftenposten* opinion pieces, the film reviews. Contemplate the day.

Sigurd has left his cup on the counter beside the sink. The kitchen surfaces are one of the few things about the house that are more or less finished, and the counter is so shiny that I can see the semicircle of coffee beneath the cup all the way from where I'm sitting. *Of course*. Perhaps it's a biological difference between men and women, this ability to see a ring of coffee beneath a cup, crumbs under the toaster, stray drops of water along the worktop. Sigurd wants everything to be done properly, is planning the house in detail, painstakingly making drawings and impressive visualisations – but he falls short when it comes to the little things. Putting his cup in the dishwasher. Wiping down the worktop. Packing up his laptop for the evening. These things are no big deal, so why do I go on about them, let them irritate me? On the other hand, they only take a few seconds – so why can't he just do them?

This is as far as I've got when I glance towards the hook on the wall where Sigurd usually hangs his document holder – the hard grey plastic tube with a black shoulder strap attached to each end which he uses to carry drawings to and from work. It always hangs there on the same hook if he's home. I frown as I consider the empty hook. Wasn't he supposed to be driving straight to Thomas' place to pick him up? Did he not explicitly say so? And wasn't the document tube hanging there on the wall yesterday evening?

I have always found it difficult to shrug off inconsistencies, although I know some people can, and I envy them for it. He wasn't supposed to be going into work – but no, maybe I misunderstood. I thought he said he was going straight to Thomas' place – well, perhaps I heard wrong, maybe he was going to call in at the office first. Maybe he left the document tube at work, and when I think I can remember it hanging here yesterday, I'm actually thinking of the day before. It would be much easier to be able to shrug it off. Those with poorer memories seem much less suspicious of the world, less argumentative. To take the current example: I remember, without a shadow of a doubt, that Sigurd and I spoke about his plans yesterday, how I got up from our sofa in the corner and went across to the kitchen nook to empty the dregs of my tea into the sink, threw the used teabag in the bin and put my cup in the dishwasher; remember how I turned when standing perhaps a metre from the kitchen island where I'm sitting now, and said to Sigurd, "So, when are you leaving tomorrow?" And I remember Sigurd so clearly – as if I'm looking at a photograph of him, one with an extraordinary resolution, billions of megapixels, every impurity of his skin rendered in detail. I remember the worn-out jumper and ripped trousers he often wears in the evening; that he ran a hand through his dishevelled curls and looked at me with narrow, tired eyes, as if I was waking him, and said:

"Oh. I'm leaving early. I want to be at Thomas' by six-thirty."

And I said:

"Six-thirty?"

And he said:

"Yes. So we'll make it up there by mid-morning, get a full day on the slopes."

Then maybe he forgot and acted out of habit, taking the document tube with him. Maybe he decided he'd do a bit of work from the cabin. Perhaps he changed his mind and went into the office at the last minute.

My memory is too detailed. I remember all too clearly the way he looked when we spoke about this; how he was wearing the beige, ill-fitting jumper with the black collar that looks like something his mother might have bought him – which in fact it is – he told me it was she who had bought it for him before he met me, when I first dared to point out how hair-raisingly awful it is. It's an insignificant detail, not something I need to be able to recall. At least, it isn't important to remember that I said, "O.K.," and turned away, and that by the time I had put down my teacup and looked back at the sofa he was already sitting with his laptop open on his knees, his eyes squinting at the screen, eyebrows drawn together, mouth half-open, and that I suppressed the urge to say, "Turn a light on, you're ruining your eyes, and take that computer off your lap, it'll ruin the quality of your sperm and we might need your sperm to be in tip-top condition some day, and don't sit there on the sofa with your neck bent like that, you'll get a bad back." Instead, all I said was:

"I'm going up to bed. Night."

All this is trivial. What's important is to be able to distinguish the important details from the rest. If you remember everything, it's harder to recall the significant things – the things you *have* *to* remember.

From the bathroom window I can see my first patient of the day walking up the path to my office above the garage. Vera bows her head a little as she walks, which gives her a distinctive gait that's easy to recognise – the gait of a teenage girl who hasn't yet grown into her adult body. Were you to ask her, though, she'd tell you she's mature enough. I take a deep breath, down into my diaphragm, following her with my gaze as she opens the door to the office. Three patients, that's all – then the weekend. I feel tired, even though I've only just got up.

I brush my teeth in the bathroom, balancing on one of the pallets Sigurd brought back from a construction site he'd visited and then used to cover our bathroom floor. The basin belonged to Sigurd's old Grandpa Torp, as did the shower cabinet, which means it was fitted before 1970 and hasn't been updated since, apart from the few modifications Old Torp carried out himself. The tap has one round handle for cold water and one for hot, and when I look at them I can almost see Old Torp's crooked,

13

arthritic hands turning them. Sigurd's grandfather didn't believe in worldly goods. According to him, it was inevitable that Norway would soon be taken over by the communists – although he must have been disappointed that it was taking so long, because he'd been waiting for this to happen since the 1950s. By the time he drew his last breath, in his command centre in the loft, his convictions had remained rock solid through the fall of the Soviet Union and the rise of China as a global economy. Still, the sly old fox must have been dispirited when his health began to decline, just as the world's communist states were succumbing to capitalistic ideas. The Cold War had been his heyday, and he was palpably proud to tell anyone who would listen – generally Sigurd's mother, or Sigurd and me – that the intelligence service had kept a file on him throughout the '70s. But last year was his final over and out, and now all that remain are the souvenirs of this house: the old radiators and taps, and the command centre, so far untouched, with its shelf upon shelf of reading matter, membership magazines from the Communist Party and Workers' Communist Party, its wall maps with small drawing pins marking locations Old Torp regarded as significant targets, and the old, rusty revolver, thought to have been owned by someone who had fought in the Russian Revolution, and which Old Torp had acquired in the '70s to protect himself – or to give the secret service a reason to keep tabs on him.

Old Torp's death gave Sigurd and me the opportunity to achieve our dream of owning a house. In the 1950s Nordberg was an area of the city like any other, but over the years it has gone up in the world. In 2014 it was utterly impossible for a hopeful young couple like us to raise enough capital to buy a house up here. On the way back to the station after visiting the old wreck, we'd sigh to each other and say, but just look at *the view*, and it's so close to *the countryside*, and just a short T-banen ride from the city, and you can see *the sea* from here. But there was no point saying anything further. A terraced house in an outer suburb without any kind of view was all that was on the cards for us. But two days after the old man was found, declared dead and sent off to a funeral parlour for the necessary preparations, Margrethe, Sigurd's mother, had called.

"Listen," she had said. "Wouldn't Grandpa's house in Kongleveien be perfect for you?" Margrethe is an only child, and lives in a modern house in Røa. Sigurd's brother Harald lives in San Diego and has no need for a house in Oslo. Sigurd's late father's cabin in Krokskogen had already been given to Harald, who had promised not to sell it before his mother became too old to use it, and one day would also be the beneficiary when Margrethe's house was sold. So Old Torp's house was given to us.

But an uncomfortable fact about Old Torp's death is that almost three weeks passed before he was found. That is, he died in his command centre in the loft, above the bedroom Sigurd and I now share, as he sat there with a flask of coffee, poring over a wallchart from a time when there was still an East and a West Germany. It was his heart that gave out – no surprise really, the man was almost ninety. Nor was he a very social person, so he had no visitors other than immediate family. Margrethe was on one of her two-month jaunts to warmer climes when it happened; Sigurd and I were supposed to visit Old Torp once a week to ensure that everything was O.K. But we were busy with work and our own lives; we skipped a week here and a week there. When we finally turned up, two weeks late, we sensed the silence from the moment Sigurd turned the key in the lock.

"Grandpa?" Sigurd called.

We had looked at each other with apologetic smiles, feeling guilty for leaving the old communist alone so long, and when I think of Sigurd's expression now I can see the tension in it, as if he had used safety pins at the corners of his mouth to pitch it up. I'm tempted to say that we already knew, although that's too dramatic. But perhaps our guilty consciences made us suspect something was wrong.

"Grandpa?"

In the end, I was the one to find him; he lay there with his face on the map. His skin was grey and rugged, dry as leather and just as lifeless, and mottled with haematomas in the way that long-dead human bodies often are. It's an image I wish I could unsee. The yellow nails that looked as if they might drop off; the vertebrae of the neck about to pierce the dead, parchment-like skin. The heavy, stifling smell of decomposing flesh. I've hardly been in the command centre since. Perhaps the distressing circumstances of his death were in part what made Margrethe decide to give us the house.

We wanted to renovate the property as soon as possible; peel the old man off the walls, empty the house of him and make it our own. Sigurd created drawings; I drew up a budget. Our new-found financial freedom gave us opportunities. Some of Sigurd's former student friends wanted to open their own architectural firm, and had invited Sigurd to join them. We no longer had a mortgage or service charge to pay, and the sale of our apartment provided the sum Sigurd needed to buy himself into the firm. I was unhappy in my job in the health service, working with young people suffering from mental illness; we now had enough space to create an office for me at home. The house was the start of something new for us. Four days before we moved in we went down to the courthouse in Oslo and got married, eating cake at the local bakery afterwards with my sister and Sigurd's two best friends and their partners. It didn't change anything – we'd still be us – but we wanted to have the paperwork in order. On our first night in the house we slept on an air mattress in the living room. We toasted ourselves with glasses of prosecco, and told each other, "The rest of our lives starts now."

But Old Torp would prove harder to get rid of than we'd imagined. The renovations took time, as did getting started at our new respective workplaces. Sigurd was working a lot of overtime, and our plan to redecorate primarily required him – his expertise, his practical hands. We had set out overenthusiastic and full of energy, ripping off the wallpaper in strips, tearing up the tiles in the bathroom. We managed to get some things done, such as fitting a new kitchen and creating a home office for me above the garage. Then we started to lose momentum. Sigurd took on more clients, worked longer days, sat bent over his drawing board. Winter came, the days becoming colder and darker, draining us of energy. When we got home from work we could no longer be bothered to paint; to go to Maxbo to look at showerheads or taps or to find tiles. We failed to mix any filler, failed to pull off the last strips of wallpaper, instead dropping onto the old sofa we had brought with us from Torshov and watching T.V. Sigurd often didn't get home until late in the evening, stooped and tired, with the document tube dangling from his shoulder.

"In the summer," we said. "We'll spend the summer holidays doing up the house." That's around three months away, and the fact that I've lost faith worries me. Something else is bound to happen, and then we'll say "in the autumn", and then the weather will turn cold and we'll have yet another long winter in which I tiptoe around barefoot, my feet stiff and heavy as frozen clubs on the pallets on the bathroom floor.

I run my practice from the floor above the garage, where I have a tiny waiting room containing a shoe rack, a straight-backed chair and a minuscule table with magazines, and then a door that leads into my office. Vera is sitting on the straight-backed chair, a magazine open in her lap, but I suspect she isn't reading it. She looks up as I enter.

"Hello, Doctor," she says. She looks refreshed, and is sporting a new haircut.

"Hello," I say. "Just a moment, and then I'll . . . I'll come out and call you."

"Alright," she says obligingly, one eyebrow arched in the expression I most often see her wearing – it complements the touch of sarcasm she adds to most of her remarks.

I go into my office and close the door behind me to prevent Vera's gaze from following me, from tainting everything I do.

Sigurd has done a great job with the office. It isn't very big, and the sloping ceiling made the optimal use of space the main concern. He knocked out one of the shorter walls, the one facing the driveway, and replaced it with glass. My two chairs are set there – two fine Arne Jacobsen armchairs, with a small table between them. When we sit there, my patients and I, we sit in the brightest part of the room. In the ceiling above us, Sigurd has installed a Velux window, so that natural light can enter through the ceiling, too. A couple of lamps make the nook cosy and welcoming, regardless of the autumn storms and freezer-box winters. Against the other short wall, the one that separates my office from the waiting room, Sigurd has placed my little white desk, and hung shelves along the walls all the way up to the ceiling on either side of the door to create plenty of space for my books and ring binders. The short wall and floor are panelled in pale, warm wood; the two taller walls are painted white, and the overall effect is so modern, so friendly. I've positioned a couple of plants where the sloped ceiling nears the floor, and although it's admittedly difficult to keep them alive – it gets cold in here when I turn off the electric heater for the day – they provide a certain atmosphere. "You can breathe in here," the room says. "In here, you can be yourself. Nothing you say in this room will be judged, repeated or ridiculed." That's what I had wanted – an office that would invite my patients in. And that's exactly what Sigurd gave me. I have to give him that.

But now Vera is sitting out there waiting for me and a tiredness starts to squeeze around the base of my throat. I don't want to invite her into my office. I sit down at my desk, turn on the computer – I'll read my notes from her last visit, although strictly speaking I don't need to, I remember what we talked about during the session. I'm playing for time – want to delay the moment at which I have to go out and tell her she can come in. Why am I doing this? I'm not sure – or perhaps I don't want to think about it. Therapists care about their patients, and I care about Vera, but there's no escaping the fact that our conversations are hard work.

Difficulties with parents, say my notes from our last session. *Difficulties with boyfriend*. Vera's problems are relational. She started coming to see me just after Christmas for help with a depressive reaction. She's of well above average intelligence – perhaps even gifted – so everything bores her. "I'm just so tired of everything," Vera said in our first session when I asked her to tell me why she had come to see me, "it just seems as if nothing matters or means anything anymore." Her boyfriend, it turns out, is a married man. Her parents are researchers who are trying to solve a mathematical theorem only a handful of people in the world are familiar with – they're always at work and often away. Her siblings are grown-up and have long since left home, and Vera, eighteen and wise beyond her years, says that the family was already complete when she arrived. Her parents had not wanted more children. She was an accident.

There's a lot to unpack here – there is real pain in Vera's life. But it's such tough material to work with.

I check my e-mails, killing time before I let her in. Mostly advertising, nothing personal. For the briefest moment I want to call Sigurd, but that's silly, it's five to nine, he'll still be in the car with his friends. I take a deep breath. Three patients, and then it will be the weekend. The entire evening alone. Lunch with my sister on Sunday, otherwise no plans. Except to go to the gym, perhaps.

"Ready, Doctor?" Vera asks when I go out to tell her she can come in.

This calling me "Doctor" is something Vera started doing in our second session. She asked me about the difference between a psychologist and a psychiatrist, and I told her that I'm a psychologist, not a doctor – that I specialise in how the whole person functions, not just the pathology – but she got hung up on this and said, "So you're not a real doctor, then?" Irritatingly, I let this bother me, let the remark prod at an inferiority complex I didn't think I had, because I answered – a little defensively – that I knew as much as any doctor about what goes on in people's heads, at which she laughed, and said, "That's O.K., I'll call you 'Doctor'." I feel a stab of discomfort every time she says it: a prickling feeling at the back of my throat that tells me I've revealed too much. Sometimes I ask myself whether she understands that it bothers me – whether it's a passive-aggressive move on her part – but she seems genuine enough. Just playful.

I let her into the room ahead of me. Vera is a little taller than average, slim, with straight hips. Her hands are quite large, hanging there like pendulums at her sides, and I look at her and ask myself – as women always do when they meet other women – is she pretty? Yes, averagely sweet. Young. But there's also something peculiar about her; her round little face, her long body.

"Well," Vera says as she takes a seat. "I've had a fight with Mamma and Pappa. And argued with Lars."

"I see," I say, settling into my chair. "Tell me what happened."

The waking sun is visible in the Velux window as Vera speaks, illuminating her hair and making it halo-like, all the hundreds of curly, flyaway hairs that have broken free from her otherwise slicked-back hairstyle. All girls have these kinds of unruly, flyaway hairs, I think. I have plenty of them myself – more than Vera has.

The pattern in what she's telling me is straightforward: Vera feels rejected by her parents, who have so many important things to do that they don't have time for her. Since she's unable to tell them how upset she is, nothing is more satisfying than a confrontation with them – afterwards, feeling even more rejected, Vera calls her boyfriend and starts another argument. The married boyfriend goes home to his wife after they hang up regardless of what happens, so in the unprovoked argument there's no doubt that Vera will be rejected – this is how Vera takes the intolerable feeling of not being prioritised by her parents and reframes it within more tolerable limits with her boyfriend. Half an hour into our session I share this observation with her.

"I don't know," Vera says, wrinkling her nose. "Isn't that a bit easy? Like, a bit Freudian or something?"

"So is it correct to say that you don't think that's the case?"

She looks over at my bookcase, as if trying out my interpretation. Her fingers pluck at the bracelet on her wrist, a thin silver bracelet with a single pearl dangling from it. She rolls the pearl around between her index finger and thumb. The piece of jewellery is too grown-up for her, I think. The girls who come to see me often wear jewellery bearing letters; they adorn themselves with words like LOVE or TRUST or ETERNITY. This bracelet might belong to a middle-aged woman.

"I don't know. I hope not. I really don't think I called Lars just because I wanted to feel bad. I think I *did* feel bad, and wanted to feel better."

"I understand," I say. "And so you ended up feeling even worse than you already did."

"Yeah," she says, and sighs deeply. "So it wasn't such a good strategy, you might say."

"What might have been a good strategy, do you think?"

"To help me feel better? I don't know. I only ever come up with bad strategies."

"Such as?"

"Self-harm," she says. "Isn't that the classic one? There's a girl in my class who does it. She blogs about it, too – takes pictures of her wounds and posts them online, it's *crazy*. But that's not my style. Unless you count Lars as self-harming, I suppose."

This last reflection is an invitation, but I let it lie. She wants to talk about her boyfriend, needs to discuss the relationship with someone and has nobody else in whom she can confide. But he is not the cause of her pain. As I see it, the boyfriend is a symptom, while the cause of Vera's depression lies deeper, in the things she doesn't want to talk about. Those are the things we have to explore. My body still feels sleepy; I fight the urge to stretch in my chair. Through the window behind Vera I can see that the mist is lifting – it's going to be a nice day.

"You were upset after the fight with your parents," I say. "You wanted to feel better, so instead of self-harming or doing something similarly stupid, you chose to do something that *could* have been effective – you reached out for support from someone. The problem is that you chose someone you knew would reject you. So what I'm wondering is, what if you'd tried to reach out to someone else?"

"Like who?"

"I don't know. Someone you can trust. A friend, for example."

"A friend," Vera says, her voice heavy.

"Do you have any friends, Vera?"

She looks at me – is she weighing me up? A kind of challenge suddenly flashes in her eyes.

"I have lots of friends. God, I've got tons of them – more than I need. But do you know what the problem is?"

"No," I say. "What is the problem?"

"They're idiots. Every last one of them."

"I see," I say, thinking for a moment, reflecting this back. "Then they don't sound like very good friends."

She inhales, her face softening.

"O.K., maybe not idiots, exactly. But they just don't understand. The girls in my class – you have no idea. They read beauty blogs and plan end-of-year parties and think the world's most important skill is to be able to pluck your eyebrows just *so*. Y'know? If you ask them about love they start going on about that one guy in the other class they messed around with at a party. What kind of help would I get from them?"

"It sounds as if, although you have plenty of people around you, you don't have very many you can turn to for support," I say.

"I have Lars."

"Yes. But Lars is something other than a friend. It sounds a little lonely, in a way?"

She doesn't like this perspective, I can tell. Vera wants Lars to be enough. She feels that she's above her classmates, but doesn't want me to pity her for it.

"But do we all have to get so fucking *personal* with each other all the time?" she says.

"I think everyone needs someone they can have a personal conversation with."

She doesn't like this, either.

"Well, do *you* have friends you can talk to?" she asks, and now there's something mean, something caustic in her tone, a stinging slap, and I feel it in my stomach, the discomfort at being subjected to an attack. "Do you even have any friends at all?"

She raises an eyebrow again. So many of the girls who come to me tell me about this fight for survival in the schoolyard, the brutal strategies used to claw one's way up the pecking order of this dog-eat-dog world. Vera considers me like this – in the way that the queen of the class looks down her nose at the quietest girl in the back row.

"Yes, I do," I say, perhaps too quickly. "Not that we talk about deep, personal things all the time, but I have people I can confide in. I think everyone needs that."

We look at one another, sizing each other up, and I'm already sensing that my tactics have failed.

"And you can work to build those kinds of relationships," I say, trying to steer the conversation in a more constructive direction.

There's an element of something I can't decipher in her eyes – she's assessing me. But then it's as if she loses interest.

"Yeah, well," she says, glancing down at the pearl she's fiddling with on her bracelet. "Maybe you need it, but it's not like that for me."

That was the wrong approach, I realise. She got angry. Threw her anger at me, as young people do. I didn't quite manage to steer it, didn't give her what she needed. Ended up defending myself instead. Vera runs her hands through her hair, a tired, grown-up gesture. But when she lets her hands fall and looks over at me again, she seems younger than her eighteen years.

"I don't need anyone to confide in," she says. "All I need is love."

Her tone is that of an obstinate child – I almost want to cup her cheek with my hand. This is Vera's blind spot. She's convinced that she's so clever, so much older and wiser than her friends, that she has no idea of the extent of all she has yet to experience. Maybe it's my job to help her understand this. But I'm tired. It's Friday – and anyway, the session is almost over.

I glance at the clock, and Vera sees me do it.

"Time to give up, Doctor?" she asks.

I scribble down some quick keywords for my notes, which I'll write up later. *Argument with parents*, I write, *argument with boyfriend. Feels rejected by her parents, provokes argument with boyfriend.* I read over the words. Cross out "provokes". Write: *starts an argument with boyfriend. Assessment,* I write, and consider – how should I assess Vera? *Fear of rejection; topic of loneliness is a sore point. Intervention: interpretation, attempt to increase reflection around own reactions. Follow up feeling of not having anything in common with those around her."*

Outside I see Christoffer's mother's B.M.W. already parked at the side of the road. I set a full stop at the end of my notes and stretch and twist my body in the chair, in preparation.

When I emerge from my office Christoffer is sitting in the waiting room, confident and with his legs spread.

"Hi, Sara, how's it going?" he asks as he gets up and enters the room, sauntering across to his chosen chair without hesitation.

This is a litmus test for a patient's first session, and I use the same routine with all my new patients. I let them into the room first. Most young adults wait for me to ask them to sit down – wait for me to signal that one of the chairs is for them. This is natural – the room is mine, they are guests. Some ask me, "Where should I sit?" Some, like Christoffer, pick one. In our first session he stopped for a moment and considered the two chairs, then decided on the one on the left, dropped into it, slung one leg over the other, and looked as if he owned the place.

I take the other chair. As it happens, Christoffer and Vera like to sit in different chairs, so now I'm sitting in the chair that's still warm from Vera's body.

"Right," Christoffer says, with a grin so broad it shows all his white teeth, from the molars on one side to those on the other. "I'm ready. Let's go."

He could almost have winked at me. He doesn't, but it wouldn't have surprised me if he had.

"How are you, Christoffer?" I say. I'm aiming for neutral: friendly, but restrained. Trying not to be taken in by his grin.

"Yeah," he says, "I'm just marvellous."

The face that surrounds his huge row of teeth is unshaven; his fringe, parted at the centre, falls almost to his chin. His hair is dyed black, and around his neck is a row of studs I can only describe as looking somewhat like a dog collar. Christoffer has taken off his leather jacket and sits there in his T-shirt, the tattoos on his arms visible and with similar studded belts around his waist and wrists. I wonder whether anyone has ever tried to hug him. He's an attractive, likeable boy, only in this outsider position because he's chosen it for himself, and I assume that girls, if not swarming around him, are at the very least interested. But to hug him, with all the spikes?

"School?" I say.

"Yeah. I'm kinda scraping the bottom of the barrel, haha. But I'm not failing anything. Thumbs up, right, Sara?"

"And at home?"

Christoffer's grin broadens further still to reveal the spaces where his wisdom teeth will erupt in a few years' time.

"Brilliant. Pappa's in Brazil and doesn't want to come home, and Mamma's trembling with fear because of all *this*."

He taps one of the spikes of his collar with a knuckle.

"You should hear her." He puts on a falsetto, his face becoming that of an animated fool, the corners of his mouth drawn down in a comical expression. *"Christoffer Alexander, are you really going to go to school with* that *around your neck? You look like a common whore."*

I suppress a smile. Christoffer throws back his head and laughs heartily.

"And that pleases you?" I say.

"Of course it does," he says, his voice smug.

"Listen," I say. "It's not that I don't appreciate all the effort you put into your personal style. But don't you think you could find a way to irritate your mum that's a little less associated with, you know, self-harm?"

Yet more laughter escapes Christoffer's throat.

"That's what I like about you, Sara, I must say. *All the effort* I put into it, yeah, you could say that. I suppose that's true. But I have never self-harmed."

"I know," I say, looking at him, serious now. His grin has reduced by a third. "But there's a hint of it in the very style itself."

"On that I think we'll just have to agree to disagree," he says.

Christoffer sometimes lapses into adult ways of speaking. He has looked like a devil-worshipper for the six months I've known him, but right below the surface is a polite young boy waiting to break free. The first time we met he shook my hand, gave me his name, and said it was nice to meet me. Christoffer is in therapy because his mother thinks it's necessary. His parents divorced with teary-eyed, door-slamming, resounding drama a couple of years earlier, and this clothing and music style, along with a certain insolence and a sharp drop in his grades, shook his mother out of her post-divorce stupor with a jolt. She called me in hysterics, and explained that her son was in need of immediate help.

This is a qualified truth – since our very first session I have been convinced that Christoffer will be just fine. He will continue with his rebellion for as long as it upsets his mother, and perhaps in the hope that it may worry his father so much that he'll return home from Brazil in sheer astonishment. But one day in the not-too-distant future, and well before his final exams, Christoffer will throw out his black clothes and studded belts and chains, put on ordinary clothes, go to school as if nothing has happened and make up for lost time. He'll leave secondary school with grades good enough to enable him to do whatever he wants in life, and he'll be absolutely fine. I know this, and Christoffer knows it, too.

The only person who doesn't know it is Christoffer's mother, and therein lies the dilemma. If Christoffer doesn't really need therapy, isn't it unethical of me to give it to him, week after week? On the other hand, I need all the patients I can get. Christoffer, for his part, is happy to come. We have a good rapport, and I would hazard a guess that being in therapy appeals to him – fortifies, in a way, the style he's trying out. Christoffer's mother, waiting outside in her B.M.W., no doubt sleeps better at night knowing that he's being "taken care of", as she puts it, by me. Is this not then an arrangement that benefits everyone involved?

I did once attempt to end the treatment, if not as resolutely as I should have. But Christoffer's mother called me in tears that same evening.

"Sara," she wailed, "you mustn't give up on him. You're our only hope."

This was just before Christmas. It was snowing, and sitting in the chair Christoffer is sitting in now I looked out into the darkness and thought: if I keep him as a patient – what harm will it do? I applied professional terms to it, for myself – there was no-one else to justify it to. I'm offering him an "emotional corrective", I said to myself. I'm a "safe adult" with whom he can explore his identity. These are the kinds of things I wrote in Christoffer's notes, consoling myself with the fact that, since I operate privately, I'm not using taxpayers' money but rather that of Christoffer's wealthy father. And from what I've understood from telephone conversations with Christoffer's mother, taking that asshole's money is nothing to feel guilty about.

Sigurd has called me. He left a message on my answering machine when I was halfway through my session with Vera. I'm now in the kitchen eating lunch: a tuna sandwich and apple juice. I play his message on speakerphone, the mobile on the kitchen worktop beside me, and listen as I eat.

"Hey, love," he says in his typical Sigurd way; the warm, melodic sound of him. "We've made it to Thomas' cabin. Here it's, oh, it's good to be here, I . . ."

The telephone crackles, and I hear the grin in his voice, a couple of bubbly stutters.

"It's just Jan Erik, he's messing around with some firewood, he looks like a total idiot, I . . . I should probably go now. I just wanted to let you know we're here, and, yeah, I'll call you later. Be safe. O.K. Bye."

I have almost finished the sandwich. I sit there with the final crust in my hands as my husband speaks and feel something

29

push against my diaphragm: I miss him. What a stupid thought – he's only been gone for a few hours. I'm actually quite happy being alone. Going to the gym; eating food he doesn't like. Watching films he thinks are stupid. Drinking white wine – which, according to Sigurd, is only for bridesmaids and old ladies. Going to bed early. Getting plenty done with my days.

It's only his voice on the answering machine. I'll call him after work. I eat the last of the crust, wash it down with water. My next patient is Trygve. I have time for a coffee while I read his notes.

Trygve comes at two o'clock on the dot, always on time, never a second too early. But unlike Christoffer he makes it absolutely clear that he does not want to be here. He doesn't sit down in the waiting room but stands with his back to the front door, folding his hands across his chest when I open the door to let him into the office.

"Come in," I say.

He walks past me, wearing a severe expression, lips clamped together so that they're almost invisible.

Trygve always chooses the same chair as Vera, but never sits down before I invite him to. When he does take a seat he doesn't settle back into the chair but remains sitting upright at its edge, ready to get up at the slightest provocation.

"So," I say. "How has your week been?"

"Fine," Trygve says in a flat voice.

"Your schoolwork?"

"Fine."

"Have you done what you're supposed to do?"

"Yep."

"Have you been gaming at all?"

"A bit."

"Have you been gaming more than within the times we agreed on?"

Now he looks at me. He has sandy hair and brown eyes, straight features, nothing unusual – he actually looks conspicuously inconspicuous, if I can put it like that. His facial expressions are eerily controlled, and only very rarely, if he becomes irritated enough, for example, does a non-calculated movement escape censorship. When I first met him, I thought it wouldn't surprise me if he turned out to be a serial killer.

But Trygve isn't coming to me because he has murderous aspirations, or because he's too controlling or because he finds life meaningless. He's in treatment because he's addicted to playing "World of Warcraft", or, more precisely, because his parents made his getting treatment a condition of his continuing to live at home. He's twenty, older than most of my patients, and dropped out of school seven months before his final exams because it was getting in the way of his gaming. Trygve's parents are worried, and they have good reason to be. We have agreed that I will call them if Trygve doesn't show up for treatment. Trygve himself has also agreed to this – only, I imagine, because it would take too much time away from his gaming should his parents throw him out and he be forced to find a job to keep a roof over his head.

"I've almost stuck to the quotas," he says.

"When have you not kept to them?"

He suppresses a snort, like someone trying not to sneeze.

"Two nights. Sunday and Thursday. Otherwise perfect."

His mouth is straight and stiff, his jaw tense, and there's something about his reluctance that makes me tired, that makes me want to throw in the towel and say, "Wonderful, almost perfect, shall we leave it at that for today, then?"

"So, how much time did you run over by on those days?"
I say.

"A little."

I sigh. With Trygve, I know that I have to be specific.

"Let's see. On Sunday you can game from seven until ten.
When did you start?"

"Seven."

"And when did you stop?"

A pause. A muscle bulges along his jaw – that's how hard he's
clenching his teeth. His jaw is strangely rectangular – that, perhaps, is a little conspicuously inconspicuous. I've read that men
with a broad jaw are often regarded as attractive, but on Trygve
such a strong jawline only adds to the impenetrable impression.
Normal, perhaps, but even this expression – his grey, flat, ten-a-
penny expression – seems calculated. It isn't impossible that
Trygve has grand plans for his life, but if anything is certain it's that
not a soul in the real world knows what on earth they might be.

"After midnight."

A blatant euphemism.

"How long after midnight?"

A new bulge at his jawline.

"Three."

"O.K., three, and on Thursday, that is, yesterday – on Thursdays
you can game from seven until eleven. How long did you game for?"

Another pause.

"Until three."

"O.K., I understand. So by my calculations you've gamed for,
let's see, eight hours more than agreed this week."

He's silent, his expression closed.

"What do you think about that?"

Trygve shrugs.

"Is it a good thing, do you think?"

He shrugs again, looks at his watch, places his hand back on the armrest, then looks at his watch once more. There's no way around it with Trygve – all I can do is push back with force against force, steering us into the discomfort he creates for us.

"Because I noticed you used the word 'perfect' when you first came in here, Trygve."

"I said 'almost perfect'."

"Yes, I remember. I'm wondering what made you choose that word?"

He exhales, quickly and loudly – not really a sigh, more in the way that a steam engine releases steam.

"I don't know, Sara," he says, and now he's seething, just below the surface. "Maybe I chose that word because I don't think it's much fucking fun to sit here every week and have to lay out all my private habits for you."

And there it is, his irritation – I realise that it's more explicit today than it usually is. Perhaps this thought occurs to him, too, because it's as if he recollects himself – he stops, his expression with its frowning brow and twisted mouth hanging there in thin air for a moment. Then it's as if he erases it, replaces it with neutral mode.

"Yes, I agree," I say hastily – perhaps I can reach him before he clams up again – "I think that you find our sessions very uncomfortable. Can you say a little more about how you relate to that discomfort during the week, when you're not here?"

Another shrug.

"Dunno. I don't really think about it."

"Let's take an example," I say, trying to be specific again. "Yesterday evening, at eleven o'clock, when you should have stopped gaming, what did you think then?"

"How did you feel?" is what I should have said – I have to avoid falling into the trap of becoming reason-focused.

"Dunno. Nothing."

"Because you knew I'd ask you about it today."

"Didn't think about it."

"I'm wondering, Trygve, whether you're really motivated to try to keep to the schedule we've set up?"

"Dunno. Well, yeah. I'm trying."

"Because I don't think I can force you to stop gaming – and nor can your parents, for that matter. You have to want to stop for yourself."

"Yeah. I do want to."

The morning's weariness rolls over me again, a hundred times stronger than when Vera triggered it. It's right that if Trygve's going to change he has to do it himself, and it's glaringly obvious he can't be bothered to. *Patients who end up in therapy always have a motivation, or ambivalence*, the textbooks say, and I know what they advise – get a hold on what's there, Trygve wants to keep his home, build on that – but my toolbox feels empty and useless. Maybe the problem is that Trygve's desire is so instrumental: not to maintain the relationship with his parents, not to stay at home because it's safe, but simply to keep a roof over his head, an electricity supply for his computer. And if I'm being honest, I'm not sure what will help Trygve. Many gamers play away years of their lives, just as Trygve seems determined to do. He's carved in stone, and part of me thinks that as long as this is what he wants, there's not much that can be done about it.

But it's Friday afternoon. I don't have it in me, another pseudo-conversation in which Trygve says whatever he needs to say in order to follow our agreement.

"O.K.," I say, "but what do you think you need to do in order to stick to our agreed times next week?"

"I'll try harder," Trygve says through clenched teeth.

"Good," I say. "Then we'll try that. Shall we say the same time next Friday?"

Before I go to the gym I call Sigurd, but he doesn't pick up.

I'm on the T-banen on my way home when my mobile rings. The train winds its way up from Ullevål, its couplings clattering. It's dark outside, the light in the carriage yellow, the seats occupied by tired businessmen and women with briefcases and smartphones, the odd skiing fanatic wanting to get the most out of the winter heading to the countryside. Otherwise, there's just me, my sweaty body causing the windowpane beside me to fog up. The mood is sullen and silent apart from the jangling of the carriage. The humming vibration of the telephone in my bag breaks the silence, Jan Erik's name lighting up the screen.

"Hello?" I say in a questioning tone, as if I don't know who it is.

"Oh hello, Sara, it's Jan Erik."

His voice is unstable, flippant, as slithering as the carriage in which I sit. I stifle a sigh. Are they drunk already? Have they sunk to an even lower level of childishness than usual – are they making prank calls?

"Yes," I say, sharply, as in "get to the point".

"Yeah, we just . . . Thomas and I are wondering whether you've heard from Sigurd?"

"What do you mean?"

Outside, the ascent becomes steeper – we're approaching Berg, only two more stations before mine. The houses are like models, black lumps with illuminated rectangles on them. They don't look real – I can't believe that people live in them.

"No, we just . . . We were just wondering . . ."

He clears his throat, and I think this is unusually idiotic, even for him.

"What are you wondering about, Jan Erik?"

"Just . . . when he's coming."

"When he's coming?"

There's a pounding at my temples – first Trygve, then my spinning class and now Jan Erik. All I want is a shower, a glass of white wine and my chicken salad.

"Yeah. I mean, he said he'd be here around five, and now it's after seven, and we just, we can't get hold of him, so, haha, well, we didn't know – but we thought you might? Know, I mean? Or have heard from him?"

There's a mumbling behind him – Thomas' voice. I straighten up in my seat.

"Yeah, I'm sure there's nothing wrong," Jan Erik says now, almost shrilly, it seems to me. "We just wanted to check."

Thomas is more sensible than Jan Erik. I'm not sure whether I like Thomas, but I certainly prefer him to Jan Erik.

"Listen," I say, in a low voice so the rest of the train won't hear me but loud enough that Jan Erik will, "Sigurd called me at around nine-thirty this morning and said that you were all there already. I haven't heard from him since."

Silence on the other end of the line. Then there's more mumbling – I can't make out what they're saying, but they're talking between themselves, I can hear them both, their almost-whispering.

"What are you saying?" I say, loud enough now that those sitting around me evidently get the gist of the conversation. "I can't hear what you're saying."

Silence again. Then Thomas mumbles something, and Jan Erik says:

"I'm not sure I understand, Sara, because Thomas and I only got here around one. Sigurd said he was going to drive up here himself, later."

36

My forehead tightens; a headache, thick and burning.

"He called at around nine-thirty, ten," I say, exhausted, tired of them and the train and this entire day. "He said that you were there already, he said . . ."

I think back: Jan Erik, the firewood.

"He said you were messing around with some logs for the fire."

Total silence descends. Even the train, now on a straight stretch, stops its noise.

"But Thomas and I only left Oslo at ten," Jan Erik says.

People's stories often contain inconsistencies, small untruths – not really lies, more shortcuts – which means that one person at different times, or several people at the same time, may tell stories that don't add up. Someone took the bus somewhere, even though the T-banen would have been easier. Someone was on their summer holiday in Denmark, but had to explain themselves in German in a pharmacy. If you don't take these things too literally it isn't a problem. Perhaps you heard wrong, perhaps it wasn't the café by the train station but one with a similar name, next to a bus stop. Perhaps they weren't taking the ferry to Denmark but to Kiel. There are usually plausible explanations. No, we *were* in Denmark, but took a day trip to Germany. It was just easier not to tell the whole story.

But fundamentally different stories – mutually exclusive descriptions of the facts – these are not so common. Even in the world of therapy it usually goes something like, "Yeah, Mamma says I was drunk, but I'd only had a couple of beers, I was just so tired, my speech was slurred – I agree about that – but I wasn't blind drunk." People stretch out the truth, embellish the story. Pull it in different directions. But people don't usually say A when B is true and B excludes A. Nobody says, "I was in the car at Sinsen," if in fact they were standing outside a cabin in

Norefjell with a pile of logs in their arms. You don't say, "Jan Erik is just crossing the yard," if in fact you're staring at an abandoned, empty yard – if Jan Erik isn't even in the same county.

Such contradictions are not plausible – are not the result of a misunderstanding or inconsistency. Only one of two options is possible: Jan Erik was at Norefjell a little after nine-thirty, and is now lying, or Jan Erik was in the car driving out of Oslo at ten o'clock, and Sigurd lied in his voicemail message.

But I don't have the energy to think about it; can only believe that Jan Erik is playing a joke on me. I have never understood his sense of humour. He once laughed so hard that beer came out of his nose because he had tricked Sigurd into taking a bite of a chilli pepper by telling him it was a sweet one. When I hang up, he'll be doubled up on the cabin floor, crying with laughter because he's tricked me, and Sigurd will come in from the outside toilet, look at him and smile, not understanding, and say: "What's so funny?"

"I'm sure there's a reasonable explanation," I say. "Listen, I'm on the train on the way home from the gym. Can't we just . . . Can't we just try to call him again? Both of us? O.K.? And then speak a little later on this evening when we've managed to get hold of him?"

"Yeah, O.K.," Jan Erik says, almost too eager. "Yeah, let's do that, haha, I'm sure it's just a misunderstanding. But. Yeah. We just wanted to let you know."

"O.K., speak to you soon, then. Say hi to Thomas from me."

We hang up. I call Sigurd, letting the telephone ring until the answering machine kicks in. The train pulls into Berg station. I look out of the window, see my reflection in the glass, still red-faced after my spinning class, and think, well, that was weird.

*

Only when I'm standing in Old Torp's shower cubicle under the stream of hot water from the hole in the wall does the illogical nature of the situation truly dawn on me. There's no other possibility than that one of them is lying, either Jan Erik or Sigurd. Jan Erik has a warped sense of humour, but this seems too much, even for him. And Sigurd is a good guy, he's my husband – he doesn't lie.

But let's just say that what Jan Erik says is true. That Sigurd is lying for some reason or other, something understandable – a surprise, for example, what do I know? Just supposing. But then why hasn't he arrived at the cabin?

Only then do I feel the fear growing cold and hard in my stomach. Where is Sigurd now? I try to assuage it: don't be stupid, Sara, there must be a good reason, he's lost his mobile or it's out of battery, he's probably on his way up there right now, I bet he called from Jan Erik's mobile while I was in the shower. It helps, makes my fear less sharp, wraps it in cotton wool to turn it into a murmuring ball of worry instead. I rinse the shampoo from my hair and turn off the water; step out of the shower, trembling and naked on the wooden pallets as I quickly dry myself and unhook my dressing gown from a pallet leant up against the wall. I wrap a towel around my hair, pull on the dressing gown, rub my arms to warm myself and hurry out of the bathroom, down the stairs and into the kitchen.

But my mobile shows no missed calls. When I pick it up the screen is illuminated by a photograph, Sigurd and me with Theo, my sister's eldest son. We have wedges of orange in our mouths, all three of us; we're grinning, orange everywhere. Sigurd's eyes are narrow with laughter, almost invisible, nothing but folds of skin with small, dark pearls inside. His smile, with the skin of the orange covering his teeth, is enormous.

A corner of the swaddled fear in my stomach pokes itself free.

I open my voicemail and replay Sigurd's message.

"Hey, love. We've made it to Thomas' cabin. Here it's, oh, it's good to be here, I . . . It's just Jan Erik, he's messing around with some firewood, he looks like a total idiot, I . . . I should probably go now. I just wanted to let you know we're here, and, yeah, I'll call you later. Be safe. O.K. Bye."

I play it again; Sigurd's voice. "Hey, love." Just as he always says it. Nothing strange. Not a cough, not the slightest tremor in his voice. The crackling as Jan Erik approaches doesn't sound like anything in particular; the hesitation before he continues seems genuine.

"Be safe." Just like he always says. "Bye."

I play the recording for a third time, more focused now. Is he indoors or outside, for example? We went to Thomas' cabin at Norefjell a few years ago, so I know the layout. Just a moment ago I imagined Sigurd standing in the doorway, Jan Erik crossing the yard with an armful of logs, trying not to drop them – that Sigurd had to hang up to help him carry them inside. But can I be certain about that? Might they just as easily be inside, Jan Erik joking around with some logs from beside the fire, lifting them up to his head to give himself big ears, for example, or raising one above his head and pretending to hunt Sigurd around the room? So Sigurd has to hang up in order to run?

"He looks like a total idiot" – is that because he's about to fall, or because he's fooling around? And would it even be typical of Sigurd to use such an expression? With a sigh I think that no, back when I first met him Sigurd would never have said that anyone looked like an idiot. This is the influence of his childhood friends – especially Jan Erik. Not the Sigurd I met in Bergen four years ago.

The fourth time I play the recording I decide that he's outside. Indoors the sounds of Jan Erik joking around would have been reflected by the walls – I would have heard him. Sound travels further outdoors. Unless Jan Erik is outside, and Sigurd's watching him through the window.

If Jan Erik is even there at all. Another sharp corner of the fear in my stomach jabs at me.

I call Sigurd again. The mobile rings and rings. "Hi, you've reached Sigurd Torp. Sorry I can't come to the phone right now, but leave me a message and I'll get back to you." A beep.

"Hi, love, it's me. Can you call me?"

I hesitate, waiting. Why don't I just hang up?

"Be safe, O.K.? Call me. Bye."

"Hi, love." We've talked about this. "Sweetie" is too childish. "Darling" too serious, unless you're saying it ironically, in which case it becomes alienating. "Baby" is for teenagers. "Honey" is too gooey. But "love" – "love" is cosy without being too sweet. From the verb "to love", and therefore also descriptive. Exactly the way we feel about each other but can't bring ourselves to say every time we speak on the phone. Sigurd and I aren't the kind of couple who say "I love you" on a daily basis. We save that phrase for special occasions, whisper it to one another with a sincere intensity when it feels as if our chests are about to burst. "Hi, love" is code.

I call Thomas. He answers immediately.

"Have you heard from him?" I say. Thomas clears his throat, says no.

"Thomas," I say, "what's going on? Are you kidding around with me?"

"No," Thomas says, sounding hurt that I could possibly think something like that. "No," he says, "we'd never do that."

"I just, I just don't understand," I say.

"Neither do we," Thomas says. "We don't know what to think. There were no footprints in the snow outside when we arrived. I can't see how he could have been here – I mean, are you sure that's what he said?"

My stomach contracts. Thomas' voice isn't as wavering as Jan Erik's. He's speaking coherently – they're not drunk. Thomas isn't mean, not really. He has a normal sense of humour – he laughs at Monty Python and stand-up comedy on T.V.

"He left me a voicemail," I say. "I've listened to it four times since I last spoke to you – I know what he said."

"O.K.," Thomas says. "Then I don't know. He must've been joking, then. Maybe he was supposed to . . . No, I don't know."

He takes a deep breath. Behind him, Jan Erik says something. I hold my breath on my end of the line.

"So what do we do now?" Thomas says.

We agree to wait and see, because what else can we do? "Just go on with whatever you planned to do," Thomas says to me, so I make a chicken salad. I open the bottle of white wine. I think, this is ridiculous. I think, it'll turn out there's an explanation for everything, Sigurd and I will laugh about it later. I imagine myself telling him about exactly this moment, the way I stood here, making a chicken salad and not knowing what to believe. But oh, you poor thing, didn't you realise that I'd just slept over at the office? No, it never even occurred to me, I didn't under-stand why you hadn't called – but that was just because, because, because. But, "love". Were you worried? I'm so sorry, I didn't mean to scare you – didn't mean to ruin your evening, the dinner and film you were so looking forward to. No, it doesn't matter, of course not. Just as long as everything's O.K.

The lump in my stomach struggles against the layer in which I've wrapped it. I pour myself another glass of wine. So Sigurd has lied to me. Or Jan Erik and Thomas are lying, though I don't think so. But why do I trust them more than I trust my own husband?

Because they're here right now. Because they're talking to me. Because Sigurd hasn't turned up to tell me his side of the story. That's what it comes down to. Why don't you, Sigurd? Can't you just show up and tell your side of the story? Tell me what that voicemail means?

I call him again. The ringing tone drones on and on, that aggressive sound, no answer, and then the tiny click as the answering machine kicks in, the moment of hope – is he picking up? – but it's the tape. "Hi, you've reached Sigurd Torp . . ."

The food is unsatisfying – I've lost my appetite. I've found a chick flick on Netflix, "Sense and Sensibility"; women in bonnets and long dresses, men with fine manners who suppress all their feelings. A film Sigurd would never agree to watch.

So he lied. So what? I might say that he doesn't lie, but then what do I know? If men do lie, isn't it first and foremost to their wives? Are there not thousands of reasons for us to lie to those closest to us?

I have lied myself – I probably lie often, even to Sigurd. *Especially* to Sigurd. I tell him that my practice is going well, that it's a little difficult to find patients now that it's winter, but that things will pick up. I say nothing about the fact that I feel lonely out there in the office above the garage – although I had so looked forward to quitting my job and leaving behind all my complaining, arguing, gossiping colleagues. I don't mention that I'm not advertising my services, that I haven't put an ad on Google, even though the guy from the year above me at university who also runs his own practice says that's the way to get patients. I say nothing of the fact that I haven't told everyone I know that I've started working for myself, don't say that I haven't created a Facebook page, that I'm not doing my best to find more work.

I say only this – that things will pick up. In fact, now I come to think of it, I lie even more than this. I say that the guy I know also thinks it's difficult in the winter – although he's never said anything of the sort, only that his first month was a little on the quiet side, before he started advertising. I turn his words around; embellish them, deduct from them. So that Sigurd won't nag me. He's mentioned it a couple of times: "You said you'd earn more – I don't mean to pressure you, but we need money for the renovations." He tends to say this whenever I bug him about the fact that work on the house has ground to a halt. Old Torp is still living in the walls – he must be rubbing his hands with glee. "I have so much to do," Sigurd says then – but is that true?

"Atkinson," Sigurd says. Atkinson is an English shipping magnate who lives in an apartment in St Hanshaugen and who Sigurd has been working for – preparing the drawings for the conversion of his cellar. Mrs Atkinson in particular has pre-sented problems – she was trouble from the start, and has only got worse as the project has progressed. No, the stairs were not supposed to be like *that*, that's not what we agreed at all, Mrs Atkinson says. She had imagined there would be "much more light" when the window was installed. Sigurd had to be friendly, understand that she was disappointed, explain, go back to the drawing board. She also quibbles about the bill. "I'm not paying for this," she says, "that's not what we agreed."

"Atkinson," Sigurd says when he comes home late and slumps down on the sofa in front of the T.V. "She's been on the phone all day, I had to go down there and look at the fucking stairs, which don't 'open up the room' as she'd envisaged." It's implied that he can't be bothered to work tonight – not on the bathroom, not on the bedroom, and especially not on any of the stairs in this old shack. He wants to put his feet up, watch a reality T.V. show about a group of Americans trying to survive thirty days alone in the wilderness as he fiddles about with his laptop. Is he not due this, at least? When he's been forced to appease Mrs Atkinson all day?

Or has he? Or is this just like when I tell him about how it's been hard to find patients?

While the people in the film just about manage to exude a polite joy at their hearts being broken, it hits me. The missing document tube.

Maybe he had planned to work from the cabin. Perhaps it's logical that he took the document holder with him. But did he really call from the cabin in Norefjell, when there were no tracks leading up to the front door by the time Jan Erik and Thomas arrived? Maybe he did see Jan Erik with the logs. But then why are his two friends not telling the truth about it now?

He lied. He must have done. Or maybe everyone is lying, at least a little. But Sigurd lied about where he was. About who he was with. I listen to the voicemail message again. I know it off by heart by now. But that's not it. What is it I can hear?

"Hey, love. We've made it to Thomas' cabin."

Is there a hint of deception in his voice?

"Here it's, oh, it's good to be here."

Now was that necessary, if it was all a lie? And with a sigh, no less! "Oh, it's good to be here." Well, you know what, Sigurd? It's not so good to be *here*, in Kongleveien, in this old house where your old grandfather lived and died – here, with the empty hook where your document tube should be, with your voice on the answering machine and your friends calling me, telling me things I don't understand.

Crackle, crackle.

"It's just Jan Erik, he's messing around with some firewood."

My stomach starts to boil, hot and violent, melting away the fear and unease – angry and strong and freeing. So it's Jan Erik, you say? Wrong! You've made it, you say? Lie! You want me to stay safe? You asshole.

Infuriated, I delete the message – wanting to be done with it, not wanting anything more to do with it, as if I could delete the memory of it at the same time. As if the whole problem will cease to exist now that the message is gone.

I put the chicken salad in the fridge; turn off the film, turn off the T.V. Set the mouth of the bottle to my lips and empty the rest of the wine down my throat.

Before I fall asleep, as I lie there with Sigurd's side of the duvet around me, trying to make the room stop spinning, I think: perhaps that wasn't such a good idea. Deleting the message. It might have been good to have the option to play it again.

Breathe, breathe. I flounder, wake with my head under Sigurd's pillow. Was something there – did I hear a sound? I listen. I hear nothing but silence.

Has he called? The telephone is blank. It's 3.46 a.m. His space is empty; his side of the bed cold.

"Sigurd?"

I say it softly, repeat it. Get up, open the door, call out, go down the stairs to the living room and kitchen.

"Sigurd?"

It was as if I heard something – as if I was startled awake. But now I can hear nothing. I go back to bed.

Sitting beside me on the sofa is a history student, prattling on and on. She has her face turned towards me, is drowning me in her words, pouring and spraying and spewing them over me so they splash around in my ears. I look over at the veranda door, which is open, and beyond it can see my friend Ronja standing there speaking to a guy she's interested in. It's Ronja who dragged me here. We were at home in our apartment drinking Sambuca from shot glasses decorated with cheaply printed religious symbols which she'd bought for me in Peru over the summer – we'd laughed until we cried when I opened them – and Ronja said, "If I drink up first we're going to that party You Know Who is going to, and if you drink up first, we'll go to your friend's place in Gyldenpris like we said we would." Ronja was the faster drinker, so here we are.

"So what do you do?" the history student asked me when I sat down on the sofa.

"I'm studying psychology," I said.

"Are you really?" she said.

"Yes," I said. I knew where this was going.

"So then maybe you can help me with something," the history student said. "You see, my dad's just got remarried, my parents divorced when I was ten, and his new wife, well, if I were to describe her in a single word? – she's a bitch."

And so it goes on. My eyes search the room for someone I know, but the party's been organised by a friend of Ronja's would-be boyfriend. He's an architecture student and sitting in the kitchen – I saw him when I put our beers in the fridge. He was in the middle of telling a girl with a face full of piercings about how he intended to "reinvent the kitchen". There are some girls sitting on the sofa across from us, deep in discussion, but they're friends – the first of them has an arm around the second; the third slaps the first one on the thigh as she speaks. It suggests a kind of intimacy I'm not party to – I can't just barge in on their conversation. Then there's the drunk guys eating salted pretzels at the dining table, and then there's the guy standing there leaning against the door frame.

Him. He's alone. He doesn't seem to be bothered by this, but of course that might be affected. He squints at the air in front of him, thinking about something, perhaps. The beer bottle in his hand has had its label torn off. His hands are covered in flecks of paint, they're fine, the fingers crooked, as hands should be. He's bitten his nails all the way down to the quick.

I watch him, seeing all this – his destroyed nails, his soft eyes, the dishevelled hair – but mainly I see that he's standing alone. He doesn't look desperate, but he's standing alone, and I just know that he's waiting to meet someone. Someone funny and smart and passably attractive. Someone like me.

"Excuse me," I say to the history student, and get up.

I go over to him.

"Hey," I say, "it's you."

I put my arms around his neck and whisper, just beside his tiny, round ear: "Pretend you know me."

"Hi," he says.

I look at him. He has a mole under his left eye; it stretches when he smiles.

"It's been a while," I say. "I haven't seen you since that day in Berlin."

"Yeah, Berlin," he says, "that must be a few years ago now."

"Did you go to France, like you said you would?" I say.

"No," he says. He smiles more, the mole stretching thinner,

longer. "I ended up going to Australia. Studied at a Panda school for two years. Became a panda-ologist."

I laugh. O.K., so he's playing along. But it was me who started it. I'm funnier.

"What a coincidence," I say, "because my panda's actually sick at the moment."

"Sick in what way?"

"A bit under the weather. Hacking and coughing. Can you help?"

"Unfortunately not," he says. "I no longer dabble in panda medicine. I teach."

We grin at each other – that's enough. He glances around, leans towards me and says, his voice lower:

"Why are we pretending that we know each other?"

"I'm trying to get away from the girl on the sofa."

He leans his head past mine to look and I observe his neck, a strong, healthy sinew in the middle of it, and I think, I like that, sinewy men.

"She looks about one metre sixty, fifty kilos maybe," he says. "I reckon you can take her."

Now he's trying to be too funny, I think, he must have something to prove – and anyway, it's not nice to comment on people's weight, although it is true that I'm almost twenty centimetres taller than she is.

"I think your name is Harald," I say.

"Wrong," he says.

"Are you sure? You look like a Harald. Well, anyway, Harald, this party isn't all it's cracked up to be. What do you say we go grab a burger?"

"I'm in," he says. "But call me Sigurd. Harald's my brother."

*

Because he was standing alone. Because boys like him stand there at parties looking for girls like me. Because I was tipsy and twenty-five years old. Because my friend was out on the veranda, talking to some boy. Because I felt so safe out and about with her, with the other girls I knew at the time, that it didn't matter to me whether he said yes or no.

Saturday, March 7: Missing

Old Torp's doorbell wakes me. The sound is piercing, like an air raid siren – appropriate should the communists see fit to stop by. My dream was restless and fluid – I think I was swimming – and there was something I had to remember to do. The doorbell. The hard, insistent cries call me back. I look around me. Sigurd's side of the bed is empty.

But there's someone at the door, and who else could it be? I throw my dressing gown over my shoulders, tie it closed as I run into the hall. I rush down the stairs, holding the banister so that I won't slip on the cardboard that covers the sticky floor that once featured wall-to-wall carpeting, lifting my feet so I don't trip on the loose treads.

He's back. He'll explain everything. It'll all be a misunderstanding, it doesn't matter what kind.

I tear down the next flight, down to the ground floor where the front door is and throw it open, expecting to see him, to throw my arms around him.

On the front step is Julie.

"How are you?" she says.

I look at her, not understanding. What is *she* doing here? Before I manage to answer she's over the threshold with her arms around me.

"Good," I say, a reflex response, but I'm no longer sure, haven't yet had time to check in with myself. I've spent all night tossing and turning, wide awake, checking the telephone only to see that nobody's called; I've pondered, slept, dreamed, woken up. And now I'm standing here with Julie before me, her hand on the sleeve of my dressing gown in an attempt to comfort me. We don't know each other very well, even though she's been with Thomas as long as I've known Sigurd. It hits me that I haven't checked my mobile since I was last awake at 3.45 a.m.

Without a word I turn and run back upstairs, to the first floor where the living room and kitchen are, then up to the second floor and into the bedroom. Frantic, I look through the items on the bedside table, knocking over a glass, shoving aside a book to find my mobile. Then I look in the bed, sit on my knees on the mattress, put my hands under his side of the duvet – still warm, but it's only my heat – until I finally feel the smooth, flat rectangle of my phone, hidden between our pillows.

There are two messages. One is from Thomas, received this morning at 07:15:

He's still not turned up. We're packing up and making our way back to town. I'll call you.

The second is from Julie, received at 07:38:

Hi, Sara, Thomas told me what happened. I'll stop by when you're awake. Hugs, Julie.

Nothing from him.

It seems that Julie could wait no longer, because it's now 8.23 a.m. and she's here in my house. I hear her steps downstairs; she's made her way up to the living room. She calls my name, probingly, as if she's not quite sure whether I'm still here. My breathing becoming shallower and shallower, straight down my throat and back up again, I tap Sigurd's name in my list of calls and put the phone to my ear. *Pick up, pick up, pick up.* The line is silent.

"Sara, where are you?" Julie says from downstairs.

The receiver crackles, and then a friendly female voice tells me that the person I'm trying to call has turned off their mobile.

The effect of this is like a punch to the gut. I fold over on the bed, although this is really no different from yesterday – his telephone rang and rang without him answering then too. It stands to reason that it would run out of battery. But yesterday there was a line connecting us, which has now in one fell swoop been snapped. I had called his mobile, and it had rung – wherever it might be. Now it no longer rings. This technical detail, a mobile with battery, a mobile without, startles me. I lie here in a folded lump on the bed and listen to Julie's footsteps. As she makes her way up the stairs to the second floor, I whisper to myself: "Sigurd, Sigurd, Sigurd."

I sense that she's standing behind me before she says anything, as you can sometimes sense that someone's staring at you – that uncomfortable sensation of being observed. Here I am in my dressing gown, the mobile clasped between my hands and my forehead against its glass surface; my feet hurt, I must have tripped on a loose tread on the way up. I lie here in our messy, half-finished bedroom, wallpaper half-stripped from the walls, the night's stale air hanging heavily over the bed, a lingering smell of alcohol from the bottle of wine I emptied. Julie stands and looks at me.

"Sara," she says, her voice uncertain, "are you O.K.?"

I don't respond. The cold screen of my mobile is smooth against my forehead. One of my feet is stinging – might even be bleeding. I want her to leave.

But Julie does not leave. Instead, she comes in, crosses the threshold and comes over to the bed, places both hands on my dressing-gown-covered back, and says:

"Come on now, you can't just lie here. Let's go downstairs and make some coffee."

She takes hold of my shoulder as if to pull me up, hoist me out of the bed, and as she does so I feel it rising in me, a column from my belly, a source of heat, an elemental force travelling from my stomach up my back and into my arms and legs and throughout my body – who the fuck does she think she is?

I rip myself free of her, pull away, want to hit her – so fierce is this force quivering through me. It takes a degree of self-control not to lash out at her. She stands there, confused, with her big innocent doe eyes, her snub little button nose, her round chin – her adorable face, with its fringe and ponytail, as if she's a teenage schoolgirl out to play the Samaritan, out to help me. How self-satisfied she is, I think, telling me that I can't just lie here. Ordinary little Julie has come to set things straight, pick up the pieces. She must have practised in the car all the way here, going over how she would act. And now she's standing there, so surprised, her face just begging to be slapped, and the only thing that stops me from hitting her is the fact that I pull away.

This is our bedroom. Sigurd lives here, and so do I. This is where we have lived and loved and fought and slept. He left yesterday morning, and since then it's been just me, alone, but now she's standing here, in our very inner sanctum – who the fuck is *she*?

The first time I met her, at a barbecue in their back garden in Nydalen, she delightedly said to me: "I'm sure we'll become good friends." But it never happened. Even then I felt an unwillingness at this expectation – we've fallen in love with two friends so therefore it's only logical for us to be friends, too. More than that – we should become close, intimate. She was wearing heart-shaped earrings and a white lace blouse; she was smiling and dumb, and I saw nothing in her that I could identify with.

That was four years ago. Sigurd has sometimes complained about it. Julie's fine, he says, you could try to get to know her a bit better. Perhaps I could, but on the other hand maybe I'm just using my common sense.

I pull the dressing gown tight around me and stare at her, trembling, heat leaching from my pores, my eyes, my mouth – I can feel it, I'm no longer sane.

"Get out," I hiss.

"But—" says Julie.

"Get out."

Her face crumples; it's as if I have struck her, after all. She turns, about to leave, hesitates, and turns back to me.

"I was just trying to be nice," she says to me, her voice thick now, full of tears and rust and jagged stones, "even though you've never been nice to me. I just wanted to *help*." She turns again and goes – I can hear her footsteps, hard and quick, as she makes her way down the stairs. I sit with the telephone in my hands, this dead, shiny object. *Sigurd, Sigurd, where are you?*

Downstairs the front door slams shut behind Julie. I try to breathe deeply, down into my stomach. It's Saturday, and I'm alone.

"Oslo police headquarters," says the woman on the other end of the line.

"Yes, hello," I say, "I'm calling about a missing person, yes, a man – my husband. He, well, he's been missing since early yesterday morning, or around nine-thirty, I don't know when exactly. He called me a little after nine-thirty. That's the last I've heard from him. He should have arrived at his friend's cabin by five, but he never made it there."

"I see," the woman says. "But current procedure is not to start looking for anyone until at least twenty-four hours have passed."

"Right, O.K.," I say, fumbling – I hadn't thought this far, about searches, that kind of thing.

"This is an adult we're talking about?"

"Yes, my husband, so – he's thirty-two."

"I understand," she says. "Of course you're welcome to come down to the station and make a report, but we won't be able to do anything until twenty-four hours have passed."

"No, O.K., then."

I don't know what else to say. Twenty-four hours. Missing, wanted.

"Most people who go missing turn up again after a few hours," the woman says, her tone a little friendlier now. "Generally there's been a misunderstanding about an agreement, or someone's misremembered something."

I clear my throat.

"He left me a message on my voicemail," I say, "telling me he was with his friends. But they say he wasn't with them."

"Hmm," she says. "Well, as I said, it's often a misunderstanding."

The economy of these sentences – he was with his friends. Of course it sounds like a misunderstanding.

"I understand," I say. I have to try. "But you see, he said he was with them, and they say he wasn't, so either, well, either he's lying or they are."

"O.K.," she says, and I hear how I must sound – like a ridiculous woman, the victim of some joke or indiscretion, too stupid to understand. "Well, it's hard to know sometimes, but when it's an adult and the circumstances aren't evidently critical, we don't do anything until after twenty-four hours. So you can call back again then, if you like. If he doesn't turn up in the meantime, that is."

"O.K."

"As I said, most people do."

I hang up. "Evidently critical." Then what are we talking about? I'm still sitting in bed in my dressing gown.

The shower makes me feel more normal; afterwards, I stick a plaster on my toe. As I dress I think that she was right, the woman on the phone. Most people do turn up. The police have experience of this kind of thing – they know what they're talking about. I need to calm down. I've always been good in emergency situations at work – administering first aid, handling out-of-control children, taking taxi rides to accident and emergency with suicidal teenagers. I know how to keep calm. It's one of my strengths.

I've let myself get carried away. Jan Erik is wobbly by nature, he jokes about everything and takes nothing seriously – isn't that a symptom of insecurity? Isn't it insecurity that makes him cower at the slightest change in the weather? Thomas, well, Thomas is sensible, but his feathers may have been ruffled by Jan Erik. Or by Julie. Yes, that's true – a man married to Julie must be the kind of man who succumbs to pressure.

But I'm stronger than that; I should be able to stand firm. Perhaps it was the session with Trygve; maybe it was the bottle of wine. It's strange, the voicemail message, but there must be an explanation. I just need to relax. Wait. Things will work themselves out. Sigurd will turn up; everything will be explained.

I threw Julie out – that may have been a bit extreme. I was angry, of course; confused, just woken up. I'd had a bit to drink. There's no getting away from it – I was tipsy last night, off balance. She caught me napping – in the most literal sense. I overreacted. I'm private by nature, and we're not close. I'll have to send her a message and apologise.

I take a long, deep breath. Yes. That feels better. Nothing but a minor worry, a troubled lump in my belly. Otherwise, I feel fine. Relaxed. It's Saturday. I should get on with my normal routine.

On the first floor something makes me stop. I'm about to go over to our kitchen nook and make a cup of coffee, but I stop, look around me. Something feels strange.

It's hard to put my finger on what. I remember yesterday in detail, what I did and didn't do, but my memories from last night are fuzzy. It was the wine – that has to be partly to blame – and of course all this to do with Sigurd, too. All the thoughts that ran through my head. To remember anything, I have to focus.

But it's peculiar.

The pan on the hob, for example. It's empty – clean, even – I put it there yesterday evening after boiling some water for a cup of tea. It has a long handle, so it can be held with just one hand. When I was little, such pots and pans always had to be positioned with the handle facing inwards. It was Mamma who was particular about it. "Small children might grab that handle," she used to say. I was seven when she died, and had no interest in things like pots and pans, but I can remember Annika saying it: "You have to put the pans like *this*, Mamma says so." Handle in. I always position my pans that way; Annika and Pappa do, too. But the pan on the hob has the end of its handle sticking out over the edge of the counter. A child – should one be here – would be able to grab it. I would never have left a pan like that.

Or would I? And by that I mean, was I really so groggy yesterday – the wine, the voicemail message – that I left the pan that way without thinking? I remember the cup of tea. I remember that I was simultaneously thinking about Sigurd: his lie, of which I was now convinced. About why he would lie. Was he carrying on with someone else? Mrs Atkinson, for example? Was he involved in something dodgy I didn't know about? Was he avoiding me because of my constant nagging about the renovations? That's what I'd stood there thinking about. My hands prepared the cup of tea on autopilot. I look in the bin – the teabag is there. I look at the pan. It twists within me, that handle sticking out over the edge of the hob. It makes my fingers prickle just to look at it. Could it have been me? Could I have been in that much of a daze?

Or might it have been Julie? I breathe, remember that I was lying upstairs on the bed with my mobile pressed to my forehead as I heard her pottering in the kitchen, calling my name. So, Julie, you were snooping around while you were here? Took a peek in my pan? Had a little look in the fridge, perhaps? Just couldn't help yourself.

I lose my sense of calm again, lose it so fast. I'm clearly not myself because of all this. I have to remember what she said, the woman at the police station who answered the telephone. Most people come home of their own accord.

As I sit there with my cup of coffee and look around the living room, it occurs to me that there's something else. I don't know what, exactly – which detail has changed – but something is different. Did Julie take a little walk around in here?

Then I remember that I woke in the night. That I was calling out to him. Was he here? Walking around in the living room, without coming upstairs?

I shudder. Shake off the thought – it's unthinkable. It was Julie, of course it was. Julie, on the prowl for gossip. I have such a short fuse. My nerves are frayed.

*

A friend would come in handy right now. When Sigurd and I met four years ago, I had many. Ronja I was closest to, but there were others – Benedicte, Ida, Eva-Lise. We shared a flat in Bergen: Ronja, Benedicte and I. A shabby apartment in Håkonsgaten, close to the cinema.

But we haven't been good at keeping in touch. Ronja is bumming around, travelling the world now, writing articles for various newspapers and taking casual jobs before she moves on again. It's difficult to reach her – if I send her an email, she answers a few weeks later. She calls me every now and again if she's here in the city, and we go out, have a few beers, laugh and have fun, but she's not someone I can depend on – not the way I could depend on her when we were students. Ida got married and moved to Stavanger. She and her husband both have hectic careers in the oil industry, and whenever they're not working they're outdoors, climbing some mountain. Benedicte has one-year-old twins. Whenever I call her, I hear them screaming and hollering in the background. Eva-Lise lives in Tromsø, and works at the university there. Neither she nor I particularly enjoy speaking on the telephone, but we do speak every now and again – it's not that. I don't mean to complain. But we all used to be so close. I could speak to them about anything – and by anything I mean the important things. But even more importantly, we could also talk about the unimportant things. Everyday things, the things that don't matter so much. The kind of you'll-never-guess-what-happened-to-me-on-the-bus type things; the did-I-tell-you-about-that-guy-at-work stuff.

When your husband doesn't answer his phone for hours on end, those are the people you want to speak to. The people who you can talk to without it being hard work. Friends the conversation just flows with, where you can say whatever occurs to you or simply stay silent. The people who can make you think about something differently. I can't just call Eva-Lise on a Saturday and say, "Tell me about something that happened at work yesterday." Because now there's all the other accumulated stuff, the kind of what's-happened-since-we-last-spoke things we'd have to catch up on. And that's exactly what I need a break from, what's happening right now. The screaming absence in this house. Sigurd.

On a whim, I call Margrethe. Maybe he's just with his mother. I can already hear the apology, hear him explaining: "Oh, my phone was out of battery, and I'd forgotten my key. I didn't want to wake you, so I went to my mum's." His *apology*? Do I really believe that explanation would constitute an apology?

While the ringing tone buzzes in my ear I consider what I'm about to say to her. How I'm going to call her up and worry her like this. On the other hand, she's a strikingly sensible woman, someone who disapproves of the highly strung and the nervous, who would tell the better part of my patients that they just need to pull themselves together – to stop thinking so much, get enough sleep, eat healthily, do their schoolwork and clean up their rooms – and then everything will be fine. But perhaps "sensible" isn't the right word. There's plenty that Margrethe doesn't understand.

The number rings and rings. No answer.

I go out. Where I'm going, I don't know, but I don't want to just sit around at home. Sigurd has taken the car, so I take the train into the city centre.

The sun is out today, pale and cold. The snow is almost gone, and the closer I get to the centre of town the less snow remains on the ground. On the train are teenage girls, heading into the city to go shopping.

I could visit my dad – it's been a while. I *should* visit him soon. But then a heaviness comes over me as I think of Pappa in his study, of us talking as we sit before the fireplace, drinking tea. And of course I'll have to have something to say, preferably about something I've read that we can discuss, a novel, although nothing too socially relevant or incendiary. To say anything about *this* – about Sigurd – this thing that's quivering within me, I'd need the words for it, a way to present it as a manageable problem. And if I don't have these things, I certainly won't be able to tell Pappa about it. But perhaps I could go there anyway, just stay for a while. The great thing about my father – who has an attention span that extends only to the most superficial things that happen in my life – is that he doesn't expect much closeness, many confidences. With him I can spend time with another person while still being left alone. But it doesn't feel quite right, not when I'm in such a bad mood. And then there's the stupid rule that we're supposed to call before we turn up, to make sure he doesn't have company and that the house isn't swarming with smitten students who think he's some kind of guru. No, what am I thinking? A day like today is not the day to visit my father.

But I can go see Annika. That's what I want to do. We've said we might meet for lunch tomorrow, but I could just go to her place today instead. Just stop by, say hello. Say that I wanted to see whether they were home.

But maybe that's too desperate. Maybe that's the kind of thing you only do if it's a matter of life and death and you can't possibly stand to be alone. I drum my fingers against my hand-bag. Should I check my mobile again, even though the ringtone is set to the highest possible volume so that I won't miss any calls?

I get off the train at Majorstuen, following the flow of teenage girls with their mobiles and handbags and long locks of hair out of the station and down Bogstadveien. Perhaps I could buy myself something? We're saving money, want to spend what we earn on the house and nothing else, but whatever, Sigurd buys drawing equipment for work – maybe I need a new pair of trousers for my job? I go into a clothing store, watch the teenage girls milling around, "Oh my God, those trousers look so great on you, eight hundred kroner, Mamma gave me the money, Amalie and the others said they're coming down to meet us." Everything seems so problematic for these girls. They speak with big, wide-open eyes and gaping mouths, chew air between their greedy jaws, everything is *so* this or *so* that, the most neutral things presented as insurmountable obstacles. They talk about their friends and boyfriends as if they don't know that this is just the beginning, that in four years' time they won't even know the boy they're currently in love with. But who am I to tell them that? They come to me when they've really messed up, yes, they sit in my waiting room when everything is going wrong for them; when they're depressed, anxious, sleepless, joyless. It all seems so easy when eavesdropping on them as they shop, but I know their secrets.

I examine a few items of clothing and feel nothing, have no desire for any of it; can't be bothered to go into a changing room, take off my jacket and clothes, untie my shoes. I go out again, wander along the street, and think that no, I can't do this, I can't be here. What if I see someone I don't want to talk to? What if I bump into Julie?

I take a tram to Nordstrand. I want to go and see Annika, after all.

I hammer my hand against my thigh as the tram clatters its way up the hill. It's almost three o'clock. Almost twenty-eight hours since Sigurd left his voicemail. Around twenty hours since Thomas called and said he was missing.

Annika and Henning live at the innermost end of a cul-de-sac. The thought which always occurs to me when I visit them is that they're proper, orderly people. They live in a proper house, much smaller than mine and Sigurd's, but a functional one. A terraced house, suitably new, suitably attractive, always messy – but messy because it's used. Lives are lived there. They have three boys between the ages of two and seven. It's always noisy, there's always someone who has hit somebody, someone who's tripped over something, something that has to be said right this second, and someone – usually Annika – who says, "Can't we all just be quiet for a while?" There's always so much to be done. Bicycles and balls and games in the garden and the drive to be tidied away. Grass to be cut, walls to be painted – always something to be getting on with. They work a lot, both of them. They should be exhausted, but they're like the Duracell bunny, always hammering away with crazed smiles. I once told Sigurd that if they ever stopped to check and see whether they needed some time to relax, they might just hit the floor.

As I round the corner into the cul-de-sac that leads to their house, it's Henning I see first – because he's hanging from the top of a tree. He's holding a huge pair of loppers, turning his body, bending this way and that. He's engrossed in what he's doing, so he doesn't see me. Then I hear Annika's voice.

"Aksel, watch out, that branch is about to fall, no, Aksel, no, I said come *here* – Henning, wait, he's under the tree, Henning!"

I stop when I see her; consider them for a moment. Henning's back visible up there in the tree; my sister in jeans that sit bulkily around her hips and a checked shirt with its tails flapping free, running at top speed after a two-year-old squealing with delight at the fact that his mother is chasing him. I can't see the other two, but this is nevertheless the perfect image of Annika's family, as if every moment is about preventing accidents that could prove fatal.

She catches the boy, throws her arms around him and lifts him up. The two-year-old begins to howl, furious. He wants to keep going, was on a mission – how can his mother simply lift him away like this? She puts him over her shoulder and he rages, twisting and squirming and kicking his legs.

"I've got him," Annika calls to Henning up in the tree.

She catches sight of me as she walks back towards the house. First she stops and stares, and that's when I think it must be true, she must be tired down to the very marrow of her bones. When she was a student she spent two years living in a legendary flatshare in Fredensborg that kept open house every day, where guests came to sit and drink coffee and wine, discussing ethics and philosophy and using words like "metalevel". Now she looks at me and I see that I should have called first, because the muscles of her face go slack and she suddenly looks old, worn out. Then she pulls herself together, the muscles tightening again, and she smiles, tired and friendly, as the boy continues to writhe and wriggle up there on her shoulder.

"Hello, Sara," she says. "What a lovely surprise."

I follow Annika into the kitchen, the smallest boy dangling from her hip but still trying to break free. I apologise for turning up out of the blue and she assures me that it's fine, it's lovely to see me, although we both know this isn't true. I do regret coming, but it's too late now, and Annika deals with her son and runs her hands through her hair, perhaps feeling bad that she isn't quite as happy to see me as she claims to be.

"You want a cup of tea or something?" she asks me, and I thank her and say that I'll make it.

"I'll just go find out what Theo and Joakim are up to," she says. "Back in a sec." She leaves the kitchen, then the stairs creak, and I hear her calling their names.

Before we moved to Nordberg, Sigurd and I had tried to get pregnant. Just for around six months, no more. Back then visits to Annika and Henning were an effective contraceptive. We would look at each other on the train home and ask, "Do you think it has to be like that? So hectic? What if we only have one?"

I look around the kitchen. The remains of breakfast are on the table – plates made of plastic and porcelain, sippy cups and mugs of coffee. The magnets on the fridge door hold so many pieces of paper that the fridge seems likely to fall to its knees under the weight of them: schedules, planners, shopping lists, memos about recycling and the clothing required at kindergarten, a note about the importance of living a healthy life and meditating for twenty minutes a day. Among these are photographs. One of Annika and Henning from ten years ago, when they'd just met. She has her arms around his shoulders and is laughing at him; he looks into the camera, resting a hand at her waist. Then there are the pictures of the kids, individually and together; a childhood photograph of Annika and me, I must be around five, she seven; and one of Sigurd and me with Theo. It was taken one Sunday on a ski trip to Linderudkollen, two years ago now. We haven't been skiing together since, but I remember it was a fun day. Another stab. But I know I mustn't start to worry until after five o'clock. And by then he'll probably have turned up. The police know what they're talking about.

Just then, Margrethe calls. The ringing of the mobile makes me jump. It's Sigurd, he's calling to put an end to this nightmare, everything is fine, he's at home – that tiny, painful moment when I think everything is about to be O.K., and then it isn't.

"Sara," a voice crackles down the line, "it's Margrethe." As if I didn't know this from my mobile's display. But she always speaks like this. She makes me think of a lost time, one I haven't experienced but have read about in books or seen on T.V. When people drove sports cars, permed their hair and wore silk scarves and red lipstick; drank aperitifs in the library before dinner.

"Hello," I say.

Her charm makes me taciturn; her style makes me clumsy. That's the dynamic between us.

"I'm visiting a friend in Hankø this weekend," she tells me. "We've been working flat out in the garden all day, so I didn't hear when you called."

It always feels as if Margrethe is waiting for me to participate, to tell her what I've been doing all day, and that whatever I tell her ought to be glamorous in some way. She seems to think everyone is like her, and she refuses to give up hope – or worse, to notice – that this isn't true. It's as if she can't comprehend how awkward I am.

And then Annika comes in, the little one still on her arm, sweat on her brow.

"Anyway," Margrethe says, when I say nothing further, "you called me, was there something you wanted, sweetie?"

She calls me "sweetie". Nobody else does – not my father, my sister or my husband. I clear my throat, need to lubricate my vocal chords, say what I need to say.

"Yes. I was just wondering," I say, clearing my throat again – it's so dry, like sandpaper and dust – "if you'd spoken to Sigurd lately?"

It goes quiet on the other end of the line.

"Have I spoken to Sigurd?" Margrethe says.

"Because," I say, "it's just that he's been gone, or, not gone,

67

but . . . He was supposed to go to a cabin with some friends at the weekend, and they say he never arrived. But . . ."

I bite my tongue and it hurts, and I know that of course I don't need to tell her all the rest of it, that really I shouldn't, but I've started now, so I keep going.

"But he called me and told me he was there, with them, but he isn't. So then we started to wonder – Thomas and Jan Erik and I, that is – it was the three of them who were supposed to spend the weekend at Thomas' cabin together. Because they say he isn't with them. But he told me that he was."

"What is it that you're trying to say, Sara?" Margrethe says, sounding a little strict now, as I imagine mothers can be when their children attempt to drag them into intrigues in which they have no interest.

My tongue stings where I bit it, tastes of blood and metallic salt. Maybe I'm bleeding.

"He never arrived at the cabin," I say. "And he hasn't come home."

Silence on the other end. I sit stock-still. Behind me I hear nothing, only the rustling of the smallest child moving in Annika's arms, but neither of them says anything. It's so silent here in this house where it's usually impossible to hear yourself think. But here stands my sister, listening intently to my conversation, and I know I'll have more explaining to do when I hang up.

"Have you called his work?" Margrethe says.

"I've called him on his mobile," I say. "That's the phone he uses."

"But have you called his colleagues?"

"No."

"No, of course."

She exhales, a quick, efficient sigh – she's solved my problem.

"Call them," she says, "or go down to the office. He's

probably at work. Sigurd is so conscientious, he's always working, you know how he is."

"Yes," I say, listless now. "And anyway, most people who go missing turn up within twenty-four hours."

Margrethe doesn't deign to respond to this; I sense she doesn't like this angle, not one bit.

"Call me when you've managed to get hold of him," she says, sharper than usual. "Speak soon. Bye."

I hang up and turn around to see Annika standing there with the boy on her arm. They're staring at me, both of them.

"Is Sigurd missing?" Annika says, and in her voice I hear the fear that I'm so desperate to keep out of my own.

I sit in the passenger seat as Annika steers us out of the cul-de-sac and onto a larger artery in the intricate network of roads that makes up their neighbourhood, a grid you have no chance of learning to navigate unless you live here. We're on the way to the police station. Annika acted with lightning speed when I told her what had happened. I spoke using small words, attempting to downplay the situation – told her how the police-woman who answered the telephone said that most people do of course turn up. I repeat this remark as if it were a mantra – I'm sure there must be an easy, simple explanation.

"Don't listen to what the police say, Sara," Annika said, aghast. "Go down there right now and make a report."

"But she said . . ." I started, but couldn't finish my sentence. Could hear how listless I sounded, bowing to the system.

"They say whatever they can get away with," Annika said, snatching up her keys from the kitchen shelf. "But if you report him missing, they have no choice but to open a case. Come on, we'll go together."

Using the arm that wasn't holding the child, she took her jacket from a chair and went out into the garden. She's impressive is Annika, when she sets her mind to something. Now her every step, her every gesture, was determined. I ambled after her, feeling a hint of the reassurance I remember from our childhood: Annika will fix it for me. I stood on the veranda and watched her call out to Henning, who was still up the tree.

"Sara and I have to go to the police," she said, before giving her husband a few logistical instructions.

"Is everything O.K.?" Henning asked from his perch. From where I stood I could see only his feet, but I heard him loud and clear.

"I hope so," Annika said.

Henning came down from the tree; the smallest boy was handed over to his father, and soon my sister and I were sitting in the family Honda, making our way up one narrow street and down the next.

"It's important to be persistent with the police," Annika says. "They do their job, but like everyone else they have limited resources, so it doesn't hurt to show you're keeping tabs on what they're doing."

"I know," I say, and I do – I know this all too well now. Of course you have to be persistent, say that you're taking the situation seriously and demand that they do the same. Have I not learned this about every public agency I've come into contact with through my work? Why should the police be any different? As Annika turns onto the motorway and shifts the car into fourth gear, a gnawing sense of self-reproach seeps through me. Why did I listen to the woman I spoke to on the telephone this morning? Why did I let her mollify me? Why didn't I trust myself, my gut instinct, my memory, reason? Of course there's no logical explanation, other than that Sigurd has lied, which in itself indicates that something is dead wrong. Why didn't I stand my ground, demand to speak to somebody there and then? What if he's in danger? What if something terrible has happened? What if I could have done something, but instead was sauntering around the stores in Majorstuen in an attempt to pass the time? Annika would never have gone wandering around the shops like that – she would have known what to do straight away. She's the one who knows how to make everything right, and here I am, the little sister again, with my snotty nose and grazed knees, and since our mum is dead and our dad always working and above such things, it's Annika who will have to find me a plaster, fix me up. Which she always did, with her slapdash movements – "Why is it always me who has to help you?"

"Annika," I say, "do you think, I mean, was it stupid of me? Not to call?"

Annika glances at me. We're driving down the long stretch of road beside the fjord.

"Sara," she says, "that has no bearing on the situation."

She means to comfort me, to lift the guilt from my shoulders, but it only makes it worse. Makes it into an even worse case of guilt – because yes, this has now become a *case*, and as soon as we get down to Grønland it will be a real case, a police case, with a file and everything, or at least I think so. It has nothing to do with me – there's nothing I could have done differently. I close my eyes and imagine myself at the moment he left our bedroom early on Friday morning. How he had kissed me on the forehead, his lips cool against my skin. "Just go back to sleep."

Before we go into the police station I throw up behind a litter bin.

*

I sleep at Annika and Henning's place that night, unable to stand the thought of going home to Old Torp's empty house. We eat tacos and watch a James Bond film on T.V. I get a text message from Margrethe in response to the one I sent informing her that I've reported her son missing, telling her that she must contact the police if she hears from Sigurd. She's short with me even in her text – of course, thank you for letting me know, she writes. It's almost acerbic, I think. The film flickers past me. I'm unable to keep track of what the action is about, and it's all the same to me. I go to bed in the study twenty minutes before it ends, on the old IKEA sofa bed that was in the living room of the first apartment Henning and Annika shared – the sofa bed they conceived Theo on, Annika once told me through a titter. I close my eyes and think: two nights ago we were in bed together. Just forty-or-so hours ago, he kissed me on the forehead before he left. He smelled of toothpaste and coffee, the bag slung over his shoulder. It almost seems as if I've made the whole thing up.

I'm so tired. It's all so strange. I almost expect to wake up early tomorrow morning and discover that I've been dreaming or hallucinating.

Every evening he comes to visit us. We're often sitting on the sofa watching T.V. when he arrives; it's late, we're half-asleep. He has dewdrops in his hair and wears a fleece sweater and woolly thermals under his overcoat. He's the only guy who forms a permanent part of the flatshare, although Benedicte has an on-and-off boyfriend. Sometimes he stops to buy something on the way over: fruit, chocolate or popcorn. He flops down onto the sofa beside me, immediately puts his arms around me and pulls me in close, as if he can't properly relax until he's holding me. He smells of cold and sweat and chemicals. He presses his lips to my hair and I smell precisely that, the cold of the building in which he stands and works all day, the frozen sweat he's still accumulating, the chemicals he works with – varnish, glue, paint. The flecks on his hands. Sometimes the odour of wood, if the model he's making calls for extensive carpentry. He smells of work.

I now know that he bites his nails when deep in thought. I now know that when he was a teenager his father died of pancreatic cancer, two months after being diagnosed. I now know that he embraces me as tightly as he can before he comes.

He's a visiting student at the school of architecture, but will be going back to Oslo once the spring semester is over. I have another six months of my course remaining. We talk about everything: about the parents we've lost and the ones we have left, about our childhoods and our studies and what we like to watch on T.V. But of what will happen when he leaves we say nothing.

"True intimacy is fleeting," I say to Ronja, "because you can only ever be completely and utterly yourself when you know it isn't going to last."

"That's the dumbest thing I've ever heard you say," Ronja says.

I try not to think about the future. I want to create some beautiful memories for myself. I skive off early lectures so I can stay in bed with Sigurd, wake with him, make small talk while we're still half-asleep so that we ask each other, "Did you just say something, or did I dream it?" Lying there with him in the bedroom as it brightens, listening to the sounds of my friends beyond the door, the coffee machine, the rustling of newspaper pages, the hum of their low-voiced conversation.

Showering with him after they leave; standing there pressed close to him, naked, wet and quick to laugh in the cramped shower cabinet. "No, I'm serious," he says, "you have to wash my back, I can't reach, it's too tight in here." Drinking coffee and reading the newspaper across the table from him, thinking that we're like a married couple, testing out this feeling, this future, all the while knowing that it won't last. There's only a few weeks left. Sauntering down to the city's main square with him, hand in hand. Spring is on its way. His semester will soon be over. And then he'll go, and I'll stay, and I'll find someone new and this will be no more than a memory.

The week before he leaves we're eating dinner in the cellar of the Naboen Pub.

"There's a girl in the year above me who did her practical training in Oslo. So it's possible, if you find a placement yourself," I say to him.

He puts down his fork and looks at me, and there's something so intense about his gaze right then, his eyes wide open, and he says, "Do you mean it?"

"Yes," I say, afraid now, unsure whether I'm moving too fast. "Yeah, I dunno, I mean, if you want me to."

And then a sunshine smile bursts through all the nooks and crannies of Sigurd's face, through all the dimples and wrinkles in his cheeks and forehead and around his eyes.

"I'm just so damn relieved," he says, "because I've been walking around for weeks wondering how on earth I'm going to convince the school to give me another year in Bergen."

I move back to Oslo that summer, and Sigurd and I rent an apartment in Pilestredet.

Sunday, March 8: White noise

I arrive home in Kongleveien just before twilight. Annika and Henning have gone on working in the garden while I've played with the boys, drawing with crayons and playing house under the table in the living room. The boys – and Theo in particular – have been excited. Couldn't believe that Aunt Sara, who usually only wants to play for ten minutes – and reluctantly at that – remained on her knees in the table house for more than an hour, let them ride on her back, play havoc with her as much as they wished. "Can't you come visit every day, Sara?" Theo says, and it warms the cockles of my undeserving heart. I greedily accept it and close my eyes, because it's false – the only time I've really let go and played with them is because it is preferable to being alone at home.

"Why don't you just stay here?" Annika says. "Spend a couple of nights on our sofa."

But I can't. My work is in my house – both my real job, and the other one. To be there when he comes home. To have the candles lit, be waiting for him. I know that, and Annika does, too, or at least she says she understands as she shakes her head. There is life in Annika's house – it's loud and exhausting, but it's alive, and I'm dreading having to go home to the abandoned building site of a house in which I live. But I know I have to. Finally, I gather enough courage to crawl out from the play-house, put on my shoes and go home.

It's so quiet when I let myself in; Sigurd's absence is palpable. I stand in the hallway, staring at the linoleum flooring worn down by Old Torp, on which Sigurd's mother would walk bare-foot when sneaking out at night during her youth, and I listen. What am I hoping to hear? Him? It's so quiet, the only sounds are those that are always there: the distant judder of the train; the creaking that can be heard in all older wooden houses, of the framework that holds us, groaning under the weight of the rooms in which we live. But I hear no sounds from him. Have to call out to him regardless, but dread doing that, too, as I stand there, still wearing my shoes. As if I've just stopped in at this house, as if I don't live here, am not about to spend the evening inside. I don't want to hear my voice, lonely and unanswered, call out his name.

I take off my shoes first. Put them on the old sheets of news-paper where we set our shoes – his are there, too, his trainers and the thin-soled shoes he's taken out for spring. So big beside mine, like boats for tiny creatures. I pluck up my courage.

"Sigurd?"

My voice doesn't echo between the walls as I expected it to. Instead it sounds small, almost imperceptible; it stops against the walls, can't possibly be heard all the way up in the living room on the floor above. So I go up, careful to avoid the loose treads, hear the wood creaking and sighing with every step I take. The living room looms large in the dusk. I say his name again, before turning on the light. Sigurd? I click the switch; see that the room is empty.

I don't want to sit down in this room – something is different, but I'm not sure what. The curtains? Is that the way they usually hang? Sigurd always pushes them as far from the windows as possible, says he wants to let in plenty of light, found it unneces-sary to buy them at all. Did I move them on Friday evening when I sat here alone? Could I – who remembers so much in such detail – have done this, but forgotten? Might Margrethe –

the only other person who has keys to the house – have returned from Hankø and been here? To ruffle our curtains?

In our bedroom on the second floor I have the same feeling, less tangible here but also more frightening because this is where we sleep, because nobody but us has any business being here. Our bed, covered by the bedspread. There are some creases in one end of it, as if someone has sat on it, or perhaps just leant a hand on it. Did I do that before I left? I brushed my teeth, I came in, put on jeans and a sweater, decided against it, got out another sweater which I laid out on the bed, and then changed. Has the sweater created these creases? Or, more to the point, am I losing my mind?

My nerves have taken over, I decide as I make myself a cup of tea in the kitchen. I've been to the police station to report my husband missing; it's been more than two days since I last heard from him. This is what I would tell myself if I were my own therapist. It's no surprise that I'm nervous. It isn't strange that my mind is spinning faster, more paranoid than usual. I'm in emergency mode – have to remember that all these thoughts of crisis I'm having are exactly that: thoughts. They're not any truer, just because they scare me. I need to understand my own reaction. I have to calm down, understand that right now, given my understandable anxiety, I'm not at my most clear-headed. I shouldn't be attempting to solve the mystery of Sigurd's voice-mail message; should not be trying to understand why the curtains look different. I should order a pizza, watch T.V. for a couple of hours before I go to bed. I have to work tomorrow. I'll call Sigurd's colleagues. Things will be easier once the weekend is over. And perhaps Sigurd will come sauntering through the door this evening as planned, and this nightmare will be over.

That's when I notice it. Sigurd's document tube. It's back. It's hanging on its hook.

*

This will be no relaxing evening eating pizza in front of the T.V. – or rather, the T.V. is on and the pizza ordered, but that doesn't mean anything. The voices from the box – reality show participants discussing their strategies and the one-notch-louder advertising voices enthusiastically recommending washing-up liquids and online casinos – are nothing but white noise. I direct my gaze at the flickering images as in my inner cinema I play the scene over and over again. Scene 1: Friday, lunchtime. I've listened to Sigurd's answerphone message. I eat my tuna sandwich. I look at the empty hook, consider it. That's peculiar, I think. Has he taken it with him? Wasn't he supposed to pick up Thomas early this morning? Cut to a new scene: Saturday morning. I look at the empty hook, again, before I go down to the hallway and let myself out. I *know* that's what happened.

Someone has been in my house. There is no other explanation. It's not Julie – this happened while I was in Nordstrand, at Annika's place.

And yet I can't believe it. I go through the reasoning again and again, sitting unseeing before the T.V. Am I absolutely – one hundred per cent – sure? Is there no other justification?

The best therapist to ever deliver a lecture at my university said: "The most important thing you can do for your neurotic patients is this: help them to see the world as it is. Not the way they want it to be, or the way they fear it will be. Not the way the conclusions they have drawn tell them it is. *As it is.* Implicitly, help them to distinguish their imagination, desires and fears from reality. For example, the nervous, newly married woman who's afraid she's married the wrong man needs help to understand that the doubt she feels need not say anything magical about the relationship she's in. The young student who buckles

79

under exam pressure needs help to understand that his fear tells him nothing about his abilities, nor anything about how he will do in the exam. Here are the truths: every now and again, you find yourself irritated by your husband. You think the material you need to learn for the exam is hard. That's all. It isn't realistic to love and admire one's spouse every waking moment of every day you spend together. It isn't a given that you will never understand all your course material, just because you don't understand it on first reading. The world isn't so simple. The truths are what *is*. Everything else is the conclusions you draw."

Sigurd is gone. He has lied. This seems indisputable. His document holder, the grey plastic tube which was gone, has reappeared. That's all I know. Does that mean that someone has been here, or is that a conclusion I've drawn? I have to try to be clear, try to prevent my terrified brain from running wild.

The doorbell rings. It's the pizza, I think, as I run down the stairs and into the hallway, but at the same time it could be someone else – it might be him, or someone who knows something? There is hope in this thought. A last hope, a luxury I still have.

I turn the lock without looking through the peephole, open the door, and then, when I see the man and woman standing there, I know.

They are wearing police uniforms. They are young, the woman around my age, the man a few years younger. He appears nervous. It's the woman who speaks – she must be his superior. Perhaps he's been brought along for some on-the-job training.

"Are you Sara Lathus?" she says.

"Yes," I say, or rather my vocal cords say, of their own accord.

"Yes, then I'm afraid that I have some sad news," says the woman. She licks the corners of her mouth, once, twice. Perhaps she's nervous, too. I imagine her at the police academy when they were given training on this, the delivery of difficult news – probably a double session, hardly more than ninety minutes. I imagine her sitting on the edge of her seat, eagerly taking notes: *Be serious, but dignified. Deliver the message quickly. Be clear and concise.*

"I'm from Oslo police headquarters," she says.

Say where you've come from.

"We found the body of a man who fits the description of your husband at around five o'clock this afternoon. We won't have final confirmation of the person's identity until a few days from now at the earliest, but everything indicates that the body is that of Sigurd Torp. He was discovered in Krokskogen, about two kilometres from Kleivstua."

She clears her throat. The man standing beside her looks at my shoulder, unable to meet my gaze. Or perhaps he's been instructed not to.

"I know this must be difficult to hear," she says. "I'm sorry."

On the day Sigurd and I got married it was cloudy and cold, a typical early autumn day in Oslo. Afterwards, we walked home beside the river and up to Torshov. I said to him, "You're mine now, till death do us part." He laughed and said to me, "Likewise."

And in this moment, that's all I can think. The police officers look at me as I stand there staring into space, watching the pizza delivery boy as he parks his car in the driveway behind theirs and then gets out to stand there looking at us, hesitating, and all I can think is: till death do us part. He wasn't mine for very long.

"Open it," Sigurd said.

I picked up the gift that lay on the bed and tore off the paper, searching among all the newspaper for the tiny real present, and then pulled the paper off that, too. In the little box lay the chain.

It was my birthday, the year I was doing my practical training at a rehabilitation centre for heavy drug users outside Oslo, instead of working at an outpatient clinic for young people in Bergen, as I had planned. Sigurd and I rented a small, ice-cold apartment in Pilestredet, and every morning I took the tram from Bislett to Oslo S, the train to Lillestrøm, and then walked in the pissing rain to the barracks-like building in which I worked. My patients were indifferent to me at best, and bordering on violent at worst. I was trained by an older psychologist two years away from retirement, who had clearly stopped caring many years earlier. On the train and tram home I tried to keep my mind occupied so I wouldn't start to cry before I was standing under the shower at home where no-one could see me.

"Sigurd," I said, "it's beautiful, but surely it isn't real?"

There was a glittering stone set in the pendant – small, but still. Sigurd's smile widened, dimples appearing all over his face. I could never understand how it was possible, but Sigurd had dimples beside his eyes.

"We don't have any money," I reminded him.

"Don't think about that," he said, "think about whether or not you like it. If you don't you can exchange it."

"Can I exchange it for money for the electricity bill?" I said, but *laughed and looked at the necklace and knew that I could never part with it.*

A silver chain, a simple pendant, the tiniest little diamond. I wept in the shower so Sigurd wouldn't see that I had been crying, but he wasn't stupid.

"Happy birthday," Sigurd said. "Here, give it to me. I'll help you put it on."

Monday, March 9: Husk

There are police officers in my house. They rang the doorbell early this morning, with a feigned solemnity that disappeared the moment I let them in and they got to work. I'm sitting at the kitchen island with a cup of coffee. I haven't dressed for the day. Nor have I showered. I haven't called anyone. A few people have called me – Margrethe, Annika – but I haven't picked up the phone. I'm simply waiting.

The police are on the second floor. They are looking for things, but for what I don't know – and nor do they, as I understand it. "Anything might be of interest," said the cocky young policeman who is now trawling through my underwear and sock drawer. He arrived with the woman who came last night – she's back, which I presume is meant to reassure me. But it's having the opposite effect. I never want to see her again as long as I live, but here she is, refreshed and with her face arranged into sad creases to show me that she feels my pain.

"Gundersen would like to talk to you at around eleven," she says. "Gundersen is leading the investigation."

"He's one of the best," the cocky youth beside her says.

I like him better, he's down to earth. She's a typical girl from the west side of Oslo: highlights in her hair, pearl earrings, and the sociolect, the diction, just like the girls I grew up with. I bet we have acquaintances in common. I imagine them having friendly evening get-togethers, her telling them about me – "You mustn't tell anyone, it's confidential, but . . ." Do I care? Would it matter if anyone found out? I search myself for the answer, but I find nothing within me to take hold of, no hooks on which I can hang theories, test how something would feel. Just a vast, empty void, ready to be filled with something. With blood, with grief, with the something or other I assume will be around the next corner.

For now, I drink coffee. It doesn't taste of anything. I can hear voices around me – the police, I suppose. The police are in my house. I haven't answered any calls, haven't attempted to contact my patients to cancel appointments. I'm supposed to see Sasha at nine-thirty, and I want to keep the appointment with her, I realise. There, yes, the shadow of a feeling. Sasha will do me good today. But stop, wait a minute – do patients exist to make their therapists feel better? Am I about to do something deeply unethical? Do I even care? I try to feel around inside the void within me, but it seems that was it. I can find no reaction to the breaching of ethical principles. Any reasonable person would understand that I'm in no fit state to be seeing patients, but now Sigurd's gone I live alone, and I'm not sensible enough to give myself the necessary advice. So I haven't called. My second patient is due at eleven, an anorexic fifteen-year-old – her I can't see because the great Gundersen has decided that's when he wants to speak to me. I should call her, but will I? Do I care? My mobile buzzes beside me – seeing as I've been waiting for it to ring all weekend I jump, but it isn't Sigurd. Of course it isn't him, it can't be, I know that now. It's Margrethe again. They've spoken to her – that's one of the few things I do know, and that's good, because it means I don't have to do it.

Here is what I know: Sigurd is dead. He was found in Kroksk-ogen forest. They think he was murdered. They've spoken to his mother. The first three of these facts were given to me yesterday evening by the policewoman I don't like, without my asking for them; the fourth I asked her about myself. It was the only question I asked. I stood on the step and stared past them, the policewoman and her colleague. Stared at the confused pizza delivery boy, who was clearly wondering whether he should bring a pizza up to a house with the police standing at the door, and I felt a peculiar kind of expectation – what would he do? – felt the need to make a bet with myself, ten kroner says he turns and leaves out of pure discomfort. In the end he set the pizza on the bonnet and waited. I turned my gaze back to the woman I didn't like.

"Will you be contacting anyone else?" I said.

She looked at me, a questioning frown cleaving her forehead, her neatly plucked brows lifting. She looked surprised. Apparently this isn't the first thing one is expected to ask on hearing that one's husband has been killed. There's something satisfying about seeing this sort of west-side yuppie surprised, because it happens so rarely – they have such boring lives, nothing unpredictable ever happens to them.

"Who were you thinking of?" she said.

"His mother."

"Yes, of course – I mean, if you'd like us to?"

And so the burden of this choice was dumped onto me. I wonder what they said about this at the lecture on how to deliver the news that a loved one has died. Or perhaps this is best practice, user involvement or whatever you want to call it. The pizza delivery boy checked his watch. I wondered why I cared about all these things, why my mind travelled down these paths, why it seemed so much easier to let it chew away on these details instead of focusing on the message I had received, the veritable elephant on the doorstep.

"Yes," I said, clearing my throat, "I'd like you to."

I took my mobile from my pocket to give her the number, and saw that Annika had sent me a message.

Hope you're O.K., let me know if you hear anything. I'll call you tomorrow. Look after yourself. Hugs.

I knew I should call her. I gave the policewoman Margrethe's address and number, and for a while that was all that happened. I read out the numbers, she noted them down, the kind of situation you might find yourself in every week, just jotting down a number. The pizza delivery boy looked at his watch again.

"We'll come back tomorrow morning to ask you a few questions," she said, "and to take a little look around the house, if that's O.K."

"O.K.," I said. O.K., sure, they could do whatever they wanted. Who was I to protest?

I was just glad that they seemed to have a plan for how to move forward, a script for what needed to be done in this kind of situation, guidelines perhaps. Yes, of course they have guidelines, probably printed in a brochure and inserted into a ring binder made available at every police station across the country, or perhaps a separate booklet, a dedicated folder, a printed publication with a spiral-bound spine. Dear God, why was I thinking about all these things?

"We'll be able to answer any questions you might have then, too," she said.

As I understood it, I was expected to be wondering about all kinds of things. But as it happened, I did not have a single question.

"Do you have someone you can call?" she said. "I mean, your parents, or a friend – someone like that?"

"Yes," I said. "Yes, I can call my sister."

"Good. It's best not to be alone in situations like this."

How would you know? I wanted to ask her. How is it possible to make such a general recommendation as to what would be good for someone in such an acute situation? But of course I said nothing. The pizza delivery boy had started to walk up towards the house. He'd decided to carry out his assigned task. He surprised me in that, I have to say.

"Thank you," I said – for what I don't know.

"You're welcome," she said.

Her eyes creased into a squint; she stretched out a hand, placed it on my arm and squeezed.

"Are you O.K.?" she said.

And I had the peculiar feeling that *I* needed to reassure *her*, that the task fell to me, the next of kin, to comfort her, the professional. *Are you O.K.?* Who was I to answer such a question, with a fresh, gaping wound?

"Yes," I said.

As he got closer to the house, the pizza delivery boy almost slowed to a stop.

"We'll see you tomorrow," she said. And that's how she told me that she would return. *Offer information about what will happen next.* They turned to go then, the police officers, and almost walked straight into the pizza delivery boy. For a moment there was confusion, they wondered what he was doing there, but said nothing; he wasn't expecting them to turn around; I was beyond providing an explanation, so he ended up speaking, "I don't mean to intrude, but I have this delivery for you . . ." and the policewoman seemed to feel that she should take responsibility for handling the situation, she mumbled something generic along the lines of it being good to eat something at a time like this, and the young policeman nodded in agreement. And then they walked back to the police car as the delivery boy held out the pizza box to me.

*

They found him in Krokskogen forest. His father's old cabin. I stood there in the hallway with the pizza box in my hands and knew what I had to do. There was one simple thing I needed to check.

Sigurd's father had always had a passion for the sea, and while the rest of the family had no connection to that kind of thing other than Margrethe's friend having a small sailing boat at Hankø, Sigurd's father had left behind a few maritime effects. One of them was a so-called *garnkule*, a hollow sphere of green glass encased in a net of crocheted twine. In the old days fishermen used them to float their nets, but now they're mostly sold as souvenirs. Sigurd's father had probably claimed that this one "was actually used for fishing" – he had bought it years ago while on holiday in the north. Sigurd attached it to our cabin key, and both he and Margrethe laughed heartily at the idea – because it's a cabin in the *forest*, he said to me when I didn't laugh, as if that explained it. He would tell the joke to people who came to the house, to my Pappa and Annika and Henning, to Thomas and Jan Erik. He never garnered more than a polite chuckle from anyone, but I don't think he noticed. The key has its own special place, in a little cabinet with hooks inside it in Sigurd's office. As long as we're not using it, as long as we're not at the cabin, it hangs there alongside the other keys. But the Krokskogen key, with its huge *garnkule*, is the one that always sticks out. All I needed to do was take eight steps into Sigurd's study.

There was the little cabinet. I opened it. No *garnkule*. No cabin key.

Later, as I stood in the kitchen with the pizza box in my hands and stared at the T.V., which carried on as if nothing had happened, I realised it would be impossible for me to call Annika as I had promised the policewoman. Annika would support me and make everything right, just as she always does, but the very thought of calling her in such raw pain crushed something inside me.

And so I went to bed. After all, why not?

It's impossible to describe what that night was like. Of course I hardly slept. That's all I can say. The first piece of pizza was eaten by one of the officers now rummaging through my belongings on the floor above me.

It's nine-thirty and I've showered, dressed for work and made my way over to my office above the garage. Two police cars are parked along our drive, I can see them through the window from where I'm sitting. I haven't yet called the girl who is due to come at eleven; I'm not sure what I plan to do about it. I should call now, before she leaves school to make her way here, as she will have done by the time my session with Sasha is over, but I don't have the energy to move from the chair in which I sit.

Instead, I count. One-hundred-and-twenty-four, one-hundred-and-twenty-five, one-hundred-and-twenty-six. I'm not sure why. I've clearly stopped caring why. Police officers may have taken over my house, but here in my office I'm still in charge. I sit in my chair, the chair that feels most mine, in which I sit opposite Christoffer, and opposite Sasha, too. One-hundred-and-thirty-one, one-hundred-and-thirty-two. Now Sasha appears, down there in the street. She's wearing a black coat, a red scarf around her neck. It feels good to see her. She's my patient. I'm her therapist. I have a job to do.

Sasha is a trans person. The name she was given at birth is Henrik, but she says she has known she isn't a boy her entire life.

This became clear to her during puberty, and now, at the age of sixteen, she's receiving hormone treatment, dresses as a woman, and has adopted a feminine name, just like that. All this might sound like a real handful to anyone else, but Sasha is actually one of my healthiest patients. She knows exactly where she stands in terms of her gender identity, something most sixteen-year-olds can only dream of. Her parents are nothing but supportive, and she has some great friends around her who accept her for who she is. She feels the need for therapy in order to "clear her head", as she puts it, which she mostly needs to do because of the stupidity of certain narrow-minded people she encounters. She's also somewhat devastated that she has to wait until she's eighteen to complete her gender affirmation surgery and have her legal gender registered as "female", but even this she manages to handle with good humour for the most part. She comes to me just once a month, and our sessions are good. The interventions I make are well received; she considers my suggestions and is active in using them. I could not have asked for a better patient to see on the day after I've learned that Sigurd is dead.

One-hundred-and-eighty-eight. Sasha stops beside the two police cars. For a moment she stands still, contemplating them, then lifts her gaze to the house, before letting it wander towards the garage and up to the window where I sit. I lift a hand and wave. She lifts hers, gloved although the weather is mild, and returns my greeting. But she doesn't smile. In fact, she looks sceptical, almost afraid. I wonder why as I watch her walk the last stretch to the garage, and realise, as she rounds the corner and disappears from my field of view, that it's because I didn't smile myself. I don't think I can manage it. I slap myself hard across the cheek with the flat of my hand. Pull yourself together – you're a professional. If I don't maintain some kind of control, I can't work. I wonder whether I really care, and feel a sharp tug somewhere deep within me. Good, so there are some feelings left in there. I may not care about professional ethics, but I do care about Sasha.

"What's the deal with the police cars?" Sasha says as she lowers herself into her chair. She has taken off her coat and scarf; they're now resting in her lap. Underneath she's wearing a moss green jumper and a tight black skirt. She sits with her legs to one side, the very picture of femininity, as if she were a secretary from the '60s.

"Oh, just a boring incident that happened this weekend," I say with a wave of my hand. I'm trying to give the impression of something trivial, a break-in perhaps, but see that her alarmed expression fails to evaporate.

"How have things been since last time?" I say.

I make myself comfortable in the chair, lean forward a little, and feel my body settle into position. Yes, I can do this. Auto-pilot takes over when necessary, carrying me into professional mode. It feels good. I fall into place. All the chaos in the house – the police officers, document holders, curtains, pizza boxes – they can be left to their own devices. Here in the office it's just Sasha and me, and we have a job to do.

"Well," she says, splaying her fingers, "things are good. Yeah, they are."

I nod, narrowing my eyes in concentration. I'm the very image of a functioning psychologist.

"It's just," she says, exasperated and exhaling up into her fringe, "oh, it's so stupid, you're going to laugh at me. I, well, I think I've met someone. Or, I mean, *I've* met *him*. Whether or not he's met me is something else."

"You mean you're unsure whether he returns your feelings?"

"Yeah. Unsure is putting it mildly."

"Well, have you asked him?"

She exhales again, in the way young people do, as if to say "yeah, right".

"He's not the kind of guy who would fall for someone like *me*," she says, then adds, her voice a little sour, "to put it bluntly."

"I assume that means that you haven't asked him?"

"You assume correctly."

"So when you say that he's not the kind of guy who would fall for someone like you, that's just an assumption?"

Look at that – I'm doing fine. I'm challenging the conclusions Sasha has drawn. I'm doing my job.

"Sort of," Sasha says. "But oh, Sara, don't say that you're sure he'll love me when he gets to know me, *please*. I don't think I can take it."

I smile, which is not easy. I manage it, but it feels a bit stiff.

"There *is* a hierarchy out there at school, y'know?" Sasha says. "Even though it's tempting to believe that all that matters is that you're nice and kind and honest about your feelings."

"And where in the hierarchy are you, Sasha?"

"Not right at the bottom," she says, "but I'm not exactly at the top, either."

"No, of course. And where in the hierarchy is he?"

Sasha glances out of the window.

"Sara," she says, "another police car just arrived."

I follow Sasha's gaze. A third vehicle is now in the driveway, but sort of across it, so that it blocks the house from the road. Two people are getting out of the car, a man in police uniform and one with a bushy moustache in plain clothes, wearing a shabby parka. They walk towards the house. As we look at them I try to remember the last question I asked.

"Sara?" Sasha looks at me. "Is everything O.K.?"

I so want to say yes, but that would be a lie, and I can't lie, not here in my therapy room, not to her, and not on a day like today when just getting in and out of the chair is hard enough. To avoid saying too much, I say:

"There's been an incident. It doesn't have anything to do with our work here, but I understand it may be frightening, or upsetting, to see the police cars."

"What's happened?" Sasha says.

"It's about a disappearance," I say.

Of course it's no longer a disappearance, but I can't bring myself to say what it really is. If I repeat what I was told on the doorstep yesterday it will become real. If I say it out loud, I might never be the same again.

"It's just, well, it's my husband. My husband has gone missing."

Sasha's eyes widen, her thick lashes sticking out into the air. Her eyeballs look as if they're about to pop out of her head.

"Your husband has disappeared?"

"Yes."

I look out of the window. The two men who just arrived have entered the house. They did ring the doorbell, but it seems to me that they went in without waiting. If only Old Torp could have seen this, I think. In the end, his house really was besieged by the powers that be.

"Sara," says the teenager sitting across from me, "I know that you're the psychologist, not me, but don't you think it would have been a good idea to take today off?"

There's no answer to that – she's right. Someone should have told me, but who, now that I'm alone?

"I wanted to work," I say. "And we had an appointment."

She looks at me, her gaze so full of pity that it seems impossible we'll ever re-establish a professional relationship.

"It's O.K.," she says, her voice bright and slow, as if speaking to a child. "We can talk another day instead."

The man with the bushy moustache and parka is in the living room. The policewoman from yesterday is with him, as are a couple of other officers. Moustache is in the middle of saying something when I come into the room; I catch the end of his sentence.

". . . so we need to ensure that forensics give us their opinion on that."

He has a broad dialect from the east of Norway; he is probably from a small village. His voice is flat and toneless, but the others hang on his every word with such intensity that he doesn't need to raise it for them to hear him. It's obvious that he's their boss.

He stops speaking when he catches sight of me, and the other officers turn and look at me, too.

"Hello," I say. "I was just going to get a cup of coffee."

The woman I don't like shakes herself free from the moment, and says:

"This is Sara Lathus. She was married to the deceased."

It sounds so peculiar – "married to the deceased". A new status, I think. Not even next of kin. Married to the deceased. It sounds like a frightful position to be in. Moustache sets his body in motion and comes towards me with his hand outstretched. He stops just in front of me, but I don't know what to do with his hand, it seems I'm no longer able to conduct myself in line with social norms. But he's quick and efficient, I can see it in every step he takes, and it's clear he doesn't intend to be deflected by my listlessness. Without further ado he bends towards me, takes hold of my right hand from where it dangles loose at my side, squeezes it and says:

"Gunnar Gundersen Dahle, but call me Gundersen. That's what everyone ends up doing, sooner or later."

"Sara," I mumble.

He lets go of my hand. It hurts, I realise – he must have squeezed it hard. But at least I feel something.

"So, Sara, I'd like to have a few words with you. Tell you a bit about what we know so far, and hear what you have to tell us."

I nod. So I'll have to tell them what I know. That's new to me. I'm not sure what kind of conversation I was expecting to have with him, but it hadn't occurred to me that I would have to speak.

"Is there somewhere we can go to talk?"

"My office," I say. "It's above the garage."

"Excellent," Gunnar Gundersen Dahle says. "Then we'll go there right away."

Before we start our conversation I call Linnea, the patient I was supposed to see at eleven o'clock, and cancel our appointment. Gundersen Dahle and another officer, a red-haired woman in her late thirties, are in the room when I make the call. I don't like it, feel under surveillance. I've never liked speaking on the telephone in front of others – not in front of anyone, not even Sigurd. I always went into the bedroom if I was going to speak to anyone about anything but the most prosaic things. All conversations relating to my patients take place in this office. But Gundersen and his colleague showed no signs of leaving the room when I said I was going to call, and I don't feel in a position to ask Gundersen for anything, so they're standing here, listening.

"Unfortunately I have to cancel today," I say.

"Oh, O.K.," Linnea says.

There's a racket in the background, voices and laughter.

She must still be at school. And there's relief in her voice. This bothers me. It is much easier to cancel sessions with my patients than I thought.

When I hang up, I see that a patient has called me and left a message on the answerphone. I play it back, pressing the receiver against my ear to prevent the police officers from hearing anything. Gundersen peers at a painting hanging above my filing cabinet, pretending not to listen.

"Hi," says a voice on the answering machine, "it's Vera. I, I need to talk to you. Before Friday, I mean. There's something I need to talk about. Can you call me? O.K.? Bye."

That's strange, I think, Vera has never asked for an extra session before. I ask myself whether I'm curious, but feel nothing, only the void again, an empty gnawing from it.

"Is this painting one of those tests you do on people?" Gundersen says. "Where you ask them what they see in it, and if they see their mother then it means, I don't know, something or other?"

"No," I say. "It's a Kandinsky print."

"I know nothing about art," Gundersen says. "Do you, Fredly?"

"No," the red-haired officer says, and it seems to me that she's suppressing a smile.

"So, what's happened?" I ask them.

"We'll get to that," Gundersen says, turning his back to the painting, "but let's start at the beginning."

He pulls out the chair from beneath my desk and sits down on it, slinging one leg on top of the other so the ankle balances against the opposite knee, his legs spread, as if making himself comfortable.

I make a note of this. I ask a question, and he says that's not where we'll start. I also note that he's the kind of person who chooses his own chair, and not even one of the two unoccupied ones that stand there, invitingly – no, he chooses a third chair, pulls it out from under the desk. We may be in my office, but he's taken control of the conversation. I don't know what that means. Maybe nothing. But I make a mental note of it.

"Tell me about what Friday was like for you," he says.

I sit down in the left of the chairs I use in my sessions – I have no choice but to take one of them. Gundersen's colleague leans against the door. I wonder whether this is a rank thing, that the subordinate remains standing.

"It was an awful day," I say.

"Tell me about it," Gundersen says.

"Well," I say, "Sigurd disappeared."

"No, no," he says. "Tell me about the day. From the beginning."

I sigh, glance out of the window, through which I can see the police cars on my driveway. A week ago it was just another normal Monday in March. Gundersen says nothing. He's said his part and now waits, confident that I'll speak.

"I woke up as Sigurd was leaving," I say. "I don't know what time it was, I was asleep, it must have been early. He kissed me on the forehead and said, 'I'm going now, go back to sleep.' So I went back to sleep. When I woke up he was gone."

Gundersen nods. Fredly leans against the door, scribbling on a notepad.

"I woke up again around seven-thirty," I say. "My first session was at nine o'clock."

"What did you do immediately after waking up?" Gundersen interrupts. I understand – the information he needs is in the details.

I feel suddenly like Trygve, like someone who speaks in general terms, always avoiding the concrete, the specific. I pull myself together.

"I showered," I say. "I got dressed in the bedroom. I went downstairs and sat at the kitchen table. I ate, I don't remember what, and drank a cup of coffee. Then I came up here – my patient was waiting for me."

Gundersen clears his throat in approval, and I think: there's a capable psychoanalyst somewhere in this man.

"Yes, and then I had another patient, and then it was time for lunch."

"Wait a second," Gundersen says. "How long were you with the first one?"

"Fifty minutes."

"So until 9.50?"

"Something like that."

"Something like that?"

"Within a minute or two."

"And the name?"

"The name?"

"Of the patient?"

Now it's my turn to clear my throat.

"That's subject to confidentiality."

Fredly looks surprised, raised eyebrows and all. She steals a glance at Gundersen, as if curious to see how he'll solve this. He holds my gaze, and says:

"We're the police. This is a criminal investigation. Nothing is confidential."

"I'm a psychologist," I say. "Unless you can prove that you will be able to prevent serious harm by knowing the patient's name, I have a duty to keep it confidential."

The room falls silent for a moment, so that it seems as if my voice reverberates back and forth between the walls. Gundersen considers me with his grey eyes. Eyes that have seen it all, I think. I don't look away, concentrate on returning his gaze, even though I'm quivering inside. The discomfort of standing one's ground. Especially against men – and especially against those who are older than me. I remember some discussions at home in Smestad when I was a teenager, the few times I raised my voice, Pappa looking at me calmly and saying, "Oh Sara," and the sense of wavering, fighting the need to give in and say whatever my father wanted to hear. It was Annika and Pappa who fought most often – I would hide until it had blown over. But right now, I have to stand my ground. I may have lost my husband, but I still have my profession, and I'm clinging to it as if it were a lifebuoy.

"Sara," Gundersen says, his voice soft and friendly, like thick cream, "think now. Before you do something stupid."

"I have a duty of confidentiality in matters relating to my patients," I say. "Take it up in court, if you must."

He gives a deep and dramatic sigh.

"O.K.," he says, "but you do understand that we're investigating a murder here? Sigurd was found with his face in the mud and two bullets in his back. There's no natural explanation for this. It's murder. And you're refusing to give us an alibi for the morning of the day he was killed."

I look out of the window again, at the police cars. I suddenly feel unspeakably tired. I want to close my eyes, lean my head back against the chair and fall asleep. Let Gundersen carry on however he wishes.

"I understand," I say in a low voice, out into the air, as I try to prevent my eyes from closing. Gundersen sighs again.

"So it's 9.50. What did you do then?"

"I wrote up my notes."

"And they're also confidential?"

"Yes."

Gundersen and his minion exchange glances. She notes something on her pad.

"And then the next patient?"

"At ten o'clock."

"And you don't want to give us the name?"

"No. I saw him too for around fifty minutes."

They exchange glances again.

"And then?" Gundersen says.

"Lunch. A tuna sandwich. Oh, yes, he'd called – Sigurd. While I was with my first patient. He left me a voicemail message."

"And what did he say?"

"That he had arrived at the cabin. He was supposed to be going to Norefjell with his friends for the weekend."

"To Norefjell?"

"Yes. That's why I reported him missing."

Gundersen looks directly at his colleague for the first time. She nods, but says nothing.

"I reported him missing," I say, my voice a little louder now, "because he called me and said that he was at Norefjell with the guys, and because the same friends called me that evening and said that he hadn't arrived."

"I see," Gundersen says, now stretching a long, thin hand towards his colleague. "Sheet."

She passes him something; he fishes a cheap ballpoint pen emblazoned with advertising from a breast pocket and writes something down on the sheet of paper, which he rests against his knee. Fredly scribbles more, even faster, as if Gundersen has rebuked her.

"So Sigurd called and said that he was at the cabin at Norefjell? What time was this?"

"Just after nine-thirty," I say, and it dawns on me that they're going to ask to hear the message. "He said it was good to be there, and that he had to go because Jan Erik was messing around with some firewood. Jan Erik is a friend of his, one of the two guys he was supposed to go up there with."

"One of the guys?"

"Yes."

"O.K.," Gundersen says, "and did Sigurd say anything else?"

"No. Just that they had arrived."

"And did you call him back?"

"No. I mean, yes, but not right there and then. I called him after my last patient."

"Fine. So after lunch you had another patient?"

"Yes. At two o'clock."

"And you don't want to give us the name of this patient, either?"

"No. It isn't that I don't want to," I begin, but he waves away my words. There's something nonchalant in his movement – or is it self-assured? He's not interested in discussing it with me because he knows all he needs to know – or, no, I think, that's not it. It's that he's convinced he'll discover what he wants to know through other means. Yes. Gundersen will not allow himself to be disarmed by a no. Only now does it occur to me that he is not necessarily on my side. He's on Sigurd's side, which, until now, I had believed to be one and the same thing. That Sigurd and I are on the same side, so whatever benefits Sigurd, benefits me.

"That gives you three hours between patient two and patient three," Gundersen says. "Three hours and ten minutes, in fact. What did you do with this time, apart from eat?"

"I wrote up my notes," I say, "and then prepared for my next session."

"How long does it take you to write up your notes?"

"I don't know. Ten minutes, perhaps."

"O.K., and then say half an hour, an hour max, for lunch. A full two hours for preparations, then?"

The feeling of being pushed against the wall drapes itself across my shoulders. I look from the policewoman making her notes – who looks up at me and scribbles some more – to Gundersen, who sits there, one leg atop the other, studying me with his unyielding grey gaze.

"No," I say. "I mean, I must have done other things, too. Little things. I went to the bathroom, made a cup of coffee, tidied up a little and checked my e-mail."

"And when you go to the bathroom and drink coffee, do you do that here?"

"No, I don't have water or anything like that here. I have to go into the house."

He nods, and his colleague jots down something else. Out of the window I see a grey Honda turn and drive up onto the grass beside the driveway and stop. Out of it comes Annika, wearing a suit and carrying a briefcase. She stands there for a moment as she gets out, her fine, high boots on the muddy lawn, and stares at the police cars, then up at the house. She's far enough away that the details of her expression elude me, but the disbelief in her face is unmistakable – the open mouth shaped like an O, the jerk of her head as she directs her gaze back to the police cars.

Gundersen casts a glance her way, but says nothing.

"When were you finished with patient number three?" he says instead.

"At ten to three," I say, remembering the habitual reluctance Trygve awakens in me. "No, wait, it was before that. I don't think the session lasted for much longer than twenty minutes."

"So, twenty past two?"

"Yes. Something like that."

Annika walks across the lawn towards the house. She has the strange, staccato gait of a duck, the heels of her boots sinking into the damp earth, but she's doing her best to be quick and authoritative regardless, her pace hurried. Were I not so numb, I would have found it comical.

"So just before two-thirty you were done for the day?" Gundersen suggests.

"No, I wrote up some notes first. A little after two-thirty."

"O.K. And then?"

"I went into the house. Had a snack. Tried to call Sigurd."

"And what happened when you tried to call Sigurd?"

"The telephone rang, but he didn't pick up. It went to voice-mail."

"And did you leave a message?"

"No, not then. I rarely do. I generally just think he'll see the missed call and call me back."

"And then?"

"I don't know. I read the newspaper. Watched a little television. Tidied up a bit, maybe put a load of laundry in the washing machine. I was online for a while, checked the online newspapers and Facebook, things like that, reserved a place at my spinning class at six o'clock. Other than that, I don't know."

"O.K. And your next activity?"

"Yes, that was my spinning class. At Ullevål at six."

"So you left the property here for the first time that Friday to go to this exercise class at what time?"

"Ten past five, maybe. I take the train down there and usually arrive at around, let's see, half past."

"So the first certain sighting of you that day, other than by these patients who you do not wish to name, would have been then? I presume that you register that you've arrived at the gym in some way?"

"Yes."

"There are cameras at Holstein station," the red-haired officer says.

This is her first contribution to the conversation, and I'm surprised to hear that she speaks with a deep, melodic voice and in a northern dialect.

"O.K.," Gundersen says, "so you exercise, you sweat, for, what, an hour, and when you're done?"

"I went home."

"Did you shower?"

"No, yes, I mean, not until I got home. I was on the train when Jan Erik called."

"Right. And what did Jan Erik say?"

"He said what I said just now, that Sigurd never arrived at the cabin."

"Did he say it like that? That Sigurd never arrived at the cabin?"

"No, no, of course not. I mean, he must have asked me whether I knew where Sigurd was. They were waiting for him."

"And 'they' were?"

"Jan Erik and another friend, Thomas."

"I see. So they're sitting in a cabin at Norefjell and waiting for Sigurd."

"Yes. He told them that he'd be there at around five in the evening. But he told me he'd be leaving Oslo before seven in the morning."

Gundersen notes something down. Then he lifts a hand to his face and passes it along his cheek, down over his moustache. I ask myself whether this is something people with moustaches tend to do.

"So, according to Sigurd, he left Oslo before seven in the morning and arrived at Norefjell around nine-thirty or earlier. He called you from there a little after nine-thirty. But around, what must it have been, just after seven in the evening, Jan Erik calls you and says he's at Norefjell, and that he's still waiting for Sigurd."

"Yes. And that he hasn't seen Sigurd all day."

"So this voicemail message, where Jan Erik's supposedly messing around?

I nod. It's as I feared. Best to just say it and get it over with. I swallow.

"So what happened was, I went home and showered, and then I thought that there must be an explanation, but then I called them again – Thomas, he's the other friend, he's a bit more . . . reliable . . . if you know what I mean – because at first I wondered whether it was a joke. But anyway, I was upset, because, you know, I didn't understand. Because Sigurd doesn't usually lie, and there didn't seem to be any other explanation than that he was lying. So then, well, afterwards I drank some wine. And I was a bit stressed, you know, I drank too much wine, and I tried to call Sigurd again and again, and he didn't pick up. And so I did something that may have been a bit stupid – or, I don't know, maybe it doesn't matter – but anyway, I deleted the voicemail."

Fredly and Gundersen look at me. Gundersen's eyes widen.

"You deleted the message?"

"Yes."

Blood rushes to my head.

"But I'm sure it doesn't matter," I say. "I mean, surely you can retrieve the message, doesn't the telephone company save things like that? They have data about who calls who and what they say, or at least for messages saved to voicemail. Isn't that what we hear about all the time, mass surveillance and everything?"

I smile against my will. I can feel it happening but am unable to stop it, my nervous grin.

"This doesn't look very good, Sara," Gundersen says. "Especially in the light of your not wanting to give us the names of the patients you saw that day."

There's concern in his voice now, that of a doctor, I think, professional concern on behalf of another.

"I was angry," I say. "He'd lied to me. I was so upset. Can't you understand that?"

Just then the door to the waiting room slams. His colleague and I both turn towards the door between the waiting room and the therapy room in which we're sitting, but I can feel Gundersen's eyes on me right until the door opens and Annika strides into the room.

The first thing that happens when she comes in, of course, is that Annika becomes the focus of our attention. She casts a glance at Fredly, who has had to move to permit Annika to open the door, and her gaze merely grazes Gundersen before she looks at me.

"Sara," she says. "What's going on?"

And I have the feeling of seeing the world through the wrong end of a telescope, so that everything happening around me becomes tiny and far away, but I look at Gundersen, who nods, as if giving me permission to share the information, so from the other end of the telescope I say to Annika:

"Sigurd is dead."

What happens next is predictable, in a way, but also so bizarre. Because Annika inhales sharply in shock, hurries across the room and puts her arms around me, pressing me to her, rocking me back and forth as if I'm a rag doll in her arms. I let her sway me this way and that, really pressing the air out of me, and into my hair she says, "Oh Sara, oh Sara, oh Sara." When she lets go of me I see that tears are already streaming from her eyes, her mascara running in black tracks down her cheeks.

And what's strange is that Annika is demonstrating the reaction I myself should have had. While I'm numb and far away, consumed by bizarre details – the pizza delivery boy and the police officers' dialects and who chooses which chair in the room – Annika goes straight to the heart of it. Sigurd is dead. It's awful, terrible. So simple. And nobody loved Sigurd more than I did. So why isn't it me that's crying?

Annika lifts the back of her hand to her face and wipes away her tears, converting the black streams into grey smudges across her cheeks. She wipes her hand on her jacket, then holds it out to Gundersen.

"Annika Lathus," she says, "Sara's sister. I'm a lawyer."

It always surprises me when people introduce themselves like this, giving their profession, as if they're so proud of what they do they need to mention it at every opportunity. Sigurd could always be counted on to do it. He expected everyone to be so impressed that he was an architect, although why I don't know, because I can't remember anyone ever responding to him with anything other than friendly nodding and the usual polite follow-up questions.

Then I realise that Annika wants to protect me. She wants Gundersen to know that someone with legal competence is keeping an eye on him. He appears unimpressed, shakes Annika's hand without getting up, but for a moment his colleague stops scribbling on her pad. And in some way Annika reaches me, on the desert island to which my pain emigrated when it dissociated from my body, because the gaping hole in my chest now feels a little warmer, a little more like home – somebody is on my side.

Annika sits with me as it becomes Gundersen's turn to speak. He gets up, stretches his hands so that the knuckles of his fingers crack. He's tall, I see now – in my office in the garage loft he has to bend his neck beneath the sloping ceiling unless he stands directly under the ridge of the roof. He speaks in a calm, mono-tone, plainly and to the point, without unnecessary adjectives. He paces back and forth as he speaks, uses his hands, casts the occasional look my way. His gaze is clear and direct; I imagine that he never concedes ground. I don't know what I would have to offer such a man – in no conceivable future, I think, will Gundersen ever have any need for a psychologist.

Here's what he tells us: a local man found the body, which they believe to be Sigurd's, on Sunday. He was lying fully dressed just a short distance from the path, but the area is popular with hikers, and he wasn't very well hidden. A cursory investigation revealed two gunshot wounds to his back, and the present theory is that he died as a result of these wounds, although confirmation from forensics is yet to be received.

He was lying face down in the mud, as Gundersen had said earlier in our conversation – as he'd spat at me, in fact, when I refused to give him the names of my patients. This detail has vibrated in my chest ever since he delivered it. Sigurd's face: the crooked nose, the dimples, his beautiful, quick eyes and the mole below one of them – all this deep in the mud. I already know that I'll never get over this image, and I hate Gundersen for using it against me. He was irritated with me over the whole confidentiality thing, but this is my life, my tragedy, and I'll have to live with it for the rest of my days. I now have the image permanently etched into my brain. Thank you, Gundersen. Thank you very much.

He had been dead for a couple of days, Gundersen says. A more accurate time of death will soon be obtained, but based on current information it is likely he was killed on Friday, or Saturday morning at the latest. This offers some relief – on Saturday morning I'd let myself be reassured by the police-woman on the telephone who believed it wasn't urgent to report him missing, but by then it was already too late.

"His family have a small cabin at Krokskogen," Annika says. "Don't they, Sara?"

"We're aware of that," Gundersen says.

Someone must have spoken to Margarethe; perhaps she gave them this information last night when they informed her of Sigurd's death.

"So I have to ask you, Sara," Gundersen says, coming to stand before me with his hands hooked to his hips – although slim, he's a wall of a man, "can you think of anyone who might have had a reason to want to take Sigurd's life?"

Here I go blank. I leaf through the people we know, through the things Sigurd talked about, things he said in frustration or when exhausted.

"No," I say, "I just can't imagine it."

"It doesn't have to be anything major," Gundersen says. "Did he have any disagreements with anyone? Did he owe anyone money, or was there anyone who owed him?"

"No," I say, "not that I know of. I know it sounds boring, but Sigurd was, well – he was just a normal guy."

Something flickers across Gundersen's face. A normal guy, I think – and what might that be?

"He didn't do drugs or have a gambling problem," I say. "He

worked – a lot, and hard. He would sometimes hang out with his friends, otherwise he was home with me in the evenings, watching T.V."

"Is there anything in particular you're referring to?" Annika says.

"Just a routine question in murder cases," Gundersen says.

"I can't think of anything," I say.

"Let me know if anything occurs to you."

He scribbles his telephone number on a corner of the piece of paper his subordinate hands him, tears it off and holds it out to me.

"You can call me at any hour."

He places a hand on the door handle, and I gather that the interview is over.

"Gundersen?" I say. The name sounds wrong coming from me, it sounds stupid, but he turns nonetheless. "Is it . . . ? I mean. I'm just wondering – are you sure it's him?"

Gundersen lets go of the door handle and turns, his eyes almost friendly now.

"We won't know for certain until the forensic report has been completed," he says, "but if I can give you a single piece of advice, Sara, it's this: don't start to doubt it. The man we found *is* Sigurd. I'm not permitted to say this for certain – but it's him."

I nod, slowly, sleepily. Gundersen turns and leaves, Fredly at his heels.

Sigurd's tiny diamond rests in the little dip at the base of my throat, where it has rested every day since he gave me the necklace. Now I fiddle with it. I'm in the kitchen with my sister. Annika has found some bread and made a sandwich, which she's set down in front of me. I look at it, knowing that, should I manage to take the tiniest bite, I'll throw up.

"Have you spoken to Margrethe?" she says.

"Sigurd gave me this chain for my birthday three years ago."

"I know," she says.

"We were living in the apartment in Pilestredet. He was still studying, we had no money – but he bought it for me anyway."

"Hmm," Annika says.

She's not interested; is stressed, it seems.

"It was so typical of Sigurd," I say. "He thought I needed this necklace more than we needed the money, and I think he was right, in a way. Because isn't that often the way, when you're scrimping and saving, that you need . . ."

I search for the right words. Annika looks out of the window. She reminds me of the doctors I've seen on T.V. programmes about the accident and emergency departments at hospitals – always trying to find the overview in chaotic situations.

"Anyhow," I say, "he used his savings to give me this necklace. It was for my birthday."

"I know, Sara," Annika says, and now she sits down across from me and takes my hands in hers. "You've told me several times, including when he first gave it to you. I think we should go and see Margrethe this afternoon. Don't you think? I think it would be a good thing for you to do."

"Alright," I say.

I'm limp as an old towel in her hands; I'll do as she asks. Even though I haven't the slightest desire to see Margrethe, and I really feel that way, I realise – it'll be a test to have to encounter her grief when I have such a poor grip on my own. But although I don't want to, I'll accompany Annika if she takes me there. I'm just grateful that someone is taking control.

When our mum died, Annika was the rock. Pappa was

crushed, and simply sat in his study among the photograph albums and piles of shoeboxes that constituted Mamma's archiving system – boxes containing baby shoes and locks of hair and postcards from old friends on holiday and bits of paper with phone numbers. "What am I going to do with all this?" he sighed. I was seven. A friend had told me that when people die their bodies are eaten by small insects, unless they're cremated, in which case the body sits up once aflame. My head was full of appalling notions. Annika was twelve. She was at Pappa's side in the meeting with the funeral home. It was she who suggested that they should play the song *"Ellinors vise"*, which Mamma had liked, since Pappa was incapable of remembering anything she had liked, other than that she used to play "Satisfaction" by the Rolling Stones at high volume when she was getting ready for a night out. Annika found Mamma's address book and called the family friends who had not been informed. She chose the dresses we wore to the funeral. And in the end, it was she who sorted through the shoeboxes, whittling the seventeen boxes down to four. She's good at things like that. Pappa became apathetic when Mamma died, and if this situation is the equivalent of that, it seems that I take after him, because I'm just as apathetic, just as helpless.

So we get into Annika's Honda. But before we leave, Annika calls the patient I'm supposed to see this afternoon, as well as those with whom I have appointments booked for tomorrow and Wednesday. I am grateful not to have to do it myself.

We park outside Margarethe's house in Røa. I wait beside the car as Annika bends in the wing mirrors; I feel nervous, don't want to walk up to the house alone. In the end Annika goes first, taking the narrow path through the front garden. She walks up the stone steps to the front door and rings the doorbell. I stand behind her, fighting the impulse to duck down and hide. A few moments pass, and then the door is opened by a woman I've never seen before, wearing a green blouse and black trousers in a glossy, expensive-looking fabric that hangs so elegantly they must be tailor-made.

"Yes?" she says.

"I'm Annika Lathus," Annika says. "This is Sara, Sigurd's wife."

She gestures towards me. I stand there, feeling small and crumpled. The woman at the door doesn't give us her name, but opens the door so we can enter.

"She's in the living room," she says as she closes the door behind us.

I'm not surprised to see a stranger in Margrethe's house. She's always surrounded by people. Her husband, Sigurd's father, died when Sigurd and his brother were very young. I know little about him, because whenever the family speak of him they do so using stock phrases and lists of values: "He was fearless, he was so honourable, he was a man of principle." Every now and again these lists of values will be accompanied by anecdotes intended to prove them: the story of how he sailed to England alone; the story of how he could have earned vast sums of money on the stock exchange after he received a speculative tip-off, but chose not to act on the information, and so on. There is never anything that humanises him, nothing of any use if you want to understand the kind of person he was, what he was like to live with. In photographs he smiles, appears mild-mannered and friendly, and I've often wondered whether his unknowability stems from the fact that he was a gentle, lovable soul who ended up overshadowed by Margrethe's loud and colourful iron will. She never married again, but she doesn't seem in the slightest bit lonely. She has so many acquaintances, goes to so many parties – it's exotic and disconcerting at the same time. Sometimes she visits the homes of celebrities, has friends who associate with the royal family, but her circle is forever changing. I once asked Sigurd whether he thought it was a bad sign that among all the people in Margrethe's circle only a few ever chose to stick around. He had not enjoyed being asked that.

She is standing next to the living room window when we come in, looking out into the garden. She turns to face us, lifts a hand and waves. She looks devastated. Sigurd was her favourite.

"Hi," I say.

"Hi," she says.

We stand there, looking at each other. There's something familiar, I think, in the shattered eyes; the quivering line I've never seen before that now tugs at either side of her mouth. As I look at her now, I feel a connection to her I have never felt before. I have always wanted to get to know Margrethe – get close to her – and now that I feel I'm finally doing so, it's too late.

I lift a hand, place it on her arm, feel that she's nothing but skin and bones and that the arm inside her blouse is shaking. We stand this way for a while, as Annika and Margrethe's companion watch us, awkward and helpless.

"Thank you for coming," Margrethe says.

"I asked them to tell you," I say.

"Thank you," she says.

I withdraw my arm. Margrethe hugs herself.

"I don't know what he was doing at Krokskogen," I say. "He was supposed to go to Norefjell. He was supposed to leave early. I don't understand it."

Margrethe shakes her head, holding herself and trembling. She does not want to hear any of this.

"Harald's on his way," she says. "He and his girlfriend are flying out of San Diego this evening."

"That's good," I say.

I've only met Harald a couple of times, during a summer when he was in Norway for a few weeks. He's like Sigurd, only taller, a little louder. And he has reddish hair, whereas Sigurd's is chestnut brown; he looks like a copy of Sigurd where the printer ran out of ink halfway through. He has a girlfriend now, Lana Mei. She's Chinese American, and somewhat of a genius according to Margarethe – she has a doctoral degree in physics and a research position at a private energy company that pays her huge sums of money. Margrethe told Sigurd and me about her this summer at Hankø – I remember where we were sitting on the veranda, how I had picked at the edge of the chequered red tablecloth as she spoke, feeling grey and boring compared with the incredible Lana Mei.

Margrethe rocks back and forth where she stands. The woman in the green blouse goes across to her and places her hands on her shoulders, whispers something to her, but Margrethe shakes her away. She straightens her neck and looks out of the window, and for a while we simply stand and look at her, all three of us. Then she turns to face us, appearing to have recollected herself.

"Can I offer you something to drink?" she says. "We have coffee, tea, water and whisky. And I have an open bottle of white wine somewhere, I believe."

So there we sit, each with our glass of water, Annika and I. Margrethe, unsurprisingly, has opted for whisky. She probably had one before we arrived, too, but she's not drunk – it isn't that. There's just something old-fashioned about the entire scene,

Margrethe a tragic actress from the '40s; Greta Garbo, Veronica Lake. The whisky seems fitting.

"We'll have to figure out what to do about the house," she says. "I don't want to live there, but Harald may, in the long term. He could buy you out."

"I'm sure we'll figure it out," I say.

"But you're welcome to that Gundersen fellow," Margarethe says. "With his cigarettes and dirty running shoes."

I say nothing. I make eyes at Annika, trying to signal that she should interrupt, us, but unable to say anything myself.

"And at Krokskogen," Margrethe says, looking down into her glass. "Would you believe it, at Krokskogen?"

"So Lana Mei is coming, too?" I say.

"Yes."

"Will this be the first time you've met her?"

Margrethe examines her glass, turning it in her hand. Then she looks up at me, suddenly irritated.

"You know it will be, Sara."

I look down.

"Maybe we should head home, Sara," Annika says. "Let Margrethe get some rest."

Before I leave, I hug her. She's stiff and wiry as steel rods in my arms. The woman in the green blouse sees us out. She still hasn't told us her name.

In the car on the way home, Annika says:

"You know, she doesn't have any right to the house."

"What do you mean?"

"You're married to Sigurd. You're entitled to stay in the house pending distribution of his estate. And anyway, you'll inherit half of whatever is his."

"I don't intend to deny Margrethe anything to do with the house."

"No, I know," Annika says as she pulls away from a junction, "but just so you know, you're entitled to do whatever you want, from a legal point of view."

I look out of the window, fiddling with the tiny diamond Sigurd gave me. It meant so much to me at the time, and I'm trying to feel something for it now, but can't seem to summon any emotion. Is it still important? I have no idea.

"Sara," Annika says. "I've been thinking about your patients."

"Yes," I say, but I'm distracted. I consider the landscape beyond the car, the rows of terraced houses and gardens and melting snow.

"If they provide consent, you can give their names to the police."

"Gundersen can't make me do that," I say. I feel like a truculent child, clinging to what's mine, what I'm entitled to.

"I know," Annika says. "But it wouldn't hurt to ask for their consent, would it? To show the police that you're co-operating."

She drives down towards the ring road, and we soon pass the turn-off to the area where we grew up. I don't want to think about it; can't imagine calling Vera, Christoffer and Trygve and asking for permission to pass their names to the police. I have no idea what I'd say should they ask why I need to do such a thing. And anyway, I don't want to do it. Gundersen has no right to make that kind of request.

"I could do it for you, if you like," Annika says. "Call your patients. Ask them whether it's O.K."

I lean my head against the cold car window; the cool pane is soothing against my temple. I'm so tired.

"Fine," I say. "As you wish."

We say very little for the rest of the journey.

Annika stays with me until nine o'clock. When she's gone, I sit on the sofa with my mobile. Maybe I should call my father? I wouldn't even have to say anything – or at least, nothing about this. Just the sound of his voice might soothe me – just to hear that he's there as usual, doing his thing, the same as always. But I don't know. Perhaps it wouldn't calm me at all. I scroll through the list of calls on my mobile, see the incoming call from Sigurd on Friday at 09:38. Ask myself, did he know that I was busy with a patient then?

There are the many unanswered calls I made to him that weekend, which stop on Sunday evening. Since then, Margrethe and Annika and Vera have called, while I've only called patients to cancel. Five of the patients Annika has called for me. I haven't heard anything from Julie, nor from Thomas or Jan Erik.

Before I go to bed, I return Vera's call.

"Yes?" she says when she answers the phone, quickly, a little too efficient.

"Hello," I say, "it's Sara Lathus. You left a message on my answering machine?"

"Yes," she says, "yeah, it wasn't anything in particular."

"Are you sure?" I say. "You said it was something urgent."

"Yeah, well, it was just the same old stuff," she says. "It's no big deal. See you on Friday as usual?"

For two long seconds I stay silent as her question hangs there between us. It occurs to me that there will be days after today, weeks after this week – so much time in which I'll continue as a therapist, writing up notes, arranging appointments, intervening, attempting to heal young people's anxiety and depression and discontent. I have thousands of ordinary days ahead of me. That's what's most terrifying – that there will be normal, grey days, in which I'll be expected to work as if nothing has happened. Such an awful, vast number of them.

"Yes," I say. "See you on Friday."

When I've hung up, I think that I can always cancel. If, in four days' time, it turns out I still can't function.

The train is swift, almost soundless. I watch the landscape that rushes past, wondering whether we'll head into the mountains soon. It's taking so long, this journey through village after village – if only it would go faster, hurry up. Perhaps it's the coffee in the paper cup before me, but I've felt this same sense of impatience all week at work, thought that everything to do with my colleagues and patients and everything else I should have sorted out but haven't managed to get done no longer matters – I'm going to Bergen. Ronja's coming, too – the whole gang is getting back together, and that's all that matters now. I'm finally on my way and I can't believe how lucky I am – for four entire days, I'll be free. The train shoots through the landscape like an arrow and still it isn't fast enough for me. Five hours remain until I'll be there; I check my watch every ten minutes.

"I've made up the sofa bed and stocked the fridge with beer, so now all you have to do is get here!" Benedicte writes to me in a text. I check my watch again, still five hours, and I have to laugh at myself – what am I, fourteen years old? – I'm so excited that I just can't wait. It's almost two years since I moved to Oslo. Sigurd and I have a small apartment in Pilestredet. He's studying, I'm working at an institution for young drug users. I've been spat on. I've been called a whore and a dictator and a Nazi pig. I try to take it for what it is: justified but misplaced anger from young people who have had more than their fair share of the crap doled out by life. I squeeze the chain Sigurd gave me between my fingers, relying on it – at least I have Sigurd, who loves me. I cry in the bathroom only when absolutely necessary, cover the tracks of my tears with make-up afterwards, and carry on.

Am professional. I don't know any of my colleagues, who know each other, who face off against each other in the trenches of their professional battles. I don't belong to any side, but that's O.K. Every morning I sit by myself on a rickety local train for half an hour, and then it's yet another half an hour on the way back, reading books, reading newspapers, until finally I'm home. Sigurd is almost never home. His thesis is due in a month, he practically lives at the university. The cold apartment in Pilestredet is always empty, but that's where I spend my time. I don't know anyone in Oslo. Why don't you give Julie a call, Sigurd would suggest at first. He's so keen on Julie, simply can't understand why I won't be her friend. Annika has had her second baby, it's impossible to talk to her. I visit my father, sit in his living room, watch the students who have practically moved in as they work and write and discuss things in the dining room. Talk to my father about books I've read and the less controversial things in the newspaper. Think that we're so alike. He's just as socially awkward as I am, but he manages this congenital misfortune by maintaining an ever-changing fan base. They don't stay long, but while they're around they're intensely loyal. It seems to be a thing in the fourth semester of their studies – to read my father's works and become captivated by them. I'm not sure what purpose these students serve for him – whether they give him company, the human contact and care he needs, or a conceited joy when he sees himself reflected in their admiring eyes. Maybe it's about sex, I think, but I don't say this to anyone, not even to Sigurd. I try not to think the thought myself. He's my father, after all. How am I supposed to sit opposite him when I visit if I'm thinking about that?

We hardly ever drop in to see Margrethe, almost never visit Old Torp. I barely even see Sigurd.

But I understand. He has a lot to do. I try to show him that I understand, try not to complain, not to whine about being lonely, the fact that most of the social contact I have during the day is with these damaged young people who believe that the intelligence service is spying on them and just want to run off to give blow jobs behind the bushes at Sognsvann so they'll have the money to shoot up. It's all so sad I could cry, for the fates of these teenagers first and foremost, and then for my own life, because what reason do I have to be sad when these kids, ten to fifteen years my junior, have already experienced so much that's so damn awful? Drugs, incest, prostitution, abuse and molestation, war and torture – there are no limits to it, and here I am, whining because my boyfriend works so much.

I cry at home, sitting on the sofa and bawling without restraint. Sometimes it starts on the local train and I lift my book to cover my face, pretending I'm short-sighted and letting the tears I am power-less to stop run down my cheeks before I wipe them on the pages.

And I call no-one. What would I say? It's so shameful. If Sigurd had hit me, I would have been able to say that, I think; had he been unfaithful or drunk too much, I could have called my friends. Ronja now lives in Madrid, but she would have jumped onto a plane to be there for me if something like that had happened. If my father had died. If I had been ill. But because I'm lonely? I daren't even say it. Who would jump onto a plane for someone who's unable to connect with others? They might provide friendly reassurance and comfort over the telephone, but they'd be embarrassed on my behalf as I spoke. We always wondered about Sara, they would think as they hung up. Nobody wants to socialise with loneliness. If I reached out they'd withdraw, and I couldn't stand that.

So I handle it myself, at home in our sad living room. Cry, shower, cook a meal for myself. Eat alone in front of the T.V. Cry during the ad breaks at how sad I am – such a cliché, the girl on the sofa with a plate of pasta balanced on her knees, dissolving into tears over a shampoo commercial. I pretend I'm asleep when Sigurd comes home. Hear him come in, pottering around out there as he makes himself a sandwich, turns on the T.V., goes into the bathroom, brushes his teeth. And when at long last he comes to bed – I've been waiting for him and now, I think, now I'll finally get it, the glimpse of love I've been longing for all day – I turn over with a sigh, opening my eyes and squinting as if I've only just woken, and say:

"Sigurd? Are you home?"

And he says:

"Yes. Just go back to sleep."

He undresses and gets into bed, all the way over on his side. I wriggle across to him, lift my head, place it in the crook of his arm. Put my arm across his chest, close my eyes, breathe in his smell – the sweat, cold and chemicals. The way he's smelled since I first met him, when he would come straight to our apartment after finishing his classes in Bergen. He kisses me on the head. He holds me, but he's tired and sleeps best alone, and I know that he's waiting, just counting down how long he has to hold me before he can let go. I can feel him waiting. Three, two, one. He gives me a hug, leans over me, pulls his arm from beneath my body.

"Goodnight," he says, and then rolls over to his side of the bed.

Sometimes, in desperation, I've lost it. I've said, not yet, I've said, we never see each other anymore, can't we just stay close for a moment? It's worse, I've learned, to be rejected as directly as I am when I try to force him – Sara, I'm so tired, I've been working all day, I don't have the energy, I just want to sleep. It's better to take the crumbs he offers me, the minute or two, perhaps, for which he holds me, before easing me back over to my side. Sometimes, it's O.K. Sometimes I'm almost satisfied. Other times it frightens me how little I'm willing to put up with, the pitifulness of it all.

My mobile beeps as I drum my fingers against the cover of the book beside the cup of coffee – it's impossible to concentrate, so it lies there, unread.

On the move, *Ronja writes, and then:* I'll meet you at the station!

It's been almost a year since we last saw each other. I look at my watch – four hours and fifteen minutes left. The train gathers momentum, as if descending a never-ending mountain. We've signed up to be volunteers at the Nattjazz jazz festival, all four of us – three whole days at the festival doing simple tasks with no responsibility, spending time together, drinking beer and going to concerts. I've taken time off work. Sigurd was eager for me to go – a little too eager for the guilt-free mini-week at the university I'm granting him. Of course you should go, he said. Have a good time with the girls, party in moderation, haha, no, but seriously, have a really great time. And I intend to.

I see her before she sees me. She's standing under the platform canopy, her gaze searching among the passengers streaming out of the train. Her hair is longer than I remember, hanging wild around her shoulders. She has a kind of infectious, nonchalant elegance that rubs off on anyone standing beside her; appended to Ronja, I'm someone who counts. She doesn't see me, even though I'm waving, and I enjoy watching her look around as she stands there and waits – it's me she's waiting for – and I love the moment she catches sight of me. Now she lights up and waves, really waves, jumping up and down and shouting my name as loud as she can.

We hug one another.

"Sara, you hussy," she says into my hair, "I've missed you, d'you know that?"

And I have to concentrate, so that I won't start crying right there and then.

"Ronja, you tart," I say, fighting to maintain my self-control. "Of course I do."

Early morning, March 10: O.K., O.K.

What was that? I'm suddenly wide awake, lying with my eyes open in the darkened room, staring without anything on which to fix my gaze. Was that a sound? Was there something that woke me? Now there is only silence. I lie there for a few seconds, on full red alert. The house creaks; the wind blows outside. In the far distance I think I can hear the rattling of the train, but I've reached the point where I'm no longer sure whether I'm really hearing it – whether I've heard it so many times over the past few days while listening into the silence for Sigurd that now I'm simply imagining it.

But I hear nothing more. I grope for my mobile on the bedside table, check the time while trying not to look at the image of Theo, Sigurd and me with orange peel in our mouths. It says 02:43. O.K., then.

Then there's a creak. Not the kind made by a wooden house in the wind. The kind of creaking when something moves – a clear, articulated squeak. I sit up. Turn on the light. Don't know what I'm expecting to see, but my bedroom is bare, just as it was. My gaze dances uneasily from object to object: the rail hung with shirts, both Sigurd's and mine, the chest of drawers, the window, his now eternally empty side of the bed, his bedside table and mine, the ceiling light, the window again. Then I hear the footsteps. They're above me. Crystal-clear steps; a rhythmic thudding. Someone is in the loft. Someone is walking around in Old Torp's study. I hear them go out through the door, hear it close, and with a shudder I know that they're standing on the landing.

Only the bedroom door separates me from whoever is up there. Lightning fast, without thinking, I jump out of bed. With a leap I'm over by the door, gripping the handle, pulling it towards me as hard as I can, holding the door closed with all my might. It's silent up there and I count, *one, two*, whoever is up there has heard me, *three, four*, we're waiting for each other, *five, six*, these hundredths of seconds in which I'm monitoring the intruder and the intruder is monitoring me, *seven, eight*, and then, as I count *nine*, the intruder makes his move. I hear the banging of his footsteps on the stairs, rushing step by step down to my floor. I brace myself against the door, hanging my entire body weight off the door handle with an ice-cold, paralysing feeling inside me – that this is it, this is life or death, just me and the stranger outside.

But the footsteps race past the bedroom door, down the stairs to the living room, down from the living room to the hallway on the ground floor, and then I hear the front door being opened, and no more.

With my pulse pounding as if it's about to explode my eardrums, I wait, still holding on to the door handle with all my strength. He must have gone out, but what do I know, there may be others out there. I wait, quiet as a mouse, trying to hear through the rushing of the blood in my head – to determine whether there are strangers in my house.

Then I let go, throw myself towards the bedside table and pick up my mobile, reaching back; keeping one hand on the door handle I use the other, my left, to call the police.

"My name is Sara Lathus," I say to the pleasant male voice that answers. "I live in Nordberg, and five minutes ago I woke up because there was someone in my house."

*

It takes the police nine minutes to arrive, and I sit like this as I wait for them, one hand on the bedroom door handle, the other clutching my mobile.

"O.K.," I say to myself to calm myself down, "O.K., O.K., O.K., O.K."

I say nothing else; can't think anything, either. Everything is pale and trembling and I periodically see the image that was burned into my cerebral cortex around a year ago on the day Sigurd and I came to visit Old Torp, and found him dead in the loft.

At long last I hear them.

"Hello?" says a man's voice from inside the house. "Hello, is there anyone here? We're from the police."

I wait, still quiet, O.K., O.K., let's see how this goes.

"Hello?" another voice says. "We received an emergency call from this address."

There's a mumbling; I guess they're speaking to each other, and then I hear them on the stairs to the living room, their voices a little louder.

"Hello? Are you here?"

And then, in a low voice:

"Do we actually know who we're looking for?"

"A woman, her name is, let's see . . ."

O.K., O.K. My pulse begins to slow. An emergency call.

"Sara?"

O.K., O.K.

"Yes," I answer, my throat hoarse.

"Sara? Are you here?"

"I'm up here."

"Can you come out?"

And so I let go of the door. My hands are shaking from the strain. I get up, and stagger out on chattering knees, through the door that has saved me.

The policemen are kind. They're both young. One speaks in a soft, refined Kristiansand dialect, which reminds me of the summers I spent in southern Norway as a child; the other is Asian in appearance, at a guess I'd say his parents are from Pakistan. He's attractive, with big, brown eyes and a small scar on one cheek. It is he who interviews me.

"When did you first hear the sounds?"

"I woke with a start," I say. "I looked at the clock, it was 2.43."

He nods; notes this down.

"And can you describe the sounds?"

His colleague is taking a look around as we speak. He goes across to the terrace door and pulls on the handle; checks that the windows are closed.

"It was footsteps," I say, "I'm sure of it. He was up in the loft. He went out onto the landing and stood there while I sat in the bedroom holding the door closed, and then he ran down the stairs and out of the house."

The policeman makes some notes.

"Are there any entrances to the house other than the front door where we came in and the veranda?" his colleague says.

"One at the back of the kitchen, into the laundry room," I say, pointing, and he disappears.

"Have you had any break-ins before?" the policeman interviewing me says, and for a moment it's as if everything stands still, and I think, he doesn't know, he really hasn't heard, and now I'm going to have to tell him.

"Well," I say, "my husband was found murdered in Krokskogen on Sunday."

His eyes widen, understanding spreading within them.

"So that's not exactly another break-in," I say, "but I'm sure you'll understand why I'm a little jumpy."

"Certainly," he says. "Yes, of course, just give me a moment."

He disappears off towards the laundry room in search of his colleague. I stay where I am, gazing after them. Alone in the living room, I look around. They're only in the other room, but I miss them already, it feels lively and crowded when they're in here. I wonder whether I can ask them to stay. Just the thought of having to go back to bed, alone up there in the bedroom, frightens me.

The policemen go upstairs, to where the intruder came from, up in Old Torp's loft. I'm suddenly talkative, telling them all about Old Torp, describing how I found him, but I don't follow them upstairs. Instead, I move across to the window. From our living room we have a view of the Oslo skyline – it's one of the property's big selling points.

There are lights everywhere down there, tiny dots. Street lights, office premises in which the lights are left on, squandering our communal electricity. Then there's the buses, snack bars, bakeries and newspaper offices where people are always awake, I imagine, and the lonely wretches who can't sleep. I wonder for how many of them this is just an average night. I want to ally myself with them.

The policemen come back downstairs.

"Well," says the one with the Kristiansand accent, "we've searched the loft and checked all the exits, and there seems to be no sign of a break-in."

"Are you sure you locked the front door last night?"

"Yes," I say.

I go back over it in my mind – did I? Can I be sure that I remember locking the door yesterday, that I'm not confusing it with the evening before? Can my nerves have been so frayed that I forgot?

"Absolutely sure?"

I do a quick assessment.

"Ninety-five per cent," I say.

They exchange glances.

"The front door was open when we arrived," the policeman continues. "So it's impossible for us to know, but he might have come in through an open window that he closed after him."

I nod, waiting. Do they have any other theories?

"And if not, there are two possibilities," the colleague says. "Either he managed to sneak in during the day, if you had the door unlocked at any point. Or he had a key."

"Is there anyone other than you who has a key?" the policeman from Kristiansand says.

"My husband had one," I say with a sigh – Sigurd had one, but he no longer exists. "But his was found on him, or with him, so the investigators working on the case must have it. Other than that, his mother has a key."

They nod.

"Might it have been her?" one of them says.

"No," I say, "no, I can't imagine her ever coming in like that, going around my house and then running."

"Well, she has just lost her son," the policeman of Asian descent says. "Perhaps she's in shock. Maybe she wanted something of his?"

I'm not sure how to respond to this. I think of Margrethe, as she was yesterday, tragically beautiful and a little drunk.

"Call her in the morning," the policeman with the Kristiansand accent suggests, "and find out whether she still has a key. Someone may have taken it from her."

Something in his tone tells me they're about to finish up.

"What happens now?" I say. They look at me, then each other, and back at me again.

"We'll write up a report," the policeman with the scar says, "and pass it on to the detective in charge of your case. The case involving your husband, I mean."

They look at me again, and I feel the panic surge from my chest, they don't understand, they're about to leave.

"I mean," I say, "what happens to me? Are you, I don't know, are you just going to leave me? Am I supposed to stay here?"

The policeman from Kristiansand stares at his hands. I look at them, too. They're covered in dense, fair hair.

"If you'll feel uncomfortable staying here," he says, "you can always go and stay with someone you know."

Annika, Pappa, Margrethe. The list isn't long. Annika would be happy to have me, but I don't know, I feel reluctant. This is where I live. This is my house. And it's illogical, but regardless – if Sigurd were to come home looking for me, this is where he would come.

Do I really think that? Do I believe it? Am I starting to lose my mind? I hear the voice of the eminent Gundersen: "The forensics report is due on Tuesday." Hear him saying, "Sara, don't doubt it." Well, Gundersen, I'm afraid I do. The forensics report hasn't been completed yet – there's still the tiniest morsel of possibility that it may be someone else. What that would mean, I have no idea, but I know that I want to be here should Sigurd turn up.

"I want to stay here," I say. "I live here. I mean, why should I move?"

"Well," the other policeman says, and something in his tone

tells me he's starting to tire of me, "that's naturally up to you to decide."

"Is there any reason to believe the intruder may come back?" the southerner with the hairy hands says.

"I don't know," I say. "I have no idea why he was here in the first place."

When the policemen leave I let myself into my office, carrying a duvet under one arm and a pillow under the other. In my left hand, I hold the keys. In my right, I hold the sharpest kitchen knife I own.

It's cosier in here, safer. Only I have a key to the office – not even Sigurd has an extra key. I lock the front door, then lock the door between the waiting room and my office. Then I drag my desk over to the door and push my office chair beneath it. If anyone tries to get in, it will at the very least wake me up. I lie down on the floor with the duvet, it's hard and painful, but I don't expect to sleep much tonight anyway. In my hand, I hold the knife.

Here's what I remember from the days at the Nattjazz festival that year:

An electric, almost compulsive first evening; Benedicte, Ronja, Ida and I sitting at Verftet, we have a table, people we know come up to us, we hug people here and there and I say, "Hi, how's it going?" to loads of old acquaintances I'd forgotten I had. I'm being too intense, I realise, so I try to hold back – to relax and take the good atmosphere as a given – but I can't, I'm too desperate, and so to camouflage this I drink too much. I'm staying with Benedicte, and she has to come home with me before the party is over. I throw up in the bushes of her neighbour's garden.

The sandwiches we make as part of the festival kitchen team: saveloy sausage, butter and rocket, or cheese, butter and grapes, for the volunteers. The artists are given nicer packed lunches. There are four of us on the shift: an emo girl from Sauda with black eyeliner, who hardly says anything; a literature student who's writing her bachelor's dissertation on Proust, but who is also surprisingly funny, "In Search of the Lost Cheese Slicer," she says over the sandwiches; and a shy engineer who pretends to follow what we're saying when we speak Norwegian, but who only thaws out when we switch to English. I'm funny, too. I can tell the others think so. I tell stories from my life, from my practical training, from Oslo, about my father. I share too much. Not just from my work – which is ethically problem- atic – but too much of the rest, as well. Not that I'm telling everyone what an awful time I'm having, but I reveal so much that's personal.. I make fun of my father. "I don't think I've read any Zinerman," says the literature student, and I say, believe me, if you had you'd remember – my father likes to shock his way into people's memories.

Backstage we organise what the artists have asked for – food, T-shirts, whatever's on their rider. The Italian engineer, Massimo, and I have a slightly embarrassing moment over a stack of porn magazines an American progjazz band have requested. Massimo blushes easily, and I find him sweet because of it.

The mornings spent at home with Benedicte. When her partner has left for work, she and I eat big, fatty cheese sandwiches and drink litres of coffee from the ceramic mugs she took with her from the apartment we shared while we watch comedy series on D.V.D., and everything is just as it used to be.

The odour of stale beer on the premises when we arrive in the afternoons, the smell of sweat, of the party, of the people from the night before which still hangs in the air, in the heavy black stage curtains. Those curtains smell of things I can only imagine, things that are fun and borderline illegal, maybe drugs, maybe sex.

A concert with an old Dominican artist who takes off his shirt on stage; he throws it into the audience and Ronja catches it and holds it up, it's white with blue flowers on it and we look up at it, both of us, and laugh, and in that moment I think, I'm never going back, here I am free, fuck Sigurd and everyone else in the grey concrete slab of a city that is Oslo.

The last night of the festival, when all the volunteers celebrate together. Ronja has snagged the festival flirt, I've drunk Turkish shots with the kitchen team, and some of the people who've worked at the festival for years – the enthusiasts behind it – get up to play. None of them are professionals, but they make up for this with their passion for the music, and it's almost beautiful when they slide into an old Billie Holiday song: "All of me, why not take all of me, don't you know I'm no good without you." Massimo takes my hand. I smile at him – am about to say, I'm sorry, I have a boyfriend. But then I don't.

135

It's as if I'm twenty-two years old and a student again. I think, don't I deserve just one night when I can be that person again? Here Sigurd doesn't exist, and if he doesn't exist, I don't live in Oslo, and therefore I'm not the girl who cries behind books on the train and pretends to be asleep when her boyfriend comes home. So I stand there and hold Massimo's hand for ten minutes. Then he places his other hand at the small of my back. Then he kisses my ear. Then he looks at me with his kind, brown eyes, and I think, why the fuck not? I've had a bit to drink, but that's not why. I'm clear-headed enough to think: we have to go now, before I change my mind, before I manage to be sensible. I drag him out of the main auditorium and into one of the band rooms I know is empty.

Here's what I remember of Massimo on that last night: that he had a surprising tattoo of a shark on his shoulder. That he was worried someone might come in, even though I'd locked the door. That we did it standing up, leaning against the wall; that it was a little uncomfortable because of the position but enjoyable enough. That I asked him to say something in Italian while we did it, and that this made him self-conscious – he didn't know what to say, he said, but didn't want to disappoint me either, and so he said, "Sara, bella," and I regretted having insisted that he say something.

That best of all was afterwards, when we went back out to join the others but didn't say anything to anyone, just smiled knowingly at one another for the rest of the evening.

Early in the morning, around seven o'clock or so, everyone took off their remaining clothes and jumped into the water. I saw Massimo's shark tattoo for the second time. The water was freezing cold and I ducked my head below the surface. Back on land I dried myself on some old stage curtains. Then I got dressed, gave Massimo a hug that was too long and encouraging, wrote a made-up telephone number on a scrap of paper when he asked for mine, and then walked back to the station with Ronja.

"What happened with the Italian guy?" she asked me.

"Nothing," I said.

I slept the entire train journey home.

Sigurd is out at the university when I get home. I stay up until I hear him come in, and then get ten minutes with him.

"Did you have a nice time?" he says between bites of a cheese sandwich, his eyes red and tired. "Tell me all about it."

"Everything was great," I say.

"Great," he says, and his gaze loses focus.

It takes a week for the memories of Nattjazz to become as faded as all my other memories from Bergen – something that happened in another time, to a girl almost someone other than me, someone I know or have read about. Sigurd is hoping to hand in his thesis during the summer. Now he sometimes even sleeps at the university; creeps into the installation he's working on with a sleeping bag and a pillow. Ronja is back in Madrid, and our e-mails to one another are light and superficial. At least I manage to hold back my tears until I'm at home in the apartment, for the most part. I apply for a couple of jobs, get my hair cut in a new style.

One day Sigurd is home when I let myself in. I'm not prepared for this, and when I hear his voice call out my name, I have to call his in return:

"Sigurd?"

As if I can't believe that it's him.

"I'm in the kitchen," he says, and I go in without taking off my shoes.

He's sitting at the kitchen table. In front of him is a postcard.

"What are you doing home at this time of day?"

"Who's Massimo?" he says.

"Massimo?" I say, and it's true that for a moment I'm not sure who he's talking about. He throws the postcard at me.

Dear Sara, *it says*, Thank you for the wonderful time we spent together in Bergen, and especially for the last night. That was really special for me. I miss you a lot, and think about you. I wish I could visit you in Oslo, or you could come here to Milan. Please write back to me, or call at any time. Many kisses, your Massimo.

"Sigurd," I say, and for the first time in many months it feels as if he actually sees me.

Tuesday, March 10: Breathe and start again

Gundersen hurries into my kitchen, a satisfied expression on his face. I'm sitting at the kitchen island and staring down into a half-drunk cup of coffee. There really is something compelling about this man, I think. When he's satisfied with something, as he obviously is now, he's pure energy. I feel small and frayed. I've spent half the night locked in my office, nodding off every now and then with my back against the carpet, the steak knife within reach. There's nothing in particular I want to do.

Without a word he slaps a slim sheaf of papers on the table. I look at it – the pages lie there, printed side down, important-looking.

"Do you know what I have here, Sara?"

"No," I say.

"Three signed consent forms granting permission to access the patient records of – let's see – Trygve, Vera and Christoffer."

He holds them out to me, and as I summon the energy to lift my hand to take the sheets of paper they simply hang there, imperative, from his hand. Sad proof of what the powers that be can achieve when busy. So I take them, see the childish signatures in blue pen, but the letters swim before my eyes. I can't be bothered to read them, but I can't be bothered to protest, either. It's all the same to me.

"All in order," Gundersen says. "I gather you don't have any other grounds on which you'd like to protest?"

"No," I say lamely, and we head out to my office.

I let us in. My duvet is rolled up and set against one wall.

"So, I heard someone paid you a visit last night?" Gundersen says.

"Yes," I say, and to my surprise he says nothing more about it. "There's the filing cabinet," I say and point, but he bats away my words. He has all the time in the world now he has the paperwork in order.

Instead, he goes across to the two armchairs by the window.

"So this is where the magic happens?"

"This is where I treat my patients, yes," I say.

"I've never been to a psychologist," he says. "I considered it once. Just after I got divorced. I don't know. I've always wondered what it's like."

"There's nothing magic about it," I say. "It's hard work."

"Yes," he says. "Yes, maybe."

We stand beside one another.

"Which chair do you sit in?" he says, and even in my deep indifference this amuses me, just the tiniest bit. So now he's asking.

"I let my patients choose," I say.

"I see," he says, and nods, "but which one do you prefer?"

"The right."

Gundersen sits down in the chair on the left, and with a commanding gesture of his hand he says:

"Sit down for a moment, Sara."

"Aren't you going to go through my archive?"

"We have time," he says.

So there we sit.

"How do you start a session?" Gundersen says. "If that's not a professional secret."

"It depends," I say. "But as a general rule I provide a bit of practical information, and then I ask the patient why he or she is here."

"And what do they answer?"

"They generally tell me what they're struggling with."

He nods.

"Perhaps our jobs aren't so very different," he says, but he doesn't look at me. It's almost as if he's pondering this only for himself.

I say nothing. He passes a hand across his chin. He must be forty-something. The decades of smoking have clearly been rough with him, but he's still a good-looking man. If he got rid of the moustache and worn-out parka, you might even be able to call him attractive. Sitting here like this there's something disarming about him, as if we could just sit here and chat for a while – as if I could ask him, "How do you usually start a conversation with an informant?" and we could contemplate our professions' similarities and differences. I wonder how much of this is calculated, a means of creating the desired mood, and how much of it – if any – is genuine.

"Do you have any patients who hate you?" he says then.

"What do you mean?"

"I don't know," he says, stretching his arms. "You've practised for what, four, five years?"

"Three."

"And during that time, have any of your patients threatened you?"

"I've worked with psychotic drug abusers," I say. "What do you think?"

He laughs amiably.

"I get it," he says. "But is there anyone who stands out?"

I sigh; shrug.

"Of course they were aggressive, but I don't think any of them hated *me*, personally. I got the impression it was more the system they hated."

"Well," Gundersen says, "the system might be enough. Just give it some thought. Whether there's anything at all you can think of."

I close my eyes, think of a couple of the episodes in which I was spat on. Angry, desperate adolescents in withdrawal or terrified by psychosis. Of the outpatient clinic for children and young people – eight-year-olds who wet the bed and teenagers who refused to go to school and who cut their arms, but little animosity. And then my private practice. I give it some reflection. Trygve.

Haven't I always thought that there's something malicious in him? Not towards me personally, perhaps, but towards what I represent for him – coercion. He's forced to come here weekly and confess, and finds it degrading. Every now and again, as on Friday, rage rips through his face. He once told me that gamers have all the power: "We could make your life a living hell and you wouldn't even know what hit you," he said. He'll never stop coming to treatment because it's a condition of his being allowed to live with his parents, but he loathes coming here. If something were to happen that made me unable to work with him – to work at all – would that not serve Trygve's purpose?

But I'm not going to tell any of this to Gundersen. First, it seems far-fetched. If Trygve really wanted to get rid of me, and if he was able to use such extreme means as murder – which is quite an assertion – why would he kill Sigurd? Why not just do away with me directly? Not to mention all the other things: why Krokskogen, what does Sigurd's lie have to do with it, and who was in my house in the middle of the night? The second reason not to mention this to Gundersen is how Trygve would be treated. I can just see Gundersen hurrying into the kitchen of Trygve's confused parents, the way he hurried into mine twenty minutes ago, and saying, "Now listen here, Trygve's psychologist believes he may have killed her husband." It would be impossible to reconstruct anything with the family after that. And although, if I'm being honest, it wouldn't be any skin off my nose not to have to deal with the weekly sessions with Trygve, I'm worried about where it would leave him – and his parents – in terms of trust in the system. Not to mention how I would feel having to see the disappointment in the eyes of these parents who are trying so hard. All this because Trygve, of all my patients, is the only one I feel expresses any form of hatred, and because of the unlikely possibility that he may therefore have shot Sigurd in the back.

"No," I say, "I can't think of anyone."

Gundersen nods.

"Let me know if that changes," he says, then thinks about this for a moment. "O.K., then. Good. Practising for several years, no animosity."

I give him a brief smile.

"So then, what about the other way around?" he says. "Is there anyone who has shown, how should I put this, an excessive interest in you?"

"What do you mean?"

"I mean, have any of your patients developed a crush on you?"

I frown.

"That's probably much more common in films than in Norwegian private practice," I say, adding, "at least, if you work with children and young people."

"Well," Gundersen says, stretching out his long legs, "no stone must be left unturned."

I nod in agreement at this, but consider the tips of his trainers as I think, is that really the direction they're taking? Nobody had reason to want to take Sigurd's life, so they reach for the most far-fetched possibilities – that one of my patients may be harbouring a burning hatred or passion?

"There's one more thing I have to ask you, Sara," Gundersen says, as if prompted.

He hesitates for a moment, then looks at me with steady eyes.

"Were you and Sigurd having any difficulties in your relationship?"

This is surely the most obvious of questions. I understand. Gundersen's amicable tone has been deployed, with care, for this purpose.

"No," I say. "The usual marital disagreements, but nothing beyond that. We've had a good marriage."

"What were the disagreements about?"

I sigh, feeling the weight of this question. To have to bring up the most trivial of disagreements with the man I love, just days after he's gone. To have these disagreements subjected to critical assessment – we're talking about motive here – to have each and every stupid act committed by either him or me blown up to billboard size, rendered suspect. It is, of course, necessary. But it's so uncomfortable, so shameful.

"We're renovating a house together," I say, "as you've seen. Sigurd was the project manager, I was the foot soldier. I was impatient, thought it was taking him too long to get anything finished; he thought my private practice wasn't lucrative enough, that I didn't have enough patients, that my turnover was too low. Things like that."

Gundersen nods, thoughtful.

"Who owns the house?"

"We do, together. I mean, it's my mother-in-law's childhood home. When her father died, she gave the house to Sigurd. Sigurd's brother took over the family cabin and will inherit the house at Røa when the time comes, so we got this."

"And now it's yours," Gundersen says quietly, to the toes of his shoes.

"Yes," I say, remembering the conversation with Annika yesterday, "I assume so. But, I mean, won't Margrethe inherit some of Sigurd's share?"

"Your mother-in-law? Well. A small portion, maybe. But she can't throw you out of the house."

"Regardless," I say, "it's Margrethe's childhood home. It was she who inherited it; she gave it to us so we could have a house."

"That was kind of her," Gundersen says. "What are the houses around here going for these days? A detached property like this one? Ten million? Fifteen?"

It squeezes my chest, the stress of being pressured. One thing I learned from working with young psychotic patients was this: to take note of my own reactions. In therapy this is known as countertransference – a good therapist can make use of it in treatment. If a patient makes you feel angry or upset or dejected, this tells you something about what's going on within the patient; what others close to him or her feel. Used with consideration, it can give the patient insight into their own behaviour, their mental defences. Under all circumstances it's important to be clear about countertransference, "what the patient awakens in you", as one of my tutors once said. Gundersen is insinuating something uncomfortable. He's awakening a need to defend myself, but it isn't like that, I wasn't interested in the house other than that I wanted to live here with Sigurd. I mean, good God, this hovel has caused me enough problems.

Breathe. And start again. This is also something I learned when working with young people struggling with psychosis. I inhale, take a deep breath, in and out. I am calm. I can handle this. I can interpret it, and hand it back.

"Gundersen," I say to him, "I'm getting the impression that

you're trying to tell me something. Can you not just say whatever it is you mean?"

But Gundersen is no patient, and this is not a session to work on his behaviour and defences.

"You've benefited greatly – financially – from your marriage to Sigurd," he says. He doesn't look away, and nor do I.

"I've lost an infinite amount these last few days," I say. "You think I wouldn't give up this house – this nightmare of a building project – in an instant, if it would give me Sigurd back?"

Gundersen shrugs.

"I'm just making an observation," he says.

"You think I would have killed Sigurd for the house?"

"People have killed their spouses for less."

"Well," I say, "I loved Sigurd. I would never have murdered him, not for anything in the world. I could never kill anyone. But I assume my telling you this doesn't help at all."

He shrugs again.

"O.K.," he says. "Finances and the house. Was there anything else you fought about?"

For a fraction of a second I think about the child we had planned to have when we lived in Torshov, how we stopped trying when we moved up here. We talked about it only once, and then it was never mentioned between us again. It wasn't an argument. But it was something I wondered about.

"No," I say.

Gundersen leans forward.

"Were you thinking about something just then, Sara? Just say it. I've been married – I know how it is."

"No," I say. "We rarely argued."

"I see," he says, looking around my office, up one wall and then down the other. "But there's something else I was wondering about. As I understand it, there was a third person in the

146

picture at one point. On your part. A little breach of the agreement, as it were. A few years ago."

I blink. Breach of the agreement?

"What do you mean?" I ask him.

"What I mean is this: did you or did you not have an extramarital affair two or three years ago?"

The quiet of the room is uncomfortable as I draw breath. They've spoken to someone. I didn't think Sigurd had told anyone about it, but he might have confided in Thomas and Jan Erik. Thomas might have told Julie, in which case there's probably several people who know – she would have been far too excited at the idea of such a secret to keep it to herself. They must have spoken to her.

"That's right," I say, looking at my duvet over in the corner, the sad remains of my bed. "Sigurd and I were going through a difficult period. I did something stupid; one single, isolated night. He found out about it. He was angry. For a month I thought he was going to leave me, but then he decided to forgive me instead."

"Hard thing to forgive," Gundersen says.

"Yes, perhaps."

"It must have cost him quite a bit."

"I'm sure it did."

"How was your relationship after that?"

"You know," I say, "afterwards it was better. We took better care of each other. Understood that we could have lost each other."

"Now listen," Gundersen says, "I'm divorced, as I've said, so I'm not going to claim to be an expert on marriage, but that's something I don't understand. One party has been with someone else, and the other party forgives them. Can you explain it to me – as a psychologist? Wouldn't you want to punish the other person in a situation like that? You know, mess around with someone else yourself? Or throw them out? Send naked pictures of them to their boss? Something like that?"

Now it's my turn to shrug. I'm being put under pressure, and this time I don't know whether I can simply breathe and start again.

"I don't know," I say. "I would think it depends on the person."

"And Sigurd?"

"He was angry with me. He was busy studying at the time, and finished his thesis almost without speaking to me. When he'd handed it in he went away for four days without even telling me where he was. Then he came home and said he wanted to try again."

"Again?"

"Yes. He wanted to be with me. We bought an apartment and got engaged."

"Well, look at that!" Gundersen says. "A happy end to an unhappy situation. Where was he for those four days?"

"I don't know."

"You didn't ask?"

"Can't you imagine the situation I was in? I couldn't ask anything of him. I was just relieved he still wanted to be with me."

"But you must have had some idea?"

I shrug again.

"I thought he'd been to his father's old cabin at Krokskogen. He liked to go there to think, and it was almost always empty. And the key with the *garnkule* was gone."

Gundersen nods.

"And now it turns out he's been to Krokskogen again. What was he thinking about this time, do you think?"

"I don't know. Honestly. I have no idea."

148

"Might property and finance worries drive a man out into the forest?"

"I don't know."

"But what do you think?"

I sigh. I haven't eaten anything since the dinner Annika forced me to take a few bites of yesterday, and I'm starting to feel it in my head.

"I don't know what to think. He was having a bit of a hard time with some projects at work, and the renovations were taking time, but other than that he was happy. I don't know what else to say. He invited me out for a surprise dinner on my birthday just over a month ago. There wasn't anything – how shall I put it – strange about his behaviour."

"I see," Gundersen says. "It's a hard nut to crack, this one."

"Do you have any suspects?" I say.

He looks down at his hands again, seeming to smile at them. The tips of his fingers have a slight orange tobacco tint. Even from where I'm sitting I can see that they must smell bad.

"It's a little too early for that," he says. "We're still exploring the lie of the land, you might say."

Then he looks up at me, clear-eyed and compelling, a man so strong it's difficult to oppose him.

"Look, can I be honest with you?" he says – as if I might object to this.

"Yes," I say, unnecessarily.

"I want to believe you, Sara. I do. You've inherited a house, but, well, that applies to almost everyone who loses a spouse, and you seem candid enough. But I just can't understand this thing with the voicemail message. I mean, if I imagine it – O.K., I'm you – I've been to the gym, I've come home, I've received a phone call telling me Sigurd isn't where he's supposed to be. O.K. I have this voicemail in which he tells me he's somewhere he demonstrably isn't – that he's with people who say they haven't seen him today. I have this indisputable evidence that he's lying. And then I delete it. Now, why on earth would I do that? Even if I'm not thinking of the situation as involving any crime, even if it doesn't occur to me that I may need to prove my innocence at some point, it's still evidence that he lied. Wouldn't I want to keep the message so I could confront him with it, if nothing else? I just . . . I just don't get it, Sara."

I close my eyes; my ears are ringing again. This overwhelming exhaustion. For a moment I wish I could go back to Saturday, when I still believed, was still certain, that Sigurd would come home and explain this whole mess.

"I've already told you," I say, my eyelids almost closed. "I'd had a bit to drink. I was angry at him. I didn't think, I mean, at the time I couldn't even *imagine* that would be the last I'd ever hear from him."

And then the tears spring into my eyes. The message, Sigurd's lie, was his final greeting to me. Never again would I hear his voice. "Hi, love." Never again would I see his smile, hear the sound of his key in the front door. It's just me now.

I cry, quiet sobs. I don't look at Gundersen, and he says nothing. For several minutes we just sit there. I cry, and he sits in silence and lets me. After a while my tears stop. I grab a tissue from the box I always keep on the table between the two chairs and dry my eyes.

"I know it's hard to understand," I say. "What can I say? That wasn't how I supposed I'd confront him. I would ask him; he would answer. It never occurred to me that I might have need of the message."

"Well," Gundersen says. "I have to say, I'm sorry it never occurred to you. I really am."

We sit for a while in silence.

"So do you want the patient notes?" I say.

"Yes. Thank you."

I log on to my computer and print out what he needs. We sit there without speaking as the printer chugs away, not looking at each other, but the silence isn't an uncomfortable one. I give him the printouts, and he confirms that I'm free to go if I wish.

"Sara?" he says to me before I leave the office. "Try to eat something, hmm? You need to keep your strength up. It'll only get worse if you mope around here starving. Do it for my sake, at least?"

And in the moment he says this, he looks kind.

The police have our car, so I wait for the train. I'm uneasy, wandering back and forth on the platform as glimpses of what happened after I received the postcard come back to me. The long month throughout which Sigurd worked on his thesis and I waited for him to decide whether or not he would forgive me. His silence when he came home, jaws clamped together, and the way he almost couldn't look at me – only as much as was necessary to ensure that he wouldn't bump into me. He never looked me in the eye. I waited; he slept on the sofa. He stayed at the university, or perhaps he was staying over with friends. He came and went as he wished, and I never asked him about anything, no longer had the right, was unable to demand anything of him. I waited. He handed in his thesis, then disappeared. I waited some more, spent the passing days in pain. Confided in no-one. I went to my Pappa's house, spent a night in my childhood bedroom – felt comforted by my father's ability not to wonder about what was going on in my life. I ate his home-made meatballs with gravy, listened to his spiel about the ignorance of the Research Council of Norway, and felt myself blessedly numb.

Other than that, I lived my life as if nothing had happened. Went to work, came home, waited for Sigurd. Thought – *knew* – that things couldn't go on like this. Sigurd would have to forgive me, or decide that he was unable to and therefore let me go. The latter was too painful to think about, and I didn't have the strength to give him an ultimatum. Nor was it necessary – I knew that he knew. Four days later he was already home when I got back from work. He sat there on the sofa, freshly showered. A vase of sunflowers stood on the coffee table, and I knew what he had decided.

We talked about it, of course. I swore that it would never happen again. "I have to be able to trust you," he said. I said, "It's just you and me." He said, "Yes, it's just you and me." One day that summer, Sigurd went to the jeweller's and bought a ring.

I never wanted to be twenty-two again – I moved into my life in the present. I no longer yearned to go back to Bergen. I missed my friends, but realised they had moved on, that I was yearning for a time that was over. I had to discover new things for myself. Sigurd. My job. I called a friend from secondary school and went for coffee with her; I made another, half-hearted attempt to get to know Julie. I got a job at an outpatient clinic for children and young people. I thought, O.K., I'm not particularly social. During my time as a student I had a period in which I was always surrounded by people, but now I move in a more limited circle. That's fine. I have Sigurd, whom I love. I have a job. We'll have a baby. It's more than enough.

As the train rattles into the station and I board it and sit down, I think about that – the potential baby. How the idea had died for Sigurd after just six months. Now there will never be a child. Now there is no husband, either.

"You've benefited greatly from your marriage," Gundersen said. "I want to believe you," he said. I understand. He's on Sigurd's side, and Sigurd's side is not necessarily mine. I feel shaken like a rag doll after our conversation, but recognise that he's been pleasant enough. And that the future may involve conversations in which he is not so pleasant.

Someone was in my house last night. When I woke up, they were in the loft, but there were no signs of a break-in. I'm not sure what that means, but I've noticed that the police team working on my property are not working to find out who was there. That the policeman who questioned me only ever asked me one question about it, and that single question was no more than a polite formality. Perhaps they don't believe me. Maybe they think I made it up.

Gundersen says he wants to believe me, but I'm not sure whether I believe him. I draw a deep breath, feel the seriousness of all this. Now, it seems, I'm on my own.

The offices of FleMaSi Architects are situated in a quiet area, in a side street in Bislett. The young entrepreneurs paid through the nose for the attractive, light-filled premises in a building from the 1800s – premises which are cold in winter and hot in summer, but refurbished with whitewashed walls and polished parquet flooring. The premises are everything, Sigurd enthused – he was the "Si" in the name – when he showed me around for the first time. Back then, it was a single, huge space; it has since been divided into three offices and a common room that functions as a workshop and meeting room in one. Each of the three architects have their own angled drawing board, and above the main entrance hangs a sign featuring the logo they designed themselves. FleMaSi Architects. Flemming, Mammod, Sigurd. An orange rhombus containing grey and white letters. The offices are on the ground floor, and from my position on the pavement outside I can see Flemming sitting there, head bent, concentrating on his work. Mammod's office faces the back courtyard. There is no-one in Sigurd's office.

I push the intercom button. Mammod's voice answers. "Yep," he says, friendly, informal, efficient – just as the three of them had decided to run their business.

"Hi," I say. "It's Sara. Sigurd's wife."

There's silence for a moment.

"Hi, Sara, come in," Mammod then says, with considerable weight in his voice. The door buzzes, and I push it open.

They come out to see me, both of them. Mammod is wearing work clothes, blue overalls flecked with paint and sawdust, holes worn in both knees; Flemming horn-rimmed glasses and a T-shirt featuring characters from an '80s children's T.V. show – half-hipster, half-nerd. Both are wearing stiff, grief-stricken expressions. Sigurd was their friend, but I imagine this mood is being created mostly for me. They weren't particularly close, and their collaboration was not without its problems.

Flemming speaks first. He comes across to me and hugs me.

"Fuck, Sara – how are you holding up?" he says into my hair.

Mammod hugs me in turn, more stiffly.

"I was so sorry to hear the news," he says.

"What happened?" Flemming says. I look at them, from one to the other.

"I have no idea. I don't know anything."

We sit down in the common room. It smells of woodwork; assorted large pieces of chipboard are leant up against one wall.

"Sorry about the mess," Mammod says. "I'm working on a model."

Flemming serves us very strong coffee, not bothering to ask whether we want any, and neither Mammod nor I say anything. We sit there, the tiny cups balanced in our hands.

"So, how are you doing?" Flemming says.

"It's completely unbelievable," Mammod says. "I still can't believe it."

"Who in the hell would want to kill Sigurd?" Flemming says. "What's he ever done to anyone?"

They look at me with wrinkled foreheads and raised eyebrows, manifesting their incomprehension.

"I know," I say. "It seems so absurd."

"The police were here yesterday," Mammod says. "Poking around the office, looking through the shelves. They took pictures of his appointment book, stuff like that."

"They asked us about work," Flemming says. "About whether Sigurd had any problems at work."

They shake their heads in unison, and I take note of the question. Gundersen, of course.

"What did you tell them?" I ask. They look at each other.

"The truth," Flemming says. "That Sigurd was a good friend, a talented architect and an esteemed colleague."

That expression says it all, I think – "an esteemed colleague". As if he's speaking at a statesman's funeral. Mammod drops his gaze, more conscientious.

"We did mention," he says, head slightly bowed, "that there had been some difficulties. You know, with earning enough to cover our expenses and, well . . . the discussion we had in the winter. About how we wanted to run the business. Minor things, really, but – everything had to be laid out on the table. That's what the policeman with the moustache said."

Flemming slams a hand against the table.

"It's ridiculous," he says. "We only started the company in August. *Of course* we've faced challenges. It would have been a fucking miracle if we hadn't."

I remember their challenges, and the discussion that took place last winter in particular. Sigurd came home upset. "Flemming thinks he's the boss," Sigurd had said, "just because he owns the biggest share." The company was distributed as follows: forty per cent was owned by Flemming, thirty per cent by each of the others. Flemming's father had put up some capital. The young architect had agreed that it was a formality – reflected in the dividends, of course, but not to the detriment of a flat hierarchy. No single one of them would be above the others. But then, at the first disagreement, Flemming had started to assert himself. Or so Sigurd said. Mammod said nothing, avoiding conflict, not wanting to give an opinion on anything – again, according to Sigurd.

Flemming wanted them to go out and market themselves through the major architectural competitions, and to build up capital with smaller projects. Sigurd and Mammod wanted rather to work on private projects, and to aim to win medium-sized public sector jobs, so that they wouldn't have to spend valuable time on competitions for which they might never see any return. At least, that's what Sigurd said. What Mammod really wanted it was hard to say, but, if you ask me, I think he just wanted to work in peace. I don't think the issue was ever resolved – I think each of them worked with what they themselves wished to work with; that further conflict would be unavoidable once money became tight. Well. It's probably all irrelevant now.

"What did he say?" I ask them. "Gundersen – I mean, the guy from the police?"

Flemming shrugs.

"Nothing. He asked us whether we'd fallen out. I told him that we most certainly had not – that we solved creative dis-agreements through hard work and hard drinking. End of story."

"Are they bothering you, Sara?" Mammod asks.

I sigh.

"They're around. Asking me all kinds of weird questions.

What we argued about, things like that. But they're just doing their job. That's how I try to look at it."

They both nod, as if I've said something important, something right. They're no doubt looking forward to getting rid of me. I down the rest of my coffee in one gulp.

"I just wanted to take a look around his office," I say. "If that's O.K.?"

"Of course," they say eagerly, almost as one.

We get up.

"I'll show you in," Flemming says.

Mammod hugs me again, and goes back to his sheets of chipboard.

Sigurd's appointment book is a physical book. This is how it is at FleMaSi Architects: no Outlook, no shared iCalendars – every man for himself. On the page for Friday, March 6 are the following entries: *11.30 a.m.: Atkinson. 4.30 p.m.: Mountains*. I consider Sigurd's characteristic handwriting – capital letters bent as if he was writing them cursively, uneven circles above the "i"s. O.K., then. Atkinson at eleven-thirty. Two hours after he left the voicemail saying he'd arrived in the mountains. I think of the evening before Sigurd disappeared, of all the details I can remember. I'm no longer sure whether this clarity is due to my recalling the evening so well or because I've gone over it so many times in my mind, but there's one thing I remember with unwavering certainty: Sigurd looking up from the laptop resting on his knees and saying, "I'm going to try to get to Thomas' by six-thirty."

I turn the page to view the week before. Two appointments with Atkinson. In the week before that: three.

"He worked with Atkinson a lot," I observe.

"Yes," Flemming says with a sigh. "Yes, they were strange.

Not very good at paying their bills, either – they have a huge outstanding invoice. Sigurd was struggling to get them to cough up, especially the wife. There seemed to be endless disagreements about whether they'd agreed to this or that."

"Do you know why he was going to see them on Friday?"

"No idea," Flemming says. "He wasn't here when I arrived."

"But might he – I mean – could he have been showing them the drawings, do you think? Would he have taken his document tube with him on a visit like that?"

Flemming shrugs.

"I don't know. I wouldn't have thought so. But there might have been something else they were going to talk about, it's always hard to tell with people like them. Difficult clients. I have a few like that myself."

I glance up. Sigurd's drawing board is bare.

"Did the police take anything with them?" I ask him.

"No," he says. "Not that I know of. Listen, Sara, I have quite a bit of work to do. But feel free to stay as long as you want, and I mean, his things are yours now, so take whatever you like. And we can talk about the other things – the practical stuff, I mean – when you're ready."

"Thank you," I say. "I'll speak to you soon."

He hugs me again.

"It's just so fucking unbelievable," he mumbles, and shuffles out.

I take photographs of Sigurd's appointment book – the Friday, the rest of the week, and the previous three. I take pictures of this week, too – the first week Sigurd wouldn't get to experience. His appointment book for this week is fairly empty; I notice he doesn't have any appointments with Atkinson this week. I turn the pages, check a couple of weeks into the future – the name isn't mentioned. The last two pages of the appointment book are filled with addresses – the Atkinsons live on a street I'm familiar with, just south of St Hanshaugen. I change my mind and put the appointment book in my handbag.

I don't know whether or not Sigurd met with Atkinson as agreed, but what I do know is this: he lied to me. He said he was going to pick up Thomas at six-thirty in the morning. When he spoke to me, he said nothing about meeting a client before heading up to the mountains.

When I'm outside again, standing on the pavement, Mammod comes running after me.

"Wait," he calls.

I do as he asks and he comes over.

"There's one more thing," he says.

He stands there in his blue overalls, his safety glasses in his hair, covered in a thin layer of sawdust.

"I don't know whether or not I should tell you this," he says, "but Sigurd is no longer here and I think you should know. There was a woman who would come and wait for him sometimes."

"What do you mean?"

"No, well, I saw her just twice, I think. The first time I saw her she was leaning against the lamp post just there, peering in through the window. It was one afternoon, around five or six o'clock, and I remember I was in Flemming's office because he needed to show me something, and I noticed her because she was staring, y'know? And I thought, good God, I can understand why people don't want offices on the ground floor of this city when people go around staring in like that. Had I not thought that, I wouldn't even have noticed her, but then I thought, I wonder how long she's going to stay there for, so I waited, and then I saw Sigurd walking towards her. They gave each other a brief hug, then they walked off together. I don't know any more than that – that's all I saw. And I just thought, jeez, that was weird – because it was. I don't know. She could have been just a friend, or a cousin or something – what do I know? Another time, maybe around a month or so ago, he came to the office by car to pick something up. He stopped the car on the street right here – illegal parking, you know – with his hazard lights on, and I noticed a girl sitting in the car. And I, I mean, I wasn't wearing my glasses, so I can't be sure, but I think it was the same person. And well, I thought it was a bit odd, so when he'd gone I mentioned it to Flemming – that Sigurd had pulled up outside the office with a girl in the car – sort of . . . insinuating, you know how guys are?"

"Yes," I say, breathless, thinking, no, I have no idea how guys are.

"And Flemming said that, now that I mentioned it, he'd seen her once before, too. In much the same way as I'd seen her – hanging around outside, waiting – and then Sigurd went out to her, and off they went. So, I don't know, I mean, it's probably nothing – maybe you even know who she is?"

He smiles – hopefully, I realise.

"I don't know," I say. "I mean, what did she look like?"

"Well," Mammod says, scratching his head. A small cloud of sawdust rises from his curls.

"She was blondish, like most girls – she looked a bit like you, actually. Average height, average build. A black coat. Maybe a bit younger than Sigurd? I don't know – as I said, I never looked at her that closely."

I can feel how empty my gaze must seem as I look at him. I have no reaction to this. A woman waiting for Sigurd, not just once, but on three separate occasions. What women does Sigurd know, apart from me and Margrethe? My friends don't live in the city. He knows my sister – Annika works in the city centre and could easily have stopped by his office, although I'm not sure why she would. And then, of course, there's Julie. She's a few years younger than Sigurd and does, indeed, have the standard issue blonde hair. I linger on her for a moment – Julie, who Sigurd thought I should be friends with, perhaps even try to be a bit more like. Julie, who was snooping around in my house. There's also Jan Erik's girlfriend, if you want to get technical about it and include all possibilities. And a couple of friends from his student days, who I can rule out because Mammod and Flemming were in the same year as Sigurd and therefore know all the girls he was at university with.

But what about clients? Do they know each other's clients? And just as I think this, it occurs to me: Atkinson. The mystical wife with the often-absent husband – a beautiful woman with increasing demands but who refuses to pay. Who Sigurd found it necessary to lie about.

Mammod looks at me, narrows his eyes in concern.

"Maybe I shouldn't have said anything," he says. "Flemming thought so. But I don't know. I just thought that – well, if I was you, I'd want to know."

"Yes," I say, nodding. "Thank you."

Mammod nods, too.

"There might be a reasonable explanation," he says. "It might be, I don't know, it could be anyone. But anyway, now you know."

He turns to go.

"Mammod," I say, and he turns to face me again. "Did you tell the police about this?"

"No," he says. "No, I mean, they didn't ask. Maybe we should have."

"Yeah. Maybe," I say.

"You can mention it to them," he says, "if you speak to them."

He turns and hurries along the pavement. I watch him as he goes back into the office. "It could be anyone," Mammod says –

and given the description I agree with him. Blondish hair, fairly young, average height, average build. A description that would fit most Norwegian women under forty. Is he being deliberately vague? It seems I no longer trust anyone.

As I walk back towards the station, I think: the police don't know about this. Mammod didn't give this information to Gundersen, although perhaps I should. But then I hesitate. I enter Majorstuen T-banen station and walk quickly past the kiosks with their tabloid newspapers, not wanting to see whether they're reporting anything further about the "Krokskogen killing", as my personal tragedy is now known. At any rate, I don't want to read anything written in that worked-up, enthusiastic, bloodthirsty tone journalists use when covering a murder. Instead, I walk towards the platform. Lean my head back and squint at the screens, the tracks leading hither and yon, east and west, and imagine how the conversation with Gundersen would go. Me saying, "Sigurd met a woman with dirty blonde hair, in secret." Gundersen's faux-naif expression, his face artificially neutral, "Oh really, is that so?" As if he doesn't understand what it means, a man meeting a woman behind his wife's back.

And then I think: I don't need to say anything just yet. I won't make a secret of it, no – and of course I won't lie. If they ask me, I'll answer. But if nothing gets mentioned, I can at least wait a while. See how things pan out. I breathe more easily. The police don't seem so terribly interested in what I might have to say right now, anyway. So isn't it understandable that I would wait before sharing this information?

I don't go home. It's too early in the day. I have no patients, so what business do I have being in the house? I take the T-banen to Smestad instead.

I don't visit my father as often as I should. If you were to ask me, I'd say that I visit him once a week, but the truth is that I often don't bother if something else comes up – and I mean something else in the broadest sense: a good film on T.V., Sigurd wanting to take a walk somewhere, or me feeling too tired and preferring to relax at home. Annika is the same. But this isn't something we ever speak about – on the contrary, we often tell each other how we visit him once a week. Pappa never calls. He's too busy, he says and too bad at planning. He's completely open about it. "But you're always welcome," he says to us, thereby handing over the responsibility for our spending any time together.

He lives in a detached white wooden house between Smestad and Holmen – my childhood home. When I see it appear between the treetops I'm filled with a tentative hope and melancholy, a combination of emotions I remember from coming home from school wearing my rubber boots and down jacket; my heavy school bag with its metal supports that dug into my back.

This is where Mamma died, but it's also where I grew up. Here I lost my virginity, smoked my first cigarette, cried myself to sleep when Annika moved out to go to college, covering my pillows with tears I didn't entirely understand because she'd be less than an hour away by train, and at the time we were forever arguing, anyway.

Hope and melancholy seem to have been built into the very architecture. The house is old, built in the late 1890s in the classical style with oriel windows and the rest, but it looks run-down. A few years back Pappa paid some workers from Poland who had come to the door offering to paint it, so the colour itself is white enough – and upon closer inspection the house isn't run-down to an extent that would indicate neglect. There are no broken windowpanes, no drooping casings, and the house doesn't appear to be on the verge of collapsing or as if it's simply hanging on until the next autumn storm. Rather, the house's condition bears witness to the owner's lack of interest. From this external inspection you might be able to guess that the owner of the house moves in the metaphysical world, rather than the physical one.

These signs of decline are most clear early in the spring. As I walk up to the front door, I can see that the lawn wasn't raked before the snow fell last autumn, so a layer of brown pulp from old leaves is strewn like a carpet across it. In a month or two, when the sun really starts to shine, this will begin to rot. Someone – perhaps Annika, or perhaps Pappa himself – will finally take pity on the lawn, give in and rake it. But by then it will be too late – perhaps it already is. Soil is strewn along the path from someone's footsteps. Perhaps there's no hope of the lawn becoming green and lush and inviting any time in the next couple of years. Annika says that's how it used to be, when we were little and Mamma was still alive, but that's not how I remember it. Maybe she's right – when people talk about Mamma, they often say that she had green fingers. But I sometimes suspect Annika of seeing family life before Mamma became ill through rose-tinted glasses. Annika talks about Mamma more than I do, seems to need to keep her alive. "Mamma did it like this," she'll say, or "Mamma used to say such and such." I didn't know her the way Annika did, and for several years after she died would have preferred not to hear anything about my mother. If Annika or Pappa spoke about her, I'd change the subject. This made Annika angry – she'd try to force me to listen, but I'd refuse, either leaving the room or putting my hands over my ears. How could I know whether what my sister said was true? I was so young when Mamma first started to get sick. So many of my memories are tainted by the uncertainty caused by her illness. I would often wonder at the strange things she said and did; was she in her right mind, or was it the disease? How was I supposed to understand these anecdotes doled out by Annika when they were from a family life I couldn't really remember?

Mamma had Alzheimer's. It's classified as early-onset when it starts before the age of sixty-five. People who develop the illness, even the early-onset type, are generally over fifty, but Mamma was only in her early forties. I've been told that it started with small things. She'd forget the odd appointment, or mix up names and places, but laugh when this was pointed out to her. It was written off as forgetfulness – a little excessive, perhaps, but when you're the mother of children who aren't yet even school-aged, you have a lot to think about. She forgot to turn off the stove. She forgot to send us to school with packed lunches. One day she set the table with only spoons instead of knives and forks. I can remember us sitting there, Annika and me – Pappa was away – with two soup spoons each, fish fingers and boiled carrots on the plates before us. I thought it was quite funny, but Annika was angry. "We can't eat with spoons," she said in a strict tone, and Mamma laughed and said, "Oh my, you're absolutely right!" She laughed. I laughed. Annika gathered up our spoons and went into the kitchen.

I suppose someone must have sat us down and spoken to us once Mamma had been diagnosed. I can't remember having any such conversation, but I know that Pappa used to say, "Mamma has sick thoughts and healthy thoughts – she does sick things and healthy things." Goodnight songs and kisses on the forehead were healthy things. Soup spoons for fish fingers and fizzy drinks for breakfast were sick things. I remember how she used to laugh in a special way when she was confronted with the sick things – a bubbling, idiotic laughter. I remember that I learned to fret about it.

She did not, of course, become ill overnight, but I've worked out that I must have been five when Mamma was diagnosed. Her symptoms must have been evident for six months prior to this, perhaps even a year, and I therefore have few childhood memories in which I'm certain that she was well. I remember one day in my grandmother's garden, Mamma and me playing with a red and white beach ball – I see this image in my mind's eye and think, *that's* when she was well, *that's* when she was clear-headed, normal. I'm sure – almost sure – because it's so hard not to let the tiniest doubt creep in: or was she?

She would have become dependent on care; the disease progressed swiftly. Had she lived, she might have been admitted to an institution before I started secondary school. But as it turned out, she died much sooner. One unfortunate day when she was home alone, she mixed up the medicines she had been prescribed, a combination of anxiety and pain-reducing drugs, thinking they were her vitamins. It was Pappa who found her. I have no idea whether before this he was as distant as he was through the rest of my childhood, or if this incident – the act of finding his wife dead on the kitchen floor – marked him for life. I was seven when it happened. I don't recall very much of my father, either, from before Mamma became ill. I could ask Annika about it. But I don't know – we don't talk about Pappa that way, and I'm not sure how I would bring it up.

I ring the doorbell and wait. I can see that the lights are on inside, but it still takes a while before the door opens, which is typical enough. The girl standing there is a few years younger than me, with long brown hair and hard eyes. She looks at me with more than a touch of scepticism.

"Yes?"

"Is Vegard home?" I ask her.

"What is it concerning?"

I've never seen her before. They do whatever they like, these students he takes in. She can't have been here long, but she obviously seems to think she's some kind of bouncer – that she needs to protect him, the sensitive genius, from the bothersome outside world. Many of his students are like this. Of course, it may well be that those he attracts are of a certain disposition, but I also have to assume that he brings this out in them. The stories he tells them about his public and academic life are undoubtedly fashioned from the David and Goliath archetype: the little man's fight against the system. While they swallow it, the students feel important. They're his tireless defenders, whether for just a few months or a whole semester.

"I'm his daughter," I say.

She says nothing more, but opens the door and lets me in. In the hallway I see shoes and jackets of various types and sizes. Many of them clearly don't belong to Pappa – he must have a group here with him. I kick off my own shoes. The student walks into the living room and I follow her, before moving ahead of her so that I walk into his study first. My little act of overtaking irritates her, it seems, and I'm not above feeling pleased at this. This is my childhood home, and I won't be led around like a guest. I enter the study without knocking.

He's sitting at his desk, a manuscript before him, reading glasses balanced on his nose and a huge teacup at his elbow. It takes a moment before he glances up at us, the student and me, as we stand there and look at him. He finishes the page he's on, his lips moving with each word in a half-expressed accompaniment to the text.

Then he looks up, and a smile spreads across his face.

"My goodness, Sara, hello!" he says. "It's so nice to see you."

I cross the room to his desk and give him a hug. He smells of tea and aftershave and wet leaves.

"Hi, Pappa," I say.

"Have you met my daughter?" he asks the student who's standing in the doorway, who answers in the affirmative.

"Hi," she says to me.

"Hi," I say, most graciously.

"Would you like something to eat, Sara?" Pappa asks me as he gets up. "I'm not sure what I have in the house right now – I'm so busy either skiing or writing that there's little time to do the shopping. And I have a group here, as you can see – a group of students who are discussing some very interesting ideas around how punishment is handled within society, so they're getting on with that, and of course things get eaten up."

"We have bread rolls," the student says helpfully.

"A cup of tea is enough," I say.

Pappa disappears out to the kitchen to make the tea, the student at his heels. They've almost moved in, these students who worship him. There's something off about the whole situation, something not quite right, and I try my best not to think too much about my father's relationship to these students – whatever it might involve.

A few years ago Pappa acquired a small flat in Bislett, so he would have a place to which he could go to write. "For when the university department gets too busy," he said. Afterwards, Annika and I asked each other whether it was so he could get away from the students who were camping out in his house. Because why else would a man who lives alone need yet another place to go to to be alone?

"Maybe it's so he can sleep with them," Sigurd once said dryly in the car on the way home. I said nothing.

The FleMaSi offices are close to Pappa's writing flat – actually, if you lean your head out of Sigurd's office window you can see the window of Pappa's apartment. I once pointed this out when we were talking about it – suggested that they might have lunch together some time, seeing as they'd be working so close to one another. Why I did this I don't know, because I really couldn't imagine them ever setting a date to meet up, and predictably enough the suggestion wasn't very palatable to either of them – they've never had much time for one another. Pappa thinks Sigurd is a glorified make-up artist, since his only occupational purpose is to make things look pretty. Sigurd has always viewed my father with the bewilderment felt by most people who get to know him: does he really *believe* all that stuff? Yes and no, I would answer. But it's best not to give Pappa too much thought – he likes to provoke, and the angrier you get, the more fun he has teasing you. Sigurd found a way of dealing with him – and as long as Sigurd didn't make too much of himself, Pappa endured him like a piece of decor he didn't much care for, making the effort because I insisted he do so. It was fine, there was no conflict between them. But the proximity of their offices was never mentioned again – and it wasn't as if they invited each other over for coffee.

While the office is empty I glance at the title of the manuscript on his desk. "The use of flogging in criminal sentencing and its preventive effect on crime, a cross-cultural literature review by Vegard Zinerman." I sigh. Business as usual.

When I was fourteen, Pappa wrote an opinion piece for the *Aftenposten* newspaper in which he argued for the reintroduction of the stocks to the Norwegian judicial system. My social studies teacher asked me, "Zinerman, is that a relative of yours?" That was the first time I understood that other people were aware of him, and later I found out that he had written such controversial columns and articles throughout my childhood. In his younger days he'd taken a different standpoint – had read Nils Christie, and believed that punishments should be minimised. But then he had evidently changed his mind. When I read

his texts I'm never sure of the level at which he's operating –
whether he's being ironic or sincere, whether he pushes
questions to the extremes to highlight society's paradoxes and
hypocrisies, or whether he truly believes what he writes. He
was extremely active in the aftermath of the terrorist attacks
that took place on July 22, shouting his opinion into every microphone held out to him.

The year after the article about the stocks, Annika said,
"Listen. I've been thinking about something. I want to take
Mamma's surname. To honour her."

"Do you not want to be called Zinerman anymore?" Pappa
said.

We were eating, I remember, in the dining room of this very
house. Pappa had his fork halfway to his mouth. He put it down
again and looked at Annika with a heavy, serious gaze. Annika
looked down at her napkin.

"I've started to forget what she looked like," she said, her
voice thick. Silence descended over the table like a blanket.

"Oh, dearest," Pappa said. "It's *your* name. You can do as
you wish. Mamma would have liked that."

Annika nodded in thanks, but there were no tears in her
eyes, I noticed. She was in her second year at law school. The
week before, Pappa had written an article in *Dagbladet* entitled
"Capital punishment and the dignity of the state".

I was too weak for him, knew that I'd never have another
chance.

"I've almost forgotten her," I said, my voice trembling. "I
almost remember her funeral better than I remember her."

"You, too?" Pappa said. I didn't look at him, endured the
silence, counted the seconds in order to make it last.

"Well, I suppose I have no choice but to understand," he said.
"And regardless, it'll be nice for you girls to have the same name."

The Zinerman name came from my father's grandfather, a Polish seaman who in Lisbon had signed on to a ship to Bergen, lied about his origins and made up a name. Pappa was immensely proud of his enterprising grandfather. Nobody else bore the name Zinerman. It was a stamp of quality, he believed, and he never noticed the embarrassment he was causing his daughters. It must have pained him that we wouldn't carry on the name, but it was just like him not to reveal this hurt to us. He showed us that he respected our choice by never mentioning it again. Annika and I went down to the courthouse and completed the paperwork, and that was that.

When he returns to the study he's shaken off the student. He's holding two teacups, and sets them on the coffee table between the armchairs by the fire. Of all the rooms in the house, Pappa's study is the most painstakingly crafted – it's large, a living room in itself, has a fireplace, armchairs, drinks cabinet and all. In the event of a national emergency he could live here in his study for several days.

"So," he says, looking at me. "How are you, my dear?"

He has clear, green eyes, my father – like those of an old man, or a baby. The skin of his face is full of furrows, blown into him by the wind and rain atop the high mountains and exposed crags he has climbed on skis. He has this friendly smile, so mild that you'd never believe him capable of defending capital punishment and flogging. Now he's taken off his glasses, crossed one leg over the other, and the look he gives me says, "Speak, you have my full attention." All of a sudden I want to cry.

When I was little, there was nothing I wanted more than to be invited to enter this room. The honour was not extended to me very often, but every now and again Pappa would ask me whether I'd like to join him for a while. Sometimes he would make tea, and we would each take a seat in one of the armchairs.

I would tuck my feet up under me, hardly speaking, terrified of disrupting the magic of the moment, as if the improbable joy of sitting with him might evaporate should I say the wrong thing. He would talk, and I would listen. He would tell me about the scientists he admired, about the great philosophers, about decisive battles of the Byzantine Empire and epic poems from ancient Turkey, songs from distant times and far-off foreign lands. I don't think I understood even half of what he said, but it didn't matter. I could lean my head against the back of the chair, narrowing my eyes until they were almost closed and my father was no more than a shadow. Listen to his voice, always rasping, as if you could strike a match along it.

It isn't that my father doesn't ask me how I'm doing now that we're both adults – it's that he forgets to listen to my answer. With him, I have only a narrow window of time into which what I have to say must fit. After a few minutes his attention begins to wander. I know this – but it's not something I mourn. My father is who he is, and a man like him can't be changed. His glasses are on the desk, but I can still see the impression they have left across the bridge of his nose, a weak, red line. Now he looks at me, tells me with his gaze that the floor is mine, that he's listening, and I steel myself to come out with it, just say the words: "Sigurd is dead." Get it over with. Then he can say whatever he likes.

For a time, when I was in secondary school, I tried to talk to him about my feelings. Told him about how my friends were going away to a cabin but hadn't invited me; went to him when I couldn't sleep at night because the boy I was in love with had got together with someone else. Felt the pain worsen on speaking with him. "Aha, I see. I'm sure things will work themselves out," he would say – the words often appearing at such an inopportune moment that I would realise he wasn't even listening, that he was engrossed in his own thoughts, probably thinking that whatever I was going on about was just some teenage drama, something that would pass of its own accord – which it often did. But I felt stupid every time. I never learned. Always thought that this time, just maybe, what I had to say would be enough.

When my grandmother keeled over and died in Husebysko- gen without warning, Pappa invited Annika and me on a cruise. He didn't ask us first, just bought the tickets. Three weeks in the Caribbean. We would leave Oslo the day after the funeral – it must have cost him a small fortune. Annika was heavily preg- nant and said, "No way." So Pappa and I went, just the two of us. The timing wasn't great for me, either – it was right before my exams, and I spent most of the trip sitting in a sunlounger on deck, a textbook open across my knees. Thought of my grand- mother in the evenings as I tried to go to sleep, tossing and turning in bed. Pappa was restless, too. Spent hours pacing up and down the ship. He had been so close to his mother. It had never occurred to him that she, too, would one day die; that it might happen so suddenly. Back and forth he wandered, agitated in his grief. Should have been out in the forest or the mountains where he would have been able to move more freely. He must have hated every moment of it; had only gone on the cruise for my sake. Had probably thought it would ease our grief, Annika's and mine. Had used his savings to give us this holiday neither he nor we really wanted.

It isn't that he doesn't care about me. But I never know what I can expect from him. Nor do I know what I need. I've just lost Sigurd, have so little to hold on to. So I say:

"I'm fine."

And he says:

"Yes? With your work and everything? And with Sigurd?" His voice is normal, almost cheerful. I feel a sting in my chest. I didn't expect him to know anything, of course, I came prepared to tell him, and still a part of me hoped that he somehow already knew, so that I wouldn't have to. But he is the same as always, and it is as if the full burden of this hits me only now: It is up to me to do it, to say the words and shoulder the response. Or at the very least to ask my sister to do it for me; when it comes to Pappa, it seems, Annika will not act before I ask her.

"I'm keeping at it," I say, trying not to sound strained. "And you – how about you, Pappa?"

For a moment he looks at me, searchingly, as if he wants to ask something more. I'm sure he can see it on me, and my stomach flips, I will have to explain. But then he smiles again, and says:

"Well, you know, I'm keeping at it, too."

It's pleasant, his smile – stories read before the fire and a feeling from when I was small, of being invulnerable as long as he was there. Endless relief washes over me. I came here to tell him. Now I won't have to.

"So what have you been up to?" I ask him.

"I've been out skiing quite a bit," he says, before adding, like a proud child, "I went out every day last week. There's enough snow if I drive up to Sørkedalen."

I lean back in my chair, longing to press my cheek against its high back as I used to when I was small.

"Have you read any good books recently?"

Pappa makes himself comfortable. Has been reading Michel Houellebecq.

"Now that guy really is something," he says. "It's dark, there's no escaping it, but at the same time, Sara, I think there's a lot one can learn from sitting in the dark and watching the world for a while. I think it's an essential activity. One just has to be sure to emerge from the darkness afterwards, and not get stuck in it."

I've been reading Sofi Oksanen.

"You should read her," I say. "I'd like to hear what you

think – I think you'd like her work. Speaking of darkness."

This is how we talk about the big things in life – love, death and pain, the absurdity of it all. If great authors have written about it, Pappa and I can talk about it. I'm so relieved at having decided not to say anything about Sigurd that I become generous. I laugh at his comments, a little bit too much. I joke with him: "Yes, well, if you're stuck in the darkness that's where we therapists come in." As he begins to tell me about the book he is reading, I lean back in the chair; in the heat from the fireplace it's almost as if I can taste the cocoa from the audiences I was granted with him as a child. And I know I will regret this later. I should take the opportunity and tell him, instead of stealing this moment of calm for myself. But it feels so irresistibly good. Sitting here listening to his voice in complete stillness, eyes closed.

When I get home, the house in Kongleveien seems to tower there upon its slope. It's cloudy, almost dark outside. There's a police car in the drive, and in the garden I see a police officer bent over, her backside in the air. The sound of my footsteps on the gravel reaches her, and when she turns I see that it's Fredly, the red-haired northerner who accompanied Gundersen at our first conversation in my office. I wave to her, and she waves back.

In the kitchen I realise how tired I am. I have barely slept since 2.45 this morning. Now that I think about it, I've slept poorly ever since Sigurd disappeared. I feel unsafe in my own house. How am I supposed to sleep?

But with the police car in the drive, with Fredly in the garden, I'm safe. I walk up the stairs as if in a trance, drift into the bedroom and sink onto my bed. On Sigurd's side.

*

The competition was called New Horizons, and the project was to design a new cultural centre for a village in the west of the country. The municipal council had dug up some money, applicants were given free rein, and Sigurd – recently graduated, out of work and hungry – threw himself into the challenge. He covered our apartment in drafts, sat in the spare room until late into the night in a never-ending dance between his computer and the drawing board.

"Expansive surfaces," he said. "Open spaces. Views."

"Sounds good," I said.

New days and nights; new ideas. I came home from work, walking up Vogtsgate and into the stairwell to the apartment we had bought in Torshov, and let myself in. It smelled of heavy breathing, of cold coffee.

"Sigurd," I called, and he emerged, his eyes shining.

"Meeting places," he said. "An arena for play, learning and conversation."

He had a drawing in his hands. He held it up to me.

"What do you think?"

"What on earth is it?" I said, and a hint of irritation worked itself into the corners of his mouth before he explained.

"This is the main auditorium, that's the foyer, in here are meeting rooms, and over here is a play area for children."

A library, multimedia room, stages. Sigurd's passion burned on behalf of the villagers. Why should everything be limited to Oslo? Why shouldn't these weather-beaten westerners have the same access to cultural experiences and beautiful architecture?

In the evening, as I sit watching T.V. in the living room, I can hear him in there, the creaking of the outdated printer that's working over-time, his feet crossing the floor to collect the printouts. Sometimes he comes out to get something to drink or go to the loo. I've stopped asking him whether he wants to sit down and watch T.V. with me.

At university, Sigurd was the golden boy. He worked longer days than anyone else, lived for his projects. He earned high praise, which always glanced off him, and criticism, at which he snorted. He'd had his eyes on the prize ever since I first met him – would make it big, design opera houses and landmarks, and take on private projects through which he could express himself as he wished. He could speak endlessly about it – the importance of what we surround ourselves with; buildings that help us to breathe. Once he got going, he would lose touch with his audience. Thomas and Jan Erik would humour him, their patience wearing ever thinner; Margrethe would tell him straight out, "Sigurd, honey, we can't stand to listen to any more about open-plan office spaces" – but he paid no attention. Yes, he would graduate with a diploma more golden than any the university had ever seen; would sail smoothly into an established but innovative firm, start at the bottom and work his way up. I don't believe it ever occurred to him that things might not turn out that way.

But in the autumn of 2013 the city's architectural firms were being cautious about taking on new staff. They had just put a financial crisis behind them, but an oil crisis loomed. In his own mind, Sigurd was already a respected and renowned architect, but on paper he was a recent graduate with no experience. He spent his first two months as a jobseeker in a state of silent, uncomprehending wonder – how could this be? On Facebook he saw his classmates taking up new positions, and blurted out:

"And even her – I mean, she's never created anything original!"

I got a job at a clinic for children and young people. Sigurd and I barely spoke about the fact that I'd changed job. We'd bought our first apartment; the Massimo affair was behind us. This was supposed to be a good time for us.

And then one afternoon the competition announcement sails into Sigurd's inbox. He immediately lights up. New Horizons. He draws; he speaks. This might be a way in. He works alone, from home. Who needs the big firms? Who needs the bureaucracy and bosses breathing down your neck? One man, alone at his drawing board, that's *all, no bothersome administration, pure creative force. Work on the project moves into our apartment. I'm just happy that Sigurd has something to do.*

The announcement comes in October. Eight submissions have been shortlisted for assessment. Seven are from the major firms, the eighth is from an experienced Dutch architect. I come home from work and the apartment smells of burning. The charred remains of Sigurd's model are in the shower cabinet. In the spare room, Sigurd is clearing away his things, tearing pages out of sketch pads.

"I'm sure it's usual to get rejected," I say. "Most people probably have to go through several submission rounds before getting selected for anything."

Sigurd stares at me, his eyes black – it's a stranger standing before me.

"Shut up, Sara," he says.

It's a slap in the face – Sigurd never speaks to me like that. And I don't know what to do with it – this wildness and rage that surrounds my fiancé like a foul smell. I don't want to prod at it, don't want to make it worse. Don't want to know what I might find in there. This isn't Sigurd. "I want no part of this," I say. "I'll be in the living room." I leave the spare room; shut him in there.

Half an hour later he comes out carrying some papers in his arms. He goes into the bathroom. Comes out to collect a bottle of whisky and matches. I say nothing.

He takes the rest of the whisky into the spare room with him; burned paper lies beside the model in the bottom of the shower cabinet. I walk past it, brush my teeth as if it isn't there. I want to wake in the morning and find that the man I'm engaged to has reappeared. I fall asleep with the firm conviction that this wish will come true.

It works. The next morning Sigurd is silent. When I get home from work, he's tidied up and bought food for dinner. Three weeks later he gets a job. We never speak of New Horizons again.

Annika comes over to see me after work. I'm sitting there limply, sorting through boxes for something I can't quite put into words. We're still partly living out of boxes, Sigurd and me. One is labelled RANDOM STUFF, SIGURD, and it looks promising. Everything that was his is mine, Gundersen said – Flemming, too. Maybe there will be something to learn about Sigurd from his random stuff?

Old photographs from his final year of secondary school: Sigurd and Jan Erik with young, soft faces and eyes half-closed in an unaccustomed drunkenness that still afflicts them to this day; mouths grinning, caps askew. Course reading lists from the Norwegian Business School, which Sigurd attended before he figured out he wanted to become an architect. Postcards of paintings in little paper bags, Klimt, Rodin, Chagall, Kandinsky, Pollock and Warhol. A wooden box containing a bone-dry cigar. Sigurd hasn't touched any of this in the past five years. I'm groping around in the dark here, I know that, but I need something to hold on to. Who was Sigurd? The page of his appointment book is burned into my memory: *11.30 a.m.: Atkinson.* I know I'll throw myself into it at some point, hold it up against my own calendar, for every Atkinson entry in the book asking myself: what did he tell me he was doing?

But the contents of these boxes tell me nothing. We have one labelled RANDOM STUFF, SARA, too, full of similar things: photographs, cards I received on my twenty-third birthday, the schedule for a language exchange programme I went on when I was fifteen, and so on. No-one would learn anything about me now by looking through what's there, other than the most banal details: she travelled a bit in her twenties, went to an exhibition in 2007 that suggests she likes photography.

"Hi," Annika says.

She looks at me with pity. In my hands I'm holding a bright green teddy bear, the kind you might win as third prize in a competition at a fair.

"Hi."

She stands there in the kitchen; I'm sitting on the living room floor. She sets a brown paper bag flecked with grease on the kitchen counter – I assume it's today's dinner, purchased at one of the many takeaways located between her office and where she parked her car. But I shouldn't complain. She has a full-time job, works regular overtime, and has three children under the age of ten – and yet she still comes here every day to look after me. And I have to ask myself: would I have done the same? For her? For Pappa?

"How's it going?" she says.

"Y'know," I say.

I look around me. Boxes, random stuff.

"I brought food," Annika says.

"I'm not hungry," I say reflexively, without thinking.

"No," she says. "But try to eat something anyway."

She's brought Indian – I don't know what made her think that chicken tikka and garlic naan would be a good thing to serve to someone with no appetite, but nevertheless I manage to get some of it down. It's not especially tasty, but my body quivers, pouncing on the tiny dose of nutrition I'm finally giving it, and something loosens – I understand, I have to eat. I take another bite.

"I went to see Pappa today," I say to Annika between bites.

"Oh?" she says.

We sit in silence, chewing our food.

"What did he say?"

"The usual. What he's been reading, what I should read. The house is full of students who wait on him hand and foot."

"I mean about what happened to Sigurd?"

"Oh. That."

I tear off a piece of naan bread, glance out of the window. It's foggy outside. The city lies there, just beyond the threshold, I know that, but I can see nothing of it now. Only fog and the closest trees and nothing else.

"I don't know," I say. "I didn't tell him."

She looks at me, eyes narrowing, but she doesn't ask why. Instead, she says:

"I understand."

I imagine myself in therapy, imagine myself in a session with a friendly, older therapist, a man around my father's age, but different – someone who listens and understands, who says: "What does it mean, do you think, that you visited your father and didn't tell him that your husband has been found murdered? And what does it mean that your sister understands this choice without further explanation?"

"I could call him and tell him for you," Annika says. "If you want me to?"

Do I want her to? I don't know, don't know anything, but why not? So I nod. But the comfort of letting go is tinged with a slight bitterness I know only too well – here comes Annika to clean up my mess once again.

"Annika," I say, "do you remember how I used to wet the bed when I was little? While Mamma was ill?"

"Yes?" she says.

I ask myself whether she's being vigilant. Is this painful for her? We chew our food.

"Do you think Pappa saw other people while Mamma was ill?" I ask.

"Huh?" Annika says, and then, when I don't answer:

"Well, you've heard what he says about adultery. The stocks have been mentioned."

"But towards the end," I say, "when she was more his patient than his wife."

Annika thinks about this. The house is so quiet – the sound of our cutlery tapping on our plates seems to ring between the walls.

We rarely talk about our childhood, Annika and I, although she would sometimes try to bring it up when I was a teenager. She invited me to have dinner with her in the flatshare where she lived; covered the table with a cloth and set it with candles, served me cheap red wine although I wasn't yet eighteen, and asked: "How is it, really, living at home with Pappa?" and "What do you remember from just after Mamma died?" It made me nervous. There we sat, surrounded by pleasantries and niceties, and this was what she wanted me to talk about? Her questions were direct; loaded. There was so much expectation in the meal she had prepared, the candles she had lit: I was supposed to confide in her. I had no idea what to say – everything would have been wrong. I more or less ended up telling her what I thought she wanted to hear. Tried to steer the conversation towards safer topics.

Later, I read about the fundamental significance of the early bond between parent and child, and reflected on how my childhood had shaped me: the loss of one parent, the twisted relationship with the other. I realised I'd like to know what Annika remembered, so I could compare her memories to my own. She was older, had understood more about the events as they were happening. But I never asked her – perhaps I didn't quite know how. And anyway, I saw her so rarely – I lived in Bergen, and she was in Oslo. I thought it was better to leave it; something to be discussed in the future.

Now Annika rubs her eyes. I wonder whether she's been in

court today. It seems so – she's smartly dressed and made-up, her hair neat, in place.

"Who knows?" Annika says heavily. "It seems as if his, what does he call it, his 'moral codex', shapes itself around whatever suits him at the time."

There's no clattering of cutlery against plates now. In the distance I can hear the sound of the train rattling its way up towards Holstein station.

"You think so?" I say to my food. "I don't."

We eat in silence. Now isn't the time to ask her these questions either, not when it's only days since Sigurd disappeared. But perhaps another day, soon. I almost finish the whole portion, and it does me good. Annika tells me that her middle son has been to the dentist today, that he bit the nurse's finger. We try to relax.

I don't remember much from when Mamma was ill. I remember her dying; remember her funeral and the period that followed. A few other things – spoons instead of forks, Mamma's idiotic laughter, sick thoughts and healthy thoughts – but can recall little of how I felt. Was I sad? Was I afraid? Did it feel unsafe to me, that Mamma was no longer an adult I could depend on?

But I do remember that I started to wet the bed at night. The feeling of waking and being wet, the sticky bed, and the feeling of shame – that I remember so clearly, the deep sense of regret, "how embarrassing, now that I'm such a big girl". I remember waking Annika. Even then I must have understood that Mamma couldn't be depended on, and I could never have woken Pappa with something like that – I wanted to be a good girl, someone worthy, for my father. So I went to Annika. Shook my sister until she woke, and then confessed with a lowered gaze. Reluctantly, she helped me. After a couple of times, she said I should be able to manage by myself. She was eleven or twelve, thought it was disgusting. I, too, thought it was disgusting. It made *me* disgusting. I didn't want to have to tell anyone about it.

During my studies I learned that bed-wetting, nocturnal enuresis, can be due to emotional stress. As I sat there in the lecture hall while a psychologist from the psychiatric service for children and young people whizzed through all the childhood disorders in the diagnostic manual, I felt a childish relief wash over me: maybe it was just stress. Perhaps there was nothing wrong with the child I had been. Maybe I was distraught because my mother was ill.

Later, I also realised that it gave me a fixed point of reference regarding how I had felt. I remember so little pain, so little fear, very little emotion at all. I know only what happened; remember it in adult phrases, so must simply have accepted the things that others interpreted and explained to me. Know so little about how this huge event, this terrible childhood grief, actually felt.

One night I woke up and felt warm and wet beneath my back-side and down my thighs, and I thought in confusion, *oh no*. I went out to the linen cupboard in the hall, found the bedding as Annika had taught me, and tried to put it on the bed. The sheet – one of the stretchy ones – didn't quite fit the mattress. When I sat on the bed and fought with the corners, it too became damp as the fluid from the wet mattress soaked up into it. I started to cry.

Why I ended up on the landing, I don't know. I must have gone there after I couldn't manage to make the bed. I didn't dare wake Annika, but I remember that I pushed open the door of my parents' room a crack. That I saw Mamma sleeping; felt an overwhelming despair at the fact that it would do no good to wake her. That my father's bed was empty – and that this was strange, because I'd heard them go to bed together, earlier that evening. Had heard them talking. But now my father was gone. I felt so alone.

I don't remember how I ended up sitting there, only that I sat there. I cried, as quietly as I could so as not to wake anyone, and then heard the sound of a key in the front door. I could see the hallway from where I was sitting. It was Pappa. He didn't see me, just took off his shoes. Stuck his hand into his jacket pocket to take something from it. He was fumbling around with something, but I couldn't see what he had in his hands. As he hung up his jacket he saw me and said:

"Sara? Is that you sitting there?"

I nodded. Didn't ask him why he had gone out, where he had been. I said nothing. He lifted me up; I rested my head against his broad shoulder. He smelled of cold air and his familiar after-shave. I never wanted him to leave, ever again.

He followed me back into the bedroom, laid me down atop the new sheet. I didn't dare tell him that everything was wet; didn't dare tell him that I'd peed myself. I lay down on the wet bed and tried to sleep.

Three weeks after Sigurd and I got married I was in my office at the clinic disinfecting my hands. I'd had a family in for therapy, and they had just left, so I had squeezed some antibacterial hand gel into my palm from the dispenser I kept by my desk. I was careful about it – had learned from working with my young psychotic patients always to shake hands, and then to wash them. I wasn't yet used to wearing my wedding ring, so put the gel on first. It created a sticky layer around the ring's edge. I took the ring off, put it on the desk and rubbed my fingers together. Then I wiped the ring on a paper towel, and it was only then, as I was putting it back on again, that what I had seen on the night I wet myself and sat on the landing of the house in Smestad and saw Pappa fiddling with something became clear to me. More than twenty years later came an experience that gave the memory meaning: my father had stood there, putting on his wedding ring.

As we are clearing up after dinner, the doorbell rings. Annika and I look at each other, and I must look afraid, because Annika tells me she'll get it.

As Annika is walking down the stairs, Gundersen comes walking up them. This is the way things are now – my house is no longer mine, the police come and go as they wish, and Gundersen doesn't have the time to wait for me to pull myself together and open the door.

They come up the stairs together, Gundersen first, taking two steps at a time. He's in his energetic mode, I see. Annika follows him, vigilant again, brows drawn together and eyes glued to him, as if she's trying to communicate that he ought to watch himself – she has her eye on him.

Gundersen greets me and sits down beside me at the kitchen island, without really saying anything.

"How's it going?"

"Yes, well," he says.

He appears to think for a while, staring into space, in contrast to his energetic entrance.

"How was the rest of that weekend, Sara?" he says. "You went to the gym, you went home, you drank some wine and deleted the message, and then you went to bed. Correct?"

"Yes."

"And then what happened?"

I think for a moment.

"I woke up the day after," I say. "Julie was here – she's Thomas' girlfriend, you know, Thomas – Sigurd's friend. She wanted to see whether I was O.K. I don't know. We . . . Yeah. She didn't stay long."

It won't look good, I think, if I have to tell Gundersen in detail about my encounter with Julie. Of course it has nothing to do with the case – semi-blonde hair or not, I can't see Julie shooting Sigurd in the back. But to say that I quarrelled with the girlfriend of Sigurd's best friend? And after I deleted the message?

But Gundersen doesn't seem interested.

"Yes, O.K.," he says. "And then?"

"I went into town. I took the T-banen to Majorstuen, sauntered around for a bit, went to Annika's in Nordstrand. There I . . . I told her what had happened, and she drove me down to the police station to report Sigurd missing. I had spoken to a woman from the police that morning – had called to report him missing – but she'd told me I should wait until at least twenty-four hours had passed."

"And then?"

"Then we went back to Nordstrand. I slept at Annika's place."

"That's correct," Annika says.

She's standing wide-legged with crossed arms, like a bouncer wearing a suit and leather boots.

"When did you get back here?"

"Sunday afternoon. I stayed with Annika for a while, and then I came home."

"O.K."

Gundersen is still thinking, drumming his fingers against the kitchen worktop, and I sit there, look over at Annika, then turn back to face him.

"Why do you ask?" I say.

"Routine question," he says. "And how about the telephone call, I mean, you told me that you called Sigurd?"

"Yes. I called him again and again, right up until his mobile ran out of battery."

"O.K., and when was that?"

"I called him on Saturday morning. While Julie was here. It went straight to the automatic message – you know, the person you have called is unavailable, something like that."

Gundersen nods.

"You see, Sara," he says, "we've found Sigurd's mobile."

"Oh?"

Annika and I stare at him.

"Yes," Gundersen says, calmly. "It was out in the garden."

"In the garden? Here?"

"Yes. Fredly found it this afternoon."

Silence descends for a moment. I stare out into the fog, at the gathering twilight, and think of the last time I called Sigurd, from up in the bedroom, as Julie wandered around in the living room downstairs. Of the footsteps in the loft that night, the open front door.

On Thursday evening Sigurd told me that he was going to try to get to Thomas' by six-thirty the next morning, so they'd arrive early and get a full day on the slopes. I've returned to this little exchange so many times that the line between what he said and what I now *think* he said is starting to blur. Can I really know for certain that my memory of this conversation reflects its actual course, just as I've always been able to rely on my recollection of events? Is it not possible, for example, that he may have been talking about six-thirty in the evening instead? That I thought

188

he was talking about six-thirty in the morning, and so have made this into the memory? Can I know that Sigurd undoubtedly, indisputably, said that he was going to pick up Thomas? Can I now be sure that I didn't misunderstand? Or that I'm not muddling the details based on all I've learned since our conversation? By recalling the memory so often have I changed it from one occasion to the next, imperceptibly, but nevertheless enough to make it different over time? Have I ground it down, honed it into shape, without even realising that I was doing so?

Without looking at Gundersen, I say:

"How's it going with the forensic report – when will that be available?"

"Yes, that was the other thing," Gundersen says. "It's back. He was killed on Friday. The cause of death is a gunshot wound. The man who was found is indeed Sigurd, no doubt about it."

I think about that Friday, of his telephone ringing and ringing. Of the message: "Hi, love. We're at the cabin." The document tube, the curtains, the pans.

"Can I see him?" I say.

"The body?" Gundersen says.

"Sigurd," I say. "Can I see him?"

"It's been several days," Gundersen says. "I'm not sure it would be advisable."

"But can I?"

Gundersen shrugs.

"Of course I can't deny you," he says. "But as I said, he's been dead for a while. The decomposition process is rapid."

"I want to see him," I say. "As soon as possible."

"Oh, Sara," Annika says, but she doesn't protest further.

"In that case," Gundersen says, "I'd recommend that we make arrangements for this evening."

*

The basement of the Institute of Public Health is tiled. I follow a woman in green scrubs with a surgical mask pushed up onto her head in the way people push up their sunglasses. Annika has driven me here, but is waiting upstairs. She looked at me, her face pale and twisted, and said, "I don't think I can come down there with you." It's O.K. I'm walking alone, following the woman in the green uniform.

I'm not afraid. I'm not sure what I am – eager, perhaps. I feel awake. I've made a decision. I remember in detail the sight of Old Torp, know what happens to a body when it's been left in a loft for three weeks. I also know that I need to know.

Sigurd's telephone was found lying in the garden. His document tube has turned up. Someone is walking around in my house. Yesterday, as I lay on the floor of my office, gripping the kitchen knife so hard that my knuckles became sore and bloodless, I thought, why don't I call out to him? Sigurd?

But why would I call out to him? He's dead. I'm not superstitious: when you're dead, you're dead. I don't believe it was an apparition's footsteps creaking down the stairs, an apparition that ran away leaving the door wide open. But in a tiny, uncertain place at the very back of my mind, I thought, what if it *is* Sigurd? And today they found his mobile.

So they found it at Nordberg. It doesn't mean that Sigurd has been here. It's the easiest thing in the world, to take a dead man's phone and throw it into the bushes outside his house. Or if you're running away in the middle of the night, you might even drop it.

But it's so hard for me to believe that Sigurd is gone. The answerphone message. The things I've learned about him since then, his lies. The woman who waited for him outside his office. Atkinson. Sigurd is dead, and I've only just learned that there's so much I didn't know about him. The staff at the Institute of

Public Health – even they can make mistakes, can't they? But I won't be mistaken. If I see with my own eyes that it's Sigurd, then it's true. So that's why I'm here. To be sure.

The woman opens a door into a room. Contrary to what I had imagined, it's quite pleasant here. It's well lit. No dark, damp cellar, no deep cabinets full of bodies, no frightening, perverted doctors. The woman accompanying me is Annika's age, she's wearing gold earrings and is wide-hipped in the way that many women are after giving birth. The room contains a sink, some kitchen cabinets and a counter, in addition to a metal table on which something is lying, covered by a kind of sheet. Had it not been for this table, I think, we could be anywhere. Throw in a dining table and some chairs and it could be the canteen of an outpatient clinic.

But the metal table is here.

The woman hands me a surgical mask.

"It can smell a bit," she says.

I put on the mask; the woman pulls hers down from her hair.

"Are you ready?"

"Yes," I say, and only now do I realise that I'm nervous.

This is the moment. Either it's him, or it isn't. The woman turns down the sheet.

It's indescribable. If anyone were ever to ask me about this moment, there's little I'd want to say about it. He's lying there with his eyes closed. He's dead, has been for several days, and there's no doubt, no doubt at all, that this is Sigurd. Looking at him this way, I remember the details I haven't recalled, or wanted to think about, over the past few days. His brown eyelashes, light at the tips. The sprinkling of freckles across the bridge of his nose. How the dishevelled hair he never had properly cut curls at his fringe.

There is no life in him. It doesn't look as if he's sleeping, as

I've heard people say. It looks as if he's dead. The blood has vanished from his face. As I look at him, a sob bursts out of me, surprising both me and the woman in green – it isn't followed by tears, it simply hangs there, all alone. I already know that I'll remember this for the rest of my life, how I stood here and saw Sigurd dead. I feel no sense of relief, no kind of closure or catharsis. Only the awareness of the situation's severity. It will never be possible to forget what I have seen.

Life potentially begins on the day a woman leans towards a man and whispers in his ear, shall we try? We're sitting on the sofa. It's a day like any other. We have just eaten fishcakes, are watching T.V. An advert featuring a dolphin comes on.

"I hate dolphins," Sigurd says.

"Nobody hates dolphins," I say.

"I do," Sigurd says.

"Why?"

"They think they're so cute," he says, "swimming around as if everybody loves them. Look at me! Look at how cute I am!"

I laugh. I kiss him.

"I mean it," Sigurd says. "You think I'm joking, but I mean it."

I put my arm around his neck. Lean towards him.

"Sigurd," I whisper into his ear, "shall we try?"

Our first attempt takes place that night. As Sigurd tightens his embrace around me I think – this is it, now you'll be made, my little one.

The following month we have sex every night of the week in which there's the possibility. Now, now, now. I work out when I can take the test, but the night before I discover a trace of blood. I stare at the stain, not understanding – surely it can't be? We've done it so many times. Tried so hard.

The month after that I manage to take the test before I see blood. The line in the test window is alone, blue and strict, like a prudish schoolmistress.

Many couples try for a long time – the average is six months, I read online. There's no need to panic until you've been trying for a year. I don't tell anyone, only imagine what I'll say when it's a fact, when I've seen two lines crossing the window of the test. Imagine how I'll tell Annika, as if in passing, oh by the way – cue the radiant smile – I have something to tell you. Wonder what I'll say to Ronja.

But not this. Not this nothing, this transitional stage. We're trying – that's not news. It's nothing, an empty promise – and hardly even that.

Three months pass. The summer holiday arrives. Margrethe travels to Italy with her friends and says to us, make sure you take care of Grandpa, go up there and see him once a week or so. We go up there on a hot, late-summer day and find him in the loft.

By the time we move to Nordberg, we've been trying for six months – the average, as it happens. I read online that many couples try for longer. Involuntary childlessness isn't a disease, roars an opinion piece in the newspaper, and I fold it and throw it out, can't read it, don't want to know how this needn't be the end, how rich life without children can be, how I should be thankful for what I have. Sigurd is working like crazy on my office, and it's in that week that I go out there to him. He's standing there, in his overalls and safety glasses, holding his grinding machine. It takes a little while before he sees me, and I stand silently in the doorway, watching him, head bent as he sands the wood below the sloping roof, everything in him focused on the new floors. And I think, shall I do it now? Seduce him, in a way, tempt him – coax him up into the bedroom, is that what I'm going to do? Me in my jogging bottoms; he in his work clothes? He doesn't know I'm here, doesn't know that I'm watching him and thinking, isn't it a miracle that it happens at all? That in between everything else, people find the time to make love to each other?

194

Then he looks at me. He turns off the machine, lifts up his glasses and takes off his ear protection.

"Yes?"

He has dust from the floor in his fringe. His lips are split and chapped from sitting out here. He thinks I've come to give him a message, he's waiting – yes, what is it? I stand there in my sweat-pants and seducing him suddenly feels like an impossible task.

"Nothing," I say. "I just wanted to say I'm going to bed."

"O.K. Goodnight."

Sigurd is doing all this for me – these floors, this office. I go upstairs, shower, get into bed. Lie awake for an hour, for two. It's gone mid-night. Still no Sigurd.

My sleep is fitful. I keep waking with a start and listening – is someone here? I've dragged a chair in front of the door; in my hands I hold the kitchen knife. I hear a creak, a car driving down the road outside; at one point I hear a child crying. I fall asleep again, wake a little later. Drift in and out of sleep.

Eight months have passed and still nothing. Our attempts during the past couple of months have been half-hearted. Sigurd is finished with the office, but there's still so much more to do. The kitchen, bath-room, bedrooms. He's busy at work, too. He gets home at around six o'clock, eats dinner in front of the T.V., and then starts hammering away in the kitchen. I've started my practice, but it's slow-going. During the day I surf the Internet, seeking fertility advice. Eat fatty fish and citrus fruits. Avoid alcohol and coffee. Put a pillow under your bum after sex; try to do it in the morning.

Our lives revolve around the house. I work and live here, almost never leave it. Sigurd disappears off to work every day, comes home again in the afternoon or evening, and then works late into the night. His face is tired; his skin grey.

It's the right time again, that golden week. Sigurd is scraping wallpaper off the walls of his study in the basement. I put on a night-gown – appropriately short, passably sexy – and shake my hair loose before I go down there. Strips of wallpaper are strewn across the floor, everything he's been able to tear off with his hands. Now he's scraping – the sound makes the hairs on my arms bristle, like the sound of cutlery against ceramic crockery.

"Sigurd?"

He turns. Glue in his hair, safety glasses on his nose.

"Do you want to come upstairs with me?"

"I thought I'd keep going with this for a bit."

"But it's the right week," I say in a small voice. "We have to do it now."

"Right."

He pushes the glasses up onto his head; rubs his eyes. He stretches, then comes over to me. His steps are heavy. He stops, leans an arm against the door frame. Stands so close to me that I can see the tracks the glasses have left in the skin of his face, the red furrows, just like those left by the pillows on the mornings we woke together in Bergen.

"I've been giving that some thought," he says. "I was just wondering, how would you feel about putting it on hold for a while? The baby thing?"

All the air seems suddenly sucked out of the room. I stand there trembling in my nightgown.

"Put it on hold?"

He swallows. He looks at me with his grey-blue eyes, the mole beneath the left.

"We're exhausted right now, Sara. We've both just started working for ourselves. And then there's everything that needs doing on the house."

"But this room," I say, feeling my voice thicken, the tears coming. Here I stand, in my short nightgown, my hair loose.

"Just for a little while," he says. "Just until we're settled at work, and until the house is finished. Or at least more finished. Hmm?"

He strokes his hand across my cheek. I swallow down my tears, am at least not going to stand here snivelling in my nightie.

"I'm dead tired," Sigurd says. "I'm running on empty. I just don't have the energy right now."

"O.K.," I say. "I understand. We can wait a while. But not too long."

"Of course not," Sigurd says. "Just until we have our heads above water."

I sit on the edge of the bed, up on the second floor, and try to figure out whether I'm sad. It's not as if I don't feel a certain sense of relief, too. I'll at least be spared all the dutiful fucking, the monthly defeats, the angry blue line. We can take it easy for a while. Make love when we want to. Get the house finished. And who knows – maybe it'll happen without us even trying. That's what all the blogs say. You try for years, and then suddenly, when you least expect it. I lean back, surprised. That would be good, too. To live in a newly renovated house as my belly grows bigger. Just wait a while, little one. You'll be able to come soon, and when you do, everything will be ready for you.

Wednesday, March 11: Empty surfaces

Someone has been in the house again. I realise it the moment I come down the stairs – something is different. As I turn my gaze on the kitchen, I see what it is: it's the fridge. Sigurd and I have pictures hanging there – some of us, some of Annika's boys, a few postcards and a couple of menus for restaurants that deliver. Now they're all gone. The fridge door is bare, clean and white, uninhabited. In addition, as if to emphasise that someone has been here, all the fridge magnets have been moved to the fridge's top right corner. I stare at the fridge door for a second or two, the time it takes me to comprehend all this, and then I scream.

I've reminded myself of it again and again – Sigurd has been killed – but I only really accept it now that I have seen him with my own eyes. Someone has moved the photographs on our fridge door during the night, and I know for certain that it wasn't him. This means that it's a stranger, but who could it be? Who else other than the person who shot Sigurd? A murderer has been in my house. Might still be here. So I scream, as loudly as I can. Then I turn, rush down the stairs, unlock the front door and run out.

As I come out a police car pulls into the driveway. Fredly is at the wheel, and from the passenger door steps the police-woman who was here on Sunday to inform me of Sigurd's death – the woman I thought looked like a typical bitch from the west side of the city. They're carrying paper cups of coffee and are about to discuss something, I think, when they see me. They look shocked, both of them, which isn't so strange considering that I come running towards them in my dressing gown, barefoot on the wet lawn still strewn with clumps of snow. But I see them and think only – salvation. I'm probably still screaming.

It's Fredly who comes to my rescue. She must see what's about to happen as I come closer, or at least her instincts are sharp, because she drops the coffee cup – it hits the grass, milky coffee running out. I throw myself against her, and she holds me.

"What's happened?" she says.

I am unable to speak. I sob, gasping for breath, almost crying but without tears, shaking with cold and fright and unable to put together a single sentence. I don't look at the west-side bitch. I feel only Fredly's shoulder against my cheek as I lean against her, shaking, letting her hold me until I calm down and say:

"Someone has been in my house."

"O.K.," Fredly says, and she seems alert, on the lookout.

"They might still be inside," I sob.

"We'll check it out," she says, and the west-side bitch gets into the car again, perhaps to call for backup. "Just tell me what happened."

"I came downstairs this morning and saw that someone had been here," I say. "They took all the pictures off the fridge door and moved all the magnets."

"The fridge door?"

"Yes. We put various bits and bobs up there, photographs, postcards, menus and stuff, but now it's all gone."

"Right. Is there anything else – I mean, has anything been stolen?"

"I don't know. I only saw that everything on the fridge was gone, and then I ran."

"Are you sure that the pictures were there when you went to bed?" asks a voice from behind us, and I see that the posh west-side cow has returned from the car.

"Yes," I say. "I mean, I would have noticed if they hadn't been there."

"Right."

"Was there any sign of forced entry?" Fredly says.

"I don't know," I say, starting to feel uneasy – why are they asking all these questions, are they not going to *do* something?

"Was the front door open? Had the lock been removed, or anything like that?"

I think back.

"No," I say. "It was locked."

They exchange glances, a kind of understanding passing between them. I withdraw, taking a step back, so that Fredly's arm, still on my shoulder, releases me.

"Aren't you going to investigate?"

There's something heavy weighing on them now – no, something resigned.

"Of course," Fredly says, amiably. "Of course we'll investigate."

Something about her voice is patronising, as if I'm a child, as if they're my babysitters and I'm asking them to search the cellar for ghosts.

They go inside. I lean against the police car and wait. It doesn't look as if any backup is coming. I wait for a while, standing there in the freezing cold, realising that I should have stopped and put on a pair of trainers while I was running for my life. I put one foot on top of the other, planning to swap them, to divide up the exposure to the cold. A little more time passes. I see the policewoman who isn't Fredly open the veranda door and close it again. I walk across the lawn and into the front hallway.

I meet Fredly in the living room. Her colleague is up on the second floor, checking all the windows. She hands me a pile of photographs and paper.

"Is this them?" she asks.

I look at them.

"Yes."

Is there anything missing? I try to remember – which photographs did we have pinned up? The postcard Margrethe sent from Budapest – did we throw it out a couple of weeks ago, or was it still hanging there?

"There are no signs of a break-in," Fredly says.

I nod. We look over at the kitchen, at the incriminating fridge magnets. I feel the blood start to rush into my face, red and hot. There was I in my dressing gown, running screaming and barefoot through slush and mud, all because of seven fridge magnets.

But someone *was* here, I know it. It would be no different if someone had taken Sigurd's laptop or gone through all our cupboards, but there's something ridiculous about the fact that they've taken photographs from the fridge door. It seems so meaningless. There was nothing of importance on the fridge door, that's obvious enough. It seems meaningless to have killed Sigurd, too. There must be a pattern.

"Check that everything's here," Fredly says. "I mean, check your documents, valuables, that kind of thing."

She's taking it seriously, I'll give her that, but she doesn't sound very enthusiastic. Fridge magnets. When they're investigating a murder. I poke through a couple of drawers; the deeds to the house, tax returns. In the top of one of them is Sigurd's appointment book, where I put it yesterday. Atkinson. Something squeezes in my chest. I take the book, tuck it inside my dressing gown. My hands are still shaking.

Breathe, and start again. I stand in the shower and let the hot water warm my body. My frozen feet finally start to thaw out and prickle with pins and needles. Stay calm. Relax. See the world as it is. Fear is natural, I'm off balance, have experienced two break-ins just days after my husband was killed. But fear cannot be trusted. It tricks the senses, turns up the heat on reason. Breathe.

Someone was in my house again last night. It seems undeniable. I know now that it wasn't Sigurd. I also know that the door was locked when I ran outside. I remember running into it, cursing the delay caused by my having to unlock the door, because I feared I had an insane murderer at my heels. Well. The house was empty, but that doesn't mean that whoever was here hadn't either broken in, or – and this is the more disquieting alternative – had a key.

My keys are in my handbag. Sigurd's keys are with the police. Margrethe has her set of keys. That's all.

But of course it's possible to make copies. I think about this. I once lost the keys to our previous apartment, and had to have new ones made. The key to the main front door was a security key that could not be copied, but the key that opened the door to our apartment had no such security. I could go to the key cutter at the Storo shopping centre and in less than half an hour make as many copies as I wanted. So Sigurd might have made copies without my knowing about it. He could have doled out spare keys left, right and centre. Why he would do such a thing I have no idea, but it seems he kept more secrets from me than I thought. What Mammod told me – about the woman waiting for him, the one with medium-length blondish hair. I have a mental picture of her, leaning against the lamp post outside the FleMaSi offices, eyes searching for him. Is she a person Sigurd might have given a set of keys to?

And then the fridge magnets. My mind is blank. All the photographs I can remember are there, but there are still some things I'm unsure about: the postcard from Margrethe, a list of items we were going to buy from Maxbo to do up the bathroom. Did we throw away the postcard? Did Sigurd take down the shopping list, or might I have done so myself? But why would anyone be interested in what Margrethe wrote to us from Budapest? Why would anyone care about what supplies we needed to buy? My head is spinning again, and I press my hands against Old Torp's dirty tiles. Codes in shopping lists; mystical postcards that might not be from Margrethe, after all. It's too far-fetched.

It's Wednesday. The day lies open before me – all my patients have been cancelled. I don't know what to do, but I am certain that I don't want to stay here, with the police rummaging around and the fridge magnets screaming at me. I could go into the city. Take a walk – around St Hanshaugen, for example. Sigurd's appointment book is in here with me, sitting beside the sink, beneath my dressing gown, and I think of the last pages, the ones containing the addresses. Atkinson. Or is that a stupid idea? Will I get myself mixed up in something if I go over there? I turn off the water. It's best to take it easy. Breathe. Start again.

When I go downstairs there is no-one in the kitchen. The police car is gone. I stand at the window and see Fredly's paper cup still on the ground where she dropped it, and I just know the police are done with the whole fridge magnet story. I see myself as they must see me: a woman in the process of losing her mind. My credibility has gone up in smoke. On Monday we talked about professional principles, the right of patients to expect that their medical records will not be shared. I saw Sasha. There's much that I have lost in just a few days.

But I would like to ensure my personal safety. I take out my tablet and search for security systems, for burglar alarms. One of the first companies to come up is called Arild's Security.

The logo is a house with a lock around it, and there's something reassuring about the image. A proper lock – that's what I need, I think.

I tap the number into the telephone, but stand there without calling. Look at the number and think, am I sure? Were the fridge magnets *really* in their usual places yesterday evening? Can I be absolutely sure? How about when I stood in the kitchen tidying up yesterday night, after Annika and I had supper? I remember how I put the dishes in the dishwasher, visualise the fridge door. I only swept it with my gaze, but yes, everything was there as usual – the restaurant menus, the photographs, a memo about recycling. Are the postcard and shopping list there? I can't focus in on these details – can't force my memory to recall whether they're there or not. But everything else is there. Or is it? Am I misremembering? Am I imagining another day? Is Annika even there in this specific memory,? I try to force my gaze out into the room, looking for her in my mind, but it's impossible to find her there. I see only the fridge door and the open dishwasher.

I remember little from after I came home from the Institute of Public Health. I must have walked up to the first floor. Probably drank a glass of water in the kitchen. Probably tidied away whatever had been left out. But these memories are unclear, they slide away whenever I try to fix my gaze on them. Me – who always remembers everything. Might I have moved the fridge magnets myself? Been so distraught that I did so without realising? Been in such a daze that I now can't recall? Am I still able to trust what I see, what I remember?

The telephone number shines from the screen of my mobile. Arild's Security. I change my mind. Save the number on my phone. I can always call later.

*

A few hours later I'm crossing the cemetery on foot. I find it oddly quiet here. No groups of schoolchildren wearing reflective vests and backpacks; no teachers counting them over and over again to be sure they haven't lost anyone, as there would have been up at St Hanshaugen. No hipster couples drinking coffee from reusable cups, jabbering away about *this* concert and *that* new bar. No post-natal groups, the rows of new mothers with their prams before them like shields. The cemetery is almost empty. An older lady with a walking stick. A girl with a dog on a lead. The headstones. Big, ancient trees.

The Atkinsons' apartment is a couple of streets up, in an old, classical apartment building. It looks well maintained. Not particularly fashionable, as the buildings further up are – just normal. The paint is peeling only a little here and there. The gate is open. I walk in, manage a peek into the rear courtyard, catch sight of a bicycle with a child seat on the back and a pink doll's pram. I go into the stairwell, which is spacious, so different from the way Sigurd and his architect friends design stairwells – today every square metre counts. The Atkinsons live on the ground floor. The door says only this – ATKINSON – on an old brass sign attached to the door with rusty screws. I summon up my courage, try to plan what I'll say. All Sigurd has told me about them is that the husband is English and works in the shipping industry, and that she's a total bitch. But I no longer trust the things Sigurd has said. The Atkinsons? They could be anyone.

I ring the doorbell. It screams out, loud and aggressive within. I hear no movement, but I wait. The paint on the door frame is peeling in places, the doormat on which I'm standing hasn't been shaken for a long while. I don't know whether or not this means anything.

I push the button again, hear the same piercing sound of the doorbell and then footsteps inside. My stomach churns. Am I about to tread on Gundersen's toes? But it's too late to turn back now, and nor do I want to. There's a click as the lock turns. The door opens a crack, held back by a thick security chain, and a voice, thin and full of air, says:

"Yes?"

I peer into the crack, see only the contours – a white cloud of hair, a light-blue eye.

"Yes," I say, clearing my throat. "My name is Sara. I'm here on behalf of FleMaSi Architects."

Silence.

"Yes?" the voice says again.

It smells sweetish in there, heavy and close, an old-fashioned smell, dirty and fragrant at the same time.

"I was just wondering about something."

I clear my throat again.

"I'm Sigurd's assistant. Sigurd Torp."

The door opens a few more centimetres and now I see her. She's small and old, at least eighty. Her skin isn't actually wrinkled, not on her face, but her white hair is sparse, almost transparent, and her throat is nothing but sinew and folds of skin. She's wearing a dress with a pattern of blue flowers, and has the kind of blue eyes that only old people have, astoundingly pale blue and a little damp, as if the sun has bleached them, worn them out over the decades. On top of all the other odours she smells of smoke. She has a small, thin mouth, and a red tongue that wets her lips. Around her neck is a heavy gold chain. Now she smiles at me; she stares and smiles.

"So!" she says. "You're Sigurd Torp's assistant." Her speech is a drawl – had I met her at the clinic, I would have guessed that she uses some kind of strong sedative. I'm a touch disappointed that I'm not standing opposite the mysterious woman with dirty blonde hair.

"Yes," I say. "There's something he was wondering about. Or rather, we were – at the office. Is it . . . I mean . . . Can I come in?"

She nods slowly, closes the door, rattles the chain and then opens the door wide. Now the smell of the apartment streams towards me – thick smoke, perfume and old lady. It seems that this is the first time in several days that fresh air has been let in. I go in regardless, taking a deep breath and diving into the hallway. She's barefoot, smoking a cigarette in a holder.

"There's something I've been wondering about," I say as she closes and locks the door behind me.

"Come through first," she says.

She walks past me and I follow her into the living room. The smoke is dense; the room dim because the blinds are closed, but the sun outside is shining so brightly that strips of light break in: one grazes the fireplace so that the ornaments on the mantelpiece are lit up; another hits the dark mahogany book-case; a third is reflected back into my eyes from a bell jar standing on a set of nesting tables beside a gigantic brocade armchair. The mistress of the house sits down on the edge of a shiny, dark-wood chair. She's put up her white hair in a plastic clip. Now she taps the ash from her cigarette into a huge ebony ashtray. I look around, mostly to avoid looking at her, letting my gaze roam across the old-fashioned suite and the paintings on the wall; a blotchy painting of two small children in sailor suits, a painting of a strict-looking man in uniform in a silver frame.

"Would you like some tea?" the woman asks.

"Yes, please," I say.

She remains in her seat, taps the ash from her cigarette again, takes another drag. I look at her bare feet – they're swollen, almost blue. She carefully extinguishes her cigarette, takes the butt from the holder and puts it in the ashtray. For a moment she holds the cigarette holder up in the air; there are intricate patterns along its length. She studies them.

"Do you like it?" she asks me.

"Yes," I say, and swallow.

The air in here is dry. I wish I had a bottle of water with me.

"I bought it in Paris," she says.

She puts the cigarette holder in a box on the table, closing the lid with some effort.

"It's just a piece of cheap crap," she says then, and pushes the box across the table.

I nod. She gets up from the chair.

"Just take a seat," she says. "I'll put the water on to boil."

She disappears out of the room behind a curtain. I look over at the chair in which she was sitting, at the cushion made of an expensive fabric, now worn thin. At the same moment something touches my leg, making me jump – a fat, fluffy cat rubs itself against my calf. It doesn't even look up when I jump. A low, grumbling sound comes from its throat, and I don't understand it, how cats make that sound – it seems foreign, doesn't sound like something that should come from an animal. The cat rubs itself. I don't move. When it has finished with me it swaggers off, tail in the air. Halfway across the floor it turns and looks at me, its eyes narrow and green. I notice something moving in the bookcase – a cat drawing itself along a row of books with red spines, one shelf above the ribbon of light. Out in the kitchen some pots clatter against one another. I turn my head, eyes searching the sofa, where there's yet another cat, this one white and just as fat and long-haired as the one that stroked my leg. I can't believe Sigurd never told me about this: the smell of smoke, and all the cats.

The mistress of the house glides back into the room. She now has a tiara in her hair, the cheap kind that little girls want for

Christmas, covered in plastic gemstones and glitter. I make no comment on it; I don't know what to say.

"I've put the water on," she says.

"Yes," I say. "Are you Mrs Atkinson?"

"Yes," she says, and smiles. She's missing several teeth. "That's me – nice to meet you."

She curtsies, her feet pointing towards each other, and for a moment she looks like a child.

"Sara," I say.

"Yes," she says. "You already said."

"Is it," I ask clumsily, "I mean, is it here that Sigurd's been designing something? In this room?"

She shakes her head. A fourth cat brushes past her legs and vanishes out into the kitchen.

"I'm not completely sure," I say, dragging it out as my mind spins in an attempt to find the right angle, "I'm not completely sure, but wasn't it a cellar extension he was supposed to be working on?"

I'm not used to obtaining information without being honest. Psychologists can ask about almost any private matter; for architects' assistants it's presumably a little different. Mrs Atkinson studies me, her small marble-like eyes rolling in her head.

"My husband is at sea," she says. "Did you know that?"

"Oh," I say awkwardly. "No, I didn't."

"He's the love of my life," she says.

She points to a photograph on a side table beside the sofa. A newly married couple, the man in a suit, the woman in a white dress that reaches her ankles. They're standing outside a small church. The photograph is too far away for me to make out their features; I can't tell whether they're young, whether they're attractive, or even whether the woman is the same as the one standing before me.

"What's he doing at sea?"

"Sailing," she says, closing her eyes. "Sailing and sailing."

I nod; she remains unmoving for a moment. Then she opens her eyes again, takes a step towards me.

"I'll show you the room. Come on."

She takes my hand – hers is small and crooked, but it's strong, squeezing mine as if her life depended on it. I want to stay where I am, don't want to go further into this apartment, want to stay close to the exit, but she pulls me after her. We go past the curtain and into a dark corridor. She leads me further and further down it, past a door, and up to yet another curtain, this one of thick velvet. With her other tiny hand she pushes it aside. Behind it is another door, which she opens.

On the other side of the door is an open, light space – an empty room with dirty windows facing the back courtyard where I can see several bicycles, and I breathe a sigh of relief, as if for a moment I believed that the dark of the apartment had no end. Outside, the sun is shining. The courtyard even has a plastic slide.

"The stairs will go down here," says my little hostess, still clutching my hand, "when my husband comes back."

There are a number of boards leaning against the walls, some large and wide, and a box labelled as being from the local council's office for home aids. There are elements of a building site here, but it doesn't look as if any construction work has started.

"Have you agreed on the final design?" I say. "With Sigurd, I mean?"

She sets her eyes on me, studies me from head to toe. We stand this way for almost a full minute – she's scrutinising me, and I let her, my hand resting in hers. Then she says:

"But don't you know?"

"What?" I say.

"Sigurd completed the drawings before Christmas," she says. "He hasn't been here in months."

I almost can't breathe as I follow her back to the living room. There is possibly more information I should collect while I'm here, but I don't have the presence of mind to keep up this act. Luckily, she has now let go of my hand, which is trembling. I just want to get out of here, as rapidly as possible, but she doesn't go into the kitchen as I had hoped when we return to the dark corridor. She walks ahead of me, out into the living room. I follow her, passively; draw a deep breath and fill my lungs with the sweet, spiced smoke that hangs above her furniture. She says nothing, but goes across to the table, opens the box containing the cigarette holder from Paris and takes out a new cigarette. I keep my eyes fixed on the portrait on the wall, and the strict-looking man in uniform. *Breathe*, I say to myself. *Breathe*. The two children in sailor suits stare out of the splotchy paint-ing, a little boy and a little girl, both blonde and blue-eyed. The same cat rubs itself against my leg again. I glance back at the man in uniform. On his lapel I catch sight of a swastika.

"You seem surprised," she says.

She's taken a seat again, is sitting there smoking. I say nothing. The tiara is about to slide down onto her forehead. She's fastened it to her hair, but her hair is thin, only strands of it remain. Her crooked fingers are full of gold rings.

"The police were surprised, too," she says. "They said Sigurd Torp told them he's been here all winter. But the drawings were finished within a month. I haven't seen him since November."

All I can manage is a nod. Another, older picture is hang-ing further away, near the bookcase – another man, another uniform. I have no wish to look any closer; don't want to know in which war he may have fought.

"Sigurd is dead," she says. "That's what the police said."

"Yes," I say.

"You're not his assistant."

"I'm his wife."

"Ah. I see."

She nods her head several times, almost rocking it.

"My husband was at sea for several months at a time. I never knew where he was. Never even knew whether he came home."

Silence falls. On the wall beside the picture of the other man in uniform is a dagger. Its blade is rusty with black flecks. Mrs Atkinson smokes with her eyes closed. Then the glass clock beside the armchair chimes, and she gets up.

"I'll get the tea," she says. "I assume you take sugar?"

As she reaches the curtain she turns to face me. She studies me again, and for a moment her sick, blue eyes are almost friendly.

"You seem like a nice girl," she says. "Sigurd Torp wasn't anything to write home about. It's better for you that he's gone."

We stand and look at one another in silence, and Mrs Atkinson has an expression of pure madness in her eyes – they're too round, too penetrating, her smile out of place. I say nothing, and she turns and leaves the room. She lets the curtain fall closed behind her and is gone. As soon as I hear her clattering around in the kitchen I tiptoe towards the exit, unlock the front door and slip out into the stairwell. I close the door behind me as quietly as I can, and then I run – out of the stairwell, through the gate and onto the street, running as fast as I can down the road by which I arrived, not slowing down until I am several blocks away.

I'm always at home. The furthest I ever get on a normal day is the Kiwi supermarket in Nordberg. Otherwise, I'm in my office or the house. Reading my e-mails. Checking Facebook. Waiting for Sigurd. Waiting for patients. Waiting for them to find me – not actively seeking them, or at any rate not actively enough. Feeling the pressure at the base of my throat, I should, I should. We don't have very much money. I should contribute more. Should be working just as much, just as vehemently, as Sigurd. Shouldn't be feeling so tired; so discouraged. Should just be getting on with it. Working hard.

Waiting for Sigurd. Waiting for someone to talk to, someone to be with. He comes home late, exhausted. Doesn't want to go anywhere. Doesn't want to talk. Only wants to sit there with his laptop on his knees. I ask him about things. When will all this be finished? The bathroom, the downstairs hallway, the bedroom? All the stairs? Sigurd says, "I'm working my ass off, in case you hadn't noticed, and it isn't as if we have loads of cash to pay for it all, either." I tell him about my workday. Try to explain the loneliness between these walls, what it's like to wander around in here, hour after hour, without anyone to talk to. Sigurd says, "Well, try having Flemming breathing down your neck, with all his idiotic suggestions about how we should run the business – the fucking little boss man who thinks he's a business genius just because he remembers something or other from his second year of business studies." We almost never have sex anymore.

One night I find a box of snus in his pocket. It wasn't as if I was looking – I pick up his jacket and it just falls out.

"Sigurd," I say, "are you using snus?"

He looks at me, his eyes empty.

"Yes," he says.

"For how long?"

"A few months."

"How many?"

"I don't know. Four, five."

I start to laugh. He simply looks at me.

"What is it?" he says.

I try to stop laughing.

"No, I don't know," I say. "I just – why have you never mentioned it?"

He shrugs.

"What would I say?"

He doesn't want to share it with me. Doesn't need to say anything. I get it. We don't speak about it again.

It's not as if I'm easy to live with, either. My morning explosions in the bathroom – it's too cold, winter is approaching, it feels as if the water in the shower will end up as icicles hanging from my chin! I do want to be kind. I'd like to take the same easy tone with him as before. Laugh together, have a sense of humour. But then I just snap, go crazy. All this damned loneliness.

In the mornings, when he's gone to work, I sit and look out across the fjord from my privileged position up here in Nordberg – lady of the house. Who am I to complain?

And then it all falls apart for me, one day in December. We've eaten in front of the T.V. as usual. I ask whether we should watch a film, there's a new one on Netflix that someone's been raving about on Facebook. Sigurd is too tired, he says, he has his computer on his

214

lap, just wants to play computer games and half-watch some mean-ingless T.V. series or other neither of us is really keeping up with and kill a couple of hours before he goes to bed. Not to be rude, but that's all he wants to do. O.K., I say, and carry the plates from the coffee table into the kitchen. On the way I stub my toe between two uneven floorboards, not hard, but I lose my balance for a moment and one of the plates hits the floor.

"Fuck," I say.

Sigurd says nothing. I don't need to turn around to know how he's sitting there, bent over his laptop, lost to the world. I've seen him like this so many times. He must have heard me. I'm only ten metres from him, and the plate smashed as it hit the ground. But still he says nothing.

Everyone wants to be loved and respected – it's only human. But even worse than being hated is being invisible. Not being seen as the person you want to be – O.K., that's one thing – but not having your very existence acknowledged? If you cry out in the woods and nobody answers, have you even shouted? If your plate smashes against the floor and your husband says nothing, has it even happened? Or is it true that the place you occupy, the tiny morsel of existence you inhabit, doesn't even register with the man with whom you share your home and bed? That's a different kind of pain. It wells up in my throat like vomit, bursts from my mouth in the form of a wretched sob, and then I start to cry.

In the seconds it takes him to come over to me I've managed to throw the other plate against the floor, too – this time with force, so that it shatters into hundreds of pieces, all across the floor. I've slumped down, am kneeling there hugging myself and sobbing among the fragments of dirty plate and cutlery.

"What in the world just happened?" Sigurd says, mainly, it seems, angry that I pulverised the second plate, as if he doesn't see how much pain I'm in, and I scream at him:

"Are you mad, are you crazy, is it THE PLATE that's the priority here?"

And when he doesn't answer, I say:

"It feels like you've stopped caring about me. I don't think you love me anymore. I get the impression I'm just another thing in this house that you have to find it in yourself to live with."

He sinks to the floor beside me, and we sit there.

Then we talk. Not about what I've just said, but about everything else. About the fact that things are hard. That we're tired. That things haven't worked out the way we expected, that we were so naive when we sat there in our old kitchen in Torshov, drawing up the plans and contours of the life we'd have in the new house, with our new jobs.

That he's exhausted.

"I feel as if I'm failing you," he says. "I was supposed to be so successful."

That I'm lonely. That he knows, but doesn't have the energy to do anything about it.

And so we decide to go away between Christmas and New Year. We don't have the money for it, but we'll scrape it together, borrow from my father, borrow from Margrethe. For our relationship, we say. Because a divorce would be much more expensive, Sigurd says with a half-smile. It's a joke, but not only that. We go online, searching, look at images of white hotels bathed in sunlight and the clear blue rectangles of their swimming pools. Maybe there, or perhaps there. First aid. My heart feels warmer already.

Thursday, March 12: The fortress

"Is this Arild's Security?" I say.

"Yes, this is Arild," says the voice on the telephone.

I'm sitting at the kitchen island at home. I slept in the office again last night, took the inflatable guest mattress with me so that at least I wouldn't have to lie directly on the floor, but I've hardly slept. I spent most of the time lying with my eyes open, looking out into the dark and listening. Twice I got up and went to the window, to the glass wall over by the chairs, and stood in the dark, staring out. The road that goes past the house is lit. We don't have lights along the drive, but even Old Torp had known enough to install a light on the outer wall of the house, and it's this light source I stare into at night, the little circle around it. Did I hear something? Can I see anyone? Is there something moving, there in the shadows beyond the circle? Is there movement in the darkened windows of the house? Did the curtains flutter, up in the living room? I don't know anymore. I clasp the kitchen knife in both hands. If anyone were to see me now, they'd think I was crazy.

But what can I do? I go back to bed, back to the blow-up mattress, which sinks under my weight and squeaks every time I turn, the sound loud in the darkness. I lie there with my eyes open. I hold my knife. I try to sleep, but really I'm just waiting. For morning to come. Or for something to happen. I can no longer trust my senses – I'm always hearing something. Cars along the road. The sound of metal against metal, the lock in the front door being opened. The creepiness from Mrs Atkinson's stifling living room has become lodged in my body, and I know that I can no longer be sure of what I hear. I can no longer distinguish the sound of my front door from the sound of a neighbour's, or from the nightmarish anxiety that my own door is being opened.

At around six-thirty I decide that it must be safe, that it's morning, that the intruder must have gone away. I don't feel certain of this assumption, but my office exile is driving me out of my wits. I take the knife with me when I cross the drive and go up to my front door. I unlock it, go inside. I stay standing in the hallway, smelling, listening – can I sense the intruder, is he still here? I hold the knife in both hands. I call out, hello, and hear how pathetic it sounds, how feeble and afraid. Not at all like the call of an armed homeowner ready to defend what is hers.

I go upstairs to the kitchen. I look around. The curtains are in disarray; something about the bookcase. I no longer know whether I can trust my memory, either. This is unknown territory – my memory is the cornerstone of my abilities. But I'm no longer able to distinguish a change in the curtains or disorder on the bookcase from the scream that is swelling in my chest. I no longer know what I'm seeing, and what I think I'm seeing.

I go up to the bedroom. Feel an intense reluctance to enter it, imagine someone lying there, that new horrors await me behind every door – and especially behind this one, the door to the most intimate room in the house. But it's empty. I check the bedside tables. Look under the bed.

Reassured at finding the bedroom untouched, I go on up to the loft. Old Torp's office is silent, there's no-one here. But someone has been here. Someone has disturbed the dust on the table. Someone has lifted the maps on his shelves. I can see the marks left in the dust where things have been moved.

Did this happen last night? Did it happen the night before

last? Could it have been the police officers when they were searching the place? I go out again, then turn on my heel on the landing. I've thought of something. There is one thing I should check, one thing I haven't checked since Sigurd disappeared. I go back into the loft, cross the room to walk straight to the furthest bookcase, crouch in front of the bottom shelf and heave away a couple of the maps the paranoid old man kept until I reach the small, flat box. There's nothing special about it, but Old Torp himself showed us its contents as he was nearing the end of his life – perhaps he had hoped that his grandson would take up the fight. I open the box, and see that there's nothing in it.

The box was where he kept his old revolver. The jewel in his crown, and worth quite a bit, too – or so said the owner himself, eyes shining, when he showed us the weapon. It had probably been owned by a man who fought in the Russian revolution, although we got the impression that this man must have purchased the revolver a good while later. It was fully functional. "What weapon could be better for putting a bullet between the eyes of communism's enemy?" the old man asked rhetorically. He had rounds for it, too – they had been in the box beside the gun. The weapon was ready to be used. When did I last check? When was I last up here? I had never thought about the revolver. It didn't occur to me to check it when Sigurd disappeared – even when I've needed something to protect myself with, it hasn't dawned on me to go and get it. I simply didn't think of it.

Someone has taken it. Was it the intruder, the person who broke into the house and wandered around up here that night? Was that what he was looking for? There are several hundred boxes in this room, most of them full of newspaper clippings and documents and Old Torp's notebooks, filled with his cramped handwriting. Most of it is pretty dull. How lucky the intruder would have to have been to open the one box contain-ing a weapon! Almost a little *too* lucky. He would have to have *known* where to look. But Old Torp didn't have many visitors. Margrethe, Sigurd, me. Maybe Harald, when he was home, his visits many years apart.

Hardly anyone knows about the revolver.

I close the door to the loft behind me – don't know where the key is, otherwise I would gladly have locked it – and run down the stairs to the kitchen to find my mobile. I try to calm my breathing before I dial. Maybe the police took it? Then I call Gundersen. He doesn't pick up, so I leave a message on his voicemail telling him what I've found, say that I hope it was his team, and could he please confirm that for me, because I'm feeling a little frightened. And then I think, fuck it, and call Arild.

"So what can I help you with?" Arild says.

He's speaking with the soft accent of people who come from somewhere just outside Drammen, from Mjøndalen or Hokksund or thereabouts. Somewhat relaxed, as if with a slight delay, and to hear him offering his help does wonders for me. He sounds safe.

"Someone keeps breaking into my house," I say.

I tell him the whole story. About Sigurd's murder, the nightly break-ins. The indifference of the police, the fridge magnets, the moment with Fredly out on the lawn in which I understood that they view me as hysterical. "I see," Arild says as I explain, "right, yes, I see." For not a moment does it seem that he thinks me highly strung, or that I'm making it all up. He listens. Sometimes asks me questions. So is it right that the front door was locked every time, and there was no sign of a break-in? Do you have any kind of burglar alarm? As I reach the end of the story, he says:

"I'd recommend one of our more comprehensive packages. An alarm with motion detectors for zones inside the house, for example, so that any movement outside your bedroom will trigger the alarm at night. A separate perimeter alarm that covers all the doors. New locks, of course, and perhaps some reinforced locks as well – we can discuss the options. And then I'd probably recommend some motion-triggered lights outside the house, too, at least outside the front entrance. Whether these are connected to the alarm is up to you."

"I want everything," I say.

"Of course, that's going to be a bit more expensive."

"I don't care. I want to feel safe."

Whether it's the money that triggers this I don't know, but Arild promises that he'll take care of it personally, with his assistant, and that they'll be here within half an hour. I should just try to relax in the meantime. I give him the address, and before we hang up, he says:

"See you soon."

These words fill me with an indescribable relief. Arild is on his way.

Gundersen calls while I'm waiting for Arild, and I tell him about the revolver.

"You had a firearm in the house, and you never thought to mention it?" he says, obviously irritated.

"I didn't even think of it," I say. "I mean, I could have kept it on my bedside table to defend myself against intruders, but I'd completely forgotten that it was there. I don't even know whether it works. Sigurd's grandfather said it did, but, I mean, it's as old as the hills."

"Under no circumstances should you ever keep a gun in the

bedroom for protection," Gundersen barks. "Guns can be extremely dangerous – *you* might end up getting shot. Or killing someone. You're intelligent enough to know that, Sara. And unless you have a permit, it's illegal for you even to have it in the first place."

"I know," I sigh. "But that's exactly what I'm saying, I didn't even think about it being up there."

There's a roaring sound behind him. Perhaps he's in his car, perhaps it's the traffic I can hear.

"When did you last see it?"

I think about this.

"We saw it when we went through all the stuff when we moved in, so maybe August of last year. Or, wait, I was cleaning up there some time in the autumn – I opened the box then, and looked at it. You know, he said it was worth something, and it had some carvings on the grip, I just wanted to see. But other than that? No, that must've been the last time. We never used the room."

"When in the autumn?"

"I was doing a sort of pre-Christmas clean. So at the end of November, perhaps."

Gundersen goes quiet for a moment. I imagine him parking, turning the steering wheel back and forth to move the car into position, looking over his shoulder as he reverses.

"I see," he says eventually. "So for all you know, Sigurd might have taken it in connection with something unrelated."

"And what would that be?" I ask.

"I don't know. Maybe he wanted to sell it, if it was so valuable."

"Well, maybe," I say. "I don't know. All I know is that it was there at the end of November, and now it's gone."

Gundersen is silent again.

"So it isn't possible that someone on your team might have taken it, then?" I ask hopefully.

It would be nice if that were the case. Comforting to know that the stupid revolver I had completely forgotten about is now safely stored at police headquarters; has been entered in the register as being in Gundersen's possession.

"No," Gundersen says firmly. "Are you sure there isn't anything else I should know about, Sara? No other weapons? Hunting rifles or flamethrowers – or what do I know? No old, attractively decorated instruments of torture? No intricate surveillance systems?"

"No," I say, tired now. "Not that I know of. But listen – this isn't information I've deliberately withheld. I just didn't think of it."

"I understand. I have to go now, but we'll keep in touch."

After we hang up I stay at the table, drumming my fingers against its surface. I daren't even touch my things, daren't open my drawers or make myself a cup of something, coffee or tea, for fear that the intruder may have tampered with whatever is in the cabinets. Instead, I sit and wait, an uncomfortable rumbling in my stomach after the conversation with Gundersen – my dawning realisation that I'm about to lose his sympathy.

Arild looks to be in his fifties, with greying, red curly hair and a broad-shouldered, stocky build that gives him a teddy-bearish appearance. At the centre of his face is a grey, bushy moustache that hangs down over his mouth like a brush. As he amiably shakes my hand and says that it's nice to meet me I have the desire to collapse against his chest, because he's exactly the kind of person I need: a safe, stable father figure, quite unlike my actual father, and equipped with a battery of effects that are to be used for my protection. He has a young lad with him who can't be more than twenty – a lanky, silent, shy kid named Kristoffer, who Arild refers to as "the apprentice".

"Right," Arild says, setting his hands squarely on his hips, "so this is the house we need to secure."

"Yes," I say. "Shall I show you around?"

We start in the front hallway, and I show them the study in the cellar that was once going to be the nursery, the laundry room, the second bedroom downstairs, and the storeroom. Then we go up to the first floor and they eagerly examine the kitchen and living room. Arild gestures to his apprentice, signalling him to come over, and they stand and study the lock on the veranda door with interest. I show them the kitchen entrance and unlock it, so they can inspect the door from both inside and out. Then we go up to the second floor and they check the bedroom – especially the bedroom window – and the bathroom, and then we go all the way up to the loft. I tell them about Old Torp, and about the missing revolver, since the thought of it has been bothering me since my telephone conversation with Gundersen. Down in the kitchen again, Arild sketches a quick plan of the four floors of the house.

"So," he says. "My first thought is that we have to secure all the doors. The veranda door has a pretty poor lock, and the timber it's sitting in is so rotten that with a little force it could be kicked in – I'm not saying this to frighten you, Sara, but we have to be realistic. At some point you should replace the door, but I think a decent lock will do the trick in the meantime. I have a buddy up in Nittedal who's a locksmith – a really talented guy. The kitchen entrance should have a new lock, too, and we should put an extra security lock on both. It seems your intruder may have a key as there's no sign of damage to any of the doors or windows, so unless they've been open – and you say they haven't – it's the front door we need to concentrate on. But we don't know what the perpetrator will do if he wants to get in but finds the front door impenetrable, so I think we should secure all potential entrances as best we can. Make it really difficult for him, right?"

"Yes," I say gratefully, "I agree."

"Good," Arild says, and a smile lights up his bushy face. "We'll change the lock on the front door, and then I think we should slap on a really good safety lock, with double mountings and full retention. A lock you shouldn't mess around with. My buddy up in Nittedal has a few options to choose from, and I suggest we go for one of the best available. With a safety chain and extra lock, for additional security. The perimeter alarm will make sure that all attempts to come in or out of the doors trigger the main alarm – you can leave the alarm on all the time, just turn it off when you're coming in or going out, at least while things are as they are. You should turn on the motion sensor alarm inside the house when you go to bed, and if you want we can secure the bedroom window against forced entry and get a proper lock for the bedroom door, so that you'll feel safe in your bedroom even if the alarm goes off in the house."

"Yes," I say, feeling the night's anxiety dissolve and trickle down to the floor at this thought.

"All the alarms are connected to our security centre in Økern," Arild says, "and that's manned around the clock. Usually we call you and agree whether we should come out or not, but in this case I think we should activate a "code red", which means that we'll come out regardless of what you say to us on the phone. I mean, for the time being. Until your . . ."

He looks towards the window, embarrassed.

". . . Until your husband's case is solved."

"Good," I say.

"The apprentice and I will get to work straight away. It'll take a few hours to install everything, so you carry on with whatever you'd planned to do today, and we'll work around you. Is it O.K. that we make a copy of the key to the front door to keep at our central security office?"

I give them everything they ask for. While they're in the house I feel safe enough to take a shower and get dressed. Only when I'm waiting for the train does it hit me that I've made myself vulnerable by giving strangers I found online full access to my home.

I see them from a distance when I come out of the station. They are standing there, waiting for me. Margrethe's slim, long-legged figure, a touch unstable for the occasion, beside a tall, stoop-shouldered man who must be Harald. Beside him stands a short, thin female figure – surely the infamous Lana Mei. I'm too far away to see them in detail, but Margrethe's silhouette is unmistakable.

They don't see me. They stand there, talking among themselves. Harald and his girlfriend pull their jackets close against the wind. Margrethe simply stands there. I haven't seen her in several days. Maybe I should have been to see her, but I don't know. Does she not have an equal obligation to call on me? Perhaps she'd rather be alone, as would I. I can't imagine we'd be any comfort to one another.

I stop for a moment and watch them – a family waiting for someone. It occurs to me that they're not waiting for me – although of course that's what they would answer were you to ask them – they're waiting for him. Sigurd's family, standing there waiting for Sigurd. I want to turn and go home. Sigurd will never come, of course. But maybe it's not him they're waiting for. Perhaps they're just waiting for time to pass. Or to start moving again.

Harald sees me when I'm fifty metres away. He lifts a hand and waves, and this acts as a signal to the two women, who turn their heads towards me as I approach.

"Hello," I say.

They look at me. Margrethe's eyes are both red and dull. I hug her; there's no strength in her body. I hug Harald, who is stiff and unfamiliar, but who at least pats my back, if only lightly. Then I meet Lana Mei.

Sweet is what you'd call her. As in the photographs I've seen, although perhaps less attractive in reality. At least here, in this car park in Smestad, where there's nobody to pose for. She takes my hand.

"It's nice to meet you," she says in her nasal American voice with a subdued smile, "although I'm so very sorry for the circumstances."

I try to smile. I've hated the thought of Lana Mei since Margrethe first showed Sigurd and me a photograph of her, when she told us how Harald's new girlfriend was "tremendously clever" and had "a PhD in applied physics" and "a really great job at one of those energy companies in California who are going to solve the climate crisis and save the world", but now that I know we'll never get to know each other – she's on the way into the family and I'm on my way out – I feel a kind of familial goodwill towards her. But I can't summon a smile.

"Well," Harald says, pulling his jacket around him, "shall we go in?"

The man who greets us is around my age, smartly dressed in a suit. He takes each of our hands in turn, holding my and

Margrethe's hands the longest, the same time for both of us. We follow him to his office.

"There are many choices to make," he says solemnly. "But I'm here to help you."

It surprises me that he manages to balance his tone so perfectly; not too sorrowful, but not too ordinary or chummy, either. He seems almost neutral. It occurs to me that I've already forgotten his name.

Then the discussion starts. Which coffin, with what kind of lining? Which flowers? Where would we like to hold the ceremony, and will it be a religious one or not? Do we have a plot for the grave, and, if not, have we thought about where we would like him to be buried? These are absurd questions – I can't take them seriously. But Margrethe, who has obviously taken some strong barbiturates to have any hope of keeping herself together, suddenly springs into action. She's thought about this. She wants a classic, elegant coffin with gold fittings. This will be expensive, but she's paying. She wants the ceremony to be held in the crematorium at Vestre Gravlund, and wants Sigurd to be buried in the graveyard there, in the grave in which her parents are buried.

"Where I, too, will be interred," she says. There is something tragic, but also a trifle theatrical, in her voice.

The director, if that's what we're supposed to call him, nods slowly, as if this is a carefully considered and tasteful choice, and then turns towards me.

"And how do you feel about that?" he says.

"That's fine by me," I say, my voice thick.

I'm grateful that he's asked me, but unable to form an opinion. Margrethe brings up the dilemma of red and white roses or white lilies.

"What do you all think Sigurd would have liked?" she says.

I have to bite my lip to restrain a sound that's bubbling up through my chest. What would Sigurd have liked? He would have liked to live longer than to the age of thirty-two. But there's no point in saying this out loud. It's hard for me to imagine him having a strong opinion one way or the other when the question is whether roses or lilies would provide the better decoration at his own funeral service.

Only once during the proceedings do I form an opinion. We're talking about the music. Margrethe suggests "Solveig's Song" by Edvard Grieg and "Bridge over Troubled Water" by Simon and Garfunkel.

"Not that last one," I say. "Sigurd didn't like that song."

"We used to listen to it when he was small," Margrethe says, hurt. "He used to sit close to me and listen."

"He didn't like it," I say. "A couple we know played it at their wedding, and he said he thought it was a cliché."

"He never told me that," she says.

I shrug.

"I don't know how strongly he felt about it, but I'm not going to sit there and listen to a song he told me he thinks is a cliché. Sigurd hates clichés."

"For God's sake, Sara, would you stop saying cliché," Margrethe says crossly, and for a moment I think I see the old Margrethe appear in the midst of the fog the sedatives have put her in. "I like that song. It reminds me of Sigurd."

The funeral director clears his throat.

"We do recommend that people choose something that everyone can feel happy with," he says, and Margrethe turns her gaze on him.

"This is my son we're talking about," she says. "He'll be with me for the rest of my life. Can you say the same, Sara?"

Tears spring into my eyes at this. Margrethe has always

known how to strike down her opponents, and like any profi-
cient poison tongue she knows that it's the truth that hits the
hardest. How will I think of Sigurd in ten years, or in twenty?
What place will he occupy in the story of my life, should it
ever be told? I haven't had a chance to think about that yet. In
the time that has passed since Sigurd disappeared – less than
a week – I've just been trying to cope. The thought of all the
years that lie ahead is so huge. What will I do with them?

Then Harald recrosses his legs.

"Mamma," he says, "I'm sure there are other songs you
listened to with Sigurd when he was small."

I look at him from the corner of my eye and feel a tenderness
towards him at the fact that he's taking my side in the matter.
Me – about to disappear from the family, and whom he's never
really known. I see now that he resembles Sigurd, a little. A
certain integrity in cases like this, matters of principle. The way
in which he tightens his jaw when he steels himself against
his mother. Perhaps they got this from their father.

Margrethe lets out a sob and looks away.

"Didn't we used to listen to Bob Dylan when he was little?"
Harald asks.

"And what would you have them play?" Margrethe says.
"'Like a Rolling Stone'?"

Harald doesn't answer. A few seconds pass in which we all
wait, and then he says:

"What about that gentle one? The one about everything
changing."

"'The Times They Are a-Changin''," the funeral director says.

"Yeah, that one," Harald says. "What about that?"

Margrethe is quiet for a moment. She rocks slowly back and
forth. Sigurd was her favourite.

"It was your father who liked Dylan," she says resignedly.

"I know a young singer who often sings at funerals," the funeral director says. "I heard her sing it once, and it was beautiful. It gives an entirely different feel from playing a C.D. More dignified, somehow. I can ask whether she's available?"

Margrethe nods.

"Does she sing Grieg, too?" I ask as a peace offering, and the funeral director says he's almost certain of it.

I should choose a song, too. It's the funeral director who says this. I choose "Blackbird" by the Beatles. I don't know why. It isn't as if it was our song or anything. But there's something simple, something light about it. And Sigurd was light, I think. Not just light – but if I'm going to get through the ceremony it's probably best to remember the good days.

The service will take place on Monday. The time and date don't matter to me, I have no plans. All I feel when we mention Monday is the terror of the long week that lies ahead after it.

The meeting at the funeral parlour has worn me out, but it's only one o'clock. From the car park Harald calls a taxi while Lana Mei, Margrethe and I stand there and watch him in silence. They're all going back to Margrethe's place. When the taxi is on its way, Harald asks where I'm heading – if it's on the way I can join them in the cab, he says. Since I don't want to impose I say I'm going to pop in to visit my father – it's just around the corner, I assure him, and I'd prefer to walk, get a bit of fresh air. Harald nods – relieved, it seems. I understand. I'm an outsider now, and they're grieving – it's best that they're able to spend time alone, just the three of them. We say goodbye; I hug each of them in turn. We say we'll see each other next week. No-one uses the word "funeral". Lana Mei says that it was nice to meet me. I walk slowly across the car park to the path that leads up to

Holmen, and when I turn, they're standing with their backs to me and looking down the road up which the taxi will come. Harald has his arm around his mother; she leans her head against his shoulder. Something twists within me.

I don't really intend to visit my father. I'm too tired, too frayed. I just want to get away from the three figures in the car park, wait until they're gone, and then walk back the way I came to take the train home. I follow the narrow footpath away from the clamour of the Smedstad junction, between the old semi-detached houses built during a time when the area was like any other, in the direction of the large, venerable detached properties and new builds.

Sørkedalsveien runs close by; Smestad's inhabitants have barricaded themselves against it with large wooden boards facing the road, the suburb's occupants trying to preserve a kind of nostalgic belief that they still live in rural surroundings, even with this main artery that leads from Majorstuen and up to Røa and Østre Bærum raging and frothing on their front doorstep.

I'm glad not to be making my way to Margrethe's house – glad that I'm not sitting in a taxi, squeezed between Harald and his girlfriend. That I won't have to enter Margrethe's living room, where I'll feel as if I'm disrupting things if I pull out a chair or move a cushion to sit on the sofa. That I won't be subjected to the ever-present, somewhat strained atmosphere of her house, which will be all the more strained now, with this huge, formless grief packed so tightly around everyone that it's impossible to breathe without pulling it down into your lungs. Yes, I'm glad I'm not making my way there. But still. They're leaving together. I'm walking alone.

There are many ways of grieving. I suppose I must have grieved when my mother died when I was small, but I remember so little of it. I have a few vague memories of crying during the night, of hiding my head beneath the covers so that Pappa and Annika wouldn't hear me. But there's another kind of grief in these memories, which I can't quite place – the fact that I can't say for certain that *this* is what they're about, that I'm crying in them because I missed my mother. And then there's also the grief that isn't for her, but for all that was lost – everything that might have been if she hadn't passed away. That's the grief that lasts longest. It never lets up, reappears at irregular intervals without warning. When I was in fifth grade and went to a friend's house after school, and her mother teased us over dinner and asked us if we were behaving for our teachers. When Ronja's mum showed us how to style our hair into a fishbone braid; how she had moved to stand behind Ronja's chair, taking out her daughter's ponytail and starting to plait the hair with tender movements, explaining as she went. When Sigurd's brother put his arm around his mother in the car park just now, and she rested her head against him.

The path along which I'm walking leads out into a passage-way, a couple of streets down from the one where I grew up. I stop. It won't be long before the taxi collects the three members of Sigurd's family from the car park; perhaps they've even gone already. I could turn around and go back. But on the other hand, I only have the one parent left. I could visit him, drink a cup of tea with him – even better, I could just go and sit in my old bedroom for a while. It's still there, almost untouched since I was a child, the large white blanket Mamma crocheted for me spread across the bed. When lying on the bed you can turn yourself into it; feel her handiwork against your cheek.

As I'm making my way towards my childhood home, walking along the road between patches of ice, tyre tracks and dirty snow that is yet to melt, my mobile rings.

*

"It's Gundersen," Gundersen says as soon as I pick up. "Sara, I have a question for you. When you write up your notes, how honest are you?"

"What do you mean?"

"I mean, to what extent do you write what you really think? If you think a client is barking mad or argumentative, for example, would you write that down?"

"That's not an easy question to answer," I say. "I'm always honest, but I'm professional. And my patients have the right to view their records, so I try to write my notes in such a way that it won't offend them should they ask to read them."

"So what does that mean? That you embellish them?"

I sigh. My exhaustion after events at the funeral parlour asserts itself.

"My notes aren't my opinion on anything. They're my professional assessment. If anyone is barking mad? Well – I don't even know what that means. But if someone is argumentative . . . well, yes, it depends. If someone complains about something within their control, something they have the power to change, I might write about that. But I also take it up with the patient concerned, of course."

"Hmm. I'm just wondering. You have a file here labelled ASSESSMENTS."

"Are you reading my notes?"

"Just a few selected excerpts. In order to understand."

"Understand what?"

A brief pause.

"Your workday. What happens in your sessions."

"That's confidential information," I say, but my indignant response to our previous discussions on the topic has deserted me. "The law is on your side in requesting access, but you also have an ethical obligation not to violate the private lives of my patients. If you have any questions about what happens in my sessions, I'd prefer it if you just asked me."

"Understood," Gundersen says impatiently, and I have a distinct feeling that he's going to do whatever he wants with my notes. "But now I'm asking you. What do you put in your notes?"

I turn down the road to my father's house as we talk. The sun is at my back; my distorted shadow falls across the gravel on the path ahead of me.

"I assess the patient. The treatment. I try to make an assessment after every session."

"So what if you think a patient is – for example – lying to you?"

"Lying to me? I rarely think that. But sometimes they exaggerate, or avoid telling me something that's bothering them. A patient might describe a childhood memory, for example, something tragic that happened to them, and say: "But it wasn't really a big deal." And then I might think that they're glossing over it, changing the subject, so there is probably something there. A five-year-old wouldn't think such and such wasn't a big deal. See what I mean? In that case I might write something about it in my assessment."

"And what might you write?"

"Hmm. *Patient appears to have a flat affect considering the severity of the episode. Consider whether there might be something more beneath this incident than apparent, will explore further in the next session.* Something like that?"

"I see," Gundersen says. "Thank you, Sara. I'll be in touch."

"Wait," I say as I walk up the drive to my father's house. "Are you any closer to finding an explanation? I mean, are you any closer to finding the guy?"

The line goes quiet for a moment. I wonder whether he's

been doing something else while he's been speaking to me.

"We're following a couple of leads," he says. "We think we know what Sigurd was doing in Krokskogen that day. But that's all I can tell you at this stage, Sara, and I'd like you to try not to think about it. Let us do our job."

"Have I prevented you from doing your job?" I say.

"I know that you went to see Mrs Atkinson," he says. "Of course, I can't prevent you from visiting her if that's what you want to do. But I think it's wiser to leave well enough alone. I really do."

The warning is a blow to the stomach. Not because it's embarrassing that he knows I went looking for the old woman, and possibly also knows that I left her apartment in a panic – although that *is* embarrassing. It hits me because he's insinuating that I'm obstructing him and his team; that I'm a silly girl fooling around playing amateur detective. "It's wiser to leave well enough alone." As if I'm incriminating myself. And why shouldn't Gundersen be interested in what happens in my sessions, what my working day is like? And so, perhaps as a kind of defence, I sputter out the tiny piece of information I've been keeping to myself, the information I didn't want to give him.

"There was a woman who used to wait for him outside his office. Were you aware of that? I talked to his colleagues, and they told me. They saw him go out and meet her."

Gundersen falls silent again.

"Is that so?" he says after a few moments. "No, I didn't know that. But it's interesting. Who told you that, did you say?"

"Mammod. At FleMaSi."

"Thank you very much, Sara."

"You're welcome," I say.

But I feel no satisfaction in throwing this information in Gundersen's face, no sense of being his equal.

"I only heard this yesterday," I therefore say, hearing how it sounds like an apology.

"I have to go now. Speak soon, Sara."

There's a click on the end of the line. I put my mobile in my pocket and ring the doorbell.

Nobody opens the door; I wait outside for a long time. When I'm certain that the house is empty, I walk down the steps and across to the four flowerpots lined up along the wall next to the entrance. Large terracotta pots, probably bought and planted by my mother, and neglected since her death. They've held no flowers in recent years, and one of them now has a crack in it, but they remain there, four pots on four saucers. In the saucer of the third pot from the door, well hidden around the back, is a spare key to the house. It's been there for as long as I can remember. I feel my way around with my gloveless fingers and take it, the small plastic figure of a dog, a chain and a key ring with a key on it.

Inside, the house is silent. Luckily, the hallway contains no dainty women's shoes – all of them are Pappa's: a pair of trainers, a pair of ski boots. I can't imagine these are his best ones, though – so perhaps he's out skiing, or maybe he keeps his good boots in the car so he can head out into the countryside whenever the mood takes him, as it often does. I set my shoes beside his spare ski boots.

"Pappa?" I call out, just in case.

Nobody answers. I go into the living room.

Pappa inherited the house from his parents, long before I was born. Mamma, Pappa and Annika lived in a small apartment in Holmen, and my grandmother believed that a family of four had greater need of a big house than an ageing couple. What my grandfather thought about the matter I don't know, but they moved into an apartment in Frogner, leaving a few things behind – an old linen cupboard, an antique chest of drawers, my grandfather's old writing desk. Mamma must have made an effort with the interior decoration, but since then little has happened on that front. Pappa isn't interested in furniture, wallpaper or art – it's all too mundane for his tastes. To walk into the living room is to be reminded of my family history. Those who know the story can scrape it off, layer by layer, like archaeologists. The large mirror hanging in the plaster stucco frame above the fireplace is obviously the work of my grandparents; the grey-flecked sofas probably my mother's. The chest of drawers against the wall, well, that was my grandmother's, as far as I know – she loved to tell us how it came from her childhood home and how her mother had promised that she would inherit it when she got married. Just the thought of this was enough to bring tears to Farmor's eyes. On it stands my grandparents' wedding photograph, the only personal image in the living room – my unsentimental father must have discovered a touch of sentimentality all the same, because he didn't put it in a box in the cellar with the rest of the photographs. The decor is otherwise spartan. Above the chest of drawers hangs a painting which for the longest time I thought depicted my grandmother's mother, probably because of the story about the chest, but I later learned its subject is actually Hannah Arendt, a Jewish author who wrote books about totalitarianism and evil. Why Pappa chose to hang a picture of Hannah Arendt on the wall I have no idea, but there is something reassuring about her gaze; she has fixed, self-confident eyes along with a gentle smile. When I thought she was my great-grandmother, I would often sit before the painting and talk to her.

Above the sofa hangs a large and ugly painting of a vase of red flowers against a bold, light-green background. Pappa was given it by his department at the university as a sixtieth birthday present, and, contrary to everything I thought I knew about him, he loved it and decided to hang it on the living room wall. He showed such enthusiasm for this painting that for a moment I started to wonder whether he was losing his wits – "Isn't it lovely," he said, enraptured, "doesn't it suit the room so well?" The painting is so awful that I almost wondered whether his colleagues had chosen it for exactly this quality. Pappa doesn't have many friends at the university due to the nature of his writings. Perhaps some of them felt that this was the perfect gift, an ugly painting for a disliked colleague. And it would be in line with my father's character if it turned out he had hung it up precisely because he saw through this intention. Pappa often takes it as a mark of distinction if members of high society turn their backs on him.

The study is the only room in the house which Pappa actually seems to care about. It's beyond the living room – you have to cross the living room to reach it. It was my grandfather's study before it was Pappa's, and Farfar built dark oak shelves along the walls, from floor to ceiling, which he filled with his books. When he moved out, he took all his books with him, and Pappa filled the shelves with his own. If he uses the flat in Bislett as his writing space, then the study is his library. He also kept Farfar's writing desk, a gigantic table made of polished cherry wood, with plenty of drawers that can be locked with small, gilded keys. I loved these drawers when I was little – they were like small treasure chambers, which to my disappointment Pappa neglected to lock. "I have nothing to hide from the world," he claimed. At the end of the study is a fireplace, in which Pappa lights a fire every day from October to April, and often in spring and summer, too. There's a basket of wood beside it, and Pappa prides himself on keeping it full at all times. Maintenance of the fire is also important, and he has a number of instruments for this purpose, all hanging from a small metal stand: more than one set of bellows, pokers for sifting through the ash, a small dustpan and brush for cleaning up when the fire has gone out. Facing the fireplace are two chesterfield armchairs, in which we would sit on the rare occasions I was granted an audience with him as a child. Between the chairs is a table with books on it, and when I cast a glance at it I see there a novel by Dag Solstad, one of his more obscure works, I think – or at least I haven't read it.

When it comes to the decor in here, Pappa hasn't held back. He has a collector's constitution, although he rarely shows this side of himself. On the window ledges are an old set of scales, possibly used by gold miners in Klondike, and a clock that was the only thing his father's father – the Polish con man who gave us the name Annika and I chose to abandon – took with him to Norway. Pappa keeps it serviced, and it still works. Beside this is a bust of Darwin, a jug he may have imported illegally from Iran, and a beautifully carved runic calendar.

Pappa considers himself a scientist first and foremost. He's a social scientist, but sees himself as a direct descendant of Newton, Darwin and Copernicus – the natural sciences are just one of several branches of his dearly beloved science, and when anyone feels otherwise about the interdependence of these disciplines he is either genuinely surprised or emphatically dismisses their opinion. Science, as far as he's concerned, is a method for seeking the truth, and he considers this the purest, most elevated path to knowledge. He therefore only allows space on his desk for objects he sees as symbols of this: an old-fashioned sextant, a copy of the Foucault pendulum, a piece of a meteorite, and a Newton's cradle. He has endless stories about these objects. He looks upon them with such a tender gaze, of the kind other men employ only when looking at toilet roll Santas and polystyrene ball snowmen made by their children. Pappa has never kept anything my sister or I made in kindergarten or school. Annika is hurt by this; I might wish that he'd done otherwise, but understand that it isn't about a lack of love, only about a lack of ability to understand what a Santa Claus made from a milk carton might mean. This is what I think as my fingers graze the treasures on his desk. My sister sees his limitations. He is a man who is unable to see things from any perspective but his own, who deep down cares mostly about himself. But I also see the little things he did for us as we were growing up: the visits to his study and the myths and legends he would tell us, or the long speeches about the sextant and the pendulum – attempts to initiate us into what he loves. To me, the awful cruise we went on when Farmor died is proof that he cares. He would give his life for ours if it really came down to it, but he's unable to do the things that mean something in the life we're actually living: visit us, show an interest in his grandchildren, ask us about our jobs and friends and marriages. It isn't his fault. He was born lacking the ability to show an interest in anything that, deep down, doesn't interest him.

Outside the window is the garden, which borders on other gardens containing other houses. Ten years ago, Pappa divided the garden and sold a piece of it to a developer, and now there's a new white detached house where my swing set once stood. The house is shaped like a cube and features a roof terrace with steel railings. Someone has forgotten to take in a grey-blue parasol for the winter and it stands there, drooping, worn shabby by frost and damp and snow. On the other side of the garden, parallel to ours, is the garden of the Winge family, who lived in the neighbouring house when I was growing up. The Winges' son was called Herman – he was in my year at school, and I loved him to the point of bursting for three long years of my youth without ever saying anything of it, not to him nor to anyone else. I wrote his name in notebooks I hid in the secret drawer of my desk, and tried to walk home at the same time as him so that we might start walking to school together.

My father's desk stands there as it always has. I know from experience that if you turn the desk chair around to face the other way, you have a good view of the Winge family's house from it. You can sit there, watching, hoping to see Herman Winge – perhaps even catch a glimpse of him. But I can't imagine my dad has ever turned his chair to look out. These distinguished houses and gardens offer him no inspiration, and he's positioned the desk so that he sits with his back to the window.

Open on the desk is a large book. It has thick cardboard covers and shiny black pages covered in newspaper clippings that have been glued into place. This is my father's archival scrapbook. He keeps all his published works, whether they are scientific articles or contributions to newspapers or journals. The cutting he has just glued in – the reason the book is lying here open, I presume – is an article that appears to have been taken from a magazine for people with a special interest. "Time and Society", says the header. I'm not sure what kind of journal it is, but those that are willing to print my father's texts are often controversial or of a limited circulation. The article is entitled "Ten things that would be improved if Norway ratified full Sharia law". I turn back through the pages of the book, scan the many colourful magazine pages. If his article has been published as a double spread he creates the same layout in the scrapbook; the two pages glued so precisely into the fold at the binding that you could almost believe they were the same page. It's almost touching how diligently he has undertaken this task; how straight he has cut the paper, how carefully he has applied the glue – there is no sticky mess beyond the edges of the cuttings, no creases in the glued pages. Much of what he's written I don't understand, paragraph such-and-such discussed in the light of the theory of theoretician so-and-so. But then there's the occasional bomb. Punishment as a means of preventing receipt of benefits. Human rights – a threat to our sense of justice? I rarely read what he writes, perhaps because Annika did so for a time and ended up raging at him or storming from the table at family dinners. Annika would stride out of the room, while Pappa, the imperturbable, cantankerous quarreller, would stick to his guns. Farmor, if she was there, acted as the Peace Corps, mediating between them.

"Vegard likes to provoke, but he doesn't mean anything by it," she would say.

I believed her. I still believe her. Pappa's trademark is to follow logic wherever it takes him, without being influenced by ethical considerations. He sets conventional morals aside, undertakes significant cost–benefit analyses with an added pinch of his special philosophy of life – a personal blend of Charles Darwin, John Stuart Mill, Per Fugelli and Rage Against the Machine, combined to create a kind of surprising, self-composed utilitarianism. He offers this up with a naive gaze, in the softest voice: if one accused innocent must suffer a long punishment, isn't that better than allowing a guilty person to walk free and letting ten innocents suffer?

"No!" Annika would scream, when she was fifteen, or twenty, or twenty-five. "The state cannot punish someone who hasn't done anything wrong – that's assault!"

"But Annika, honey," Pappa would say in his friendliest, most innocent voice, "isn't it true that we, as a society, must prioritise the solution that brings about the least possible overall suffering? Is that not logical?"

"Vegard so likes to stir up the things we disagree on," Farmor would say, "but let's talk about something nicer now, shall we?"

Of course Annika was right, every single time. You can't dole out sentences and harsh punishments to people who may not have done anything wrong. Of course we shouldn't flog criminals or punish the wrong person. But I just wanted to believe that my grandmother was right. "Let's talk about something nicer, shall we?"

I turn the pages of the scrapbook, thinking of all the hours he must have spent archiving his works. I imagine how he must have sat here before I was born: Mamma sitting in the living room, or here in one of the armchairs, perhaps, crocheting my bedspread as my father, with the utmost care, placed a clipping covered with the thinnest layer of glue against the page, concentrating on achieving the right angle before passing his hand across the paper to stick it down. Perhaps my parents looked at each other. Maybe Pappa smiled, self-conscious at having been observed in his ritual, and maybe Mamma teased him, or simply laughed, thinking to herself: Vegard and his archive.

What was Pappa writing around the time Mamma died? I'm sure he must have continued to write; must have sat here and cut and pasted deep in concentration while she was ill – if not in the days before her funeral, then at the very least afterwards, while the house was in mourning. It's never occurred to me to find out. I have never been interested in his work, haven't wanted to know anything about it – have actively avoided it, in fact. I've heard Annika scream at him, seen her run from the table in tears and felt the tension of the house in my body for days afterwards, when they weren't speaking. Pappa making a point of being cheery and indifferent; Annika working through her hostility until she could stand to be in the same room as him again. So I've steered clear, figured that the less I know about what Pappa believes and writes, the better. But he must have been writing around the time he lost Mamma. And now I'm here, and I've lost my partner, too.

244

I know where he keeps the rest of his scrapbooks. On the bottom of my grandfather's old oak shelves, right beside the fireplace, is book after book like the one on the desk, meticulously dated since the end of the '70s. Mamma died in June 1988. I pull out 1986–91, set it on the table between the armchairs, and open it. Turn the thick, heavy pages filled with old printer's ink and graphics. 86–86–86–87–87–87–88. February. The next clipping is from October. In February: "On corruption legislation". In October: "Moralism and what's best for the herd". I'm not interested in corruption, but I might be interested in moralism and the herd.

The article starts with a story about a kind of wild dog that lives in packs on the African plains. In these packs, Pappa says, what's best for the group is the greatest justice. Sick, old and injured individuals leave the group so as not to hold it back. The dogs realise that they are a burden and accept the consequence of this: to die alone, of hunger or at the jaws of other predators. So the pack will manage more effectively.

In certain cultures, we also often find this sacrifice among humans, Pappa writes. And then:

But in western, individual-oriented societies, the rights of the individual outrank what is best for the group. We are like baby birds, each and every one of us screaming: Me! Me! Me! The noblest act, which we know of from the morals taught by the world's religions, the moral we teach our children and the rest of the coming generation, is to put one's own wishes aside for the common good. And where do we see this nobility more clearly than within the family, society's most important unit? Parents and grandparents sacrifice time, energy, money and other resources in order to support the next generation. A mother will throw herself in front of an out-of-control bus, giving her life to save her children. We are well versed in the nobility of

245

putting others before ourselves, but we shrink from taking this maxim to its logical, existential conclusion.

Elderly individuals in ill health expect to be cared for, tended to and looked after by their children, even though these children often have more than enough to do in providing care and guidance to their own children, the generation that will inherit the earth. They, the ill, use the community's resources to keep themselves alive, living year after year with their illness, although they will never be cured. They have no future other than further sickness and a slow death, but still think they have the right to abuse the resources that the young have more need of and can make better use of. Would it not be economical for society – not only for the health and welfare services, but also for the individual family – if the elderly were to do as the wild dogs of the plains? Would this not be the noblest of acts? The same could be said of the terminally ill; those who have chronic mental disorders or degenerative brain disorders.

But since it is unlikely that individuals will make the choice of the wild dogs voluntarily, should there not be a body that can assist them? I imagine a committee to which one could apply when a given individual has become too great a burden. For the benefit of their family, their pack, relatives would be able to apply to this committee to have the individual removed. Children would therefore be spared having to grow up in the shadow of illness. Spouses and other relatives would have the capacity to use their resources on supporting those who are able to contribute to society, rather than on sitting beside hospital beds or in institutional waiting rooms. In the absence of such a committee, some individuals will take this upon themselves as a private responsibility, and I ask myself – can I cast moral judgment upon these individuals? Is it not perhaps they who ultimately commit the most noble, exalted act?

*

The article goes on, but I've read enough. I close the book, and twice drop it on the floor before I manage to set it back on its shelf. I get up and go to the desk, close the book that's lying there, too, and pick up the tiny sextant, holding it in my hands and trying to calm myself.

He doesn't mean anything by it. He likes to provoke. Let's talk about something nicer, shall we?

I wish the sudden idea to investigate my father's writings had never occurred to me. Especially now, when my house has been broken into and my husband is gone; when the police are in and out of my home and I've spent the night in my office with a kitchen knife in my hands. When I so sorely need a little peace, a little comfort.

I try to breathe normally. This clipping has been in the book on the shelf since the 1980s. I could have come in here at any point during my childhood, opened the book and read it. There's nothing new about it, nothing sudden.

I wish I'd never read it, but now that I have, I can't stop thinking about it. The most important thing now is not to panic. I have known for years that my father has written plenty of crazy articles.

I put the sextant down. Pick up the meteorite, my finger gently stroking its rugged surface. Breathe. And start again.

My father wrote this article only months after his wife had died. And his wife had been suffering from what he so insensitively terms a "degenerative brain disorder", a diagnosis which, according to his logic, should inspire the individual to take themselves off and die. I almost can't believe how he could dare to write such a thing, write it and publish it, so soon after his family had experienced such a tragedy. And not only that – he believes that if people like Mamma fail to kill themselves, then the state should do it for them. And since the state doesn't do this, he goes so far as to defend those who would kill their relatives. Which leads me to a question I would have preferred not to have to ask: does that mean that he was capable of doing so?

But this is crazy. I put down the rock. This isn't why I came here. I came to his house for a sense of peace, to feel at home – to feel safe. I don't need this, not now. I leave the study, hurry up the stairs and run into the room that was mine, closing the door behind me.

Everything in here looks just as it did when I moved out. The patterned wallpaper. White lace curtains. The ornament shelf on the wall, the wicker chair and its frilly cushions in the corner. A white desk. A family photograph, from when I was so small that Mamma's illness had not yet progressed very far. The crocheted bedspread. A straw hat hung on the wall for decoration, a porcelain doll on top of the bookcase. There are more teenage elements, too – a picture of Leonardo DiCaprio hangs on the door, cut from a teen magazine with less care than that exhibited by my father in his scrapbook. A Dorothy Parker poem written out on lined paper in my childhood handwriting hangs above the bed, and in the bookcase are the books I read during my teens (books for adults, of course): Bjørneboe, Dostoevsky, Plath, Woolf, Kafka. There are even a couple of shot glasses on the ornament shelf. But overall, the room looks as if it belongs to a little girl.

It was she who decorated it for me, and that's why I could never change it. As I sink down onto the bed it resurfaces, the heavy, hollow lump in my chest which is the grief for everything that might have been. The family life I never had. She must have been so loved, the child for whom this room was made. How painstakingly her mother must have decorated the walls with exactly the right flower-filled wallpaper. How she must have pondered – which curtains would be best, what kind of bed?

How many hours it must have taken to crochet the bedspread. All to create the best childhood bedroom for her daughter. Before she fell ill. Before she took too much medicine and collapsed on the floor of the hallway of this house.

If she took too much medicine, that is. I mean, if it was an accident. I lean back on the bed. This is a monstrous contention. Do I really want to continue this train of thought? To follow this logic through to its final conclusion, as my father would say? Do I want to go down that road?

But what if it wasn't an accident? What if Pappa, based on the arguments he set out in such detail a few months later, decided to take her life? Helped her to make the noblest of sacrifices, as he himself would put it. Might that have been possible?

She took many medicines. I've never altogether understood why a woman with Alzheimer's had access to medications potentially so dangerous that a mistake might kill her, but perhaps she was often very fearful, maybe they gave her anxiety-suppressing drugs – and then there were all the analgesics. I've asked myself how an overdose might have happened. How on earth is it possible that a person suffering from a disease that by definition causes confusion and disarray was responsible for taking their own medicine?

But of course she wasn't. There were nurses here, they came and went. Some of them chatted to me. One used to give me soft mints to chew on – they would often get stuck in my teeth. I remember the nurses and I remember their pill dispensers: the plastic trays divided into many compartments – the Monday compartment, Tuesday compartment, Wednesday compartment, and so on. When I was little I thought they looked like the ornament shelf I had on my wall. The nurses counted out and divided up the pills that Mamma would take outside their working hours. Then the family was responsible. My father, that is.

How easy it would have been for him to give her more or less medication than she should have had. She understood nothing. Everything around her was messy and difficult. She knew she was supposed to take some tablets, so if her husband had said, "You have to take these ten," would she not just have done it? As she did everything he told her to do – crossed the street when he said it was safe to do so, went to bed when he said she should, got up when he said it was time to get up. Stayed indoors even if she wanted to go out because he said it was the middle of the night or pouring with rain, or for some other reason she didn't understand, but which she accepted. Because the world had become so hard for her to grasp. Because she needed help with so much. She accepted that's how it was. We eat what he says we should eat. We use the cutlery he says is the right cutlery. When he puts a handful of pills in front of her and asks her to take them, she does it. Of course she does. If she were to start to ask questions about everything he asked of her, where on earth would she end up?

To the question of how it was possible that this accident happened, why there wasn't sufficient control of the medications to prevent an Alzheimer's patient taking a lethal overdose, the answer was this: it was human error. How the medicines were stored, perhaps, or a problem with the dispenser. Pappa avowed that she had been given exactly what she should have been given that day. He had needed to go out, run a couple of errands. She must have got into the medicine cabinet on her own. She must have got it into her head that she needed to take more. She was like that. Might all of a sudden decide she wanted to take a walk in her underwear. Might want to go and buy groceries in the middle of the night. The medicines should have been stored in a locked cabinet to which she didn't have access – but she deteriorated so quickly. The safety procedures hadn't kept up with the progression of the disease. The system had failed, as systems sometimes do. Maybe the nurses should have foreseen the coming danger, maybe the doctor should have seen how much worse she was at her last appointment, maybe Pappa should have taken the initiative to lock up the medicines. But who wants to point the finger in such a situation? She was seriously ill, was never going to get better. This was a sorry incident within a family already wracked by the tragedy of this awful illness. The father and his two small daughters would be left to grieve in peace. The enquiry into the matter was closed. The hospital would review its procedures. And so on.

The response was standard, acknowledging that accidents happen. But it was also unsatisfactory. If she was so ill that she might be capable of something like that, why had nobody noticed?

But if Pappa wanted it that way, well, that's another thing altogether. That would explain a lot.

There's something else, too. That time I wet myself during the night, when Pappa came home late and put on his wedding ring – it was while Mamma was still alive. I'm sure of it. Why would Pappa take off his wedding ring? What reason could there be, other than that he was going out to meet another woman? But Pappa despises infidelity – by definition, infidelity involves putting one's own needs before those of the family. And the family is the herd – the pack. Society's most important component. The hearth and home of humanity and humankind. Individuals must always do what's best for the group. Risking the eternal family for one's own temporary satisfaction is the crowning example of selfishness. Extramarital relations are a crime against family, and the individual who commits any crime against the family should be punished. He's told us in no uncertain terms that he believes this. Several times. This was what Annika was thinking of when I questioned her over our takeaway.

But what if he no longer regarded Mamma as a person? That's what I was thinking, what I was really asking Annika about. Whether he thought that when Mamma got sick, she was no longer a member of the family or society, but a burden of which we needed to rid ourselves. The sick wild dog. In that case, there would have been no deceit involved in entering into a relationship with someone else. Under my father's logic, he would have been as morally irreproachable as before.

But is this too far-fetched? I no longer know whether I can trust my conclusions. I begin to feel so tired. The flowers on the wallpaper start to move and whir before me. I close my eyes. Just for a moment, just to rest them.

Sigurd and I went to Tenerife. One week, departing between Christmas and New Year and staying into early January, paid for by Margrethe in the form of a loan. A package holiday to the Canary Islands. It wasn't exactly us.

We were picked up and driven to the hotel in a minibus, along with a family from northern Norway and two friends, a pair of women in their sixties, from Løten. The hotel was old, nice enough, although it seemed that the only renovations since the '70s had been undertaken for the sole purpose of improving the facade. Our room featured wall-to-wall carpeting – all the air fresheners in the world couldn't hide the smell of cigarette smoke that clung to it. But we had a sea view, and a small veranda.

The hotel rate was all-inclusive, and since we didn't have any money, eating all our meals there was the obvious strategy. There was a pool, tennis courts, a small sandy beach and a gym at the hotel. The so-called spa was just a sauna and jacuzzi. The local shopping centre, advertised by the hotel, contained nothing but a cheap jewellery shop, a Chinese restaurant, a bingo hall and a Scandinavian pub. Once we'd seen all this on our first day we looked at each other searchingly and tried to laugh a little, pretend that we didn't both see the entire holiday collapsing before our very eyes.

And then the opposite happened. Despite the circumstances, we ended up having a really great time. We slept in late, made love in the mornings, Sigurd holding me tight. We'd go downstairs and raid the breakfast buffet, then sit on our veranda and eat. We played tennis every single day – we were both terrible at it, but we laughed until we cried. One day we rented a car and drove around the island; on another we borrowed bicycles from the hotel and cycled along the waterfront. We even went to the godforsaken shopping centre, ate dumplings and sweet-and-sour chicken at the Chinese restaurant, and played a round of bingo. We spent much of our time lying by the pool reading books, each reading aloud excerpts we thought the other would find interesting. We swam in the pool, gliding up alongside one another and putting our arms around each other under water. Sigurd sneaked a bottle of beer from the bar into the spa, and we sat in the jacuzzi and watched the sunset, a little tipsy and giggling. We had long, deep conversations at the dinner table and I was convinced that everyone in the restaurant must envy us; we were the most infatuated couple there. We bought drinks at the bar and sat by the pool after dinner, or played cards and drank white wine and got drunk on the veranda of our room. There was no boundless elegance or luxury; the hotel wasn't refined. But it was exactly what we needed. Wall-to-wall carpeting and all.

I'm dreaming about when Sigurd and I went to Tenerife, but in the dream the holiday isn't as it was. This is another hotel, whiter, with shiny, carpetless floors. I'm there with Sigurd, but Sigurd is dead. He isn't dead in the way that people are dead in reality – he walks around beside me, doing the things I do, but he's so pale, almost transparent, and says nothing. I decide that we're going to go on holiday regardless. I decide that nobody will notice it. I speak for him, on behalf of us. He sits there with me, is beside me, there's no reason to worry about the fact that he's no longer alive. I order for him in the restaurant – he'll have the steak, please, I say, and a glass of red wine – and the waiters look at us with concern. They say nothing, but I shrink under their collective gaze. I'm more anxious that they can see us than I am at the fact that Sigurd is dead. I smile as best I can, so they won't see how unhappy I am. I stroke Sigurd's cold hand, which isn't completely real, isn't completely touchable. He says nothing. He looks irritated, but I can't manage to make eye contact. I can't get through to him at all, and yet I pretend that everything is fine – I smile and laugh, conducting both sides of the conversation so that nobody at the hotel will understand just how bad things are.

And because I wake up so suddenly I remember the dream, so short and bizarre. We're on holiday. Sigurd is dead. And I act as if I'm unaware of this.

There's a buzzing noise. I hear it in my dream. At first I think I'll just ignore it, that it'll disappear if I pay it no heed, but as soon as the thought of the buzzing has occurred to me it seems to get louder, and then it's too late. I realise it's my mobile. I wake up, blinking, looking around me.

I'm lying on the bed in my childhood bedroom – it takes me a moment to understand this. Evening is falling – the sun must have already set, or be on its way down. The shadow the window casts against the wall is long, and it appears to be dusk around me. I fumble around with my hand and find the buzzing, trembling mobile beside me on the bed.

"Hello?"

"Hi, it's Arild here," the telephone says, "from Arild's Security."

"Oh. Hi."

"Well, we're almost done up here. Took a little longer than expected – we had to wait for the locksmith and such – but everything's installed now. We're just packing up, but, I don't know, are you far away? I need to show you how the system works."

"Yes, of course," I say, glancing at my watch and realising that it's almost six o'clock. "I'm in Smestad, I – well, actually I fell asleep – I didn't get much sleep last night. Anyway – I'll head home straight away. I'll be with you in around twenty minutes, thirty tops."

"O.K., great," he says.

I sit up in bed, rub my eyes, experiencing the uncomfortable sensation of having lost track of the time – I've slept deeply, as if it was night, and then woken to early evening. Perhaps Pappa is already home. The unpleasantness from before I slept churns in my stomach. I would prefer not to see him now. I sit with my mobile pressed to my ear, and it occurs to me that Arild is still on the line. It seems as if he's hesitating.

"Was there something else?" I say.

"Actually, yes," he says. "There was one more thing."

He falls silent again. I rub the back of my hand across my face and wait.

"I just wanted to ask you . . . Were you aware that there's surveillance equipment in your house?"

"Huh?"

"I mean, you know – cameras," he says. "And microphones. Surveillance equipment. I just wanted to ask you, because I thought, well, it might have been you who installed it."

"What are you saying?" I say. "I don't understand what you're saying."

"We've found surveillance equipment," Arild says again. "A camera in your front hallway, a camera and microphone in the kitchen. If they're not yours, then it looks as if someone has been watching you."

"Oh God," I say, and then I say nothing further.

"Is everything alright?" asks Arild.

I imagine hundreds of minor situations. Me waiting for Sigurd. Me drinking coffee in the kitchen. Me, perhaps picking my nose. Julie snooping around down there. Annika trying to get me to talk. Gundersen slapping his search warrant on the kitchen table. All kinds of embarrassing, private things. Have I gone downstairs to get something to eat in my underwear? Been singing songs to myself? Plucked my knickers from between the cheeks of my bottom through my clothes, or scratched my crotch? Have I cried over Sigurd, have I screeched in anger or broken anything?

"Do you know how long it's been there?" I finally ask Arild, my voice thick and dry.

"It's impossible to say," he says. "Maybe two days, maybe two months."

"Perhaps it's the police," I mumble, more for my own sake, but Arild says:

"I doubt it. I think they'd use better equipment. This is the kind of stuff anyone could get hold of. You can buy most of it for a few hundred kroner. There's several stores that carry these kinds of things in Oslo, or you can order them online."

A shiver travels the length of my spine. The kind of stuff

anyone could get hold of. I clear my throat. Try to breathe, and start again.

"Arild," I say, "have you checked the whole house for equipment?"

"I've got a pretty good overview of the cellar and ground floor."

"Could I ask you to do something? Could you search the entire house? Go through the rooms as thoroughly as you can? I'll pay for the extra time – I just need to know that nobody can spy on me."

"Of course," Arild says.

"I'll see you soon."

"Yes. See you."

I'm shaking so much my knees threaten to buckle under me as I get up and cross the floor of my room. If I didn't want to see my father before, I have even less desire to do so now. Two days or two months. Two months is an eternity in a life as it plays out in the kitchen; how much might someone have learned about me, about us, from spying on us for two months? All the things we talk about. All the things we *don't* talk about. All the tense, uneasy silences, all the hints that go unacknowledged – half-questions, half-complaints, a half-joke that doesn't quite manage to hide the pain and sadness beneath the surface. That go unanswered. Me with my invitations, asking Sigurd, "Are you coming to bed soon?" Him answering, without looking up from his computer, "Yeah, I'll be up soon." And then it takes two hours for him to get up, to move. And someone has been able to sit and watch all this.

I creep down the stairs. I hear nothing, but I know that he's here. I can see it down in the hallway: the smart shoes, the trainers, the ski boots. And now a pair of winter boots, too. I shove my feet into my own shoes and then, hearing the sound of footsteps somewhere, I grab my jacket, open the front door, and leave as quickly as I can without running. Take brisk steps down the drive. For a moment I think of my flight from Mrs Atkinson's apartment. As soon as I'm out on the street, I start to run.

But it's no use letting fear get the upper hand. It's about staying composed; trying to understand. You often realise you know a lot if you just stop and think for a moment. For example – when I spoke with Gundersen this morning and told him that Old Torp's revolver was missing, he asked me, almost irritated, whether there was anything else I'd forgotten. "No other weapons?" he asked me. "Hunting rifles or flamethrowers – or what do I know? No old, attractively decorated instruments of torture? *No intricate surveillance systems?*"

I'd interpreted it as sarcasm. I'd hung up, thinking he was losing patience with me. But it was a peculiar example to bring up. From a revolver, via flamethrowers and instruments of torture, to surveillance systems. How did he end up there? What did that have to do with anything?

I've reached Smestad station. The board indicates that my train will arrive in five minutes. A group of teenagers are standing and chatting in a cluster a little further up the platform from me. They seem absorbed in their discussion and there's nobody else around. Fuck it, I think, and call him.

"Gundersen," he says.

"What's the deal with the surveillance system?" I say.

"Sara?"

"Why are there surveillance cameras in my house?"

"Just a minute."

I hear footsteps, sounds as if he's opening and closing a door, and then he says:

"Yes, the cameras. Yes."

"Are they yours?"

He sighs.

"No."

"But you knew about them?"

"Yes. Fredly's team found them when they were searching the house."

That was several days ago.

"Right," I say, and then it's thundering through me, the injustice of it, of someone watching me when I thought I was alone. "And it didn't occur to you that you ought to tell me? It didn't occur to you that I might be interested to know someone was watching me? Listening to me?"

He's silent. Uncharacteristically silent, I'd say.

"What the fuck, Gundersen?" I yell.

The teenagers further down the platform look over at me now.

"You let me just keep on as before, wandering around in a house that's been broken into several times – *you let me stay there* without my knowing that someone might be watching me."

"I understand that you're angry."

"You *understand* that I'm angry? Oh, well, that's O.K., then. I really don't give a fuck whether you understand that I'm angry – I just want to know who's been spying on me! I want to know who's installed fucking cameras in my house!"

"Sara, just calm down. Listen to me."

"You mentioned it to me earlier today, when we spoke on the phone and I told you about the missing gun. You asked me. Sarcastically. Almost as a joke, I thought. 'Any intricate surveillance systems?'"

"Yes," he says with a sigh. "It was stupid of me. But I wanted to check. Whether you knew anything about it."

"I see. And I didn't, and so you thought it fine to leave me in a state of blissful ignorance?"

He sighs again, heavily. My anger is starting to ebb away, too. There's no point to any of this.

"We did find the surveillance system. Fredly called me. I had to make a decision. Someone had set up some cameras. It might have been you, to watch Sigurd. It might have been Sigurd, to watch you. It might have been a third party, who wanted to spy on one or both of you. Or it might have been there for our benefit – you might have set them up so that we'd find them. Might have wanted to give us the impression that someone was spying on you."

"And what good would that have done?" I say, very tired now.

"I can think of several possibilities," he says. "The point is that when we found the cameras they could have meant many things. Fredly asked me what we should do with them. And my thoughts were as follows: if I asked you about them, you'd say you didn't know anything about them. And that wouldn't get me very far. But if I didn't mention it, just waited to see what would happen, their significance might reveal itself."

"And has it revealed itself?"

"Well," he says, "I'm still not a hundred per cent sure why they're there. But I've ruled out a few alternatives. Let's put it that way."

"And while you've been ruling out alternatives some sicko or other has had access to my private life?"

"Maybe so. And I'm sorry about that, Sara. I really am."

"Yeah, well," I say resignedly. "The fact that you're sorry doesn't help me. But while you're being so open about all this, perhaps you can tell me how many cameras you found?"

"Three. One in the hallway, one in the kitchen, and one in your bedroom."

"One in the bedroom?"

"Yes. That one had a microphone attached to it."

On the train on the way home, I cry. First silently. And then not so silently.

Nobody says anything. Nobody looks in my direction. I've become the woman nobody wants to acknowledge. The embarrassing woman crying loudly in public. Maybe they think I'm drunk. Maybe they would have more compassion for me if they knew that my husband died less than a week ago. But perhaps most worrying of all, I don't care what they think. I just bawl my eyes out, all the way from Smedstad to Majorstuen, the entire time I stand on the platform at Majorstuen, and then on the Songsvann line towards Nordberg. Nobody sits next to me.

Arild has taken down all three cameras and set them on the kitchen counter so I can take a look. They're small, the size of the tiny erasers on the end of mechanical pencils, with a short cable attached. At their base is a flat circle the size of a one-kroner coin. That's the transmitter, Arild explains. It sends data to the recipient's computer, or even to his mobile. For a moment there's an inkling of admiration in Arild's voice – just think what's possible with modern technology! Then he shows me the pieces of black tape used to hold the cameras in place: the one in the hallway on the edge of the ceiling lamp; the one in the kitchen on the inside of the refrigerator grill; the one in the bedroom on a lamp. The microphones are just as small, and the cameras in both the kitchen and the bedroom had microphones attached. If they're cunningly hidden, they're extremely difficult to spot. Arild isn't sure whether he'd say these were cunningly hidden – they were half-hidden, perhaps – but they're easy to overlook if you don't know what you're looking for, and especially if you have no reason to suspect that they would be there at all. He has conducted a thorough search of the house. He can't rule out the possibility of something being in the loft, but the cellar, stairs, and the ground and first floors he's sure about. The rooms in which I spend my time are now surveillance-free.

Then he shows me my security system – and it consists of some serious equipment. Outside the front door is a light with a motion sensor. If anyone comes within range of the sensor, the light will turn on. There's another one of these by the terrace door.

"Don't be scared if one of them gets triggered," Arild says. "Very often, it's just a cat. But if you're a person looking to break in somewhere, and you suddenly find yourself lit by a floodlight, you'll be in for a real shock."

There's also a camera outside, attached just under the roof above the front door. All this gives me a wonderful sense of satisfaction: now I'm the one installing the cameras. The camera continually records and sends the footage to the security centre in Økern, as well as to me. Arild helps me to download an app so that I can watch the video on my mobile. We log in, and see the empty front doorstep.

I now also have the mother of all locks on the front door, a huge thing with several keys and a fat safety chain on the inside. Arild shows me how motion detectors have been installed in the hallway and the kitchen, on the veranda, and on the stairs up to the first floor. They were installing these when they found the cameras. He's attached a camera to the wall outside my bedroom, so that I can also have eyes on the stairs and outside my bedroom door. He shows me how yet another hefty lock on the bedroom door works, and hands me a set of keys that looks as if it might belong to a caretaker. The bedroom window now has a reinforced hinge, so that I can leave it open at night, sure that it's almost impossible for anyone to crack it open. If the alarm is triggered it'll howl like a banshee throughout the entire house, as well as at their constantly manned security centre, where one of Arild's two apprentices, Kristoffer or the other trainee, will be sitting, keeping an eye on things. The instant the alarm is triggered the apprentice will jump into the car and call me on the way. Arild shows me how I can turn off the alarm, but recommends that I let it scream for a couple of minutes to scare away the intruder. Kristoffer will say "octavia" when he calls, to which I will answer "risotto". The code words have been set by him, in case the intruder is someone who knows my way of thinking. It all seems very complex, and I like it. I like everything about it – the bunch of keys, the app for the surveillance video, the code words. I feel safe.

It's almost eight by the time Arild is ready to leave. It must be way past his normal working hours.

"Thank you for being so kind," I say.

He shrugs, looks young all of a sudden.

"I have a daughter," he says. "If it was her . . ."

We say our goodbyes and he drives away. I go back inside, lock the front door, put on the safety chain and go upstairs. Look around me at my house, secured like a fortress.

I'm home.

Now things will be different, we promise each other. We raise our glasses of cheap bubbly as the New Year's fireworks colour the sky red and blue and green. We'll take Tenerife home with us – all this, which is who we really are, which is really us, we say to each other. After all, this is how it used to be. We've always had fun together. Always taken care of one another. It's just that there's been so much that's happened over the past year – the house, the money, the work. But things will be different now.

"I'm going to stop using snus," Sigurd says. "It's a stupid thing to do anyway."

"I'll stop nagging so much," I say. "I know that all the work on the house takes time, that you're doing the best you can."

"I'll stop bugging you about finding more patients."

"I'll support you when you're busy at work and have to work long days."

"I won't work as many long days," Sigurd says. "I'll make sure that improves. I'm done with Atkinson."

We seal our agreement with a kiss. Things will be different now. But we're already afraid. As if even mentioning our everyday lives in Oslo, while here on holiday where we're having such a good time, threatens to ruin everything. Afterwards, we say no more about it.

It starts well. Sigurd works fewer evenings; I stop mentioning the fact that our bathroom isn't finished. We go out together every now and again – not anything expensive, but we eat dinner at a pub and go to the cinema occasionally. On my birthday Sigurd books a table at a mid-priced restaurant and we have a few drinks and try to resurrect the atmosphere from Tenerife. We sort of manage it. We're home by half past midnight; make love before we fall asleep.

When does it change? When Sigurd starts working more? One day in February when he comes home late he says he's been to the Atkinsons' again – "She never fucking gives up," he says. Now there's less light in the stairwell than she'd imagined, and he has to start all over again. I find a box of snus in his jacket pocket.

"Are you using snus again?" I ask him. He sighs heavily.

"It helps me stay focused when I'm working late," he says.

It won't be like before, he says to me – it's just for a while. I brush my teeth wearing sandals because the concrete floor of the bathroom is freezing cold, and then I think, why should I hold back when he doesn't?

"Not to sound the way I used to," I say, "but it's so cold in the bathroom, I don't know how much more I can take. Couldn't we make an effort this weekend – have a look at tiles and heating options for the floor? Just to get started?"

"And how are we going to pay for that?" Sigurd says. "My pockets aren't exactly overflowing with cash these days – maybe yours are different?"

Not like before, we say. We won't hold anything against one another. We have to be able to mention the challenges of everyday life.

I'm not sure when we slid back into our old ways; I think it must have happened gradually. Just as we gradually stopped talking about how things were different from how they'd been before Christmas, things gradually stopped being different, too.

Sigurd working longer hours – sending a text: I'll be late. Home nine or ten. He eats leftovers in the kitchen, or a sandwich if I haven't made anything. I prepare a proper dinner more and more rarely, *because what's the point? He sits in front of the T.V., his laptop on his knees. I go to bed first. He says he'll be up soon. I'm often asleep by the time he comes to bed. Even if I'm still awake, we're too tired for anything other than a quick kiss. He's out of the house in ten minutes in the mornings. I never go anywhere; am always at home.*

He tells me he's taking a cabin trip with the guys, and I suppress the urge to ask him how on earth he has time for that when the bathroom is still unfinished. I get an e-mail from Ronja – she's in Argentina, teaching English and learning the tango. I have no-one to take a cabin trip with.

It's dark outside when he leaves, early that morning. I wake as he leans over me and kisses me on the forehead.

"I'm going now," he whispers. "Just go back to sleep."

I hear his footfall on the stairs, but must be asleep before the door clicks shut behind him.

Friday, March 13: Krokskogen

The ringing shakes me violently awake. Although ringing isn't right – the sound is more invasive than that. More a roaring or howling. I jump into a half-sitting position, fumbling half-blind through the objects on the bedside table for my mobile so I can orient myself, but give up and cover my ears with a pillow first. I clamp the pillow over both ears with one arm as I manage to find my mobile with the other. It's four-thirty in the morning and the display says *ALARM! ALARM! ALARM!* in capital letters and irascible exclamation marks. I get up, bare feet slapping across the cold floor and still holding the pillow over my head as I cross the room to the control panel Arild installed for me. I have first to identify myself by fingerprint and then enter a code, and all the while the alarm continues to shriek its stabbing thrusts, angry and threatening, so loud that it hurts my ears when I can no longer keep them covered with the pillow. I enter the code incorrectly the first time because the pillow slips, and the panel emits a high-frequency, piercing beeping that can only be heard in the space between two blasts of the alarm. On my second attempt I get the code right, and the howling stops.

The silence is unfamiliar after all the racket. I have to hand it to Arild – he's installed a proper alarm. It wouldn't surprise me if half of Nordberg were on their feet after this. I sink down onto the bed, feeling deaf after the blaring siren, as if I can no longer hear the usual sounds of the night – the creaking of the timber, the wind outside, a car moving down Carl Kjelsens vei or the train down at Holstein station – because my hearing has been muffled by the noise. Then my telephone buzzes.

"Hello," I say.

My voice is small in the silence left in the alarm's wake.

"Octavia," says the voice on the other end.

"Risotto," I say.

"This is Kristoffer from Arild's Security."

"Hi."

"Is everything O.K.?"

I haven't managed to check.

"I think so," I say.

"Where are you?"

"In my bedroom."

"Is the lock untouched?"

I go across to the door and check. The thick chain is hanging there, just as it was when I went to bed. I tug on the door; it's firm in its frame.

"Yes," I say. "It seems so."

"Good," says Kristoffer. "I'm on my way down to the garage now. I'll be with you in around fifteen minutes. Just stay in the bedroom for now – I'll check the house when I arrive."

"O.K.," I say.

For someone so young, the apprentice seems to have a great deal of authority in a crisis.

"In the meantime, you can take a look at the video footage," he says.

It feels good to have something to do. I open the app as soon as I've hung up. Sitting on the bed, I can see what happened at the front door from five minutes before the alarm was triggered. Arild's system has an element of empowerment in it. From having been so unprotected, left to a police force that hasn't communicated with any noticeable care for me, I now have control myself. I tap the playback icon and see a dark screen where nothing has happened just yet, and feel a certain satisfaction at the fact that I'm now spying on my spy.

For the first minute I stare at the empty screen. Then, out of the blue, the light comes on. I see my front step, and on it a figure dressed in black, a hand stretched out towards my door. The figure freezes in the light, stands there for a moment, very still. Then it pulls out of the camera's field of view. A few minutes pass, and nothing happens. At the bottom of the screen a text appears: *Automatic light activated 04:33.* After two minutes the light turns itself off. I wait. Almost another two minutes pass. Then the light turns on again, an object passing across the screen so quickly that I almost can't see it at all, it's gone, and then the text *ALARM!* appears below the image, in the same warning script as when I checked my mobile. Nothing else happens. If the spy has gone or attempted to break in somewhere else I don't know, but since the alarm hasn't gone off again it seems he hasn't managed to get into the house. I change the view to the camera in the stairwell. It's empty.

Several minutes pass, and nothing happens. The worst of my tension begins to fade, and with my mobile in my hand, sitting in my secured control room, I feel fairly safe. I have the kitchen knife there on Sigurd's bedside table, in case I should need to defend myself, but it seems unlikely I'll need to use it. Just the thickness of the security chain keeping the door in place puts the idea to shame. I've fortified myself. Have got myself the protection I needed.

I watch the video again. This time I notice that the dark screen isn't totally dark; the glow of a distant street lamp makes it possible to see the outline of the figure dressed in black before the sensor is triggered. Then the image is flooded with light, and the black figure, moving until this point and stretching out a hand, stands still, then pulls away. Quickly. Backwards. As if he'd burned his fingers on something. I play the video back again. The sequence is so short; just six seconds. I watch it over and over again.

The figure dressed in black isn't frightening. First, he's terrified of the light – there's something pathetic about it. It isn't what I would have expected from a psychopathic murderer. Second, he's thinner than I imagined, more limp. In fact, the more times I watch the film, the clearer this becomes. Perhaps he's a young boy, or maybe my spy is a woman. I can see nothing of the figure's face; it's wearing a hat pulled low, and from the moment the light comes on it keeps its face looking down. Perhaps this is a clever move, to prevent its face being seen by the camera. But it's also cowardly. To withdraw, head bowed.

Yes – the more I watch the recording, the safer I feel. So this figure is what's been scaring the pants off me since Sigurd disappeared. This skittish, slim person has made me so paranoid I'd started to fear for my sanity. This figure – who freezes as soon as a light is turned on him, or her. Who backs out of sight, head bowed, like a scolded dog. Who I now have control over, have scared away – have captured on camera.

First it makes me want to laugh. I pause the video at the moment in which the black figure takes its first step back, away from the door. Then anger surges within me, from my stomach and up my throat. My arms and legs are filled with energy and intent; my breathing is hard and heavy. I take the kitchen knife from Sigurd's bedside table, get up from the bed, disarm the alarm, and go across to the door and unlock it.

The house is dark and silent. I walk quickly down the stairs, the knife in one hand. Once I've seen that the living room and kitchen are untouched I become braver, truly tearing down the stairs, stamping my feet as I go. I'm so eager that I forget about the loose treads; painfully stub the toes of my left foot against one of them.

The frosted glass panel Sigurd put in the front door has been shattered; through the round, gaping hole I can see out towards the trees at the bottom of the drive. The cool night air seeps in. On the floor is an object, surrounded by a few shards of broken glass. I go across to it, squat down before it. Pick it up. Hold it in my hand.

It's a *garnkule* made of glass. Hanging from it is a key and a paper label. The key is shiny. On the label, written in Margrethe's careful, slanting handwriting: *Krokskogen.*

I'm sitting at the kitchen table when Kristoffer arrives. I hear him parking his car; letting himself in; crossing the floor down there and opening a couple of doors. Then he makes his way up the stairs. He starts when he sees me.

"Hi," I say.

"Hi," he says. "Is everything O.K.?"

"Yes."

"I saw blood down there."

"Oh," I say, looking down at my foot, "that's just mine. I mean, I stubbed my toe. Nothing to worry about."

He nods.

"I thought you were going to stay in the bedroom?"

"They threw something into the house. I had to see what it was."

He doesn't look convinced, so I keep going:

"It could have been a firebomb, or, a what-d'you-call-it – a Molotov cocktail."

"What was it?"

I gesture towards the key, which lies on the table before

me. He moves closer to it, squinting at it, stooping to take a proper look.

"What is it?"

"It's a *garnkule*. They're used as floats on fishing nets. They come in different sizes so you can manoeuvre nets of different weights."

I hear the echo of Sigurd as I speak. The misplaced and incomprehensible pride he took in the souvenir that had been his father's, as if neither I nor anyone else he told about it could understand. Kristoffer looks at me, confused.

"Our cabin key is attached to it," I say.

"Oh. Right."

Kristoffer goes out to secure the house, looking upstairs, downstairs, in the loft and cellar, in cupboards and storerooms. It takes him just over half an hour. I feel so calm – I'm in control. The *garnkule* lies before me and I stare at it – it's as if the answer might be found there, in the dark green glass that reminds me of the sea.

"Have you called the police?" Kristoffer says once he's finished securing the house.

"No," I say, without looking up from the glass sphere.

"We probably should."

"Soon."

I don't move. The key has come back to me, an intruder has thrown it through the glass panel, and yet it looks so innocent, there on the table. Just a bubble of glass, some twine and the key to a front door. What does it mean? Why was it returned in this way? Is it a challenge, or an invitation? Or a hint?

I'm not afraid. *Krokskogen*. It seems so easy, so simple. Inside the sphere, behind the mesh of the crocheted twine, it's as if I catch a glimpse of something. But it only lasts for a moment, and then it's gone.

"O.K., then," the apprentice says.

He looks at me; I look at the glass ball.

"I should get back to the office," he says.

"O.K.," I say.

He waits. Wants me to say something more, to look at him, but I feel so far away. Out of the corner of my eye I can see that he's observing me, standing there with his arms at his sides and waiting for me to come to my senses, and somewhere, in the very back of my mind, it dawns on me – there are social norms to be adhered to when someone is a visitor in your house – you should listen to them, respond to what they say, see them to the door. But I have no time for that. Because if I just concentrate on the *garnkule* long enough, that glimmer of understanding might come back.

"You should call the police," Kristoffer says.

"Hmm," I say.

"Do you feel able to do that?"'

"Yes," I say, momentarily pulling my gaze away from the object on the table. "Yes, I'll call them when they're awake."

"There'll be people on duty there now – you can call them right away."

"I mean, Gundersen," I say, returning my gaze to the *garnkule*. "I'll call Gundersen in a few hours. When I'm sure he'll be awake."

There's no rush. I'll call the police when I'm ready. They'll get the message, but not before I feel it's time. And I have all the time in the world.

"O.K.," Kristoffer says. He stands there for a minute or two, but when I say nothing more he shoves his hands in his pockets and leaves. Does he say goodbye? I don't know. I'm not paying attention. I hear his car start. Outside, the sky is starting to brighten.

At around six, I get up from my chair and make breakfast. I eat well. The *garnkule* is lying beside me, and I glance at it every now and then. The fridge door is bare now – I've taken down the magnets – but I don't feel afraid looking at it. If anything, I feel content. The key has come back. There's no denying that there's something threatening about its return, but at the same time it feels as if something is about to become clear to me. As if the answer is now so tangible, so close, that I need only reach out and touch it. I know what I have to do.

I drink a large glass of juice. I shower and get dressed. I make the bed; put my plate and glass in the dishwasher. I take a rucksack from one of the hallway cupboards. Put the kitchen knife in it, just in case. Take the *garnkule* with me, too. But before I put it in the bag, I hold it up in front of me. Smell it. Does this trigger anything? I'm not sure. I stand this way for a while, the coarse net pressed to my nose, and in the end think it smells only of salt water.

At seven o'clock I put on the alarm, go out, and lock the door behind me. Feeling calm, and with my bag on my back, I set off towards the T-banen.

It's the kind of early spring day when it feels as if summer might be just around the corner. I'm in a hire car, driving out of the city, against the general flow of the traffic and with my sunglasses on. It's good to drive – the car does my bidding. I should have brought some music with me, that's the only thing that's missing, but soft rock is playing on the radio and that's good enough. I hum along, feel a wonderful energy coursing through me. I know what I have to do. I also know that I'm taking a risk – the slim figure dressed in black with a hat over its head is certainly more foe than friend. Looking at it like that, Kristoffer is right – I should call the police. But on the other hand . . . I need to know what happened. Whatever the cost. The road before me is lit by the sun as I drive alongside Tyrifjorden, bare birch trees clinging to the rocky mountainsides. Up ahead, at the edge of the forest, there's still snow.

This is the road taken by Sigurd almost a week ago – I can't believe coming up here has not occurred to me before now. I imagine I am him, and at the same moment feel a pang of uncertainty. But it feels as if I'm getting closer to him. As if I'm starting to understand.

I park on the road a short distance before Kleivstua, sling the bag onto my back and start to make my way into the forest. It isn't far to walk, fifteen minutes perhaps, twenty at a stroll. There's a slight uphill climb at the start. In some places the path is almost grown over, and every now and then the occasional stone pops up in the middle of it – I'm forced to step aside, walk off the track. Only the path is clear – snow still lies around it – and I step into half-melted snowdrifts several times. I get a little out of breath.

It's a long time since I've been here, and I've maybe only been three or four times in total. I have never much enjoyed being at the cabin, which doesn't have running water, so you have to go to the loo in a freezing cold shack. After about a quarter of an hour I start to wonder whether I may have taken a wrong turn – I don't remember the pile of stones I can see beside me. Nor do I recall the trees being quite so dense – and wasn't I supposed to pass a bog? My self-confidence from the drive up starts to slip away. I'm sweating. This isn't what I imagined, the way I thought this would go. I had the idea that I would sail into the forest; that the cabin would be standing there, bathed in sunlight, and enlightenment would wash over me the moment I touched the handle of the front door. Gundersen would never have let me come up here, and that's why I haven't called him. Now I'm starting to wonder whether I should have told him what I was planning, after all. I consider taking out my mobile and giving him a call. Maybe I could check the G.P.S. at the same time. But then I see the cabin, a little further up the hillside, shielded from the path by some tall spruces. My memory was correct.

Krokskogen forest is dense, but the cabin itself lies in a clearing atop a knoll, with a kind of view – at least, you can catch a glimpse of the Tyrifjorden from the veranda. Sigurd's father, the principled woodsman with the mild smile, had it built before Sigurd was born. It's small and spartan. The solar panel that provides electricity was installed after his death. The cabin's timber is stained brown, and it has the small, square windows that are typical of cabins all across the country. When I make it up onto the stoop I stand there for a moment, leaning against the railing, to get my breath back.

It's so quiet here. The cabin is isolated – I can see nothing but trees and glimpses of the fjord between the treetops. I hear no sounds from the road, nor any birds. Were it not for the slight breeze gently rustling the bushes, there would be no sounds to be heard at all. The spruces are so dark – I've always disliked them, this dense wall of forest that encloses the cabin. But now that I'm standing here, watching the surface of the Tyrifjorden glitter between the trees, I have to admit that the forest can be beautiful, too. I hope that's how it seemed to Sigurd – that his final hours were beautiful.

I dig around in my bag and fish out the *garnkule*. It sits satisfyingly heavy in my hand, the key just a tiny appendage to the sphere of glass. I look at it, trying to recall the calm I felt earlier in the day, without success. I feel a little uneasy now; the darkness of the forest has lodged in my chest. But the key slides into the lock without friction. The heavy door swings open on its well-oiled, well-maintained hinges.

Everything is quiet inside, too. In the living room the items of furniture stand there, turned towards one another, as if deliberating a question. Along the wall facing me is the kitchen counter, and on it a plate and an empty glass. One of the chairs around the kitchen table has been pulled out, as if whoever was using it has just popped out for a moment. Nothing suggests that half a dozen police officers in heavy boots have tramped their way through here. They must have taken great pains to put everything back in its proper place. I stand there with my back to the front door, hesitating. Then I pull myself together.

The air isn't as stuffy as you would expect. I set down my bag beside the front door and cross the floor. The floorboards creak as I step on them; they're getting old. I go over to the kitchen chair, the one that's been pulled out. Is this where Sigurd sat that morning? Or did a police officer take a seat here, and forget to push the chair back in upon leaving?

A narrow passage leads off the kitchen to two bedrooms: one for Margrethe, one for the boys. I walk down to the doors; enter Margrethe's room. There's the uncomfortable double bed with its pine frame, a patchwork quilt spread across it. There's the pine wardrobe, and the small iron wall lamps with their checked shades. I trail my fingers across the bedspread. There are no indentations in the duvet, no sign that anyone has sat on the bed.

The door to the boys' room is locked. I tug on the handle, but it's stuck.

This surprises me. I didn't even know it could be locked

and have never seen a key in it – but it has a keyhole, so there must be a key. I try it a couple more times, shoving my weight behind the door.

Why would it be locked? Did Sigurd lock it? Or did the police?

I go back to the living room. There's something I can't quite put my finger on, some detail I'm missing. I look around. Trail my fingers along the mantelpiece. Not a fleck of dust.

The plate on the kitchen counter has been used – there are crumbs on it. In the sink are a few drops of water. The empty milk glass beside the plate has a white ring around its edge, and above this a faint layer of condensation, as if the glass was recently filled. As if the coldness of the milk still hangs there within it. I press a finger against a breadcrumb on the plate; roll its coarseness against my thumb. There's a small piece of cheese beside it – I press my finger against this, too. It is soft, gives way. Has no crust, no beads of sweat. Is cold, as if it's just been taken out of the fridge. I press it down against the plate.

I have to get out of here. Have to take my bag and run, as fast as I can. But I only stand there, as if my eyes are glued to the worktop, staring at the crumbs. My body is so heavy, as if it would take infinite energy to move it. Or maybe it's just that the moment is over so fast. Because the second I realise, it's already too late.

A tinny sound reverberates between the walls in the silence: the click of the lock on the boys' bedroom door.

It's too late to run. I hear footsteps coming down the corridor and it feels as if the moment lasts and lasts, as if, as I stand there beside the kitchen counter, my back to the living room, I'm waiting.

The footsteps stop behind me. I hear breathing, feverish and quick, and then she says:

"Turn around."

I don't want to face her, but it can't be helped. I turn as slowly as I can. See her stockinged feet on the polished wooden floor, the tattered cuffs of her sweater, the bracelet with its tiny silver pearl, her hands wrapped around something metallic. The blonde hair in a ponytail. Am I surprised? I don't know who I was expecting to see. It's as if my mind is too thick, too viscous.

"Vera?" I say, and I say it as a question, as if I can't quite believe this is happening.

We stand there facing each other, staring. Vera is focused. Her jaw is tense. Then she slowly raises her hands. The metallic object they are holding is a revolver. I can't be sure, but it looks like the revolver that belonged to Old Torp. I feel cold looking at it – I'm not sure why. I've never had a weapon pointed at me before, and this frozen feeling is unlike anything I've ever experienced. As if I'm sinking into an ice-cold mountain lake. Only the sensation is coming from inside me.

"Vera?" I ask again. She says nothing. Presses her lips together. I take in every detail about her, have never before examined anyone so intently. The curls at her temples that have escaped from her ponytail; the light flush in her cheeks from clenching her jaw. There is what looks like an acne scar on the side of her nose – it must have been there a long time, so how have I never noticed it before? The nails of the fingers clutching the revolver have been bitten to the quick, but I can hardly see them because I can't look straight at the revolver – it's like trying to look directly at the sun. But she's aiming it at me, I can see that. This is more than just a threat, more than just a play for attention. She concentrates on holding the weapon level, has me right in the line of fire. She's only eighteen, a secondary school student. I can't imagine what good it would do her to shoot me.

"Wait," I say.

I stretch out my hand. Want to say something. Stop her. Help us out of the situation.

"Don't move," she says.

Her tone is sharp with the obstinacy that sometimes flares up in her, "Do you even have any friends at all?" I withdraw my hand. She's already decided.

She cocks the weapon. The silver bracelet around her wrist slips down her forearm to the cuff of her sweater.

Now I have to be smart, be the adult. Be the therapist. Find an opening, the right words for the moment. Hit exactly the right note. There must be a way out, must be words I can say that will reach her. I take a breath.

"No," she says, before I can say anything. "Today we're not going to fucking talk."

She aims. Concentrates. Narrows her eyes. Her jaw quivers. She's afraid, too – she must be, or agitated at the very least – but she doesn't want to be helped out of this. Especially not by me. She knows better than everyone else, needs no-one.

My breath comes faster, shallower. I know that I should do something. Appeal to her compassionate side, to the person behind the gun. But I'm losing my grip – the words seem to be slipping away. I can't think – not like this, with a revolver pointed at me. I'm weak at the knees. So small. Have nothing to say.

"Vera," I say again.

There's nothing more to do. Is this how it all ends? I close my eyes.

Saturday, March 14: Waiting, spinning

I wake with a start, my neck aching. I didn't intend to fall asleep.
I was tired, so decided to lie down on the uncomfortable sofa.
The clock on the wall beside the door says it's ten past midnight.
It's Saturday, technically. My neck has been twisted, my head
halfway up the armrest. Not the ideal position to sleep in. But
I've been in this room for almost nine hours. I've tried sitting
quietly on the sofa, sprawling in the armchair; I've tried wander-
ing around, stretching, lying down.

I haven't asked anyone whether I can go home – I'm afraid
of the answer. They're the police. They might decide to transfer
me to a cell. In the meantime, I've been left in this room, in
limbo. Not detained, nor free to go.

I was questioned in the middle of the day. Two police officers
interviewed me, a man in his sixties, grey and ordinary as sliced
bread, and a younger one, a woman who looked to be of South
East Asian descent. They were professional. Serious. They asked
me to tell them what had happened, so I told them. Started with
Arild's Security. Told them how the break-in had bothered me,
how the city police had failed to take it seriously. They were
impressively expressionless, nodded to indicate that they understood, but didn't show any embarrassment on behalf of their
organisation, seeing as I now have photographic evidence of the
intruder – that I was right all along. I tell them about the alarm
being triggered, about the figure in black on my front doorstep;
about the key to the cabin in Krokskogen. About Vera aiming
Sigurd's grandfather's revolver at me. This they were less

interested in, but they had a few follow-up questions about the break-in.

Attempted break-in, we should say. I sign a form that grants them permission to obtain the video footage from Arild Security. They can have whatever they want. The woman accompanies me to this room. On the way I ask her where Gundersen is.

"The investigation is in a critical phase right now," she says. "That's why you've not been given much information up to this point."

This doesn't answer my question. Or maybe it does. I don't know, and daren't ask any more questions. I'm already so tired, so heavy-headed. I've been thinking, my mind racing since the early hours – since the moment I stood there in the kitchen while Vera pointed the revolver at me. It's been a lot of work, all this thinking – I no longer have it in me to be logical. The investigators with their stern expressions said nothing about their opinions, about what they thought. When the woman has gone, I start to shiver again. Do they think I killed Sigurd? I didn't dare ask.

As Vera cocked the weapon I closed my eyes, and just then, when I thought she was about to pull the trigger, we heard footsteps on the front porch – I hadn't locked the door after me and it was thrown open with full force. We looked towards it, both of us. Into the room stormed Fredly, red in the face and sweaty-browed so that her dark auburn hair curled at her temples, in full uniform, tie and all. The three of us stood there, taking each other in, it couldn't have been for more than a hundredth of a second, but to me it seemed that time had stopped, as if I could return to it now and look around, examine all the details of that instant, Fredly's skin, the way in which her nostrils flared, how she stared at us with wide-open eyes. And Vera. The acne scar, the ponytail. Eyes huge, mouth open, but with no air moving in or out of her. She stood stock-still, holding her breath.

Fredly lowered her hand to her hip and drew her weapon; cocked it and pointed it at Vera.

"Drop the gun," she barked.

Two figures came into view behind her, both also in uniform. I saw something flit across Vera's face with raging speed, but it happened so fast that I was probably the only one who noticed it, because time had started to move so glacially from the moment at which I thought I was going to die. I saw that she reconsidered. She contemplated what she was about to do. Then she let go of Old Torp's revolver – it bounced on Margrethe's rug and lay there. Her eyes narrowed unhappily; she squeezed her lips together and cried:

"Oh my God, stop her!"

She turned to Fredly. Took two steps towards her, wanting to throw herself into her arms, it seemed, but Fredly continued to aim her weapon at her.

"Stop right there!" Fredly shouted.

Vera checked herself; she did stop, in the middle of the room. Her arms hung empty and redundant at her sides. She gave two hiccup-like sobs. I stood there, motionless. The two officers behind Fredly came into the room, one of them stepping on my rucksack, which was still lying on the floor. Both of them were armed. They turned their weapons on me.

Fredly split us up. I was sent into Margrethe's bedroom, with one of her colleagues. He was in his mid-twenties, perhaps, and appeared nervous. He had put me in handcuffs. I let him – not that I could have stopped him, but I didn't even protest, just held out my arms when he asked me to. His face was covered

283

in moles. They would have been repellent had they been pimples, but were not unattractive once you saw them for what they were. His hands were clammy. Afterwards, he walked about the room, still holding his gun in his hand. He didn't take his eyes off me, which was uncomfortable for both of us.

I thought: Vera was planning on shooting me. Was she angry? Was she afraid? Could it be that she had been genuine when she shouted to Fredly, "Oh my God, stop her!"? But there had been something about her when she had aimed the gun at me – pure determination – and that sentence, "Today we're not going to fucking talk." No. The plan had been to shoot me. It must have been she who threw the key through the glass of my front door, to lure me up here. She hadn't looked scared. She was angry – but ready. She had a job to do. And had the police not turned up, she would have finished it.

Fredly entered the room.

"How are you doing, Sara?" she asked, and without waiting for an answer turned to the officer with the moles. "You put her in cuffs?"

He mumbled something about an unclear situation.

"Is she armed?" Fredly said.

"I don't know," he said.

"Then check!"

The officer removed the handcuffs, asked me to hold out my arms, and patted me down in a way that made me think of airport security checks. He was thorough. I just stood there. Fredly checked something on her mobile. When the officer had finished, he withdrew to stand beside the window, leaning against the sill. Fredly continued to look at her telephone. I sat down again, waiting for her. The officer waited, too.

"We're going to get you out of here as soon as we can," Fredly said to me. "We're just waiting for backup."

I nodded. She was efficient, her gaze jumping from one point to the next, looking for unforeseen elements, trying to obtain an overview. I wished she would say something reassuring. "We have her, you're safe now" – something like that. Or: "We've finally solved the case." But then her mobile vibrated.

"We'll talk more later," she said, and left the room.

The officer with the moles returned to pacing around the room, but he kept his handcuffs away from me. Another hour passed before we were able to evacuate the cabin.

The two officers who had burst into the cabin behind Fredly drove me back to the city and accompanied me into the police station. They sat in the front of the vehicle; I sat in the back. Someone else had been detailed to return my hire car. For the entire journey, I did not say a word.

When I arrived, a woman named Janne attended to me. She was wearing plain clothes – I think she was a kind of receptionist. Her name was on a small badge attached to her sweater with a safety pin. She offered me a soft drink and a baguette.

"There's either roast beef or prawn," she said. "But I'd have the prawn if I were you." I did as she suggested.

"Try to eat something," she said. "There's no saying how long you'll be here."

I am grateful for her concern and eat the baguette – which is dry, but I get it down. For the first hour I comfort myself with the fact that Fredly had reprimanded the officer who had put me in handcuffs.

But after my encounter with the serious-faced investigators I find less comfort in the thought. They were so expressionless. It was impossible to know what they were thinking, and nothing they said was reassuring – nothing along the lines of "Relax, you'll be home soon." Wouldn't that have been a reasonable thing to say to someone who's almost been killed?

And so the hours pass. There's nothing to do here. Janne has brought me a stack of old magazines; I browse through them, read about celebrities who have had babies or divorced, but none of it interests me, nothing sticks. I wish Gundersen were here. Wish Fredly would come. Wish somebody could tell me something. Vera's cry floats at the edges of my awareness, popping up at regular intervals, "Oh my God, stop her!"

Janne brings me a cup of coffee. At around four o'clock she gives me a novel which she heartily recommends, its title in a looping font on the cover. It's the story of a British noblewoman who falls in love with the stableman, she says, which makes her family furious – and then the First World War breaks out. I take it. I have no desire to read it, and know that I won't, but I'm just glad someone is being kind to me. I want to ask her straight out – what is my status, how long does she think I'll have to sit here. Or what – in her experience – the usual outcome is, in cases like these. But I say nothing.

At around five o'clock, Janne is replaced by an older, crabbier woman, who is much less solicitous. I try to interpret this turn of events – am I now under stricter surveillance, one step closer to a cell? But none of it has to mean anything. *Breathe and start again*. I only partly manage this. At seven-thirty, I begin the novel Janne gave me. It's actually quite gripping, I have to give her that.

Why would Vera want to kill Sigurd? Why would she spy on us, install cameras, break into the house? Why would she want to shoot me? Gundersen asked me about my patients. Anyone who might hate me, anyone who might be in love with me. I'd responded with a resounding no. But then I had gone back through my list, and although at a stretch I might have had cause to wonder about some of them, it never occurred to me to suggest Vera.

We've had maybe eight therapy sessions together. She comes once a week, never cancels. Her reason for coming is that everything feels meaningless to her – and her relationship difficulties. The older, married lover. Was that Sigurd? Was he having an affair? The fact that Vera is young and has dirty blonde hair hasn't escaped me. Did she decide to seek out the wife for help with the problems she'd encountered as the husband's lover? I get up, pace around the room. Don't want to think about it, but am unable to stop myself.

They meet each other at a bar. Vera is in fact too young to be there but has managed to get in – nobody has asked her for I.D. She's excited, takes a seat at the bar and looks about her, high on her own overconfidence. Sigurd is there with a friend. Passing the time. The friend – probably Jan Erik, yes, surely Jan Erik – wants to go home, and Sigurd says no, stay, just one more beer. He doesn't want to go home to the unfinished house and everything that needs to be done. Doesn't want to go home to me. Goes instead to the bar to buy one last beer, and there she is.

He initiates the conversation, I think. Maybe he says something about the room – "Can you believe how dark it is in here? If they knocked down that wall and put some bigger windows in, the light would be so much better." Something like that. Vera nods, as if Sigurd has said something exceptionally insightful. She agrees. Does he know a lot about that sort of thing? Oh yes, Sigurd says – actually, he's an architect. He smiles, coy and shy – he's only a miserable little cog at a small firm right now, but he has his opinions on current trends. He shares his vision for how the room could have been better designed – it's probably no more than a couple of minutes before he's spouting airy phrases about creating spaces for effective interactions. Jan Erik comes over, I'm going home, he says. Sigurd nods, Jan Erik leaves, and then it's just Sigurd and Vera. Sigurd speaking. Vera listening. And is she not a better audience than me? Does she not listen with real enthusiasm, whereas I stopped listening long ago? Does she not ask follow-up questions, whereas I simply hope that he'll run out of steam? Can he not see it, how she nods with parted lips and attentive eyes, as if she's still ruminating on what he just said – how easily captivated she is by his words? He thinks that she's intelligent. Purely because she listens to him. Maybe he tells her this, too – you're smart, you know. This must hit Vera deep in the chest. She gives him her best smile, yes, thanks, she is indeed pretty smart.

Am I being too mean? Painting them as caricatures – the self-centred man, the naive young woman, the stereotypical encounter? Perhaps it didn't happen like this at all. Maybe Vera's parents are friends of Margrethe. Maybe they met at the summer house she rents in Hankø, that one weekend he went out there alone.

But it doesn't matter how they met. All the scenarios I im- agine are just a prelude to what's next. They rent a hotel room close to the bar. They lock themselves into the annexe at Hankø. They go up to the bedroom of our house in Kongleveien together, or they can't keep their hands off each other as they walk the last stretch of the trail up to the cabin in Krokskogen, where they are finally able to throw themselves at each other, tear off each other's clothes, and my entire body is aflame as I think of it, burning so intensely that I have to increase my pace as I stride from wall to wall in the little room, trying to use up this useless, pounding energy. Why her, Sigurd? Why this – how could you do something like this? How could you have gone behind my back? How could he have met someone else, night after night, every single meeting that was supposedly with Mrs Atkinson? Yes, I know, I'm not completely innocent myself – there was that one unfortunate night in Bergen – but Sigurd, that was just a one-off, and I paid for it. I collapse onto the sofa, don't have the energy to get up again. Lie down. Close my eyes. Just want to sleep, but can't, it's too light in here, the sofa is too hard, and my stomach churns, forcing me to lie almost doubled up in pain. Sigurd, Sigurd, what have you done?

At some point around nine, the crabby woman is replaced by a young man. He doesn't come in and introduce himself, but I see him when I go to get a cup of water from the dispenser beside the reception desk where he's sitting. He's reading, only glances up when he sees me come out. Says nothing, gives no indication one way or another – will my waiting soon be over, is anyone coming to get me? He looks down at his book again. But when I open the door to the waiting room to go back in, I turn and see that he's watching me.

One week ago, on Friday, Vera sat in my office talking about trust. She had ranted at me, "Do you even have any friends at all?" Because she was angry at me, I had thought at the time. At our first ever session, she had taken my hand and squeezed it. Most of my patients look around when they come in, consider the large window and the chairs, the way people do when entering a new space. But not Vera. She had stared at me. Squeezed my hand for longer than is usual. Held it for so long that I had to concentrate on not pulling away, my wedding ring cutting into my crushed fingers.

Had there been the odd moment or two during our sessions in which the discomfort of our first meeting recurred? Once, when the weather was bad, she had come into my office cold and wet. I handed her some tissues and turned up the heater while saying something about the heat making sure she'd dry faster, so she wouldn't get sick. She had flung the tissues on the table and, voice quivering, said, "That's bullshit."

"What is?" I said, but she didn't answer.

Afterwards, once she had dried off a little, I asked her what she had meant. She only shrugged. I interpreted for her: it's as if you were angry at me because I showed some concern for you.

"I was just cold and wet," she said

"You said it was bullshit."

"I meant the weather."

Our sessions were demanding, a struggle – this isn't unusual with patients who are depressed. The weight of the depression, the hopelessness, can be transferred to the therapist, so that both parties end up being left with the feeling that nothing helps. But it wasn't like that with Vera. It was more that we never seemed to get anywhere. She only wanted to talk about her lover. Or the big questions – love, the meaning of life. She wasn't interested in talking about anything else – her parents, school, her friends, her *actual* life. She kept me at a distance. Was she testing me? Was she trying to find out who I was? Or did she want to know things about me, learn something about my life with Sigurd? I try to remember, a little panicked. I tend not to say much about myself to my patients – that kind of information doesn't belong in therapy – but I sometimes mention the odd thing here and there. What have I told Vera about the life that I live?

And then she had called me this week. The answering machine message: "I need to talk, could you call me?" It was untypical of her. Why would Vera need to talk to me right away, before our next scheduled appointment? Could it be that she was finally taking my advice; seeking support when she was struggling? When I had called her she'd said no, it wasn't anything important. At the time it had given me pause, but then it got lost among everything else that was going on.

But I can't think straight when it comes to all this. It's so painful. And I'm tired, worn out by all the waiting, and I'm afraid. I must have fallen asleep on this sofa at around eleven, must have slept for an hour or so with my neck bent, and now it's after midnight, and I'm still banished to this room.

Outside the room in which I'm sitting is a corridor consisting of mainly closed doors – to offices, perhaps, or meeting rooms, or maybe more waiting rooms like this one in which other people like me are sitting and wondering how long they'll have to sit there before someone comes to collect them. Halfway down the corridor is a kind of reception where the young man on night duty is now sitting. I walk up to him. The floor I walk on is curiously frictionless, my shoes don't make a sound against its soft surface. It makes me wonder whether I've been altogether erased.

When I'm standing right in front of him, he looks up. He's reading – the book open in front of him looks like a textbook of some kind, judging from the binding, although I can't be sure.

"I'm just going to the bathroom," I say.

He nods, and points towards the two doors opposite us. As if I haven't already managed to find the toilet after almost twelve hours here.

Above the basin is my reflection. I'm pale, tired, and there's something about my eyes. They're large, the pupils dilated. Maybe it's down to the garish light in here, but I look as if I've seen something truly terrible. After I've been to the toilet I splash water on my face, trying to wake myself. It's the middle of the night, and I haven't slept properly since the alarm went off at around half past four in the early hours of yesterday morning, but who knows when I'll have the chance to go to bed?

At the door to the waiting room I meet an officer in uniform. He's in his forties, with thick, brown hair and round glasses.

"Sara Lathus?" he asks me.

"Yes," I say.

"Right, we're ready to let you go now."

I exhale, my sigh audible.

"Sorry that we've had to keep you here so long," he says as I gather together my few belongings – a sweater, a jacket, my backpack. "There were a few details we needed to clarify, but everything's in order now."

"Good," I say, wearily. I suddenly feel a little indifferent about the whole thing – all I want is a bed.

He sees me out, shows me the way. I shuffle along after him.

"I know you've not been given much information," he says as we walk, "but you will be filled in, I promise. It's just that at this stage of the investigation it's important we keep our cards close to our chest."

"A critical stage," I mumble.

"Exactly," he says. "But you'll be invited to a meeting at which we'll explain the course of events to you – in more detail, that is, than you were given at the interview today."

"O.K."

We take the lift down to the ground floor in silence. We're almost at the main entrance when he speaks again.

"Oh – by the way," he says. "It's best that you don't go home for a few days. We need to carry out some investigations there. Do you have somewhere else you can go?"

"Yes," I say.

"Good. Then we'll be in touch. I'll call a taxi for you."

He turns and goes back inside; I stay standing there. It's cold, and I pull my jacket tighter around me. It occurs to me that I forgot to ask him where Vera is.

The car arrives moments later. An elderly Pakistani man is sitting behind the wheel. I sink into the shiny leather seats of his car.

"Where to?"

"To Nordstrand," I say.

Saturday, March 14 – Monday, March 16: Nordstrand

All I want to do is play with my nephews. I don't want to spend any more time thinking about Sigurd and Vera, about the police investigation or surveillance or revolvers. I want to build Wendy houses; play with Lego and fire engines and pirate ships.

I take the boys to the store to buy sweets, the youngest in the pushchair and the other two babbling away on either side of me, speaking over one another – "Do you know what? Do you know what? Do you know what? Did you know that a witch lives on this street?" I pull a long, surprised face. No – really, a witch? The boys are eager, pointing and explaining, telling me about the time they cycled past one of the houses and she came out onto the steps and called out after them. It's so nice, this. These lovely kids. So concerned with these kinds of things – cycling and football and neighbours who might be witches or wizards. I've never before understood the sheer variety that exists within them.

I become crazy about them. Sit on the floor and build an intricate railway around the coffee table. Get out the plasticine and Perler beads and paper and pens, settle down with them. Surprise myself by remembering old tricks – I can fold a piece of paper into a fortune teller and am good at drawing dogs. I offer to put them to bed, tell their parents to relax while I sit in their rooms with them until they fall asleep. The two older ones sleep in the same room, and I sit on the edge of the bed of one of them and read books and tell stories. Keep it going for longer than they're used to, because it's usually just one book and then lights out, but I tell them as many tales as they want. Deep down, I don't want them to fall asleep. I just want to stay sitting here, telling them stories and chatting with them. But in the end they doze off, and I stroke their hair for a while before I leave the room.

The nights are hard. I don't go to bed until I'm so tired that I'm almost falling asleep in front of the T.V., but once I'm lying on the sofa bed in the basement I find myself wide awake. I try to find strategies to stop my thoughts from churning – I count backwards from one hundred hopping over every third number, try to think of as many city names as I can that start with each letter of the alphabet. Try to trick myself into sleeping with little success. The more tired I become, the more easily Sigurd floats to the forefront of my awareness. As does Vera – I can't stop thinking about her. When I do manage to sleep, I sleep fitfully. I wake without feeling rested, stiff-shouldered and thick-headed, but when I get up the boys throw themselves at me and I tell their parents to go back to sleep, I'll watch them, and sink down onto the floor with the kids, grateful for the respite they give me. On the second night, I wake up thirsty. Annika and Henning's house seems strange and unfamiliar in the dark. It's so quiet. The family are asleep on the top floor, and when I make my way up from the basement to get a glass of water I hear only my own footsteps. Is there nobody turning over in bed? Nobody snoring, or coughing in their sleep? No indication that people are up there, no signs of life? There's not a sound to be heard, other than a car on the road somewhere outside, and the noises I make myself.

As I get myself a drink of water I have the sense that I'm being watched. I don't know how I come to realise this, standing there with the glass under the jet from the tap – but it's as if I catch a glimpse of something out of the corner of my eye. For five freezing seconds I stand stock-still, staring through the window – the dark glass, the outlines of the trees outside, a street lamp and the lights of the neighbouring house. I think: is it Vera? I narrow my eyes, try to focus on the darkness, but see only myself in the light above the kitchen counter. As I take a couple of steps towards the window and see my dressing gown swinging around me, I realise that it was my own movements that caught my attention. I try to smile at this, but without managing to reassure myself. I go on looking at the window, at my reflection as I stand there in my dressing gown. Meet my own gaze as I think how disquieting it is that what I at first thought was Vera was in fact me.

The police are still busy at my house, so I have to borrow a black dress from Annika for the funeral. It hangs baggily around my hips, but that doesn't matter.

While I'm standing in the bathroom of the house in Nordstrand and getting ready to leave, my mobile rings.

"It's Gundersen," the voice says. "I was wondering whether you could come in tomorrow? To the police station? Say at ten o'clock?"

"Yes," I say, adjusting my tights around my waist. "I can do that."

I don't particularly want to. I wish he would just tell me whatever is on his mind right now, over the telephone.

"Good," he says. "Then I'll see you tomorrow. And – good luck. With the funeral service today. I mean, I hope it'll be a nice ceremony."

"Thank you," I say, and then we hang up. And only then do I think, what a bizarre thing for him to say, he's not the type.

The chapel at Vestre Gravlund cemetery is full. Margrethe leans on the son she has left. The area in front of the casket is thick with flowers. Other than that, there's not much to say. Only that the man at the funeral home was right – "Solveig's Song" works. The girl singing is young, with messy red hair and a deep voice. *"Om det skulle gå både vinter og vår."* It's the loveliest moment of the entire ceremony.

Afterwards we stand out on the steps: Margrethe, Harald, Lana Mei and I. We take the hands of everyone who has come. Flemming and Mammod; Thomas, Julie and Jan Erik; Pappa, Annika and Henning. All Sigurd's student friends – their names merge into one another, I no longer remember them. For a moment I think I see Mrs Atkinson at the back, there among all the people, but I can't be sure. And if it is her, she does not come over to greet us.

But Benedicte and Ida do. I didn't know that they would come. I hadn't said anything to them, didn't really know how to tell them. It's probably Annika who called them – she told Pappa, too, sorting things out as usual. Benedicte runs up to where I'm standing on the church steps to hug me and squeeze my hands. "Sara, honey," she whispers into my hair, and only then, in her bear hug and the familiar, dear scent of her, do I start to cry. When she releases me I try to say something about how happy I am that they have come, but all that emerges is a garbled muddle. "Of course we came," says Ida, putting her arms around me, too, and they don't understand, don't know how little I feel I can expect of them.

The most surprising guest is Fredly. She presses my hand, quickly, looking about her, obviously still trying to form an overview of the situation. She's on my side. I can see it in her eyes now, she fixes me with her gaze, as if she wants to tell me something, but when it comes down to it she only offers her condolences.

I spent the entire ceremony wondering whether Vera was

there. I didn't see her before we started, but it would have been just her style to sneak in and observe us, unseen, from a dim nook or hidden gallery. Many times, as we sat there and the priest spoke, and Harald spoke, and the red-haired girl sang, I turned, trying to make out her face from among the rest. I felt her presence in the walls – I couldn't see her, but was sure she was there. Unless the police have her in custody. I have no idea whether this is the case; I didn't ask Gundersen. But if she's free, she will have been here today, watching me. Guaranteed.

Once every last hand has been shaken we go to the car park to make our way to the reception. Annika's boys are bickering a little; Pappa puts an arm around my shoulders. I'm sure this is meant as a supportive gesture, but it's an unfamiliar one for both of us, and neither of us quite knows how to handle it. His arm lies heavy and unmoving against my shoulders, like a dead animal – it's a relief when he removes it. I try to smile at him as best I can, and he smiles back. A little anxiously, it seems to me. Perhaps Annika has told him he has to show me that he cares.

Later, at the reception at the restaurant, Harald speaks again, telling childhood stories – it's like hearing about the life of a stranger. I try to say something, but don't quite manage it – I lose the thread of what I'm trying to say, so wrap it up as quickly as possible, cheers to Sigurd, the best husband I could have wished for. Annika takes my hand when I sit down again; people clap and say cheers regardless. It's an odd atmosphere. Some of his student friends clearly want to celebrate him. One of them speaks, says something about it, "Let's celebrate Sigurd's life, rather than mourn his death." His other friends cheer. We members of the family don't. I catch Mammod's eye. He's not cheering, either – in fact, he looks a little embarrassed.

We leave shortly after that.

Tuesday, March 17: Confirmation bias

He must have been waiting for me, because he appears almost the second the receptionist calls him. He's wearing a faded shirt and worn jeans, and has a kind of plastic card featuring his name and photograph on a lanyard around his neck, but I've never seen this on him before. Otherwise, he's as he usually is, but as I follow him into the building, through the labyrinth of corridors it must take years to learn to negotiate as effortlessly as he does, I ask myself whether he looks the tiniest bit paler than usual. As if he's worn out. Perhaps after several days of hard work with little sleep.

We get ourselves some coffee from a small kitchenette nestled between open-plan offices and corridors of cubicles, deep in the underbelly of the animal that is this building. As Gundersen goes through the cupboards to find mugs, a woman wearing a shirt and blazer comes over, takes my hand and introduces herself as a police prosecutor.

"I'm working on the case," she says. "Gunnar here will fill you in. Unfortunately I won't be there, but I'm sure Gunnar will be thorough and answer any questions you may have. And if you need anything further, you can always call me afterwards."

I nod. Gundersen and I exchange a glance so fleeting as to be imperceptible to her, but we both appear a little embarrassed that she's using his first name. Something about him makes me think that even his mother calls him Gundersen.

He shows me into a meeting room just as spartan as the one I waited in on Friday: pink chairs covered in a woollen fabric of the kind favoured by institutions in the early '90s, a Respatex table with steel legs, a cheap-looking desk lamp on top of it, and a long, rectangular ceiling light suspended on two steel wires. In the corner there's a rubber plant that may be artificial, its leaves covered in a layer of dust. Gundersen takes a seat and indicates that I should sit on the other side. There are two chairs there, and for a moment I think of my office. I take the one on the right, at random. Gundersen sets my cup of coffee in front of me, and there we sit.

"So," he says.

"So," I say.

We look at each other.

"I expect you've given some thought to it," he says. "To what happened on Friday."

I nod.

"Can I – before we start – may I ask you a question?" he says.

"Of course."

"Did you know that it was Vera you were looking for? When you went up to Krokskogen on Friday?"

"No," I say. "Honestly. I had no idea that it was her."

"So as far as you knew, it might have been any old crazed murderer who invited you out into the wilderness? To the scene of a crime?"

"I didn't know it was Vera," I say, looking at my hands, trying to explain. "But I saw her on the video from the security firm and . . . well. There was nothing threatening about the figure on the film. It seemed more . . . pitiable than anything."

It isn't as if I haven't been thinking about this since Friday. But it isn't easy to explain, either. I take a deep breath. Try again.

"I'm not sure you realise just how afraid I've been," I say. "Of course I knew that it might be dangerous. But I just . . . I needed to understand. So I decided to let things play out in whatever

300

way they would. There was a kind of arrogance in that – and, I mean, it isn't as if I still think it was a good idea. But I felt like I was losing my mind there at home, with the cameras and the footsteps in the loft and the fridge magnets. It wasn't only about finding out what happened to Sigurd. It felt like it was about survival."

He looks at me, his head cocked to one side.

"Well, everything turned out fine," he says. "But if I was to tell you just one thing, I'd say you should be eternally grateful to that young lad who works at the security firm. Arild's Security? That young whippersnapper there? He called us in the early hours and told us what had happened. Explained how he thought you might go up there. Sounded as if he was really struggling with the decision to contact us – as if he were breaching confidentiality. Sort of like you, when we spoke about your patients and their notes. Anyway, this boy notified us. Fredly threw herself in the car and was able to get help from a couple of officers from Hønefoss. Thank God, we might say. It could have ended very badly."

He gives me a meaningful look. I nod. Gundersen has worked for the police for a long time. He's probably seen all there is to see. A warning that you shouldn't put your life on the line isn't something to be taken lightly, coming from him.

"Anyway," he says, straightening some papers on the table in front of him: a folder containing sheets of paper, something that looks like printouts of Excel spreadsheets and some pages of printed text, all with notes scribbled in the margins and blank spaces in a cramped, illegible handwriting. "Let's start at the beginning. Vera. Do you have any thoughts about her? I mean, what do you think of her role in all this?"

"Well," I say. "I've thought – I don't know. The most likely explanation is that they were having an affair."

Gundersen nods.

"Yes," he says. "They were. I'm sorry to say."

I receive this news as an expected punch to the gut. The pain is dull, although I know that I'll come to feel it just as intensely as when I sat in the waiting room on Friday night. Only later. Right now, there is only this – a fist in the diaphragm that confirms my suspicions. I take a couple of slow, deep breaths.

Gundersen looks at me over his papers. I wonder how long he's known. I think back to some of our conversations. The one when we sat in my office, and he asked me whether Sigurd and I had had any problems. "We've had a good marriage," I had said. Did Gundersen know even then?

"She met Sigurd when he was drawing up plans for an extension at her parents' house," Gundersen says. "They live in a semi-detached property in Sogn. Sigurd had to stop by a couple of times to take some measurements while her parents were away, and they said, 'Vera's home, she'll let you in.' So."

I don't want to think about what happened next. Don't want to imagine how it happened but know that I will, later tonight, when I've gone to bed and am trying to sleep – as I will every night for the foreseeable future. Instead, I think about everyone else. About the police officers who searched the house, going through our drawers last Monday as I listlessly sat there, trying to understand what had happened. Did they know? And did Jan Erik and Thomas know? Were they aware that Sigurd was having an affair when they called me that night because he hadn't arrived at the cabin? And if they knew, did Julie?

Gundersen clears his throat.

"And I understand, Sara – and I hope you won't mind me saying this – that there were difficulties in your marriage. In such a situation it isn't up to me to decide what's right or wrong, God knows being married is more than hard enough, but in order to understand how this relationship developed, I had to ask myself: what was it that made Sigurd go in for this? A grown man, married and all? With a schoolgirl? I mean, she's eighteen, over the age of consent and an adult in the eyes of the law – but she was, after all, still a teenager.

"It isn't up to me to tell you why, but if you want to know what I think, I'd guess he was frustrated. Marriage wasn't as he had expected it to be. I've seen it many times – especially with men. You know, relationships are full of things you have to do, have to deal with. Parents-in-law and property and jobs and payslips. There are so many ways in which a couple can disappoint each other. And in which you can disappoint yourself. Then along comes someone else. Someone young and open, who doesn't demand anything. Who thinks you're a great guy simply because you are who you are. Who thinks you're brilliant, without demanding that you earn more or take on more assignments or improve your performance. If you've been feeling inadequate for a long time, it's so tempting to accept this more generous interpretation of yourself. And if she's young and pretty to boot, well."

This is Gundersen's analysis of Sigurd. Would I too have viewed him this way if I'd been looking at him as an outsider? I don't know. I just want to hide my face in my hands. I think of previous cabin trips with Thomas and Jan Erik. Sigurd in the evening, worked up and red in the face after a couple of beers and the heat of the log burner, "Should I tell you guys a secret? Well, only if you promise not to say anything to Sara . . ." See them grinning, both of them – yes, tell us, we won't say anything to Sara.

Gundersen continues:

"At the start it was a physical thing, at the house in Sogn when Vera's parents were away. But then it developed into a relationship. E-mails and messages. Meetings at his office late in the evening when the others had gone home, sometimes in the car, and after a time mostly at the cabin in Krokskogen, where they were guaranteed not to be disturbed. Vera falls head over heels for him; it isn't long before she's convinced that they're made for one another. One of the upsides to our age's almost boundless opportunities for communication is all the traces we leave behind us. Mobile technology has transformed my profession. It's no longer about searching for the incriminating letter that may or may not exist. When two people enter into a relationship nowadays, there are always tracks. They open secret e-mail accounts and Skype and Facebook profiles and whatever else. We had already discovered the e-mail addresses and Skype profiles, but Vera showed us communication on a couple of other platforms. I have three students undergoing their training working their way through it all, because it truly is massive: page after page of chat logs. Through these logs, we can take the temperature of Vera and Sigurd's relationship. Watch it unfolding.

"Not long after their first meeting came the first e-mails. Vera declares that she loves Sigurd. She doesn't hold anything back. She's never met anyone like him, she writes, what they have is unique. Their love is special – that kind of thing. At first, Sigurd plays along. He reciprocates – not in such a florid way, perhaps, but he follows her lead. Sometimes he tries to tempt more from her: "What do you think about when you're missing me?" And – let me put it this way – she could be counted on to reply."

I nod, my head heavy. Sigurd, who needed a code word to tell me he loved me. "Hey, love." And me – who needed the same.

So Vera, who in her own estimation is more intelligent than the rest of us, underestimated the importance of lived experience. She probably entered into this adult affair with self-confidence, perhaps just to see what it was like. Perhaps she thought she was stronger than the kind of people who fall in love with someone they can't have. Didn't understand the potent situation she was in before it was too late. Her parting words to me at our last session, on the Friday Sigurd was killed: "All I need is love." I think: that must have been just before she went up to Krokskogen to shoot him.

"But little by little it seems that Sigurd cools off," Gundersen says. "He doesn't ask Vera to stop, but he no longer responds to all her declarations of love, or not unless she asks him to. This is a few months in, around November, perhaps. Her declarations are now more specific. She wants them to run away together, and this isn't just a metaphor – she actually has plans for how they might do this. A savings account, a friend of the family who has an apartment in London, that kind of thing. She wants him to divorce you; she wants to marry him. This, I have to say, is the predictable continuation of the story of the man who falls in love with a young girl who demands nothing. And Vera is more intense than most. When she writes to Sigurd to thank him for a piece of jewellery he gave her, she calls it 'a symbol of the very deepest love'. I don't think it ever crossed her mind that Sigurd might feel differently."

"What was it, the piece of jewellery?" I mumble. I already know the answer, but need to hear him say it, nonetheless.

"The gift? A bracelet with a pearl on it."

I say nothing more. Again, I know that I will feel the true weight of this later.

"Anyone reading their exchanges can see that he starts to tone it down as the autumn progresses," Gundersen says. "All three students agree on that. As Christmas approaches Sigurd only ever says 'I love you' when prompted to do so by Vera. And in the middle of December he ends their relationship."

It must have been just after we decided to go away between

Christmas and New Year in an attempt to save our relationship, I think. When, beneath the fireworks in Tenerife, we'd promised to turn over a new leaf, and Sigurd had said: "I'm done with Atkinson." I'd listened and nodded, still believing it was all about architecture, about work. Didn't understand what he was actually saying to me.

"The break-up itself doesn't happen via electronic communication," Gundersen says, "but the chat logs enable us to follow its repercussions. Vera begs him to take her back, declares her love for him, and threatens suicide. Sigurd tries to explain himself, asks her to speak to someone if she's finding it difficult, becomes shorter and shorter in his replies.

"When I speak to Vera about this period, she puts all the blame on you. Sigurd broke up with her because he was worried about you, she says. She was worried about how Sigurd was doing – even feared for his life. While you were on holiday in December she installed tiny, wireless cameras in your house, so she could make sure that he was 'doing O.K.'. She also says that she made a copy of Sigurd's house key fairly early on in the relationship. Her explanation of how that happened is a little sketchy, so I'm guessing that she stole it from his pocket."

I know all too well what's coming next. The start of our therapy sessions, in which I believed myself to be her psychologist. In which I acted as the therapist while she sat there knowing all kinds of private things about me. Had seen me naked, quite literally, given that she had access to surveillance footage of my bedroom, had also seen me crying in bed while Sigurd was still downstairs on the computer. Heard me tell Sigurd that I was lonely, taken note of this, and thrown it in my face in a moment of anger – "Do you even have any friends at all?" Able to hit me where it hurt the most. No wonder I often felt uneasy before our sessions. She sat there in the chair in my office, knowing that

I'd been betrayed by my husband. What could I have said, what kind of wisdom about life and love could I have offered her, while she sat there nodding, accepting my advice, all the while knowing the most intimate aspects of the man who was mine?

"In January, contact between the two of them resumes," Gundersen says. "Vera takes a different tone in their chats; she's more measured. She just wants to be friends, nothing more. But over the course of a few weeks they slip back into a relationship. Then Vera calls you and asks for an appointment. To see who you are, she says. To understand what Sigurd sees in you."

I don't have the strength to talk to Gundersen about this. No matter how understandable it is that I believed her, it still feels as if I've been taken in. As if I've been gullible, revealed too much. Since I don't want to explain this to him, I quickly say:

"But why did she kill him? Did he try to dump her again? Or – what was it that triggered it?"

"Ah," says Gundersen, straightening the papers in front of him. "Well."

He remains quiet for a while, looking at his papers and saying nothing. Then he looks up at me with the expression that crosses his features from time to time, his eyes honest, crystal clear. I'm unsure whether this is some kind of technique, whether it's something he learned at the police academy, or whether it comes naturally to him, but it's impressive – it's impossible to protest when faced with that kind of honesty.

"Unfortunately, Sara," Gundersen says, "I don't think Vera did kill Sigurd."

At the weekend I sat on the floor of Annika's living room, playing with a train set with my two eldest nephews. Building bridges over the tracks that curved around chair legs, immersed in this activity and nothing else: to think like a child with my sister's two little boys. I was part of a simple world: ice cream and fairy tales and a neighbour who might be a witch. And now, as the consequences of what Gundersen is saying begin to dawn on me, and I think of my frightened eyes in the kitchen window that night in Nordstrand and start to wonder whether I *did* see something outside, after all – whether someone is still out to get me. This is all I want: to go back to that moment with my nephews on the living room floor, when all that mattered was how to get the train tracks to lie flat across the edge of the rug.

"I don't understand what you're saying," I say.

There is something almost apologetic in Gundersen's expression. He presses his lips together into a thin line beneath his moustache, all the while maintaining that honest gaze.

"She was watching us," I say. "She threw the key to the cabin through the glass panel of my front door, lured me up there, and I *know* she intended to kill me. I mean, I'm sure she's saying it was self-defence or something like that, but, Gundersen, you didn't see her."

"I know what you mean," he says. "And if it's any comfort, you have an ally in Ingvild Fredly. She said the same as you – that it must be Vera, because she wanted to shoot you up there in Krokskogen, without a doubt."

"But," I say, and now my voice is trembling, it's a struggle to stop the tears coming, "but then who could have done it? Because, I mean, surely it's pretty unlikely that Sigurd, a common architect from Røa, would know not only one but *two* potential murderers?"

"I understand your objections," Gundersen says. "But the facts simply do not indicate that Vera killed him. It would have been almost impossible for her to manage it."

"But surely there must be a way she could have done it? Something you haven't considered?"

Gundersen is silent for a while – he's waiting for me to calm down, I think, and I try to regain control.

"I'm a simple man, Sara," Gundersen says. "I look at what I have in front of me, and I ask: is it possible that X could have done it? Did X have a real, physical opportunity to perform this act? And if not, well, either we have to find a way in which X *did* have the opportunity, or we have to set aside that hypothesis. In my line of work, it's easy to be blinded by the answer that seems most obvious. When you first have a suspicion, you see only the evidence that supports it. You disregard everything that indicates you've made a mistake, and selectively look for the details that suggest you are right."

"Confirmation bias," I say. "That's what it's called. The tendency to look for evidence or information that confirms what you already know."

"It's a very easy mistake to make," he says. "A fundamental error, but that doesn't stop experienced investigators storming head first into the wrong conclusion. It would be fitting if it was Vera, wouldn't it? But the trouble is that it just doesn't add up."

He leafs through some of the documents in front of him and pulls out an Excel spreadsheet.

"Let's start with what we know about Friday, March 6; we can summarise that fairly quickly. Let's see. Sigurd gets up at five-thirty in the morning. He showers, gets dressed, gathers up some of his things, gulps down a cup of coffee and says goodbye to you – we can see from Vera's footage that he leaves at 06:10.

"We know that he then arrives at FleMaSi around six-thirty. He parks his car at the kerb, well within view of the camera above the entrance to the office. He's in there for around an hour and a half, until 07:53 – when the camera shows that he returns to the car.

"At a couple of minutes past eight the car is registered on the toll road at Majorstuen, on its way west. Sigurd goes through the toll on the road to Kleivstua at 08:44. This is the last hard evidence of Sigurd's location that we have.

"But we can follow the G.P.S. on his mobile. This isn't idiot-proof, because a person's mobile isn't part of their body. But we have a witness – you – who puts Sigurd with his mobile at 09:40. The G.P.S. on the mobile indicates that Sigurd stops the car on the road below Kleivstua nine minutes after he goes through the toll, and that he then walks through the forest for fifteen minutes before he reaches the cabin a little after nine. From this point on, the mobile doesn't leave the cabin.

"Sigurd and Vera have agreed that she'll come up to the cabin at around eleven or twelve. A little after nine, Sigurd sends Vera a message via Skype, letting her know that he's arrived and asking her to message him before she gets on the bus, so that he can drive down to the bus stop and pick her up. And then there's an outgoing call made from his mobile to yours at 09.40, which aligns with your statement about the voicemail message. Unfortunately, the telecoms company have been unable to retrieve the message, Sara, so I'm still upset that you chose to delete it, but as things stand, I'm inclined to believe you regarding its content. But this deleted voicemail message is the last trace left by Sigurd. The pathologist and our forensic physician agree that the murder took place no later than three, so he must have been killed just a few hours after that call.

"Vera says that after her session with you, she walked to Holstein station, took the T-banen to Oslo Central Station, and tried to contact Sigurd to say that she was ready to make the journey up to Krokskogen.

"She had accidentally left her mobile at home that day, which meant that we couldn't trace her via G.P.S., as we did with Sigurd. Fredly has pointed out on more than one occasion that this is *very convenient*, so before you draw any similar conclusions let me just say that Vera's chat logs make clear that she had a habit of leaving her mobile, wallet and keys here and there – but yes, noted. So Vera tried to get hold of Sigurd in another way – she rented a computer in an Internet cafe at the station; she borrowed the telephone in a clothing store and tried to call – but was unable to get hold of him. She let one bus go, and when she'd waited so long that the next bus had also gone, around two hours later, she went back to school. She therefore arrived at Nydalen Secondary School at around 11.45.

"Luckily for Vera, that day was the day on which students at her school were having their school photographs taken. And the image files contain information about exactly when each photograph was taken. For Vera to make the round trip to Krokskogen to kill Sigurd after her session with you would have taken her two and a half hours. With luck and no delays at any point along the way, she might have managed to get back to school at 12:15. At the absolute earliest.

"But the first photograph of Vera's class was taken at 12:03, and in it is Vera, standing right there between your average Kari and Ola Hvermansen, smiling wanly towards the camera."

Gundersen places the palms of his hands on the table. I look at them, trying to gather myself to make a counter-argument.

"Now," he says, formulating it for me, "you may be thinking that the margins here are fairly narrow. If the first photograph was taken at 12.03, then we're only talking about twelve minutes. But I've performed the calculation using the minimal time required at every step of the way. A couple of red lights, a queue in the traffic through Sollihøgda, a conversation to lure Sigurd out to the forest, just one slow-moving driver a little further along the road beside the Tyrifjorden or an extra trip around the car park in Nydalen to find a vacant space – any of these and the timeline shatters. I'd say it's improbable that she could have been at school by quarter past twelve, even if it's technically possible. And I've spoken to the photographer. If the first photograph was taken at 12.03, that means that all the students had to have been getting into position a few minutes earlier. Vera is in the middle of the group. She hasn't dived onto the end of a row as the last person to arrive.

"So I don't know. If I were a prosecutor, I might be able to build a case on this. But if you ask me, I don't think she did it. She didn't have the time. It seems she *almost* could have done it. But not quite. Unfortunately."

"But," I say, "you said before three. She could have done it after the class photograph was taken."

"Yes," Gundersen says, "but the thing is that the photographer wasn't finished after the class photo. Between 12:24 and 12.29 the photographer took at least four portraits of Vera. And between 14.19 and 14.30, he took a range of pictures of all the students at the school together. After the last whole-school picture was taken, she wouldn't have made it up there until well after three o'clock – by which point Sigurd was already dead.

"Furthermore, we can follow all her attempts to reach him from Oslo city centre. All the logins, all the calls to his mobile – they fit with her story as she tells it."

"But she could have got someone else to do it," I say. "A friend, or someone she manipulated, something like that."

"Well," he says, shrugging. "Of course, she *could* have. But there's nothing to build a case on until we have a candidate. There's nothing that gives us reason to believe that Vera's been in contact with a hit man, and when it comes to friends, it doesn't seem as if she has many close ones. Certainly nobody she could go to for help to commit murder. And besides, the bullets found in Sigurd's body are not from a revolver like the one that was stolen from you. Of course, this means nothing more than that if Vera killed Sigurd, she must have had two weapons – and she may well have done – but it doesn't exactly support your hypothesis, either."

I sigh deeply, glance at the dusty rubber plant in the corner.

"So what now?" I say. "Does that mean that I'm still a suspect?"

"Actually no," Gundersen says, and he smiles now, albeit faintly. "You know, despite how violated you must feel by the surveillance, that is in fact what clears you here. Technically, you could have gone up to Krokskogen and killed Sigurd between, what were their names?"

He turns to his papers.

"Between Christoffer and Trygve. But thanks to Vera's surveillance cameras, I have video footage of you pottering around in the living room, preparing meals, surfing the Internet, emptying the dishwasher and so on, all during that period. I'm guessing you don't feel any particular gratitude or warmth towards Vera right now, but if you ever find yourself wanting to reconcile with her, you might bear this in mind: she gave you an alibi."

"Confirmation bias" is the seeking of information that confirms what you already believe. As I did that Friday when I waited at police headquarters. It's about ignoring information that doesn't support what you believe. Just as everything within me now wants to dismiss Gundersen.

But the more he explains, the harder this becomes. While Gundersen goes on talking my mind tries to rationalise away everything he has told me. It's certainly possible that Vera did it. She had an accomplice. She killed him somewhere else, then moved the body. There must be something we haven't thought of. She must have killed Sigurd – because who else could have done it?

As I refuse to believe him, Gundersen tells me what that week was like for Vera. If we accept her version of events, as he says. He tells me that she went home from school that day and waited all evening for Sigurd to call and tell her why he broke their agreement. That she started to worry when she didn't hear from him. She watched me via her surveillance equipment, heard me speaking to Thomas on the telephone, and to the police the next day when I reported Sigurd missing. On Saturday afternoon she took her mother's car without asking and drove up to the cabin; found Sigurd's things, but the cabin was abandoned. As if whoever was staying there had just popped out for a moment, Gundersen says. Sigurd's mobile lying there on the table. The document tube containing his drawings leaning against the window. His bag open; a plate with a half-eaten sandwich on the kitchen counter. As if he might come back and finish eating it at any moment.

She took his mobile phone and document tube, Gundersen says. She took the cabin key. Of course it was Vera who put the tube of drawings back in my house. It was she who left Sigurd's mobile in my garden. She had been trying to cast suspicion on me – or help the police, as Gundersen says she puts it. She's sure that *I* killed Sigurd. Gundersen says that when he confronts her with all the reasons why it *can't* be me – her own video surveillance footage, for one thing – she just scoffs. She's convinced that I had an accomplice. I was jealous because I found out that Sigurd was seeing someone else, Vera says with conviction when questioned – I killed him to take revenge. She says that I must have known about her cameras, walking around the house playing the role of the worried spouse while my co-conspirator went up to Krokskogen. When Gundersen presents her with objections to these claims, she dismisses them. She doesn't believe him when he says it's impossible that events unfolded that way. Her response is: "Well, who else can it have been?"

Little by little, my resistance wanes. It's too hard to maintain it.

Gundersen tells me that Vera admits to breaking into my house. She took Old Torp's revolver – Sigurd had previously told her about it, she knew roughly where it was. That's what she was looking for in my loft that night when I heard her. Through her microphones, she heard what the police said. And how they said it. Here, Gundersen looks a little embarrassed.

"We may occasionally have expressed ourselves in a way that wasn't becoming for professionals – I'll admit it. My staff, and myself too. Before we knew that we were being watched. When you didn't want to release your notes. The fact that you deleted the voicemail message. I'll be big enough to admit that it irritated me. I, erm, I may have let my irritation influence what I said to my staff when I thought nobody else was listening. But Vera heard me. And that may have influenced her."

Then the police discovered *her*. That is, they hacked Sigurd's computer and found out that he'd been having an affair with a young girl. Gundersen says that his team interviewed her, and she had to explain herself, because there were periods of Friday, March 6 for which nobody else could confirm Vera's asserted whereabouts. Suspicion was turned towards her. She wanted to put it back on me. And so she started to get involved. She understood that I was afraid when I discovered that someone had been in my house. She was watching me. She heard what I said to the police – and that they were coolly indifferent towards me. Wanted to worsen the relationship between them and me.

"The fridge magnets were a clever idea," Gundersen says. "It seemed so idiotic. It *was* idiotic. To professionals, people who have been investigating murder for several decades, it sounds so trivial. It's meaningless, easy to attribute to hysteria. To someone losing their grip. At the same time, it terrified you."

"But I don't get it," I say, hurt. "Why nobody understood that that might account for the behaviour of the intruder. That if someone wanted to discredit me, that would be a good way to do it."

"Well," Gundersen says. "Let's just say that the thought did occur to me. There were several possibilities. Either you were mad and paranoid, or you were trying to appear like a victim – in a pretty stupid way. Or someone was indeed trying to diminish your credibility. So I stationed an officer in front of your house, just to be on the safe side. On the night of Friday, March 13, Vera wasn't just captured by your – or, that is, Arild's – surveillance system. She was also observed by my man. He followed her when she ran off, but she disappeared into a garden on Carl Kjelsens vei and got away."

A shadow of security draws itself over my memory of that evening. There was someone keeping an eye on me, after all. I hadn't been left entirely to fend for myself.

Gundersen speculates that Vera began to realise that she was a target of the investigation. She could see from her surveillance footage that they visited me less frequently, and until Fredly found the cameras she heard them speaking about other persons of interest, including the "mistress", when they thought nobody could overhear. Vera had no autopsy report or digital image files containing times and dates – she didn't know she had been cleared. Of course, had I been charged with murder, it certainly wouldn't have been any skin off her nose. But as time passed, it must have occurred to her that it wouldn't be such a bad thing if I was killed. According to Gundersen, Vera believes I took Sigurd from her twice: first because he chose me over her several times, and then because I murdered him. If she had shot me and claimed that she did so in self-defence, it would have been easy for her to redirect suspicion of Sigurd's murder from her onto me. The fact that I wouldn't be able to protest would only make her argument more convincing. And my death would be a fitting punishment for both of the ways in which I had taken Sigurd from her – or so Vera might have thought.

The cabin was a good scene for the crime. She had to get me out of the house – there was no reason for her to be at my place. She took the chance of sending me an invitation: "Here's the key, the answers you're looking for are at Krokskogen."

"But all this is speculation," Gundersen says. "We can speculate that she lured you into a trap, planning to kill you. But we can't prove that was her intention."

I sigh. What does he need? A note on which she'd scribbled down her plan? A confession?

"Her story is that she wanted to let herself into your house and return the cabin key, but that she was frightened when the alarm went off, so panicked. She says you were furious when you found her at the cabin in Krokskogen; that you stood there in the kitchen and threatened her. That she thought you were going to kill her."

"That's ridiculous," I say. "*She* pointed a weapon at *me*."

"Yes," Gundersen says. "But she didn't shoot."

"She *would* have! If Fredly hadn't turned up, she would have killed me."

"You could say that," Gundersen says, unperturbed. "And then her lawyer would ask how you could be sure. Her defence would give the same old speech, she's eighteen years old, no previous convictions, never so much as held a gun before, blah, blah, blah."

"And so, what?" I say, my voice thick with tears. "You won't even try? She tries to kill me, but since we can't prove anything we just say, 'Oh well, that's a shame'? And let her go?"

Now it's his turn to sigh. The exhaustion is suddenly apparent in his face. He rubs his eyes and when he takes his hands away the movement seems to hang there in the skin; the wrinkles, the thin, swollen skin below them quivering after the rubbing.

"Whatever we try to charge her with will be up to the public prosecutor," he says. "The police prosecutor you just met will submit a recommendation. Whatever you might say about her, she's damn good at her job. If she recommends going after Vera for attempted murder, and they decide to do so, there's a good chance she'll win the case."

"If."

"Yes. And if not we have plenty of other violations we can charge her with. Breaking and entering, stalking, illegal surveillance. Theft of a firearm. Intimidating and harassing conduct."

"And what does an eighteen-year-old with no prior offences generally get for those violations?"

"Possibly a prison sentence," Gundersen says. "But in all likelihood a suspended sentence. Maybe community service and a substantial fine."

We're silent for a long time. I think about my first meeting with Vera. Her tone when she called me "Doctor". I wonder what it will be like to start working with new patients after this. Will I look at each and every one of them – the troubled youngsters who venture up the steps to my garage office in the hope of getting the help they so sorely need – and wonder what ulterior

318

motives they may be harbouring? Will I be able to work clin-ically again? Is it even ethically responsible to do so?

We have come to the end of the road, Gundersen and I. Before I leave, he assures me that the case is still a priority. He admits that when they don't have any suspects after a week there's a chance they may never find the perpetrator, but he assures me that it's possible the case may still be solved – he'll do his personal best, and they're already looking into other possi-bilities. FleMaSi, for example. Sigurd's ownership stake there. They're also investigating Margrethe's circle of acquaintances, and still checking out certain individuals linked to Vera. A lot can come out of wiping the slate clean and starting again, he says – optimistically enough, but something in his tone indicates I shouldn't get my hopes up too much. As I follow him out through the labyrinth of corridors and locked glass doors, back to the reception desk, I think that it stops here. Some time will pass, and then I'll receive a letter or someone may call to inform me that the investigation is being scaled down. Then the case will be closed, or it will be marked as inactive, pending new evidence – a new angle, a smoking gun, an incriminating e-mail. In vain, most likely. I'll probably never know what hap-pened to Sigurd.

As he's about to let me through the final glass door, Gunder-sen says:

"Sara? Can I offer you a piece of advice?"

"Yes?"

He clears his throat; wipes the back of his hand across his mouth.

"From now on, spend your time with those who wish you well. Be with your family. Your father. And your sister, who seems prepared to stand by you through thick and thin. A lovely woman, if I may say so. Prioritise spending time with them."

I nod. I thank him for the advice. We take each other's hand, and then I go out through the glass door. When it has clicked into place behind me I turn to watch him walk away, but he has already gone.

One Sunday in May: Sitting in the dark

It's impossible to avoid getting soil on my hands; I should have worn gloves. In my dirty fingers, earth pressed into their ridges and cracks, under my nails and behind the wedding ring I still wear, I hold the purple osteospermum – an African daisy – which looks far too delicate and beautiful for the Norwegian spring climate. I've never been interested in gardening, not like Annika, not like Mamma. I'm like Pappa – the weeks pass, suddenly it's winter, and I still haven't mown the lawn. Sigurd was the same way. But according to the man at the Plantasjen garden centre, African daisies do well in Norwegian soil, if they're properly cared for. So I've bought some compost and a trowel and have got to work.

The silver-grey car appears at the corner of my eye as I'm attempting to ease the plant into the hole I've dug for it. I have to backfill the hole with a mixture of potting compost and the soil in which the plant will grow, while taking care not to damage the poor thing's roots. This is what I'm practising – this balance, unfamiliar to me, but I'm doing the best I can. At the edge of my field of view I see that the silver-grey car has stopped down by the road, at the bottom of the drive. The engine is turned off. At the sound of one of the car doors slamming shut I straighten, the African daisies abandoned on the ground. I make a futile attempt to wipe the soil from my dirty hands, then shade my eyes and look towards the road. It's an unusually sunny May day, and it's warm, a foretaste of summer. The kind of day on which you take off too many layers and stay outside too long; on which it's almost impossible not to become arrogant about your clothing choices – and then to come down with a cold afterwards. With my hand before my eyes, I can see him. He hesitates, lifts a hand and waves to me, but stands there longer than necessary before walking towards me. As if he would rather get back in the car and drive away again.

"Hi," he calls to me as he finally walks towards me.

"Hi, Thomas," I say.

I put my hands on my hips. When I look down, I see that my T-shirt has flecks of dirt at my waist.

"So you're doing a bit of gardening?"

"I am," I say. "Not that I really want to. But the estate agent thought it would be a good idea. Help to create a homely atmosphere, or something like that."

We smile a little.

"So you're selling up," he says.

"Yes," I say. "In the end, I decided that would be best. I don't want to stay here after everything that's happened."

"I'm sure it's hard to feel at home again."

"Yes."

We look up towards the house, the two of us. The sun faces the windows, flaring brightly within them. It's a fine house when you look at it like this – majestic, even. Whatever you might say about Old Torp, he had dignity. His house has it, too. But I'm done with it.

"What does Margrethe think?" Thomas says.

"She's not keen on the idea. But what can she say? It's my house. I can do what I want with it."

He nods, as if thoughtful. He's wearing a sweater, is smarter than me – waiting until summer truly arrives before stripping down to his T-shirt. His hair is neat, combed down against his head with some stuff or other in it to keep it in place. He looks

so – what's the word? – so respectable. But I don't mean anything negative by this. He doesn't look boring – although Julie
has probably done her best to make him so. I just mean he looks
rock solid. Dependable and trustworthy. No fuss.

"So," he says. "How's it going?"

"Good," I say. "Or, I mean, up and down. But good enough."

We stand in silence for a moment, both looking at the African
daisies between our feet. I suspect that Thomas has something
he wants to say. I should really get finished with the plants as
soon as possible, so I can go in and take a shower in the cold,
still unfinished bathroom, wash the earth from my hands and
get dressed, and then make my way to my Pappa's for what has
recently become a weekly habit – Sunday dinner with the
entire family. But I wait. I give him time. It seems like the right
thing to do. Thomas has made the trip all the way up here to
tell me something, and he isn't the type to gossip or speak out
of turn.

"About what happened," he says, finally. "I just wanted to
say. I'm sorry."

"Sorry for what?"

"For, you know – the thing with the girl."

Yes, I think. I do know.

"Sigurd told us about it – Jan Erik and me. And we never said
anything to you. We wanted to – or, at least, I wanted to. I didn't
think it was right, what he was doing. And I mean – I really
had no idea that she was so *young*. But . . . well. I knew that he
was carrying on with someone. And I should have told you."

I close my eyes, tilt my face to the sun. I don't want to think
about it, have always sort of known that they knew. I've gone
over the conversations I had with them on the night Sigurd went
missing a thousand times in my head – something evasive
in their tone, something that slipped past me, as if they were

holding something back. Of course they were reluctant to call me, because he might be with her – they tried to downplay the obvious lie, because they knew why he had lied. And still they told me nothing – not even when it turned out he was dead. I'd had to find out that he was having an affair on my own. I am not particularly impressed by Thomas' apology.

We stand like this for a while, in silence. Whatever you might say about Thomas, there is at least this – that he understands when he should stop talking, and he can endure a silence. And it's not as if I don't understand Thomas' motives, either. Sigurd was his friend. Most of all, I'm just so very tired. I don't want to have anything more to do with it. It's a nice day, it's sunny, will soon be summer, and the estate agent has promised me that the house is worth a fortune. It's been valued at 14 million kroner, but she thinks it might go for more than 16 million. I'll be rich. I'll have money to do whatever I want. In a little while I'm going to go inside and shower, and then go for dinner at my father's; next week I'm going out with my new colleagues. These are the kinds of things I want to think about. All I care about, really. I sigh deeply, open my eyes again. Thomas is standing beside me. We look down at the daisies.

"I'm sorry," Thomas says finally.

"It's O.K.," I say. "He was your friend."

"Yeah. But it was a rotten thing he did."

Good old Thomas. I never liked Jan Erik, and Julie sets my teeth on edge, but I have a certain amount of sympathy for Thomas. In some ways he's like me – the social awkwardness, the quietness. But he's more reliable than me. I've often thought that if it had been him whom I had met at the party in Bergen, I might have been a lot happier. But I don't know. Maybe I wouldn't have fallen for him. Maybe he wouldn't have fallen for me.

"While it was going on," Thomas says, "Sigurd told me that he was looking for a way out. Just a few weeks ago, he said that he was tired of the whole thing. That it was a mistake. That it was you he wanted."

I sigh; take a deep breath. Am I supposed to be grateful that he's telling me this?

"I don't know whether this is something you want to hear," he says. "But I wanted to tell you. Just in case."

"Thank you," I say, rubbing a grubby hand across my forehead to get rid of the irritation.

"So what will you do now?" he says. "Once you've sold the house? Will you rent an office somewhere and continue your practice?"

"No," I say. "I'm giving it up. I have a couple of patients left to wrap things up with, but once I'm done with them, I'll be done with being a therapist."

"So what will you do instead?"

"I don't know," I say, enjoying just how good this feels. The world is open. "I've got a part-time position at a psychology journal – I read articles and give feedback to the authors, things like that. Otherwise – I don't know. Travel, maybe. I've always wanted to try living in a French château."

Thomas smiles.

"And now you can," he says.

"Yes."

For a brief while we're silent again, but it's a more comfortable silence this time, and I think that this is quite nice, actually, the fact that he's come here to see me. Until now, none of Sigurd's friends have come to visit – not Jan Erik, nor Mammod or Flemming. Nor his brother. Only Margrethe, furious because I'm selling her childhood home; also furious at everything that's happened. I think she holds me morally responsible for Sigurd's infidelity. "If only you had been a better wife," she said to me. But she'd had quite a bit to drink. Annika had warned me that this might happen, and asked me to stay calm, say as little as possible. And I did. I'm done with Margrethe, too.

"And what about you?" I ask Thomas.

"Oh, you know," he says. "Same old, same old. Or, well – Julie's pregnant."

"How lovely," I say. "Congratulations."

"Thank you."

He smiles, as if to himself. He'll be a good father, I think. He'll do whatever it takes. Take parental leave, get up in the middle of the night. Be the referee for the football team and take on the role of volunteer coordinator at school. Get involved.

"I'm sorry about what happened with Julie," I say.

"Oh God, don't even think about it," he says. "It's she who should apologise. She meant well, but . . . Let's just say she can be a bit much sometimes."

I smile. It's good to hear him say it. It paints me in a generous light.

"Do tell her I said hello," I say. "And say congratulations from me."

"I will."

"Thomas, I . . . I'm grateful you came."

"It's the least I could do," he says. And then he hugs me, loosely, so that he hardly touches me. "Take care of yourself."

And that's advice I'm going to take.

At the dinner table, while Pappa and Annika bicker about something in the newspaper, and Henning hushes the boys, who are quarrelling over the salt and pepper pots, I think that I'm grateful for what Thomas told me, too. About the fact that Sigurd had chosen me. At the end of the day, it's a good thing to know.

Annika and Pappa clear the table. I offer to help, but Annika says it's fine, they can do it, I can go and sit down.

"Why don't you go into the study and I'll put the kettle on," Pappa says.

Henning and the boys are in the living room, watching children's T.V. – from Pappa's office I can hear it in the background: merry songs, adult voices adopting a child-friendly pitch, speaking in the way that actors speak when performing the voices of cats and dogs and elephants. The boys are quiet as mice, bewitched by the T.V., and Henning is just as silent, all his attention probably focused on his mobile. From the kitchen I can hear the clattering of pots and containers, the sounds of Pappa and Annika clearing up. Their voices don't reach me in here, although I expect they're still going on about some disagreement or other they were discussing at the table. In here it's calm. Pappa's oasis.

I put some logs on the fire in the way that Pappa taught me, on top of each other in squares, as if I'm building a notched timber cabin. Place paper and smaller bits inside. Consider whether or not I should light it. It's still warm, not yet fully dark, but the cold will soon arrive. I think Pappa should have the honour. I straighten up, my gaze grazing the books of newspaper cuttings, and I remember the Thursday in March when I read them, Pappa's hard words. How afraid I had been. But today is a good day, and I'm not going to think about it.

Instead, I cross the room to the window behind Pappa's desk. I set the palms of my hands against the wide frame and look out, at the neglected garden with last year's leaves still strewn across the fresh grass. Out at the neighbouring houses. The new one that was built when Pappa divided up the plot, and the old one to the right, where the Winge family lived. The house from which Herman Winge – whom I was in love with, even though we hardly spoke – would emerge each morning to stand on the front porch and zip up his down jacket before setting off for school.

Some nights I would stand here, in Pappa's study, and look out towards Herman's house in an attempt to catch a glimpse of him. I would turn off all the lights in the room so that nobody in the Winge house would see me standing there in the dark, spying on them. I would see Herman, too, sometimes. On occasion I'd borrow Pappa's binoculars – I almost blush to think of it.

I wonder who lives in the house now. There's a blue trampoline in the garden. Maybe it's Herman himself, who now has a family and has taken over the house. But in all likelihood it's been sold. Pappa hasn't mentioned it, but on the other hand it would never occur to him that I might be interested to know.

On a whim, I turn off the lights, as I would do back then, clicking off the reading lamp on the desk. In the dark I set the palms of my hands on the windowsill as I lean against it; look out towards Herman Winge's old house.

Stand here where nobody can see me.

As I stand this way, I think I catch sight of something. Is there something moving out there, or is it just my own reflection? I focus my gaze, staring at the Winge house. Change focus, see only myself and the empty study behind me, just a glimpse of it in the mirror image in the glass. And it's as I shift my focus again that it occurs to me, and it's as if all the air has been sucked out of the room. For a cold second or two I stand there, holding my gaze between the two points of focus, and see both sides simultaneously – the garden outside, and me here in the study. Realise that I know. And that nobody but me would ever think of it.

It's so quiet, all sound absorbed by the vacuum. The only thing that can be heard is the low, rhythmic sound of my own breath against the window.

From Pappa's writing flat it's possible to see the pavement outside Sigurd's office. Sigurd must have thought of this when he asked Vera to meet him at the office. He must have taken precautions, been careful.

But Pappa always works outside normal office hours – works weekends, evenings and nights. I can just imagine him wandering around in the unfurnished flat at night-time, turning off all the lights, the street lamps outside providing just enough light for him to see by as he pours whisky into a tumbler in the dark, then sits on the windowsill. Looks down at the street from his apartment, considering the lit scene below him, the few people walking around Bislett on a Wednesday evening at eleven-thirty. And then Sigurd and Vera appear, on their way into Sigurd's office. Together.

My hands are shaking so much that I can no longer lean my weight on them. What would Pappa have done if he had found out that Sigurd was having an affair? I sink down onto the chair by his desk. Pappa, who sees the family as the only thing that is sacred. Who believes that infidelity should be punishable. Who believes in vigilantism and the neighbourhood watch and the right to take the law into one's own hands to defend the herd. In the twilight of the room my gaze flits across the scrapbooks. Pappa, who believes in extreme measures. The way of the dogs.

Beside the cold fireplace are the armchairs, like big, sleeping animals. Where we sat on the day I came to Smestad, but then left without telling my father that Sigurd was dead. We had talked about books. Pappa told me that what he'd been reading was dark, but he'd learned a lot from it regardless – "I think there's a lot one can learn from sitting in the dark and watching the world." I might not have the same faith in my memory as I once did, but I know that I remember this word for word. "I think it's an essential activity," he'd said. And now, as I'm quite literally sitting here in the dark, my gaze flits from the archival scrapbooks across to the bookshelves and back to the armchairs; from the Foucault's pendulum to the Winge house and the world beyond the window, to finally land on the mantelpiece with this knowledge: in that moment, he was telling me what he had done.

Pappa knew about Sigurd and Vera. An echo of the humiliation from Gundersen's office burns in my stomach – everyone other than me knew, even my father. But Pappa didn't just shrug and look the other way. Pappa observed them. On March 6, he sat in his apartment early in the morning while Sigurd parked his car at the curb with the hazards on. Pappa had looked down. Seen the *garnkule* on the dashboard. And understood.

Pappa, who hasn't kept a single drawing I made as a child. Who has thrown out chopping boards made in woodwork classes and ornaments from ceramics classes as soon as he received them as Christmas gifts. Who never remembers the names of my friends, never calls on my birthday, who visited me in Bergen just once in six years. But who would still do anything for me – should he deem it necessary.

Perhaps he waited for an opportunity. Sat there in the dark, watching Sigurd live his double life. Took his time. And then, on that Friday in March, seized the opportunity. Sigurd parking his car early in the morning. The *garnkule* resting on the dashboard, clearly visible through the front windscreen. Pappa got up, went down to his car and drove out of the city. To Krokskogen? Perhaps, but it could just as easily have been another place. To Sørkedalen. He keeps his skis and best ski boots in his car, regardless. If anyone were to wonder, he was simply going skiing in the middle of the day, as he often does. But who would question his movements? His colleagues don't know how he spends his days, nor do his students. When we sat in the armchairs before the fire that day, he told me that he'd been out skiing every day for a week, because if he drove up to Sørkedalen there was enough snow. I had thought nothing of it at the time – I had enough on my mind. But why would he go there, when his favourite place to ski is Østmarka? And it was unlike him to be so specific – he never usually tells me where he goes.

Yes, he went to Sørkedalen. Strapped on his skis, and crossed the fields to Krokskogen. So that he wouldn't be recorded by the toll station cameras. So nobody would see his car parked along the road that leads up towards Kleivstua. How long does it take to cross the fields on skis? For a man in good physical shape who skis regularly? Three hours, three and a half?

I count on my fingers, get to ten, ten-thirty. Remember Gundersen's timeline. Vera tried to call Sigurd a little after ten-thirty. That was the first call he didn't answer.

I imagine it. Pappa skidding up to the cabin on his skis. Sigurd coming out onto the front step upon hearing that someone was there, thinking that Vera must have made it all the way up to the cabin by herself. Pappa adopting an easy-going tone, "Oh

Sigurd, I didn't expect to see you up here, in the middle of the day on a Friday." It must have been the easiest thing in the world to persuade Sigurd to leave the cabin. Getting his father-in-law away before Vera turned up must have been the only thing on his mind. Of course he left his mobile in the cabin – because what if Vera called him while my dad was there?

Together, they make their way to the clearing in the forest, Pappa on his skis, Sigurd walking along the path where the snow had melted. Does my father ask Sigurd to point something out to him, then shoot him while his back is turned? Or does he tell him what he intends to do before demanding that he turn to face the forest?

Did Sigurd beg for his life? Was he afraid when he was shot, or was he unaware that death was coming for him, until it came?

What would Pappa have done if Vera had been at the cabin? If she'd been there with Sigurd when he skidded into the yard? That I'm unable to think of – that's the limit, the point beyond which I'm unable to go.

Then Pappa makes his way back across the fields. Maybe he throws the gun in a lake where the ice has melted, or perhaps he takes it home with him. I have no doubt that he has a weapon, believing as he does in taking the law into one's own hands, and since he's not a member of any club I know of it's probably not registered in his name. Maybe it's lying hidden in the cellar of this very house, or perhaps it's in a drawer of the desk at which I'm sitting. This is a house full of secrets, with hidden rooms and deep closets and loose panels. He would be able to hide the revolver here for as long as he wished. Should he get cold feet, he'd be able to borrow a boat one summer evening and drop the gun into Bunnefjorden. But he doesn't get cold feet.

He returns through the forest, gets back to the car, straps his skis to the roof and drives home. Feeling so uplifted. I'm sure he must have been unafraid – because what did he have to be scared of? There are few people on the trails on a Friday morning in March, and even if he were to pass other skiers it's unlikely they would notice him, let alone know and recognise him – and even more unlikely that they would remember him several days later. The only thing he might have feared was that suspicion could be cast on me, but he would have assumed I'd be with patients all day, one after the other. Because I don't think I ever admitted to him the state my practice was in. I'd wanted to appear successful, a clever girl, for my Pappa.

I hear the clanking of pots and pans out there, and then I hear footsteps, and Annika's voice, along with those of Henning and the boys. Soon Pappa will come in, with a cup of tea for each of us. It's a little chilly in here now – it would be good to have the fire lit, to be able to warm myself before it. But I don't move. I can't explain this away. I might have been able to write it off as only my imagination, were it not for what he said that afternoon before the fire. We sat here, in the armchairs, and he talked about looking at the world from the darkness, effectively telling me how he had found out what Sigurd was up to. Was careful to mention that he had been skiing in Sørkedalen on the day Sigurd disappeared, in order to reveal how he had done it. Told me that it was important not to get stuck there, in the darkness. You had to do what you had to do, and then move on, he'd said. That's how easy it was for him to dispose of a person.

I had laughed it off. "Yes, well, if you're stuck in the darkness that's where we therapists come in," I'd said.

I hear steps out in the kitchen. There's so little time, just a few seconds before he'll be here, then what will I do?

What if I just ask him? I so want to hear him deny it, so want to be reassured – I'm wrong, Pappa was away that day, he can prove it. There was nothing to the things he said. I want to be able to put this all behind me and never think of it again.

But my father believes in uncompromising honesty. Suddenly it's as if I never grew up – as if I'm still that little girl in her nightgown sitting at the top of the stairs. Who sees Pappa come home in the middle of the night, but doesn't dare ask where he's been. The girl who knows the weight of that question – how asking is to risk a dangerous answer, something you'll have to know and live with for the rest of your life. All my memories of my father are tainted by this feeling: that it's best not to ask too much, best not to know.

Because if I ask him where he was on that Friday and he answers, I will lose him.

Light falls across the floor as he opens the door.

Even in the twilight I can see his smile. It's too dark to see the details, but I know all too well how his face creases, his green eyes small forest lakes in the folds of leathery, weathered skin.

"Oh, Sara," he says, in his rasping voice. "Are you sitting here in the dark?"

HELENE FLOOD is a psychologist who lives in Oslo with her husband and two children. *The Therapist*, her first adult novel, was the winner of Norway's Best Crime Debut Prize and Iceland's award for Best Translated Crime Novel. Film rights have been sold, as well as translation rights in twenty-seven languages. It will be followed by *The Lover*, to be published in English in 2022.

ALISON McCULLOUGH is a Norwegian-to-English translator based in Stavanger, Norway. Previous translations include *Restless* by Kenneth Moe, *Theatre of the World: The Maps That Made History* by Thomas Reinertsen Berg and *Edvard Munch: An Inner Life* by Øystein Ustvedt.